Halo Halo

Michael Kaye

Rainbow Valley Books

Rainbow Valley Books

First Published in 2021 by Rainbow Valley Books

Bula Matra House
205 Sanderstead Road
South Croydon
CR2 0PH

www.rainbowvalleybooks.com

Main Text Set in Times New Roman 11.0

Published by Rainbow Valley Books
ISBN: 978-1-9999829-4-2
ff

Printed and bound by CPI Group (UK) Ltd

'Come on, Pete,' Hal filled the doorway, the epitome of impatience. 'Let's get out of this bloody place. It's beginning to give me the creeps.'

'You have to have beautiful thoughts before you can have beautiful surroundings. To have clean surroundings, a clean house, a clean backyard, you have to think of it before you can actually do it. So, this is the true meaning of 'The New Society' that the President is trying to put into the hearts and minds of the people.'

Imelda Marcos

Chapter One

In the darkness Peter tripped and almost fell down the final five steps leading into the crowded car park. His ankle turned and his eyes pricked with pain and fury. He groped in his left trouser pocket, found his precious wad of fiduciary issue and transferred the notes to his right pocket.

He limped across the courtyard, reached the side of the car and sought to extricate his keys. The money now formed an obstruction. A fluttering came from the direction of the solitary armoured night-light and a large bat swooped low over Peter's head. He ducked.

He would have preferred to avoid the gymnastic climb into the vehicle. He was uncomfortable enough already. He hesitated, then, with a sigh of resignation, swung his left leg forward and over the door of the Healey – only to feel his right ankle give way. He slumped. The door frame between his thighs was surprisingly cold. Peter cursed and prepared to hop into the driver's seat.

As his right foot left the ground, he thought he detected a low susurration. The bat returned and Peter ducked. The whistle crossed the courtyard once more. Someone, he concluded, was trying to attract his attention. Peter peered into the penumbra beyond the pale pool of light. Something glowed and then gently expired in the residents' parking area.

'Pete,' called a soft voice. ''Ere, Pete.' The voice had a familiar West Country burr.

Peter remained immobile.

''Ere, Pete, me old mate. Over 'ere'.'

The cigar tip glowed once more. In the wing mirror of the other parked car Peter detected the reflection of a gold watch strap.

Peter shifted his weight back onto his right foot. The pain leaped up his leg. 'Shit,' he yelped.

'Tut-tut,' Hal's voice murmured. 'Think of the neighbours, Pete. Sound travels at night.'

Peter hobbled towards the glowing cigar. He reached the side of Hal's Granada.

'You weren't sneakin' off before we 'ad a chance to 'ave our little chat, were you Pete?' A cloud of smoke materialised outside the driver's window.

Peter shifted his head to one side. 'You took your time getting back, didn't you?' And even as he put the rhetorical question, Peter realised that Hal must have been there for some time. Waiting. He must have cut his engine at the top of the hill and drifted down silently and into his car space.

Peter's eyes were becoming accustomed to the gloom. Hal set his face in profile, his pink shirt glowed in the darkness. So did his teeth.

'Boy, 'ave I 'ad to do a lot of fast-talkin', Pete.' Hal leaned further towards the open window and looked up.

Peter nonchalantly read the face of his watch. 'What took you so long? I reckon it's been an hour since you left.'

'Well, Pete, when Nigel gets 'is dander up, there's no stoppin' 'im.' Hal shook his head. 'And no calmin' 'im.' Hal shook his head and winked at Peter. 'He was really set on reportin' the driver of that Healey to the cops.'

'And did you succeed in dissuading him?'

'Yeah.' Hal patted his car door reassuringly.

Peter managed to rustle up a smile. 'Thanks. That was good of you.'

Hal returned the smile. 'I told Nige there was no rush. After all, he's got forty-eight hours to report it to the police.'

Peter winced. Hal was all concern. 'What's up, Pete?'

'Twisted my ankle on that death-trap of a staircase.'

'It doesn't pay to rush about in the dark, Pete. You need to watch your step.'

'I'll take your advice.' Peter looked down. 'This ankle needs a cold compress, so I shall take it home.'

'You sure you're gonna be able to drive?' Hal peered over the edge of the window. 'We can give you a bed for the night. Ah Yeot could do with a bit of company.'

'I'll be fine.' Peter bit his lip as he made as if to leave.

'Nigel's not a bad old stick, really.' Hal looked into Peter's eyes. 'You'll enjoy workin' with 'im.'

'I said I'd think it over.'

'On the other hand, he can be a mean bastard if he's crossed.' Hal shook his head.

'Get stuffed, Hal.' Peter turned and started to limp away.

'You can take your 'and out of your pocket, Pete.' Hal called after him. 'Nobody's after your money.'

Peter paused, devised a riposte and then thought better of it.

''Ere, Pete,' Hal lifted his voice a notch. 'What do you think of Hil's knockers?'

Peter's anger overcame his discretion. 'Do you want your neighbours to think that you're pimping for your wife?'

Hal gurgled from the darkness. 'There's not one of the blokes in this block who wouldn't like to get his leg over.'

Peter winced at the resonance of Hal's voice in the parking area. With not a little pain, Peter managed to clamber into the Healey and lower himself behind the big steering wheel. He glanced back towards the Granada. 'You know, Hal, you're nothing but a big prick.'

'That's what all the girls say.' Hal laughed. 'What do all the girls say about you, Pete?'

As Peter turned the key in the ignition, the bat swooped low over the Healey.

The big, long-stroke engine rasped into life. Ignoring the searing pain in his leg, Peter gently increased the pressure on the throttle. As the long bonnet edged into the darkness, the wall above his head was pierced by two shafts of vexed light. Bugger the neighbours.

Spinning the wheel, Peter forced himself to throttle down hard. The Healey's tail swung round in an arc of sand and grit. Then he was free, the car roaring through the night, headlights blazing. Peter licked his lower lip. It tasted of salt.

Here was the main road. With relief he released the pressure on the throttle. The Beast coasted down the slight incline. Peter swung the car to the left and into a lay-by. He felt the front tyres gently bump against a kerb. He switched off the engine and the lights. The Healey lurched once and then all was peace. He relaxed his right foot until the pain had declined into a dull ache. His head sank back against the seat. It wasn't just the physical pain that troubled him. His evening, and the events that had led up to it, jostled in his inebriated mind as a blurred montage. He might have dismissed the whole business as a bad dream were it not for the money nestling in his trouser pocket.

Everything had happened at such speed. When had it all begun? He stared into the night. The previous Tuesday. Not his good news day.

Chapter Two

Peter had spotted her outside the Honkers and Shankers. She was wearing something pink which set off her tan. As he continued his progress along Des Voeux Road, Central, Peter wondered how she could remain so cool on such a day. The humidity trembled on the brink of precipitation. Peter felt the sweat, trickling down his sides beneath the short-sleeved shirt, dam up against the waistband of his trousers. All around him scurried the Central District tumult, preponderantly Chinese but with a sprinkling of European decoration; all intent on the pursuit of the elusive dollar.

The distance between Peter and Hilary narrowed. A very tall blonde overtook him on the edge of the pavement and then darted across Hilary's path to clatter up the front steps of the Bank. To his right a dark green tram swayed past, clanging – at each open upstairs window the white-shirted arm of an office worker.

Another twenty paces and they must meet. Peter fingered the small, damp bundle of notes in his left trouser pocket. At ten paces she spotted him and could not disguise her confusion, her indecision about the appropriate style of greeting. Her eyes narrowed for the splittest of moments before the smile broke out.

'Hello, Peter.' She resumed her progress.

'Hello, Hilary.' He returned the smile and swung into step beside her. 'Hot enough for you?'

They moved in lockstep across the narrow alley dividing the Bank of China (the former local H.Q. of the Cultural Revolution) from the Hong Kong and Shanghai Bank (the running dog of imperialist capitalism with paws in Peking and London). Peter glanced across at Hilary's unwavering expression.

'Where are we going?'

As she continued to look straight ahead, Peter dropped his eyes. Yes, they were still there. Hilary possessed the most perfect breasts Peter had ever seen. When was the first time he had allowed his eyes to wander? Yes, it was at the Ladies' Recreation Club. A nervous Hilary – a callow, newly-wed secretary, fresh to the Colony – had been grateful to be offered a drink and some light banter. Since then their fortunes had moved in opposite directions.

'Just window shopping in the Hilton Arcade,' she said. He lifted his eyes to meet hers. 'It's my lunch hour,' she added.

'Quelle coincidence,' Peter rejoined. 'That's Ionesco.' Peter could not resist teasing Hilary. It made up for no longer trying to bed her.

On closer acquaintance Hilary's pink jacket had the iridescence of Thai silk. Its clever cut flattered her café-crème complexion. Peter allowed his gaze to drift lower to her legs. Pity about the flat, white shoes but – as she had informed him on an earlier occasion – Hilary was 'a happily married career woman whose prime requisite is comfort, not allure'. Yes, she had actually said 'allure'.

'Have you lunched yet?'

Hilary turned her head in response to the question. Peter was a split second late in lifting his eyes. Peter noted that she had noted the lag.

'Your Hilton or mine?' Peter enquired and gestured to the right. The pavement curved towards the hotel in question. Across the tram tracks lay the manicured cricket ground.

The temperature beneath the leaden, baleful sky had to be in the nineties; the humidity even higher.

'Taxi!'

Peter waved at a grubby red Mercedes which had paused by the pedestrian crossing at the end of Queen's Road.

'Peter, are you crazy?'

Peter ignored the question and swung open the cab door.

'After you, milady.' He indicated the back seat of the cab.

'But the hotel's just over there!' Hilary remonstrated, half amused, half angry. She held her ground.

Peter feigned puzzlement. 'So, we're not going back to your place?'

'No!' Hilary clasped her pristine white leather bag more closely to her midriff as though that were the object of Peter's strategy.

'Where you go?' the angry driver shouted, as the vociferous traffic behind him gave vent.

A dapper Chinese, one inch below five feet in height and wearing a brown, light-weight suit with chalk stripe detailing insinuated himself between the couple and the railings at the kerb edge. He disappeared within the cab, slamming the door behind him.

'*Diu chat lei lo mo hai la*!' the driver yelled at Peter.

'What did he say?' Hilary wondered.

'It's untranslatable.'

To Peter's gratification, the cab, its glaring driver and triumphant passenger came to a squealing halt at the next traffic jam twenty yards further on.

'Peter.'

'Yes?' He turned to consider his hostage and captor.

'You're an idiot.' She bit her lip. 'No wonder they can't bear the sight of us.' Then the hint of a smile lifted the corners of her mouth.

She had lowered her bag. Did that mean he was forgiven?

Assuming the best, Peter supported Hilary's elbow to steer her through the stalled traffic towards the hotel on the corner of Garden Road.

They reached the portal of the Hilton coffee shop without further ado. Peter waved Hilary through yet another open door. As he followed her into the conditioned air, the sweat immediately began to congeal beneath his Pringle tennis shirt. The cold was Siberian. Twenty minutes of this and his teeth would start chattering. The micro-climate of the Mandarin Mezzanine was more equable and its club sandwiches more generous but the Hilton was kinder on the wallet. In the days when he had still been part of Solly's merry troupe they would adjourn here after some of their more wearisome parties to do battle with omelettes and toast at five of the dawn. There were consolations in being unemployed. Correction; self-employed.

Crammed into a tight scrum at the entrance to the café, they awaited their chance to escape. (Hilary was convinced the entire congregation of the café was staring at them.) In the furthest corner by the window a 'gwailo' couple was vacating a table for two. Peter just pipped two young Chinese rivals to the post. He grinned at them and shrugged. Hilary arrived, looking embarrassed, and avoided the eyes of the losers as she took her place. She flicked a vagrant crumb from the leatherette before lowering herself before him in a deep curtsey.

A diminutive, bow-legged waitress surfaced beside them. She proffered a menu. Peter waved it away.

'I couldn't cope with more than coffee, could you?'

Before Hilary could offer a rebuttal, Peter turned to the waitress.

'Leung booi gaafei, m goi lei-a.' For emphasis he raised the relevant fingers in a victory sign.

The waitress sniffed and elbowed her way back through the deafening throng.

'Why do they have to shout when they converse?' Hilary shouted. Peter glanced through the window overlooking the street. A gleaming Mercedes 600 disgorged another dapper Chinese, an Arab in a flowing white burnous and a tall European in silk shirt sleeves and shorts.

The group disappeared off to Peter's left into the Hilton Arcade, with its expense-account tat. The Mercedes waited; its driver unconcerned with traffic violations. He did not pay the fines.

'Did you know there are more millionaires per square kilometre in Hong Kong than anywhere else on earth?'

'Don't look at me,' Hilary said with a moue.

'Gaafei ma?' The little waitress almost elbowed Hilary aside as she poured overheated coffee into the waiting cups. The overflow in the saucers would save her a second journey.

'M goi sai,' mumbled Peter with an unconvincing approximation of Cantonese tones. The waitress cleared her throat. Had Peter inadvertently made an improper suggestion?

Hilary leaned sideways and placed her handbag on the floor beside her chair. The waitress left, vexed.

'You'd better slip a chair-leg inside the loop of the strap,' Peter advised. 'A friend of mine had her bag nicked in the Pen lobby.

Never saw it go. Only took a second or two.'

Peter's jaw twitched with cold. He raised the coffee cup. It dripped into the saucer. Through clenched teeth he muttered. 'Here's to us.'

'To Aggie,' Hilary rejoined, with a knowing lift of the eyebrow. Peter wondered which film had inspired that tic. Something starring Lauren Bacall and Bogey, no doubt?

'Aggie?' His face expressed blank ignorance. The name was certainly familiar.

'Your little lady friend,' Hilary murmured, lowering her cup with delicate care.

'Oh, that Aggie.'

Throughout his previous affair, Hilary had without fail enquired after Sarah's well-being. Now it was Aggie's turn for concern. Peter placed a sincere hand over hers.

'Hadn't you heard?'

'What?'

Hilary had forgotten to recapture her hand.

'She moved in with Solly. A 'professional arrangement' I am reliably informed.'

Hilary's eyes softened. 'I'm so sorry. I didn't mean to pry.' She squeezed Peter's hand. 'That's sad.'

'Who knows?' Peter shrugged. 'Perhaps it's for the best in the long run.'

Another squeeze. A bead of suspicion began to form somewhere at the back of Peter's brain. He raked through his memory in search of the last occasion when Hilary had offered any sympathy, with or without coffee. Then he remembered. He carefully removed his hand.

'How's Halford?'

Peter knew how Hilary loathed anybody referring to her husband by his full first name. She carefully arranged both hands in her lap.

'Hal's very well.'

'Of course he is,' Peter acknowledged with a crooked grin. 'He's got you.'

This was quite the wrong rendezvous for bitter-sweet, erotic badinage.

Hilary's arms were beginning to develop a rather pinched look. From this distance he could detect goose pimples. Peter took another sip of coffee. It was already tepid. With his left hand he fingered the congealed bundle of notes in his pocket. He was down to his last two hundred and seventy-three dollars. Seventeen measly pounds. He determined that if Hilary offered to pick up the tab, he would let her. After all, Hilary had a wealthy husband and a highly lucrative job, while Peter had neither. This was not a moment for false pride.

From beneath her lashes Hilary asked, 'Are you keeping busy?'

'Busy enough.'

'There's no need to be proud, Peter.'

'I shall always be too proud to work with Hal again.'

The temperature plummeted further. Hilary reached down for her bag. Peter's inspection of her cleavage affected contempt. The handbag clicked open and a compact was extracted from its innards. Peter averted his gaze from the public powdering; just in time to spot the waitress waddling in their direction. She paused to allow a group to pass. Peter lurched to his feet.

'Nature calls.'

Hilary did not respond. She had embarked on a cosmetic circuit of her lips. Peter hustled past the waitress and muttered, '*Ngor tai-tai bei chin.*'

Up the steps to the breakfast bar, a smart left turn, through the swing doors and out into the arcade. Breathing hard, Peter extracted the bank roll from his damp pocket. With careful affection he shuffled the red, green and brown notes into their respective groups and counted them. No. No change. Still two hundred and seventy-three dollars. Sixteen to the pound.

The Eternal Ivory Company disgorged the trio of one Chinese, one burnoosed Arab and one silk-shirted gwailo. They jostled in front of the boutique window and – jabbing fingers at contortions of distressed-cow-horn-masquerading-as-ivory – continued to haggle. It was clear that the dapper Chinese was the owner of the boutique.

Peter checked his watch. Long enough. He re-entered the refrigerator. Hilary rose to meet him. He gave her his most boyish grin; perhaps a doomed attempt at thirty-five. Hilary led the brief Indian file towards the exit. She awaited her escort at the door. As Peter brushed past her to open it, Hilary murmured in his ear, 'I don't mind paying for the coffee but there was no need to tell the waitress that I was your wife.'

'Sorry. I don't know the Chinese for 'mistress'.

'Don't even bother to find out.'

Hilary swept out into the sauna. Peter plunged after her and felt a thousand pores erupt. Hilary seemed unperturbed by the sudden change of environment. He relented.

'Look, let me pay you back for the coffee.'

Peter produced his re-configured bankroll. Would it stretch for another eight days?

'All right. You may.' Hilary seemed pleased.

Peter found a responsive look of pleasure quite beyond his power. A Hilton doorman brushed past him and crossed the pavement to open the Mercedes door for the arcadians. Peter felt a knee press gently against his leg.

'You can repay me by promising to come for dinner.' Hilary's chin tilted and she bestowed one of her most winning smiles on Peter, ignoring his extended (and soggy) twenty-dollar bill. Hilary's knee had not yet departed from his leg.

'Tuesday evening?' She raised a Bacall eyebrow.

'Who's on the menu?' The knee was gone. He had been caught again.

He watched as the Mercedes slipped away from the gutter with the gesticulating trio still gesticulating. A battered Austin coughed its way into the 600's place. There was a flash of pink silk, white leather and tanned knee. The diesel coughed black smoke. Peter coughed in response as he thrust his meagre stash deep inside his left trouser pocket.

Chapter Three

In the dark, the green Austin-Healey cut away from the lights and turned sharply up towards the University. As Peter swung the wheel to meet the big right-hander at the brow of the hill, he cursed his profligacy. Gone were the days when he could afford to roar about in this debilitated, ancient monster. Yet he smiled as the wind blew a neat, rear parting in his hair. Peter knew these bends so well. He changed down from third to second and the Beast gurgled in eager response. Listen to that roar. It sounded like the former lorry engine it was. A killer of a car with too much weight up front and too little behind. Drivers who steered their Healeys through the bends of the Mille Miglia would dump damp bags of cement in the boot; the only way, they claimed, to prevent their tails wagging. He changed back up to third.

Peter felt sure that the car had been pranged before he'd bought it. At times it sat uneasily on the road, particularly during the rainy season. Peter smiled. A garage owner had once taken it for a quick spin from North Point to Central. He'd set off in a hurry. The round trip should have taken three minutes at most. The garagiste returned, shaken and pale, after fifteen. He pronounced the Healey. 'The most dangerous car I've ever driven.'

Peter knew that the tyres were now bald and that the car had needed its three-monthly oil change three months ago. But there just weren't the funds. He shook his head ruefully. Twelve miles to the gallon. Ridiculously wasteful, even with petrol being so cheap.

At least the road to Pokfulam was pretty clear. This was one of the few stretches of drivable road on the island. The roads in Mid-levels were usually chock-full of tai-tais sawing at the wheels of their husbands' sex substitute Cadillacs or Oldsmobiles. Impossible to pass. He wished he had not introduced the thought of Mid-level hold-ups. It was tempting fate in the form of a slow-moving obstruction. He double-declutched down to second again behind the ageing Sunbeam Alpine. A woman's idea of a sports car. He cursed beneath his breath, waiting for the obstruction to draw over or accelerate. The Rapier did neither. He flashed his lights.

After two slow, processional bends, Peter gunned the Beast past the Sunbeam with full-beam headlights and a jeering stab of his horn. He was past. His elation turned to dismay as other headlights began to sweep round the next bend towards him. Without checking his speed, he flung the Healey to the left, narrowly avoiding the Alpine and scurried on into the darkness to the accompaniment of screaming brakes and howling horns.

Stupid to try to overtake on a blind bend. Still, no harm done. No need to stop. He was already late. The racing-green projectile hurtled towards the street lamps outside Queen Mary Hospital. Peter stamped on the brakes. He had almost overshot the right turn. He wound the big wheel and allowed the Beast to drift gently down the hillside road. Flame of the Forest leaves patterned the sky. In the distance the placid sea, veiled in a blue mist, embraced the reflection of a full moon. He drove with great care into the car park beneath Hal and Hilary's apartment block.

After Peter switched off the ignition, the Beast gurgled twice, lurched once and began to tick. Peter's knees were trembling. He had to pull himself together. He was getting too old for boy-racing. He reached inside his safari suit top pocket for his Pall Mall. His hands were shaking and the Zippo resisted his coaxing. With the cigarette finally lit, Peter sucked in a lungful of smoke. He closed his eyes as the smoke drifted from his nostrils.

Hilary. Twice in a single week. That hadn't happened for a while. He ran over their most recent meeting. It was almost as if Hilary had set it up. Of course, that was nonsense. But then – she had his number. She could have called. No need for any elaborate subterfuge – any 'fancy-meeting-you's'. Then he remembered. His phone had been cut off two weeks earlier. Well. who needed a phone anyway?

Even if their meeting in Central had been sheer coincidence, she had certainly seemed eager enough to invite him to dinner, in spite of his declaration that he would never work with Hal again.

He imagined Hal felt the same about him. But there had been no question of, 'I'll have a word with Hal and get back to you.'

He could hear a car slow at the top of the hill before its headlights dipped, turned and soared, before dipping once more. Flickering through silhouetted shrubs, the lights descended the hill. A tiny thought blossomed in his brain. Suddenly panicky, Peter flicked away the cigarette and clambered over the side of the Healey. He really must get the driver's door lock repaired one day. When he was back in funds.

A solitary light illuminated this side of the car park. The stairwell was pitch black and Peter stumbled as he tried to take the steps two at a time. He guessed the headlights were now well on their way down the hill. For some unaccountable reason panic was rising in his throat. He reached the second landing and fumbled for his lighter. It spat into life. The printed visiting card, athwart a small frame beside the door, declared 'Halford Puckle, Publisher, Hong Kong Weekly.' A current of air licked the orange and blue flame down towards Peter's fingertips. He flicked the hot lighter lid shut and reached out for the doorbell. Below, car doors opened and slammed shut and voices were raised. The tone was distinctly conjugal.

'I tell you it is the same fucking car!' Suburban. Home Counties.

'Stop swearing! People will hear you.' Suburban. Midlands.

'He all but killed us and all you can say is 'stop fucking swearing'.'

Shoe leather scraped on the sandy concrete of the forecourt and Peter leaned his full weight on the bell. An irate amah's voice called out in Chinglish.

'You *waitee, daung ha, daung ha.*'

Peter was subjected to inspection via the spy-hole. He heard heavy foot-steps begin to mount the stairs below.

'You'll lose that bloody hand-bag one day.'

The door swung open and Peter blinked in the light. He strode into the apartment and wrested the door from the amah's fingers to shut out the sound of ascending footsteps. He burst into the living room and a startled Hilary rose from a rosewood armchair.

Her hand flew to a bosom of black, figured silk.

'What on earth's the matter?' she demanded.

'Just carry on regardless.'

Peter spotted a half-consumed glass of golden liquid on a coffee table.

'Excuse me.'

Grabbing the drink, he slid into the matching armchair opposite Hilary's and assumed a casual pose. He raised the glass at Hilary and took a slug. 'Just what the doctor ordered.' He nodded towards his hostess. 'Love the dress.'

The doorbell rang. The amah, who had only just shuffled back into the living room, turned about and shouted an order in Cantonese.

The door rang once more. The amah called for silence. '*M ho chou. M ho chou.*'

'Will you open this door?' a male voice demanded.

'Something's eating Nigel,' Hilary murmured.

'No such luck,' Peter muttered, taking another sip. He hoped he was giving a fair impression of composure.

They all listened to the sudden silence. Hilary tried again. 'Everyone's arrived.' She tilted her head. 'I can hear him.' Nary a sound did Peter detect. Hilary returned and resumed her seat, smoothing her skirt. 'Hal's on his way.'

Two minutes later the woman whom Peter now knew as 'Susan' turned and nodded her approval at the man Peter now knew as 'Nigel'. Hilary got to her feet and slalomed around the rosewood settee towards the kitchen.

Susan extended an arm in Peter's direction. 'I'm sorry but, with all this fuss, I don't think I caught your name.' Her arm dimpled at the elbow. Peter remained inert.

'I'm Susan Thompson.'

'Peter Nicholson.'

Peter got to his feet, accepted the presented limp fingers and, for lack of anything better to do, kissed the tips.

'And this,' Susan resumed, ignoring the osculation. 'This is my husband, Nigel.'

'Haven't we met?' Nigel half-closed an eye and looked

sidelong at Peter. A tinkling sound announced Hilary's reappearance as she backed through the swing door from the kitchen. Peter, seated once more, lost interest in Nigel's question. Nigel lost interest in Peter.

Hilary bore a diminutive drinks tray in her hands. Like an amateur juggler on a heaving cruise ship, Hilary retraced her passage around the settee and across the perilous intervening space, a smile fixed on her lips and her gaze fixed on the drinks.

'Brandy dry,' Hilary announced, offering one side of the tray to Susan. 'And bourbon. Straight,' A demure inclination towards the appreciative Nigel. It was clear that she was already familiar with the couple's poison.

'Really, Hilary,' Susan flashed, all indignation. 'Why are you serving the drinks? You must take Ah Yeot in hand.'

'Oh, Ah Yeot's quite a character.' Hilary smiled. 'Quite one of the family.' She searched for a vacant space on a coffee table already cumbered with an onyx lighter, a shot marble ashtray, a table-lamp in the shape of an alabaster nude and several shot glasses. Placing the tray on the parquet floor beside her, Hilary resumed her previous position in the rosewood chair. She turned towards Susan.

'How's Ah Ha?' Hilary enquired. Peter stifled a yawn.

'Gone,' Susan lamented. She shot a sharp glance at her spouse. 'Nigel got rid of her.' Finger and thumb removed an offending speck from the laméd bosom.

'I should think I did,' snorted the said Nigel. He dropped into falsetto. 'Oh, missy, I no likee washee window. I no likee clean floor.' He restored his habitual over-ripe baritone. 'What the hell was she doing for her five hundred bucks a month, I'd like to know?!'

'Well, Nigel,' Hilary's voice assumed the tone of someone on secure ground – the expert in the mores of the domestic classes. 'Ah Yeot doesn't wash windows or polish parquet any longer and we pay her five hundred and fifty.'

Nigel snorted.

'It's the going rate.' Hilary frowned and then smiled.

Nigel ignored the smile. 'It's employers like you who are

ruining the market for the rest of us. It's bad enough having the Yanks and the Japs paying a thousand a month or more. Someone's got to make a stand.'

Peter blew across the rim of his glass. Nigel swung round. 'I beg your pardon.'

'That's quite all right.'

'I didn't catch exactly what you do in Hong Kong, Mr. Nicholson.' Susan wrinkled her brow. Before Peter could reply, a new voice interrupted.

'He's gonna do us all a good turn… ain't you, Pete, me old mate?'

The broad Bristolian vowels bounded across the living room, followed shortly thereafter by the impressive appearance of Halford Puckle, the esteemed Publisher of *Hong Kong Weekly.*

Chapter Four

'She really is a treasure, your Ah Yeot,' Susan sighed.

Nigel pushed his empty plate away as though it still tempted him. 'That was a fantastic nosh. Absolutely fantastic, old sport.'

Hal was working a cigar between wet lips.

'Ah, she is a right little wonder, that Ah Yeot. And a wonderful comfort when Hilary's indisposed.' This observation was concluded with a wide and winning smile.

Hal's bon mot was not greeted with the fish knife in the conjugal gullet it deserved. Instead, Hilary smiled in response to Hal's little jest.

Peter covered his irritation by lighting a cigarette. He wondered, as he had often wondered in the past, what this formerly rather proper girl saw in such an agglomeration of vulgarity. While she continued to smile, Peter covered his irritation by exhaling. Through a haze of smoke, he contemplated the grinning Hal.

The publisher's black hair curled over a low brow and luxuriant dark eyebrows. If the eyes and nose were unexceptionable, the teeth and jaws were frightening instruments of mastication; perfectly designed to consume two gigantic helpings of Ah Yeot's sweet and sour pork. At the slightest provocation Hal's full lips parted to reveal a picket fence of white-on-white teeth. Peter wondered how nature could cram so much calcium into one human jaw. As if in response, Hal's lips parted and his teeth clamped down on the cigar. The Lord and Master tilted his rosewood dining chair backwards.

'I reckon Ah Yeot can clear away now, Hil,' Hal said, inhaling deeply. Hilary's bare arm, like a snake responding to a charmer, stretched across the table to lift the silver bell. Once it tinkled; then twice; then thrice. Hilary, her exasperation plain for her guests to see, made as though to rise. Her ascent was intercepted.

'Ah Yeot!' Hal roared, offering a vision – not just of teeth, but of uvula. 'Get your bloody arse in 'ere, you old turd!'

The kitchen door was flung open. Peter winced at the prospect of the amah brandishing a razor-sharp kitchen cleaver. What came crashing through the aperture was a serving trolley followed by the wrinkled old retainer. Her creviced face assumed the rictus of a smile as she muttered and began to heap fresh fruit cocktail into cut-glass bowls. The first portion, piled high with pineapple, lychee and mango, was placed gently before the master of the house. Without pausing for his guests to be served (and without dispensing with his cigar), Hal set about consuming his fruit at record speed. Munching mango and his cigar in turns, Hal finally sat back to survey the company of guests. His chosen victim was to be Peter.

'So, Pete.' Hal beamed. 'How's tricks?'

Peter paused in his own skirmish with the slippery salad. 'Oh, could be worse.'

''ow long is it since they kicked you out of U.N.I.?'

'U.P.I.' Peter corrected. 'And I wasn't kicked. I walked.'

Hal smirked. 'Kicked, walked – what's the difference? Come on – how long is it?'

Peter felt his cheeks glow. Why should he submit to a humiliating assault by this Neanderthal in front of Hilary? Or in front of people he had only just met? At least Susan had the delicacy to look embarrassed. He did not feel inclined to evaluate Nigel's reaction.

'No, come on,' Hal encouraged, ''ow long is it?'

Then Hal's attention was diverted to Nigel. Hal lowered his cigar.

'Come on, Nige. Eat up. There's a good boy.' Hal's grin became a frown. 'What's the matter, Nige?

Peter twisted round to see Nigel on his feet peering down out of a window. 'I'll bet it's still down there.'

'Don't be so bloody rude, Nige.' Hal pointed his masticated cigar at Nigel's chair. Nigel trudged back to his seat. Hal leaned back and waited until his victim had obediently settled back in his place at the table.

'Now, what's still down there?'

Nigel sulked.

Peter, face impassive, explained. 'Nigel says the driver of a car parked downstairs almost wrote him and Susan off on their way here this evening.'

'Yes,' Nigel took centre stage for the punch line. 'And all I've got to do is wait here for the chap who owns it to show up, haven't I?'

Susan chose this moment to pat her husband's hand. He snatched it away.

'It was dangerous driving,' Nigel muttered. 'Fucking dangerous. And I've got a witness.' He glared at his wife.' Haven't I?'

Susan did not look overjoyed at her election as the star witness in the forthcoming prosecution.

'This mango is perfect,' Peter interjected, smiling his approbation at Hilary. She took her cue.

'Thank you, Peter. Ah Yeot buys them at Central Market. I drive her down there and she haggles away and gets all the best fruit and veg. Seems silly to get them out of tins.'

'The Philippines,' Hal interjected. Hilary's shopping narrative halted as heads of guests swivelled towards their host. Hal gazed at the end of his cigar whence rose a curlicue of smoke.

'Yeah. The Philippines,' Hal repeated dreamily. He looked up. ''Ave you ever been to the Philippines, Nige?'

Nigel's response was cut short by the sound of a car engine coming to life. Nigel was half-way to the window before Hal's stentorian bellow pulled him up short. 'Where the 'ell are you goin' Nige?' As Nigel turned, Hal's voice resumed its conversational tone. 'We are here to discuss a very important matter of business that could bring us all a nice, tidy packet.' As the invisible car coughed its way into the night, Nigel's head turned once more towards the window. He made as if to rise.

'Nige, keep your bloody arse on that chair.' Nigel complied but with a great show of reluctance. Hal resumed, giving Peter the benefit of his attention. Nigel exchanged a nervous glance with Susan.

'Now, as you know, Pete, I run this nice little magazine called *Hong Kong Weekly*.'

Hal was all affability.

'How could anyone be more aware of its existence?' Peter's rhetorical question drew a smile from Hal. Peter searched for his Pall Mall. Hal's grin broadened as Peter lit his cigarette. Hal pointed a forefinger at Peter and shook his head in apology.

'I was forgetting that the first edition was your baby, Pete. It was much appreciated.'

Peter nodded his acknowledgement of the compliment.

'But it's grown up since then.' Hal paused. ''Hil. Why don't you take Susan into our bedroom and show her that nice lingerie I brought back from Singapore last week?' (He pronounced the Singaporean booty as 'lonjerie'.)

Hilary gave Susan a weak smile and led the way out of the dining room. As Hilary passed his chair, Hal pinched her right buttock. She gave a little shriek then skipped ahead of Susan out of the room. Hal smirked as the door closed.

'She's a real trouper that Hilary.' Hal bared his teeth at his male guests. 'She can type too.'

'What were you saying about the Philippines?' Peter asked, dragging Hal back to the fork in the conversational road.

Hal ground out the butt of the cigar in the onyx ashtray. 'Pete, I'll be straight with you.' Peter shifted uncomfortably at this blatant untruth. Hal leaned confidingly towards Peter. 'Without your input for the first three editions of the *Weekly*...'

'I think you'll find it was four.'

Hal paused. 'Three? Four?' (Hal spread his hands) 'Anyway, without you 'The Weekly' would not be in existence today. I'll always remember that.'

Nigel interrupted. 'Oh, I don't know, Hal. I seem to recollect that it was mostly through your efforts that the mag got off the ground.'

'No, Nige. Credit where credit is due.' Hal considered Nigel. 'Come to think of it you 'elped too. With the ads.'

'And the advertorial,' Nigel offered.

Hal's expression radiated sincere gratitude. 'Yeah, you took care of the ads. But I did 'ave a bit of trouble finding top quality writers for the articles.'

Peter raised his fork and pushed the final slice of pineapple to the other side of his dish. Thoughtfully considering the fruit, he murmured. 'Unfortunately, writers have a nasty habit of requiring payment for their work. You know…that inconvenient business of keeping body and soul together.'

He smiled at Hal, whose nod reflected sympathy. 'Yeah, Pete, that's true. But I was 'avin troubles of my own just getting' by from month to month.' He glanced in the direction the women had taken. 'If it hadn't been for Hilary's salary, I'd 'ave been right up shit-creek without a paddle.'

'Look, Hal,' Peter slid his fork into the bowl. 'I appreciate reminiscence as much as the next man but…'

'All right, Pete. I can take a hint.' Hal pointed across the table at Peter. 'Ow much do you reckon the magazine owes you?'

Peter lifted the fork and prodded the lone surviving morsel.

'C'mon, Pete. No messin'. 'Ow much?'

'You can work it out.' Peter looked across at Hal. Pique enabled him to hold the other man's gaze. 'There were three long interviews with pics. Then there were the four features…'

'With pics,' Hal added and Peter went back to playing with his fork.

Suddenly he remembered. 'Oh, and five photo calls for other people's articles.'

Hal nodded judiciously. He reached into the inner jacket pocket of his grey silk suit. With narrowed eyes he unfolded his wallet and counted out six pristine red notes in a neat pile on the damask tablecloth. Peter relished the sight.

'Three thousand.' Hal squinted at Peter and produced another cigar. He searched for and found his guillotine cutter. Peter licked his lower lip.

Hal smiled. 'Does that make us even?' Hal produced a gold Dupont lighter and lit the cigar. The smoke drifted across the table.

Peter had suffered a pang earlier in the evening. He had spent twenty-five of his remaining dollars on petrol to drive the Beast to Hal's place and back. Only two hundred and forty-eight dollars remained. Peter's fingers twitched. It was all he could do not to snatch the notes and bolt. Instead, he said, 'We're talking about a couple of weeks' solid work. That's worth at least four and a half.' He knew it was madness to accept Hal's opening gambit.

Hal lifted the pile of notes and balanced their pristine stiffness between finger and thumb. Closing his left eye against the spiralling smoke. Hal murmured. 'Of course, you may 'ave been earning better money at U.P.O...'

'U.P.I.' Peter corrected. To be frank, the agency hadn't paid that well but Peter had loved the work. It was that and the prestige attached to working for an international press organisation which made up for the miserly rewards.

'Be sensible, Pete.' Hal leaned forward, the epitome of the reasonable man. 'You know that freelances don't make big bucks in this town.' The bundle of notes swayed between the fulcrum of Hal's finger and thumb. 'Even when they deserve it.'

Nigel looked angrily at the ingrate. 'Three thousand's not to be sneered at, Peter.'

'Who asked for your opinion?' Peter snapped. Who was doing the negotiating here?

'Now, Pete,' Hal cooed. 'Be nice to Nige. He works for Kleinwort Benson and he's got all the connections we need.' Hal beamed through the cigar smoke at the grinning Nigel. 'We're gonna need 'im. And he's gonna need us.' He pushed the wad of notes across the table until they rested beside Peter's dessert bowl.

'Which 'need' are you referring to?' Peter realised immediately that asking the question had been a mistake. He'd taken the bait. Hal took a deep drag of his cigar. He exhaled and announced, *Hong Kong Weekly's Philippines' Edition.* Hal settled himself more comfortably. He waited for the announcement to have full effect before continuing. His tone was conversational.

'I was in Mohan's the other day over on the Kowloon side. I was trying to pitch them an 'alf page ad in the mag. You know, the usual deal. An ad this month; a bit of a puff the next. Next thing I know this little brown bloke walks in and I'm forgotten. The entire sales staff swarmed round this bloke.' He paused and drew on the cigar. 'This one, I thought, has to be a really good customer. He had a ginormous bloke with 'im, wearing shades and a straw 'at. I figured the big bloke was some kind of bodyguard.' Hal paused for another inhalation of smoke while his captive audience waited. 'Since I still 'ad 'alf my spiel left, I 'ung about while this bloke got his suit or whatever.' Hal paused again and considered the wet end of the cigar. Then he resumed his tale. 'It turned out that the little bloke had ordered not one – not two – not five – but ten suits. Ten. I kid you not. All the staff came from the rear of the shop with the clobber.' Hal paused for effect. 'Ten suits. All silk.' Hal glanced down approvingly at his own suit. 'Anyway, while we were both waitin' like, we got chattin'. I just 'appened to have a sample of the Weekly ready and he took a gander. It was the April edition with the crackin' cover.'

'The harbour at night. The one I shot.' The words left Peter's mouth before he could stop them. He could have kicked himself.

Hal feigned surprise. 'Is that right?' Hal grinned. 'I told you we needed Pete, didn't I, Nige?' Hal's smile departed as rapidly as it had arrived. 'Well, to cut a long story short, I goes with this bloke to the Pen. 'E 'ad one of the hotel's Rollers waiting outside Mohan's. I love that shade of green. Mind you, I prefer my Granada.' He grinned at Peter. 'It turns out that the little bloke is stayin' in a bloody luxury penthouse suite. You should 'ave seen it.' Hal's arm described an arc over the cluttered table. 'Before I know what's 'appened, this bloke has invited us over to the Philippines to devote a whole issue of *Hong Kong Weekly* to his country. All expenses paid.'

Nigel threw in his two cents. 'The Philippines isn't Hong Kong or Singapore, Hal. It's a real Third World country. Who's going to supply us with ads? At our prices?'

'Don't worry about a thing.' This was Hal, the smooth salesman, at his most reassuring. 'This bloke is some kind of big shot over there. All you'll 'ave to do is go round dishing out invoices and bring the plates back to Hong Kong.' Hal took another drag of the cigar. 'It'll be a doddle.'

'And what about the copy and the pics? Will they be a doddle as well?' Peter looked into Hal's gleaming eyes.

'Pete, me old mate... this should solve all the money

problems... you are going to be in complete charge of all editorial.' Hal brought a fist down on the table. A startled fruit knife sprang into the air. It landed on Nigel's plate with a clatter.

Peter looked down at the crisp red notes. 'Hal, are you ready to discuss remuneration? Seriously?'

'Remuneration?' Hal feigned disgust. 'Remuneration? You won't be freelance any more. No more working for peanuts. This is for a third share of the profits from the issue.' The publisher pointed at Nigel and Peter, and finally, himself as he identified each partner. 'Share and share and share alike.' Hal leaned forward and placed his palms on the table. 'And if this comes off, who knows? We can do the same thing everywhere else in the region.' He grinned. 'Full-time partners.'

Peter resumed playing with the fruit fork.

'All right, Pete. Be suspicious.' Hal leaned towards Peter. 'Look. You won't 'ave to spend a penny in the Philippines. I've said we'll go thirds on the profits.' He leaned back. 'Well, in addition I'll pay all the usual fees for any articles or pictures you provide. And any expenses.' Hal pointed his cigar at Peter and squinted. 'Now, I can't do better than that, can I?'

Peter slowly reached forward and rescued the three thousand promises to pay. He folded them twice before thrusting them into the recesses of his left trouser pocket. He had given up using his superfluous wallet. Tonight, he might take a taxi to carry him home and another in the morning to pick up the Beast.

'Okay. Let's call this a down payment.' He held up a warning hand as Hal broached a smile. 'But I'll still need time to think about it.'

''Ow about you, Nige?' Hal turned towards the vision in purple.

'Oh, I'm in, Old Sport.' Nigel grinned. 'The firm owes me oodles of leave.'

Hal grinned back. 'You'll need plenty. I 'ear tell there's an island there where there's seven girls for every feller. It's a paradise for men, the Philippines.'

'Well, you know what I always say.' Nigel threw a stealthy glance in the direction of the master bedroom. 'A change is as good as a rest. And I deserve a really good change.' He inflated his flushed cheeks.

'Look, Nige.' Hal was on his feet, holding out his right hand. 'I reckon me and Pete 'ave got a bit more chattin' to do. It's been a long day.' Nigel approached Hal and offered his paw. Hal grinned. 'Nice of you and Susan to drop by.' He winked.

'But what about that bugger in the Healey?'

'Pete and me will keep a lookout for the driver, won't we, Pete?' Hal delivered another clamorous wink which Peter felt sure Nigel must have seen.

The unwanted guest snorted. 'Now, look here, Hal. Maybe I should...'

'Hilary!' Hal bellowed over his shoulder. 'Hilary!' The bedroom door opened and Hilary reappeared. Susan peeped around her hostess. Hal frowned. 'I don't know 'ow you too can go on gabbin' about clothes all night. Nigel's fit to fall over with tiredness. Ain't you, Nige?'

Nigel nodded reluctantly. Hal rose and slapped his partner's back. 'Come on, Susan, before Nige gets too tired for bed.' Hal laughed.

Nigel had moved over to the window. 'It's still there,' Nigel grumbled, peering into the darkness. 'Here, wait a minute.' All heads turned sharply at the note of anguish in Nigel's voice. 'I don't sodding well believe it.' He clapped his palms to his temples. 'Our bloody car has gone.'

Hal, grinning from ear to ear, seemed unconcerned. 'Stop foolin' around, Nige.'

'I'm not fooling. Wait.' Nigel clicked his fingers. 'Of course! I was so sodding furious with Susan's nagging when we got here that I must have left the sodding key in the sodding ignition.'

Susan could not have chosen a worse moment to step between Nigel and his anguish. 'There's no need to use such coarse language, Nigel.'

'Sod off!' Nigel responded, his voice thick with emotion. He was having difficulty in drawing breath. Hal was struggling against a grin.

'Never mind, Nige. It's only some kid taking it for a joyride.

The cops'll find it in the morning.'

Nigel refused to be comforted. Hal slapped him on the back. 'With a bit of luck, the silly bugger will write the old banger off. Think of the insurance and cheer up.' He placed a protective arm around the miserable Nigel's shoulders. 'Come on, old chap.' His other arm snaked around Susan's shoulders. 'I'll drive you two back 'ome.'

Peter made as though to follow in the wake of the departing group.

'Where do you think you're goin' Pete? Sit down. 'Ave another drink. I'll be back in half an hour or so. 'Ere, Hil.' Hilary joined the group by the door. Peter breathed in the fragrance which seemed to emanate from Hilary's breasts as she stood obediently beside him.

'You entertain Pete for me, Hil. He still needs some persuadin' to come on our Philippines trip. 'Elp him make up 'is mind.' Hilary nodded at Hal then smiled up at Peter. She returned to the dining room.

Hal murmured to Peter. 'I love that dress. Gives me a nice, warm glow.' Hal patted Peter's arm. He caught up with Nigel and Susan and passed them on the next flight of stairs.

Peter slowly closed the door as Nigel and Susan continued to grope their way down the stairwell in the wake of the breezy Hal. The door clicked shut on the sound of Hal's laughter and Peter turned back towards the dining room.

'I think you really prefer this to wine, don't you?' Hilary stood, poised, with a bottle of single malt in her right hand.

'You have a good memory, Hilary,' Peter said with a smile.

Hilary began to pour, then paused with a frown. 'Ice.' She turned on her heel and exited to the kitchen. Peter mused.

Yes, of course he would find the Philippines' project fascinating. The archipelago was only four hundred miles away and yet he'd never been near the place. This wasn't the first hint that Puckle had dropped about a work-trip to the Philippines. So much so that Peter had already embarked on some leisurely research. Of course, travellers' tales about corruption, violence, sexual exploitation and yawning disparities of wealth were legion. His curiosity had been aroused sufficiently for him to begin collecting articles on the islands from the *Far Eastern Economic Review.*

According to Derek Davies, Ferdinand Marcos had had a tough job getting to the top in Manila. He was an Ilocano. A Northern country boy. Of course, being the most decorated allied soldier of the Second World War had not done Marcos any harm. Now the war hero President spoke eloquently about bringing the Philippines into the 20th Century. If even half of Marcos' promises came true, the islands would truly become the paradise they already claimed to be. In any case, it would be a fascinating place to visit.

He knew that Hal would have no compunction about demanding copy from him which would be little more than advertorial for the regime. Peter wondered whether he would have the courage to stand up and be counted. He still dreamed of working for a real newspaper one day with his own by-line. Or maybe he could return in triumph to UPI. Or even join the BBC as a Hong Kong stringer. Deus vult. Or vult not.

Peter sighed and closed his eyes. Then he reached for his cigarettes. As he allowed the smoke to drift from his nostrils, he wondered about the identity of the ten-suited, small brown man who would be bankrolling the Philippines issue of Hong Kong Weekly. Was he a corrupt crony of the ruling elite? Or was he an outsider trying to buy his way in? And how would Hal and Nigel react if Peter refused meekly to sing the praises of the faultless Philippines? Nor, he was sure, would their sponsor welcome an honest, 'warts and all' appraisal of his country.

Peter had already sketched out plans to return to the U.K. Since leaving the American press agency, his life had been insubstantial in more ways than one. He had been reduced to propping up the bar at the *Foreign Correspondents' Club*, waiting for old hack acquaintances to stand him a drink and introduce him to new old hacks who might be willing to offer him a miserly stipend to mind their phones while they swanned round South Vietnam or Thailand on expenses. Peter performed miserable tasks for chicken-feed.

His one-bedroom flat in Causeway Bay was a cramped cell far-from-far-enough away from a cockroach-infested, noisy, dangerous warren of streets despoiled by drugs, disease and poverty. And death. Every dark corner and every stinking public toilet in these culs would boast their share of silver foil cigarette wrappers, tainted by the faecal, dark brown stains of dissolved heroin. The locals called it 'chasing the dragon'. Until the dragon caught them. Hong Kong had a major drugs problem.

All this was too close to inferno for comfort. He hungered to return to his old apartment in mid-levels. Would Hal's siren song restore Peter's fortunes? Was it worth a final fling?

The darkness gathered round him. The ticking of the cooling engine had stopped. Lights flickered in the distance between the shifting leaves of palms. The incised silhouettes of sampans dotted the moonlit sea. Their lights were lures to attract fish to the small boats whose hungry nets awaited their arrival.

Peter exhumed his damp packet of Pall Mall. Last cigarette. The wavering flame of the Zippo was reflected in the dark face of the speedometer. He drew smoke into his lungs.

The Philippines. It was the place the typhoons came from. Everyone in Hong Kong knew about typhoons. They were procreated in the mid-Pacific and swept westward across the waters, increasing in strength as they went. Think of it. A storm with the power of a hundred atomic bombs. And the Philippines was right in the path of the furies of nature.

He would never forget the deep thespian voice of Ralph Pixton on Radio Hong Kong warning, 'A tropical storm has been reported passing through the Balintang Channel.' After abusing the islands, the storms roared on towards the coast of China.

He had already experienced several of these 'dai feng' or 'big winds'. On one unforgettable occasion he had been trapped in this very flat with Hal. 1962. Wanda, wasn't it? Winds with gusts of over one hundred and eighty miles an hour. He and Hal had watched, breathless and impotent, as the large, wooden constructor's hut across the road had begun to collapse in slow motion. The sunburned worker in the singlet, shorts and flip-flops had just managed to reach the ground via the exterior staircase before the whole structure was reduced to a flat-pack. The next day's journey into Central had been blocked by a freighter, lifted high and dry onto the quayside of the harbour. There was no way round. He had backed the Beast up the hill.

Peter knew that the Philippines did not only have more than their fair share of typhoons; the islands also had a thriving prostitution industry. Cebu was the island Hal had referred to where women outnumbered men by seven to one. With odds like that the women stood little chance of avoiding their fate. Old hacks in the FCC brightened as they launched into their travellers' tales of three or four in a bed. The country also had 'rum and coco-cola' a-plenty.

After the Spanish-American War of 1898 the island chain had dropped into the United States' star-spangled apron like so many ripe durians. Teddy Roosevelt's Rough Riders charged up San Juan Hill and into the book of American military myths. After the victory, the anti-imperialist 'Land of the Free' forgot all about anti-imperialism and took the place of the defeated Spanish colonialists. But before the U.S. of A could lay hold of the islands, an inconvenient local rebellion against Spanish rule had broken out in 1896. It failed; the Filipinos would have to wait until 1935 before they achieved a form of independence. But the Americans did not leave.

Marcos talked big about the glorious destiny of the Philippines but the U.S. of A. still carried the bigger stick. Even today the Americans had a major air force base here. Clark Field, wasn't it? And there was always the U.S. Sixth Fleet. Their R & R visits to Hong Kong kept the bars of Wanchai wealthy, if not healthy. The Philippines, along with Taiwan, Guam, South Korea and Japan formed part of the advanced defensive ring against Communist China.

You could not remain long in Hong Kong without picking up travellers' tales about neighbouring countries in South-East Asia. Singapore, with its benign dictatorship, rapidly enlarging its trade and influence, and trampling on the economic heels of Hong Kong. Malaysia, divided between Malays and Chinese; the former with the political power and the latter controlling the economy. Thailand, with its sex trade, its temples with their excitable Buddhist monks, and the picturesque vegetable and fruit markets, floating on the canals or *khlongs*. Yes, even without having travelled much further than the bar of the FCC, Peter had picked up more than sufficient information about the area. Including the Philippines.

For the world beyond the region, there was only one surname up in lights; the main attraction of the Philippines was a married couple – President Ferdinand Marcos and his flamboyant, glamorous wife, Imelda. They lived a life which rivalled that of any Hollywood star. Together they had fought their way from a distant province of little political account to lord it over the millionaires of Manila. Rumour had it that Imelda could persuade the millionaires to support her schemes with generous donations 'for national improvement'. In exchange, the First Lady would persuade her husband to grant permission for the donors' ambitious capital investment schemes.

Imelda and Ferdinand had made it to the top of the Philippines hand in hand. But Marcos was now the ex-war hero whose wife was also his main political rival.

Imelda bore the sobriquet 'The Queen of Tondo'. 'Tondo' was the name of the sprawling slum in the heart of Manila; the domain of the poorest of the poor.

Was Imelda really the guardian angel of the poor? Casually tossing small change to the excitable, scrabbling hordes as her immaculate limousine passed through their excited ranks, Imelda's glamour and open-handedness trumped her husband's undoubted bravery and political ability. After her regal progress it was back to the Malacañang Palace and the hundreds of pairs of shoes the 'Pirst Lady' secreted in her suite of rooms.

No. *Hong Kong Weekly* stood no chance of getting within camera distance of the stars of Manila, let alone meeting them.

Of course, all the journos in Hong Kong were obsessed by China and Vietnam – nobody gave the Philippines a second thought. And for Hong Kong businessmen the Philippines were a bad joke. Now Peter – if he took up Hal's offer – would be obliged to treat the place as he would – say – Malaysia or Thailand. He would have to flesh out the facts he already knew to bring the place to life. At least he had made a start of sorts. He knew that neither Hal nor Nigel would lift a finger or turn a page to lessen their ignorance. They would rely on him. But could he rely on them?

Peter opened his eyes. He flicked the cigarette butt into the night. He felt sure that Hal would not permit Nigel to go through with any of that dangerous driving nonsense. It was all bluff. But. Nigel, worryingly, was an unknown quantity. Peter blinked and frowned and then relaxed. He knew that Hal would not wish anything untoward to happen to his favourite writer cum photographer. So reliable. So cheap.

The only person at this evening's dinner that Peter had been glad to see was Hilary. They had first met soon after she and her husband, Halford Puckle, had arrived in the Colony. There had been no tan in those days. Just a pale, anxious little secretary from Godstone, clutching a glass of orange juice to her bosom.

Hal soon absented himself. No sooner had his chukka boots trodden on Hong Kong's colonial soil than Hal was off on his peregrinations. To Malaysia; or Singapore; or South Korea. Another country, another scheme; leaving lonely, little Hil to tan slowly in the Hong Kong sun by the pool of the Ladies Recreation Club. Between poolside drinks and confidential chats, Hilary climbed from her lounger into a secretarial post in the assistant manager's office of the Kuayleh (Happiness) Hotel. Over the following years Peter would run into her in the foyer of the City Hall Theatre or at the occasional amateur thespian dinner party. But they always managed to meet each other alone at the LRC. He also knew that she found his attentions flattering. If resistible.

In those days he had still been working for Butterfield and Swire. In the advertising department. He made a point of inviting business contacts to the LRC for lunch. It was so convenient. After his guest had departed, he would impress the watching tai-tais with four fast lengths of the pool. He prided himself on his crawl.

Among the competitive matrons who invited him to join them beside their poolside loungers, he was considered a prize catch.

They vied to catch his eye while discussing his siege of Hilary's virtue with a mixture of amusement and envy. Peter discovered that the gently gilded Hilary was not entirely displeased when this eligible bachelor set out to amuse her.

He quickly discovered that Hilary was lonely. So, no need to rush matters. He knew a direct approach might frighten her off. He could rely on Hong Kong's whirligig of time to bring her within reach. Sooner or later, he felt sure, Hilary would follow the way of all flesh.

He carefully constructed the relationship; word by word; whisper by whisper; light kiss by light kiss. Hilary's tension was eased by sun, brandy alexander and parties. They shared many friends who loved to throw parties. On boats; in hotels; in apartments; or on a midnight beach. If Hal and Hilary arrived together, she was soon abandoned by her knight errant.

Peter benefitted from Hal's insouciance. Occasionally, secreted within the darkness of a living room given over to the pleasure of very slow, close dancing, Hilary would respond to Peter's pelvic pressure. His confidence grew. When she expressed a wish to call a cab, shamed by the drunken Hal's dionysiac antics, Peter would offer to drive her home. The route became familiar. He also became familiar with Hilary's breasts, the tautness of her buttocks, the perfume of her skin and the taste of her lips. Yes, it was only a matter of time and opportunity.

How misplaced his confidence had been. It was clear that Hal was the only beneficiary of the tumescence Peter had laboured to inspire. Peter began to wonder whether, when Hal finally arrived after one of his foreign jaunts, Hilary amused and aroused him with anecdotes about her would-be seducer's fruitless advances. Was the recitation by Hilary-Scheherazade of her impregnable desirability the device she deployed to recharge Hal's sexual batteries?

Peter flushed as he recalled the events of the previous hour. Even after Hal's departure the flat stank of the stench of his cigars. Still smarting at Hal's parting shot, Peter had gracelessly accepted Hilary's offer of a drink. While they made bland conversation, Ah Yeot barged in and out of the kitchen to clear the debris of the meal. Hilary ordered her duenna to leave the task until the morning. Ah Yeot glared at Peter and barged back into the kitchen. The door to the rear balcony where the amah had her own room banged shut.

Clearly, Hilary had simply waved Peter's whisky under a closed tap. The drink's kick was vicious. Peter was invited to resume his seat. He took a second mouthful and grimaced. Studiously avoiding Hilary's eye, Peter brooded over the glass. Finally, as he had intended, she wondered aloud what the matter was. Peter's eyes wandered past the drink and focussed on Hilary's feet. In their delicate, black, high-heeled sandals, her toes were golden-brown and bare. The perfect nails were painted the palest of pinks. Peter sighed.

There was absolutely no point in complaining to Hilary about Hal. Peter had given up trying to understand how an attractive, and, by now, relatively sophisticated woman would prefer Hal's company to his. Instead, he muttered something self-pitying into his glass about Aggie. It was intended to evoke sympathy. Thinking about Aggie always made him sad, especially when he had been drinking straight whisky. The viva voce mention of the name simply saddened him further. He drained the last of the booze. He was desperate for a pee.

Hilary had slipped out of her chair and crouched before him, eyes wide with sympathy. Peter could have predicted the gesture. Peripherally, he was aware of her cleavage, tan fading into glittering gold, dipping wickedly beneath the silk of her dress. Her hand brushed his but, instead of reaching for her, he heard his slurring voice pouring out a sorry lament.

Peter related the rows with Aggie about his demand that she should leave Solly. He detailed the events of the false dawn of their reconciliation. Yes, in the end she had left Solly, as requested. And immediately everything turned turtle. For seven harried days they had fought or sulked.

Hilary's grip tightened as he continued his tale. He felt the corner of one eye moisten. Hilary's eyes moistened in sympathy. She sighed. He found her sigh very affecting.

The break-up with Aggie was three months old. Correction;

three months and one week. He rubbed his eyes. Surely, he had told Hilary all this before. His mind felt somewhat loose on its hinges. Whose fault had it been? His or Aggie's? Mea culpa? Tua culpa? Was that correct?

He excused himself, rose to his feet and weaved his way to the smallest room, bumping against the dining table en route. He apologised to no-one in particular and perched his empty glass on the table. The lavatory stank of stale cigar smoke.

Peter was hypnotised by the flow of his urine. He belched. He yawned. Focus came and went. Who cared about Aggie? True, he was still occupying her old flat, alone on a truckle bed. Meanwhile Aggie was back with Solly, wallowing in a life of invigorating luxury.

Peter zipped up with exaggerated caution. Then he sighed and considered his face in the mirror while he washed his hands. He rubbed his chin. He could do with a shave. He gave himself a nod. Time to return to the living room. Time to hit the road.

Hilary was nowhere to be seen. Peter resumed his previous position. He waited. After some moments spent humming to himself, Peter checked his watch. Hal had been gone for fifteen minutes. Where was Hilary? Peter rose, swaying a little. He went in search of his hostess. There was a slit of light beneath the master-bedroom door. Why on earth was he creeping along the parquet floor on tiptoe? The bedroom door was ajar.

As he now shifted his weight in the Healey, he recalled the sight of Hilary, inclined over an open drawer below the built-in wardrobe. He also recalled Hilary's wide eyes as she turned in alarm, clutching something pink and flimsy to her breasts. Why on earth was the woman undressing? He remained rooted to the spot. Surely, he was expected to move towards his prey. Peter hoped his smile was reassuring. She smiled in return. Nevertheless, he remained rooted to the spot. She relaxed her tense grip on the protective garment. Ignoring her state of deshabille, Peter asked politely whether she approved of the idea of his accompanying Hal and Nigel to the Philippines. He remembered the warm assurances that he was the most important element in the scheme. Peter had persisted with his questioning.

How pleased would she – Hilary – be, personally, if he consented to go? Back in the car he leaned back, closed his eyes and pictured her breathy assurances.

Then he recalled their classic love dance. Her hands on his shoulders, his on her hips. Honour your partner, honour your corner. First, a chaste kiss to the corner of her full lips. Now slip one hand down her silken back. Hilary's protestations. These were de rigueur, as would be her confused memories of what was happening now and the subsequent attribution of blame to a superflux of booze. Another gentle kiss. Her worried glances over his shoulder at the bedroom door. His breathless promises that he would come to the aid of any party she cared to nominate. He was her Bayard, 'sans peur' and 'sans reproche'. A third kiss, full on the lips, and the first inkling of a response. Another of Hilary's worried glances towards the bedroom door presented his hand with the opportunity to rove freely over her left breast. (In the car Peter could again recall her cool hand closing over his.) One more clinch, a stumble against the half-open door and then onto the bed. What a relief to get off his feet. His ankle inflicted a delectable pain. Then it was half-forgotten. Pain and pleasure commingled. Mouth to mouth resuscitation; tongue to tongue excitation.

Then his left hand finds what it has been seeking. Hilary moans gently as the garment begins to drift from her shoulders. Somewhere between Peter and the dashboard of the Healey the vision of Hilary reclines and one perfect, golden breast – a mammary Aphrodite – rises from the dark foam of the black silk. He shifts his weight on the seat of the car as he remembers the feel of her erect nipple against his lips and tongue. As his hand strokes her thigh, commingled with the thud of the pulse in his temple, he detects the sound of the returning Granada.

The sea joined the orchestration of the scene; the basso continuo of Peter's soundscape. Ebb and flow. Tumescence. Detumescence.

The sound of the Granada brought Hilary to her feet. With one practised movement she restored her dress to its original respectability.

Peter sighed deeply at the memory of something which had

occurred, it seemed, just seconds ago. He patted his breast pocket and retrieved the crumpled package of Pall Mall. The last one? He thought he had already finished the packet. The Zippo flared in the darkness. From where he sat Peter could still see the light in the master-bedroom of Hal's apartment. He drew deeply on the cigarette. The bedroom light went out. Against his will Peter pictured Hal and Hilary in the conjugal bed. He flicked the freshly lit cigarette into the darkness. He reached forward and turned the key in the ignition. As his right foot pressed down on the throttle, a sharp pain made him gasp. He cursed and edged the Beast forward until he was sure it was out of sight of Hal's flat before switching on the headlights. He allowed the Beast to drift down the incline to the first bend. He really needed a shower.

Chapter Five

The big jet banked, and Peter shut his eyes tight. His heart began to thud. An electronic bell pinged and the Angel of Death began to drawl over the public address system. Peter opened his eyes again. He frowned. He had always been an anxious flyer. But on balance he would rather be a witness to the end.

The speaker emitted a belching squark. Then nothing. Nothing but the gentle hiss of life from above Peter's head. As the wing swung back towards horizontality, Peter narrowed his eyes and glanced out of the window.

Although Manila lay hidden by cloud beneath his feet, Peter could have drawn a map of the city and its 'principal monuments'. Ever since he had confirmed his acceptance of Hal's offer, he had been gorging himself on a gargantuan feast of back-numbers of F.E.E.R., skipping over unimportant matters such as anti-nuclear demonstrations in Japan or the latest debacle in the Vietnam War, while greedily consuming even the most microscopic crumb of information concerning the Philippines, the country the plane was now fast approaching.

Ferdinand Marcos and his Thoughts were almost as familiar to Peter as those of Chairman Mao (May He Live Ten Thousand Years!). Perhaps more intriguing than the President in his military uniform or traditional Tagalog shirt was the striking figure, also dressed in a fashionable version of traditional Tagalog costume, who appeared beside her husband in photographs. They were the epitome of glamour, a relief in a world of bloody entanglement between opposing political blocs in South-East Asia. But Peter's researches revealed that the rumours among journalists about the real Imelda contained more than a grain of truth; behind her poised and tranquil appearance Imelda engaged in a whirlwind of frenetic, and not always disinterested, politico-financial-eleemosynary activity. The 'Pirst Lady' cut a swathe through Filipino public life like the heroine of a Chinese-language martial-arts movie. Or like a dervish; in one hand the fruits of charity; in the other a Biretta.

Peter felt grateful that there was no chance of an interview with the First Lady. *Time* magazine or *Newsweek*, yes. But, *Hong Kong Weekly?* Hal had already assured him that no interview with the President or his wife had been requested. Peter pretended to be disappointed.

The plane broke through the lowest layer of cloud. The airport hangars and storage buildings, familiar from Peter's travels in other parts of Asia, flashed past the wings. Now that he was finally arriving, Peter was looking forward to the visit. An impressionistic overview of the Philippines as a tourist or business destination would not ruffle any feathers.

Hal had exhibited distinct signs of nervousness about the forthcoming trip. Late-night calls in which Hal laid out the ground rules for hacks scribbling for *Hong Kong Weekly* had disturbed Peter's sleep several times in the previous week. His sexual fantasies, involving a hybrid Aggie/Hilary, fled at the sound of the phone.

Peter knew he would have to park his journalistic aspirations for the duration of this edition of the Weekly. Sightseeing, resorts, hotels, restaurants and a few mildly suggestive remarks about the local talent would more than satisfy the none-too-rich, none-too-curious and none-too-tired businessmen who flicked through the magazine.

At 02.10 Hal's phone call woke him for the last time before their departure with a disquisition on the right of the Filipinos to do as they wished with their own country. Even under martial law. So, *schtum's* the word, Peter.

As the wheels made noiseless contact with the runway, Peter exhaled and smiled. He reached under the seat in front of him for the familiar, large, green canvas hold-all containing his two Nikon cameras and their associated lenses, a Sony tape recorder and some of his lighter garments. Luckily, the air hostess had been susceptible to his charm and allowed him to guard his property.

Manila airport proved to be a nostalgic experience. It recalled Hong Kong's venerable Kaitak airport with its echoes of Empire and the odd Vampire jet permanently parked near the former location of R.A.F. quarters. A British passport had been a potent magic wand back in the Sixties. Immigration officers at Kaitak had nodded through any bearer of the stiff, dark blue booklet with barely a glance. As in Kaitak, so in Manila. The airport officials merely nodded him on his way.

When he departed from customs, he could have sworn he heard his name being called over the public-address system. He shrugged. Pure imagination. As he fidgeted through the next barrier, he heard the call being repeated. Unsure how to respond, Peter paused. The crowd flowed around him as he lowered his bag, raised an arm and announced. 'Here. I'm Nicholson.' To his amazement, two smiling, young Filipinas approached him. Their eyes questioned him. He nodded. The slighter of the two girls raised a garland of white flowers and manoeuvred it over his head. Still wearing their fixed smiles, the girls about-turned and departed in lock-step whence they had come.

Peter, somewhat non-plussed, responded to the smiles of passing strangers as he stood, his shoulders wreathed in sweet, white blossom. Peter searched the crowd for any sign of his partners-in-crime. Then he sensed out of the corner of an eye someone crouching down to reach for his bag.

'Hold it,' Peter commanded, rather too loudly. Passers-by glanced aside. The man, his left hand still on the bag, remained in a crouched position and glanced up, 'Mr. Nicholson?'

Peter nodded and waited. Would this mean trouble? 'Yes, I'm Nicholson.'

The man straightened, without the bag. He was brown, tall and well-built. 'I'm Chico. I'm Mister Agustin's driver. I'm here to take you out to the resort.' Peter recalled Hal's description of the Filipino bodyguard he had met in the Pen.

Peter relaxed and gave Chico an apologetic smile. Once more the driver bent and retrieved the bag. Somewhat embarrassed, Peter followed both of them through the concourse. He wished he could jettison the flowers but sensed that it might be more diplomatic to stay bedecked.

He followed Chico to a vehicle which looked like nothing so

much as an old turbo-prop engine. Peter guessed that the car had a V8 under the bonnet. Once they were securely inside the car, Chico pointed its green nozzle towards a waterlogged, six-lane highway, lined with sagging power cables. Peter nestled into the leather back seat. He was beginning to relax when he felt something prick the back of his neck. He eased the wreath further back on his shoulders. He lowered his head and sniffed the garland.

'Sampaguita,' a voice announced. Peter caught sight of Chico's eyes in the rear-view mirror. 'Nice smell, huh?'

Peter nodded, 'Nice.' He carefully removed the garland and laid it beside him on the wide seat. 'Very nice.'

A notice on the non-driver's side of the dashboard announced, 'Passengers are requested to keep all windows closed at speeds of over one hundred and twenty miles per hour.' Peter noted that the speedometer climbed up to one hundred and forty. Perhaps the printed warning notice was a trifle '*de trop*' in a car that had to be at least ten years old.

He felt his interest grow as they passed along the wide avenue. He noted that the side streets were awash. There must have been a summer storm. It looked as though the sewers had not been able to cope with the deluge. Hong Kong may have lacked many of the attributes of a tourist destination but at least its civil engineering was more than competent. With cars stirring up bow-waves, Peter began to worry about the conjunction of water and the sagging cables and wires lining the highway.

Peter searched for a cigarette in a breast pocket of his safari jacket. In the damp air the jacket clung to him like a rag. He felt in another pocket for his Zippo. He paused. 'Would you like a cigarette, Chico?' Peter spoke, slowly and loudly, as he leaned forward towards the driver.

'Thanks.' Hands were switched on the steering wheel. Chico's right hand reached back over his shoulder for the cigarette.

Peter extended the Zippo towards the driver. Chico waved it away and indicated the cigar lighter below the dashboard.

'Where are we bound?' Peter wanted to know. Silence. Peter tried another tack. 'Where are we going?'

The tall buildings began to shrink and age before his eyes. The car surged onwards, creating its own bow-wave.

'Is it much further?'

'We are going to the resort,' Chico announced. 'Out of town.' Did Peter detect an American accent? Maybe Chico had worked at Subic Bay. Wasn't that a playground for the Yanks?

Peter settled back and drew on his cigarette. He wondered what manner of man was their host, Agustin. Hal had dismissed him as 'a little feller'. Was that in stature, importance or both? Peter had assembled Hal's snippets of description of Agustin into a picture of a wealthy entrepreneur. He allowed his head to rest on the back of the bench seat. It should not be long before all was revealed. After all, wasn't he an ace reporter?

Through half-closed eyes, he peered through his cigarette smoke. He tried to picture his partners. Hal and Nigel had already been here for three days, taking the measure of the commercial landscape and savouring the fruits of paradise. How had Hal put it just before he left for Kaitak? – 'Sussing out the suckers.'

Peter removed his cigarette and asked, 'Have you come across a couple of English guys at the resort?'

'Sure,' Chico half-turned his head. 'Mr. Agustin asked me to drive them round while they're here.'

And here Peter was – the third caballero. He became aware once more of the perfume of the abandoned garland. Was its odour fatal to all those who came to the islands for nefarious purposes? Did sampaguita unman the descendants of the Conquistadores and leave them at the mercy of Rizal and the revolutionaries. Or was that just a prelude to the American takeover?

Hal and Nigel should not be deluded into thinking the Philippines was a virgin waiting to be de-flowered. Yet he knew they needed no encouragement to go over the top. Much of their conversation was laced with sexual innuendo. And if it wasn't sex talk, it was talk about money and the acquisition thereof. He supposed that, whether he approved or not, they would behave as they wished. It might prove a little awkward when they realised he was not intending to join them.

Of course, all his 'reading-in' on the Philippines had not prepared him for the actuality of the place; the heat, the torrential downpour, the mad traffic and the sampaguita. Had the same girls welcomed Hal and Nigel at the airport? It seemed as if there was no need to visit Cebu to find smiling, welcoming women.

'Tell me, Chico. Does the name of these flowers have a meaning?'

'Sampaguita?' Chico caught Peter's eye in the rear-view mirror. The driver smiled. 'Sure. It means 'the flower of love'.

'Is there a story to go with the name?' Grist for the touristic 'local colour' article.

'Yeah, there's some story behind the name.' Chico paused and slowed for an even deeper stretch of water. 'I think it was about some princess a long time ago.' Chico's eyes flicked back to the road. Any potholes in this road would be hidden by the flood. Until the car ran into them. End of front axle.

'A princess, you say?'

Chico kept his eyes glued to the road. 'She was supposed to marry some prince. Then the Spanish arrived and the prince left to go and fight.'

'Did he win?' Peter looked round for an ashtray.

'No, the Spanish guys won. The prince was killed, the princess died of a broken heart and this flower grew from the place where they were buried.'

Peter recalled the final scene of *Wuthering Heights*. His time at Oxford seemed as distant as the Brontës.

Chico's head twisted awkwardly towards his passenger. 'Took another three hundred and fifty years to get rid of the Spanish.'

'I guess they must have liked it here,' Peter joked. He lowered the window a few inches and flicked the cigarette butt out and into another puddle.

'Folks say it's like paradise,' Chico added with another glance in the mirror. Not a joking matter then.

'What does Mr. Agustin do for a car while you're driving Hal and Nigel around?' He had concluded that the sampaguita subject had been exhausted.

Chico uttered a gentle laugh. 'Mr. Agustin don't need this old car. He's got two Fleetwoods.'

Peter had an animus against Cadillacs.

'Do women drive in Manila?'

Chico's shrugged. 'I guess some do.' He laughed. 'But as soon as their husbands make it, they hire a chauffeur.'

Peter rubbed his temples. In the grey, afternoon humidity, a headache was forming. He loosened the knot of his tie; drew the silk over his head; and bundled it into a jacket pocket.

'Have Mr. Puckle and Mr. Thompson been busy since they arrived?'

Between roadside shacks, low, fronded palms had begun to line the road.

'They sure have,' Chico drawled.

'Doing what?' Peter kept his voice light.

'Drinkin'. Chico paused. Another glance into the mirror. 'Puckin'.'

Peter tried and failed to keep the embarrassment out of his voice. 'Sorry?'

'Puckin'.'

Chico's Tagalog accent was so light that Peter had forgotten about the substitution of P's for F's. But Chico, for all his Yankee drawls, was a Filipino. Or, as he would say, 'Pilipino'. Peter recalled the cockney police inspector in Hong Kong whose Filipina wife featured prominently in the cop's misogynistic anecdotes. He always referred to her as his 'Puckin' Pilipina'.

'Car broke down. Half-way up Garden Road. In the bloody rush hour. On our way to a presentation at Government House. I told the Puckin' Pilipina to see to it. She took ten minutes sortin' it, while I sat sweatin' in the car. And me in my dress uniform. I wish the puckin' 'ood had fallen on 'er puckin' Pilipina 'ead.'

Peter wondered what Hal and Nigel's abandoned wives would make of 'drinkin' and 'puckin'? Then he remembered the protracted and pointless siege he had laid to Hilary's chastity. He had surely forfeited the privilege of righteous indignation.

Agustin's Number Three car swung between the open gates of what Peter supposed was 'The Resort'.

'How far are we from Manila?'

'Twenty K.'

The skyline consisted of dense greenery. Could it be jungle? Close by the entrance, the view of trees was blocked in part by a neat brick building, bearing the legend, 'Sauna – Massage'. The ancient Pontiac bumped slowly along the asphalt drive. To the left a swimming pool with changing cabins. There were reclining bodies. Just a few. He heard two or three splashes and a vagrant scream of excited, childish pleasure.

The car swung to the right behind a larger building. Through plate glass windows Peter observed two men and two young women speeding silently in pursuit of some species of projectile.

'What are they playing?' Peter wondered. The car slowed. Chico glanced across at the quartet.

'*Jai alai.*' Chico replied with a shrug. 'I think it's from Spain or somewhere.'

'Oh, like pelota. Looks fast,' Peter observed as one of the girls threw her arms around the shorter of the two men. Her partner? Who knew? Even if he had known how to play pelota, Peter also knew that he no longer had the wind for it.

'Yeah. Fast.' Chico shrugged. 'I wouldn't play with women.' He grinned at the mirror. 'Too dangerous.' The car leaned on its springs as it came to a halt and settled.

Peter pushed open his door and creaked his way out into the heavy humidity. He wondered aloud. 'Does the sun ever shine in the Philippines?' Chico was rescuing his bag from the boot.

'Sun in the morning, rain in the afternoon, cool in the evening.' Chico's weather report seemed to cover every eventuality that mattered.

The tall driver led the way to an open staircase which climbed up to and around the rear of the building. Their shoes clattered on the wooden stairs. On the first floor they stepped onto a balcony which ran along the width of the building. Chico, still leading the way, pushed open the second door they reached. He waited for Peter to pass and precede him into the room. The driver followed, lowered Peter's bag to the wooden floor and made as if to leave.

'Thanks, Chico.' Peter felt cross-footed. Should he offer Chico a tip? But the driver did not seem to expect one. Peter decided a generous tip at departure would be the best solution. 'Oh, by the way, Chico… where's the key?'

'No key,' Chico responded with a shrug. 'No need.' Then, silently shutting the door behind him, he was gone.

A country of open doors. No danger of theft or mayhem in the night? He could see the headline of his 'colour piece': 'The Land Without Locks'. Cute, but not sexy.

Travellers to Mainland China enthused about the honesty of the Chinese Communists. At first sight there wasn't a thing that was communistic about the Philippines. Could there be such a thing as a Capitalist/Communist Shangri-la? Like Hong Kong – but with a heart?

The room – airy but strictly functional. Peter lifted his precious belongings onto the large, firm double bed. Something in the far corner caught his eye. He checked. Behind a discoloured door lurked a sink, a toilet and, behind a lime-green flowered, plastic curtain, a shower. The walls and the floor were covered in tiny dark-green tiles.

Peter experienced a surge of elation. He was here. In the Philippines. The idea was absurd but Peter, if asked for his first impressions, would have replied 'I like it here'. It was absurd but he almost felt at home. He re-crossed the bedroom and stepped out onto the balcony. He rested his elbows on the wooden balustrade.

To his right a door opened, disclosing a boy of alarming obesity. Peter judged him to be sixteen or so. The boy's lower lip, very pink and very wet, drooped over a dimpled chin. The apparition was clothed in a bright yellow T-shirt; baggy blue shorts reached down to his knees. His feet were bare.

'Are you Pete?' the boy asked without preamble.

'Yes, that's right.' Peter turned towards the lad. He caught sight of a girl he judged to be in her late teens, peeping shyly round the door of the boy's room.

'You want some penicillin?' The boy's open hand revealed an enormous yellow capsule.

Peter's composure was slipping. Penicillin in Paradise? He blinked and responded, 'No. No thanks.'

The fat boy shrugged and thrust the capsule into a pocket.

'I'm Miguel.' Then, with great emphasis. 'My father is the owner of this resort.'

'Is this where you live?' Peter was trying his best not to stare at the girl's careless state of undress.

'Only in the school holidays.' Miguel announced. 'I hate school.'

From somewhere below a strong smell of garlic assailed Peter's nostrils.

'Hal and Nige are in the next room,' Miguel informed him, indicating the room beyond Peter's.

As Peter turned back to thank the boy, he saw the shy girl being pushed back into Miguel's room by a fat arm.

'Thanks,' Peter called. The door slammed shut.

Peter's mouth set in a thin, grim line as he strode past his own room. He came to an open door. He peered into the room at the unmade bed. No-one. He moved on four more paces. Another door. He tried the handle. It turned. He pushed. He had found his partners.

Chapter Six

The reception committee was assembled in what turned out to be Hal's room. Peter's publishing-partner sat to one side of a small bamboo and glass table. Peter's advertising-partner was seated on the opposite side. Between the two clustered a dozen or more empty San Miguel bottles. Each partner's lap bore the weight of a nubile Pilipina.

Peter awarded Hal the laurels for his choice of the carnal spoils. The publisher's hand rested lightly beneath breasts that compared favourably in heft with Hilary's.

Nigel's escort was short – of brow, of breast, of waist and of leg. She awarded Peter a warm, welcoming smile with a hint of gilt.

'Hi, there, Pete, me old mate.' Hal beckoned Peter into the room. Hal belched. Peter stepped into the room and held his breath. The atmosphere was fetid with a sickly-sweet melange of ancient cigar-smoke, beer fumes, garlic – and something familiar, yet indefinable. The combination of odours turned Peter's stomach. He placed his hand over his mouth, eructated lightly and attempted a smile.

Hal affected to be unaware of Peter's reaction. Nigel's expression, on the other hand, was one of sour disapproval of Peter's all-too-evident disapproval. Peter chose to ignore Nigel and concentrate on Hal. There was something odd about the publisher's appearance. Peter leaned forward.

'Gosh, I've never seen you wearing glasses before,' Peter said, tilting his head to one side.

Hal raised a forefinger and thumb to shift the heavy, black frame into a more comfortable position. He wrinkled his nose to assist the resettlement of the spectacles.

'I don't wear specs for socialisin' – only for business. Looks more serious.'

'And is your lady-friend a business associate?' Peter nodded at Hal's burden. She too sported a stern pair of black-framed spectacles. She was staring at Peter with warm timidity.

'Who?' Hal gave his captive a sidelong look. 'You mean Maria?' Hal pointed at Maria's bosom, straining the seams of her cotton dress. Hal grinned and flashed his teeth at Peter. 'Well, in a manner of speakin' she is. Maria works 'ere at the resort. She is a very professional masseuse.' He pronounced Maria's occupation to rhyme with 'Seuss'.

Peter's earlier sanguine mood soured at this sub-Hogarthian scene of tawdry licentiousness. His partners were blokishly sporting shorts and flip-flops. The evidently older woman on Nigel's lap was the only member of the quartet who did not require the services of an optometrist.

Peter took in a deep, preparatory breath. This was really not good enough. He anticipated lots of excuses from the partners but he was not in the mood to accept any. Before he could exhale, Hal announced.

'We've done nothin' but eat, drink and fuck since we got 'ere.'

Peter exhaled and shook his head. 'Terrific.' He mustered all his resources of irony into the single epithet.

'Yeah, you're bloody right,' Hal concurred. 'Fuckin' terrific.' He patted his professional masseuse on her buttocks as he bounced her on his bare, hairy knees.

'This is Maria. Maria, say hello to Pete,' Hal commanded.

With a hint of embarrassment, Maria did as she had been commanded. She sensed that Peter was not happy. 'Hi.'

'Hi, Maria. Nice to meet someone who is so enthusiastic about her work.'

Hal's hand directed Peter's attention towards Nigel and his soul-mate. Nigel's look could only be described as baleful.

'And Nigel's little friend,' Hal announced with a grin and a backward sweep of his arm, 'is Consuela.'

Peter bowed elaborately to the embarrassed girl. He was awarded another glimpse of dental gold.

'*Como esta Usted hoy, Consuela?*' Peter rattled off his one complete Spanish sentence.

It was just one sentence more than Consuela could understand. Nigel sneered and muttered, 'smart-arse' before raising his glass to his lips. He gave his burden's butt an encouraging pat. Bottom-patting seemed to be a local sport.

'Off you get, Sue,' Nigel commanded. 'My leg's gone to sleep.' As the girl complied, Nigel stamped his foot on the bare boards. He rose and adjusted his rumpled shorts.

'Nigel calls Consuela 'Sue', Hal glossed. 'For short,' he added. Hal pronounced the girl's name as if it belonged to a trio of sisters. Con. Sue. Ella.

'Pete, I can see you're in need of a refreshing whistle-wetter.' Hal leaned round Maria, who giggled as he solemnly inspected several empties. Holding one such aloft, Hal adjusted his spectacles and said, ''Ere, Maria. We're right out of booze. 'Ow about a few more beers?'

In response Maria rose. The promise of her bosom was confirmed. Peter guessed her height to be five foot five. She rose above the ill-fitting dress and plastic flip-flops – an indigent Venus. Her rich hair framed her warm brown eyes. Her lips were full – perhaps a little too full. For Peter she recalled Sophia Loren. As she turned to face Hal, Peter noticed some faint pock-marks on her chin. Hal sent her on her way with another affectionate pat.

Hal stretched back in his chair and yawned. Peter perched on the end of the bed. The sheet looked as if had been deployed in a game of tug-of-war.

'So,' Peter paused to make way for Hal's cavernous yawn. Then he asked, 'What's our first task, chief?'

'If you mean 'work',' Hal rejoined, arms flopping into his lap. 'What do you call five times a night for three nights?' He pointed at the table. ''Ere Nige. Pass me my glass, will you, me old mate?'

Nigel did so with a sidelong sneer at Peter.

Maria really goes for it.' Hal drained the glass. 'Can't get enough.'

'We all know how irresistible you are, Hal. I've brought a supply of yeast tablets.' Hal responded with laughter. Not so Nigel.

'There's no need for you to assume superior airs. It hasn't just been fun for the last three days. I've done my bit.'

'That's not a kind way to refer to Consuela,' Peter said. As

Nigel bridled, Hal produced another tremendous yawn.

'No, Pete. Nige is right.' Hal's smile broadened. 'Nige and me 'ave earned the right to celebrate. We got Agustin to agree to purchase the entire issue. At cover price. No discounts. Fifteen thousand copies for the Philippines alone. Sixty thousand bucks. And if we manage to offload another few thousand in Hong Kong and the rest of the region, that's bunce. So...' He made a washing gesture with his palms. 'Deal done. All we need is your copy and some pics.'

Hal looked at Nigel. They nodded to each other approvingly. The toilet flushed and Sue re-appeared, adjusting the flower arrangement on her dress.

'And what about the ads? Who's arranging those? Sue?'

Nigel lumbered to his feet and towered over Peter, who gave him a sweet smile.

'Calm down, Nige,' Hal cooed. 'Go on. Tell 'im.'

Nigel grimaced before he bit on the bullet. 'Agustin's cousin runs one of the best advertising agencies in Manila. He's guaranteed us some fantastic clients.'

'Such as?'

Nigel told off the ads on his fingers. 'Filsyn, Seiko, Bulova, Bancom, Dior, Rolex...'

Peter raised a restraining hand. 'O.K. All right. You win. I'm impressed.' He patted his jacket pockets in pursuit of his cigarettes. He extracted and lit one. 'Now.' He exhaled smoke. 'What's the catch?'

Hal waved his hand in the air. 'There ain't no catch, Pete.' Hal waved a hand in the air. He twinkled. 'You just write a few hundred juicy words and snap some sexy pics. Then we're home and dry.' He adjusted his business spectacles.

'Done and dusted,' Nigel concurred.

Maria reappeared, smiling, in the doorway. In her hands was a wet tray supporting six bottles of San Mig.

'There's my little beauty,' Hal announced, extending his welcoming arm towards Maria. The hostess lowered the tray and descended onto Hal's thighs in one movement. Hal grunted. Peter smiled. He had to admire Maria's aim. He looked away as Hal's hand enveloped Maria's left breast, only to witness Nigel performing a similar manoeuvre on Sue.

Peter rose. The palm trees looked dejected in the grey humidity. He drifted towards the doorway overlooking the long balcony and flicked his cigarette over the balustrade. He turned.

'I think I'll take a shower and a have a zizzette.' He began to move.

'Ain't you 'avin' a drink? Hal had raised his face from Maria's neck.

'I think I'll pass.'

''Ere, Pete. You don't 'ave to worry. You can order anything you want.' Hal was the personification of largesse. 'Seriously. Just pick up the phone and order anything you want. They'll bring it up.' Hal spotted something on the bedside cabinet. He retrieved the small green card covered in stains and waved it at Peter. 'Look,' Hal enjoined, waving the card. 'This 'ere's the menu. It's all on the 'ouse.'

Nigel, concentrating on the beer that Sue was pouring, suggested, without turning, 'You should try the breast of chicken.'

'With or without garlic?' Hal grinned at Peter's feeble quip.

'And don't forget to try a massage,' Hal exhorted, the quintessence of generosity. As Peter escaped onto the balcony, Hal promised to 'see you later'.

Nigel muttered something incomprehensible and Hal bellowed with laughter.

Peter lingered outside his room. He leaned over the balcony and took in the resort beneath. Down by the pool, what appeared to be a perfectly normal Filipino family went about their innocent pleasures.

Everybody except Peter seemed to be having a great time. Then, from the room of the obese boy came a muffled shriek, Well, perhaps not quite everybody. He wondered whether he should knock on Miguel's door and see if the girl was all right. On second thoughts, it might not be the perfect moment to confront the priapic teenager. Peter imagined that any interference on his part might bring condign punishment down on the girl's head.

He was feeling more than tired – he was psychically exhausted. He hoped he would see things in a less lurid light after a good night's sleep. From somewhere below, the strong scent of frying garlic assailed Peter's nostrils.

A trio of large, black birds flew slowly along the fronded horizon. Why were such omens always described as 'ill'?

Hal and Nigel would not be best pleased at what was puzzling Peter at this moment.

At this moment Peter was wondering why a wealthy Filipino would offer to lay on wine, women and song for the dubious pleasure of buying out a complete edition of 'Hong Kong Weekly'. Peter had not the slightest doubt that no-one in the Philippines (apart from their host) had even heard of the wretched rag. And it wasn't just the Philippines where the magazine was a nonentity. Not one of Peter's friends in Hong Kong had so much as glanced at one of Peter's 'Weekly' articles. And even the back-street hotels found it impossible to *give* the wretched mag away to indigent, back-packing Australians during their two-and-a-half-day sojourn in the Colony.

The fact that Peter was secretly convinced that HKW was a terminally ill patient did not reduce the amount of effort it required to keep its feeble pulse pulsing. He contended that it was just as arduous to find enough plasma to maintain a failing patient like 'the Weekly' as it was to fill the arteries of *Time* or *Newsweek*.

Now, having briefly observed Hal and Nigel at work on location, Peter began to comprehend why the circulation of *Hong Kong Weekly* was in the tens rather than the thousands. He had always averted his gaze from the dust-gathering copies on the reception counters of the back-street hotels. He had only once seen a copy on the street; it lay, covered in wet footprints, beside a rubbish bin in Nathan Road. Not exactly a fitting symbol of the Golden Mile.

Peter sighed and entered his room. He discovered a vagrant cigarette, lit it and lay back on the double bed. The top sheet felt damp. From the room of the boy next door came another muffled shriek. Peter closed his ears and resumed his ruminations.

If Agustin wished to waste his wealth on a loss-leader, that was his privilege. Obviously, he had some ulterior motive. Was it commercial? Political? Or mere vanity? Whatever his motive, if Agustin was a successful businessman he would soon see through the sham of professional competence and probity that Hal presented. How long would it be before it was too long? How long before the consumption of wine, women, time and money told on Agustin's patience? Having purchased the complete issue and generously laid on the advertising and the costs of production, he surely no longer required Hal and Nigel to linger. He must eventually become weary of their continued presence in Manila. Or perhaps they served as unwitting hostages. And not just Hal and Nigel. He knew he would not be excluded. The traveller's tales of violence in the Philippines were legion. He had no wish to become the protagonist of one of them. The longer Hal and Nigel lingered, the greater the chance of disaster.

Peter left the bed and flicked his cigarette butt over the balcony into the deepening darkness. He retrieved another pack of Pall Mall from an inside pocket of his bag. Then he went to lock the bedroom door. Wait. There was no key. No lock. No bolt. He forced open the awkward window beside the shower to allow his smoke to escape in exchange for a little fresh humidity.

Back in the room, Peter stripped off his clothes and padded over the slightly sticky floor to the shower-room. Tentatively he tested the temperature of the water. It was blessedly cool. He revelled in the needles striking his skin and, later, the roughness of the fresh white towel. Once dry, he sprawled across the bed, face down.

Behind closed lids, he recalled Hal pawing Maria's breast. And her compliant smile. He shifted his weight. Ever since the breach with Aggie, Peter's dreams had become intensely erotic. Aggie appeared, slim and fair, and was summarily dismissed. In her place came Maria, slipping into his room, wearing the same black dress Hilary had worn on the evening he became enmeshed in a web of Hal's devising.

Maria unveiled her breasts. Bemused, Peter reached for her

and, as he did so, she caught his arm by the wrist, raised it and tied it to the bed-head. She grasped his other arm and, laying a cool hand on his groin, murmured in his ear, 'You want massage?' Throwing out his free arm, Peter mumbled, 'No. No massage.' He felt himself spiralling downward as Maria, once more in her familiar cotton frock, disappeared through the floor.

Peter awoke with a start. He was cold. The room was in darkness. He groped for the small bedside lamp, knocking it over with a curse. He righted the lamp and found the switch at last. His erection rapidly lost heart.

The room somehow looked more welcoming than it had by day. Almost friendly. His stomach rumbled. How long was he going to stare at the opposite wall?

Peter lifted the stained, once ivory-coloured, receiver. There was no dial. He placed the phone against his ear and waited. No dialling tone.

''Ello?' The female voice was not melodious.

'Hello.' Peter realised he had no idea of his room number. 'May I have some chicken, please?'

'Plied chicken?'

'Oh... yes. Yes, I suppose so.' Peter needed to explain something. 'I'm afraid I don't know my....'

There was a click and the line fell silent. The clicking continued. It was an insect trying to penetrate the lamp. Peter hurried to close the window. He shuddered and made his way towards the shower. Two showers in a day. Such extravagance. The now warm water was welcome.

He was attempting to dry himself with the larger of the two small towels when something made him pause. Had that been a knock on the door? Impossible to make himself respectable. He bunched the damp cotton against his groin and shouted at the bedroom door.

'Who is it?' Hal or Nigel would surely have barged straight in. Timidly, the door crept open. A brown face with wide, luminous eyes appeared. Then came a tray bearing a steaming breast of chicken which perched on a hillock of white rice.

With a swift intake of breath Peter stepped back behind the

shower-curtain. The girl's diminutive size was only emphasised by the tent-like cotton dress she was wearing.

She hesitated. Peter called from his sanctuary, 'Thanks. Just leave it on the table, please.'

Without so much as a glance in his direction the girl deployed the plate and cutlery on the table. She took up position behind the chair Peter would occupy. In her left hand she held the tray; in her right a slip of grease-stained paper, which she now offered to the naked diner. There was a pause. 'You sign,' encouraged the girl, holding out the paper.

'Just leave the paper on the table. You can come back later.' Peter smiled reassuringly as he waved his hand towards the open door. As if on cue, a large moth glided into the room.

'Shit,' Peter muttered. The girl was imperturbable and inscrutable. Peter concentrated on the moth. It circled the room once and then departed.

The girl stared fixedly at Peter.

'Look, young lady,' Peter forced a smile. 'I'm very hungry and I want my supper. I can't come out with you standing there.' Her eyes were unblinking. Peter repeated, more emphatically. 'I simply can't come out with you watching.' He extended his bare arm by way of illustration. 'I have no clothes on.' Still no reaction. 'I am naked.'

'You want massage?'

Peter's mouth opened, then shut. The girl's question was so matter-of-fact. He realised that his state of undress might possibly have suggested his need for a different order of sustenance.

'No, thank you. No massage.' His attempt at a smile was a failure.

The girl blinked.

'Really!' Peter insisted. He wondered whether Hal had put the girl up to this. It would be just his idea of a practical joke. Now she was trapped between displeasing one or other of the two foreigners. Or both.

Peter was irritated with Hal and the girl. He tried to soften his tone.

'Look... er... what is your name?'

The girl's lips parted and revealed the tip of her tongue.

'Look,' Peter raised his eyes to the shower-head. 'Look. I'm tired and I'm hungry. I just need to have some food and rest.'

The girl, exhibiting signs of increasing nervousness.

'Please go,' Peter implored. No response.

He raised his volume. 'Go… now!'

Without another word, the girl turned on her bare feet and departed. Peter hurried to shut the door behind her. Then he remembered that there was no key. Flinging the damp towel onto the bed, he scurried to the table, grabbed a chair and returned to the door. With a sigh of relief, he found he was able to jam the chair under the doorknob. His heart beating, he crossed to the table. This was absurd.

He reared back at the overpowering stench of garlic. Revulsion and hunger locked horns. As he tackled the foul chicken, he simultaneously attempted to breathe through his mouth. What horrors did the excess of garlic disguise? Had the chicken been healthy when it died? Or had it expired from unnatural causes?

After half-a-dozen mouthfuls, he took a deep breath and paused. It occurred to him that a beer might mitigate the stench. He rose to reach for the phone when he recollected the mishaps that befell unwary callers. He had had enough of waitress service for one evening. The beer could wait.

He pushed aside the plate. He belched. He grimaced. He surmised that the girl was the innocent agent of a silly charade concocted by Hal and Nigel. She was the innocent piggy in the middle.

He glanced down at his nakedness and then quickly up at the flimsy curtain partially covering the window. What with the heat, the food and the girl, his thoughts were in knots. Now that she had departed, he wished he had not been so peremptory.

In spite of prostitution being a major industry in Wanchai and Tsim Sha Tsui, Peter had never been tempted to dip a toe (or anything else) in those waters. There had always been an ample sufficiency of European wives (and their visiting daughters) to supply his needs. He shuddered at the very thought of the consequences of bedding a bar-girl. His stomach churned.

Damned chicken!

He realised with a start that he was still naked. He had better don some covering or other before the girl returned for his 'empties'. Ruefully, he considered the chair guarding his privacy. It was absurd to lock himself away like this. He had nothing to fear. Since there was no question of coercion, so there was no need for anger on his part. All Peter had to do was simply refuse her other services, politely but firmly. Now all he need do was get dressed and everything would be fine.

He tidied the table and slipped into his clothes.

Was that someone trying the door? No, false alarm. From the distance came the faint sound of music. It reminded him of the Filipino band who had played in the Mandarin. Those were the days. Not to mention the jazz group at the Blue Heaven. Back then he had been part of the 'In crowd'. Now he had been cast into outer darkness. Out of a regular job; out of regular friends.

He reached down for his bag and retrieved one of his two cameras. He found his blower brush and played air into the nooks and crannies of the Nikon EL body. He started to hum.

Had that been a sound outside, somewhere along the balcony? The door. He placed the camera on the bed and crossed the room. He removed the chair and carefully returned it to its station by the table. The door had swung slightly ajar. Careless of moths and room service, he left it open. He returned to the bed and took up the Nikon again. He resumed his blowing operation.

Peter woke with a start. He conferred with his watch. Eleven o'clock. He glanced down and was relieved to see his camera was still there. It lay on its back, the lens staring up at him. He looked across to the table. The plate remained where he had left it. He felt slightly irritated at the sight. One might suppose that the girl might have come back and cleared up the residue by now.

He lifted the camera and replaced it in the bag beside the other EL with the 80-200 mm. zoom and, easing himself off the bed, casually crossed the room. He stepped out into the warm night. He leant on the balcony rail and inhaled. Below, the flickering water of the pool reflected the dull lights of the cabanas ranged along its edge. A bat flickered past each light in turn.

Peter started. Suddenly the cabana lights had been extinguished. Why should his pulse race? He grasped the rail and leaned back. Above his head stars filled the darkness. Back down on earth dim lights revealed other buildings in the resort. To accompany this evocative scene came the familiar rasp of cicadas, sawing their love songs among the palms.

He stared at the gentle ripples fragmenting the reflections in the pool. Cool water was tempting. Then he remembered that he had deliberately left his swimming costume in Hong Kong.

'No need for swimming gear on a professional assignment,' he had told himself sententiously.

He strained to hear any other sounds of life but nothing could penetrate the swelling cicada chorus. He crept on tip-toe along the balcony past Miguel's den and thence down the stairs to the courtyard. The jai alai court was still lit, if dimly. Peter began to pass along its semi-transparent façade when something moving within froze him in his tracks.

A shadow was flickering quickly about the court. The solitary player was not holding a racket or bat of any kind. Yet Peter could hear the sound of an object being struck and then, in turn, striking a hard surface. Peter concluded that the mystery game must be a variation on fives.

He remained still. As his eyes became accustomed to the gloom, he calculated that the player was around five foot five and of indeterminate age. Whatever his years, the man was very fit.

Peter moved on. He still wished to fulfil his mission. He held his breath and tip-toed until he had reached the darkest shadows by the changing rooms. Taking off his moccasins, he eased himself into a sitting position beside a metal ladder which descended into the stygian water. He detected discreet slapping sounds as the water filled the gutters. He started when the lights went out in the *jai alai* court.

Peter rose and gently tried one of the cabana doors. It was unlocked and its spring offered little resistance. He entered and was immediately pitched into darkness. He shuddered. He wondered what arachnid horrors lurked in the crevices of this place. After a few silent seconds he slipped out of his clothes.

Naked, crouching, he hobbled to the edge of the pool and slipped, rung by rung, down the ladder into the cool, oleaginous water. Taking a deep breath, he plunged beneath the surface and pulled for the further side. After a few seconds his fingertips came into contact with the tiled wall. He rose, gasping for breath, and rested his free elbow in the gutter. Taking gulps of air, he wiped the water from his eyes and blinked down the pool towards the diving boards. As his sight cleared, Peter gave a start. There, apparently suspended in mid-air, was a ghostly figure wearing a familiar, pale cotton dress. He rubbed his eyes with the back of his hand. When he next looked down the pool, the apparition had disappeared.

Chapter Seven

Peter struggled upwards, his lungs at bursting point. The weed enveloped him and threatened to hold him under. Ahead, through a cone of refracted colour, he could discern a pale shape. He knew it was the girl. She was drifting further away from him. He had to reach her before it was too late. He could feel his eyeballs starting to roll as, with a final frenetic effort, he clawed his way towards her. He reached her and grasped the thin wrist. It oozed between his fingers as the arm slowly detached itself from the girl's body. Peter kicked away from the putrefaction and watched in horror as the arm and the white dress sank towards the dark mud far below. He pulled for the surface but the entangling weed still clung to his thighs. He knew he could not hang on for a second longer. His pulse drummed in his ears. The sound grew louder and louder.

'Come on, get up, you silly bugger.'

Peter had reached the surface just in time. He blinked in the air and gulped in lungfuls of life. The drumming had not stopped. Peter came to. Perplexed, he recognised that he was back in the room at the resort. Someone was banging at his door. A sense of dizzy relief flooded through Peter's exhausted limbs. He attempted to swing a leg out of the bed only to find he was unable to move. The sheet had somehow wound itself around the lower part of his body.

'Come on, you silly sod. We're waitin'.' More loud bangs at the door. Peter finally managed to extricate his legs. He lowered them to the floor and wove his way towards the door, the sheet wrapped round his waist and groin like an oversized dhoti. He removed his protective chair from below the door handle and scraped it back towards the table. It unbalanced as it turned, toppled over and came to rest at a tipsy angle in its original place.

He opened the door. He rubbed an eye. 'Oh, hello, Hal.'

Hal grunted as he pushed the door against Peter's chest and marched into the bedroom with his entourage of Nigel, Maria and Consuela in close attendance.

Hal took in the empty bed. He leered at Peter and then marched across to the shower-room. He called as he walked.

'Okay. You can come out now.'

No response. Frustration welling over, he tugged aside the shower curtain. He turned very slowly; brow puckered.

He saw Peter, who had taken up a position at the end of the bed, and who was now inspecting the curled toes of his left foot.

Hal, fists on hips, struck a pose over Peter. The pucker still corrugated Hal's brow.

'What the bloody 'ell's the matter with you?' His voice took on a note of concern. 'Are you some kind of woofter?' Peter glanced up as Hal thrust his face close to Peter's. 'What's the problem? Don't you like girls?'

Peter held Hal's accusatory glare. 'Yes,' he replied mildly. He grinned at Hal. 'Girls I choose to like.'

Peter became aware of Maria inspecting him with not entirely unsympathetic attention. He also noted that one of Sue's hands was entwined with one of Nigel's. With her free hand the girl rummaged in her mouth. She extracted something, inspected it and then popped it back whence it had come. She crossed her flip-flopped feet and masticated her discovery.

'Oh, who gives a shit about Peter's sexual hang-ups?' Nigel glared at Peter who replied to the glare with a wink. Nigel harrumphed like a retired taipan and snapped. 'You'd better get dressed. We're all going into town.'

'O.K.' Peter responded with what he hoped was infuriating insouciance. 'But I would appreciate a little privacy.'

'Well, don't keep us waitin',' Hal warned as he approached the door with Maria in tow. 'We've got a meetin' with Mr. Agustin.'

The avoirdupois with which Hal invested the name of their host impressed Peter. Agustin, Peter realised, had Hal by the balls. And not just Hal.

It was Nigel's turn. 'In any case, we can't eat breakfast here. Even the cornflakes taste of garlic.' Nigel breathed against the palm of his free hand and grimaced. Sue was busy chewing some loose skin inside her left cheek.

'Downstairs in five, Pete.' Hal ordered with a wink. His teeth gleamed, none the worse for their encounters with the local allium.

Chico was waiting by the Pontiac. Peter and he exchanged smiles. Hal busied himself revealing his ignorance of the topography of Manila by giving the hotel the wrong name. Chico gently corrected Hal and opened the rear doors of the car.

Once in the vehicle Peter was able to relax. His eyes started to close, lulled into slumber by the flickering of passing palms and what appeared to be derelict telegraph poles. Nigel was gazing intently at the passing scene with Sue squeezed between him and Peter. Meanwhile Hal, with Maria perched on his lap, was conversing sotto voce with Chico. The car jerked, slowed and then resumed its former speed.

Peter started and his eyes opened. He blinked. Where was he? He recognised Chico and Hal. He swallowed. What had he done with his gear? Had he left his precious tools at the resort? As he turned to look back through the rear window, his right foot struck something unyielding and metallic. He looked down and sucked in a deep, relieved breath. There was the canvas bag containing his kit. He unstrapped the bag and placed it on his lap over his seat-belt and checked the cameras, spare lenses, film, sound tapes and the Sony cassette recorder. This was the bare minimum he would need. If anything went awry or missing... he rejected the thought with a shudder.

It had been his mentor on the *Tiger Standard* who had advised him always to be ready for those mythical, unpredictable street shots or to record the sound of rioting crowds. Regrettably, he had never once grabbed a genuine scoop, in spite of living through the Cultural Revolution in Macao and Hong Kong; nevertheless, he was comforted by always having his gear at the ready. He smiled inwardly. Linus's blanket. At least he no longer felt the urge to sleep.

The dusty road ran on before them in the moist sunlight. The plantations and isolated resorts gave way to shanties, replaced in their turn by perfunctory, modern buildings and the graffitied hoardings of modern life.

'Ah, civilisation,' Nigel beamed, as they entered the coffee shop at the *Intercontinental.* Peter had read the description in the foyer. 'Bright rooms and suites, a rooftop spa, pool and gym.'

'Now, where's a bloody table?' Hal enquired of nobody in particular. His eyes scanned the dining room. 'Come on. Follow me.'

And he was gone, swerving this way and that between the crowded tables as he made for the furthest corner of the enormous space. Peter saw him reach his objective, tip three chairs forward in the 'occupied' position, sit on a fourth, while crossing his ankles over a fifth. As Maria arrived, he removed his feet.

Hal blessed a couple of geriatric American tourists, three tables distant, with a winning smile. Maria assumed her rightful place by Hal's side, exhibiting rather more cleavage than met with the ancient dame's approval. The blue-rinsed head wagged at the morose husband, who continued to stare at Hal's table without responding to her plaints. Peter was the last to take his place.

Hal rubbed victorious palms together and insisted, 'You can't afford to let the grass grow under your tootsies in this neck of the woods.' He drew a packet of menthol cigarettes from his pocket. 'It's dog eat bitch.'

Nigel uttered a brief, barking laugh and hoisted a menu from the stand in the centre of the table. 'I could eat a horse,' he announced and speed-read the contents.

Since Peter had already chosen, he was free to consider his surroundings. Two bulky men at an adjacent table were hacking their way through what seemed to be raw meat. Peter judged them to be American.

Hal leant towards the nearer of the two men. 'That steak?' Hal flashed his teeth.

The addressee was sporting a green, black and red tartan sports coat. He turned towards the questioner and jerked his head.

'Sure is!' The dissection over, the man pinioned a dripping hunk of flesh, before thrusting it between his jaws.

Hal played his next pawn. 'You 'ere on business?'

The American's nod was strongly affirmative. Meanwhile his companion paid no heed to this exchange, continuing to saw at his own meat.

'What's your line of work?' Hal addressed the more informative member of the duo.

'Security.' The man's eyes were still fixed on his plate.

Hal raised his eyebrows and gave Nigel a conspiratorial wink.

'So, what's the security business like 'ere now?' Hal smiled at the American.

The question gave pause to the tartan-wearer's mastication. The feeder's arm was lowered beside its owner's plate. He looked closely at Hal before responding. He then glanced at his colleague whose eyes were still fixed on his steak.

'Waal,' came the drawled response to Hal's question. The man half-turned towards the questioner. 'Since Marcos brought in martial law things have really quieted down here.'

'Yeah, you're right.' Hal nodded vigorously. 'I was 'ere in sixty-nine.' The American returned to feeding. Hal's accent thickened as he went on, 'My God! You should 'ave been 'ere then!'

'I was here then,' the American responded and nodded firmly.

Undeterred, Hal ignored the response. 'Yeah, you should 'ave been there then.'

'I told you,' the man paused and looked directly at Hal. 'I was here then.' Hal slipped around the conversational obstruction by turning to Peter. 'I was in this little restaurant in Quezon City, see?'

The tartaned one pointed his fork out of the window at the distant, passing traffic. 'Say, that's just down the road a-ways.'

Ignoring this interruption, Hal concentrated on Peter.

'There was I, just 'avin' this quiet little business discussion.' He winked at Peter. 'All of a sudden this bloke gets up and brings out a bloody ginormous shooter.' The West Country vowels were really rolling now.

'Smith and Wesson?' The American's interest had been aroused.

'I didn't ask 'is name.' Hal, somewhat miffed, replied. He held his hands about a foot apart. 'As big as that.'

The American gave a light shrug and returned to his food. His companion had all but finished. Out of the corner of his eye, Peter saw him eructate.

Hal clicked his fingers in front of Peter's eyes and resumed his narrative.

'Yeah, well, this little wog starts poppin' off at another bloke on the far side of the room. Before you could say 'the only good Injun is a dead Injun' the place was covered in smoke and blood.'

The Hibernianed Yank looked concerned at Hal. 'Were you OK?'

Hal looked down at his body with affection and patted his stomach. 'Yeah,' he grinned. 'They weren't shootin' under the tables.'

The taciturn American uttered a strangled cough. His talkative companion was judicious. 'Well, that kind of shit's all done now.'

'I bloody 'ope so,' Hal replied with a firm nod. He could not resist a final flourish. 'Mind you, you can never be sure. There's no knowin' with these little buggers. I wouldn't trust 'em as far as I could throw 'em.'

In response his American interlocutor pushed away the bloodied plate and offered_his verdict. 'Well, all I know is, you can't get steak like this in the States. Not now.' He indicated his empty plate. 'If this is martial law, then Marcos is welcome to introduce it to the U.S. of A. any time.'

His companion's cheeks inflated in another belch. Peter wondered whether this flatulence would finally prove to be the prelude to speech. Rolling his shoulders like a wrestler, the large American looked directly at Hal and finally spoke. 'Yeah.' He nodded.

Peter noted the red gums and the mottled teeth.

Hal frowned and demanded, 'Where's our bloody waitress?'

Nigel cleared his throat and raised his menu. 'I was wondering when we were going to get around to ordering.'

'Well,' said the more informative American, rising to his feet and extending a hand. 'Nice meetin' you all. Have a nice day.' He withdrew the unshaken hand, turned and pushed his companion ahead of him.

Hal nudged Maria. 'Go and get a waitress before we all starve to death.' He grimaced. 'Fuckin' Yanks. Got no fuckin' manners. Did you see 'ow the big feller was eatin' that steak?'

A waitress arrived, closely followed by Maria, who resumed her place beside Hal. Hal and Nigel ordered. Peter deferred to Maria and Sue. The breakfast was ordered at last. Within ten minutes Nigel was pouring syrup on his waffles and Hal was gorging on his bacon, eggs and toast. Peter had ordered a 'halo halo'.

Nigel and Hal looked on in disgust as Peter explored a fresh, green coconut filled with lychees, papaya and other unidentified fruits.

'This is rather terrific,' Peter announced to Nigel's evident disbelief.

'Terrific prices too,' Nigel grumbled, tapping the plastic menu with his knife. 'I blame the Yanks. They're all on expenses and wherever they go they bring their expenses with them.'

'Don't worry, Nige'.' Hal grinned at his disgruntled comrade-in-arms. 'Agustin's footin' the bill. Remember, this is all on the 'ouse.'

But Nigel was not to be deflected by the reassurance. He was still fuming at the breakfasting Americans. 'Yanks! They are a bloody bane.' He sneered. 'I pay my amah five hundred bucks a month and she still complains. She' s always quoting the stupid Yank in 2B. He forks out a thousand a month for the useless twat.' He pointed his egg-laden knife at Hal. 'And she's just a makee-learnee kid.'

'Use your imagination, Nige,' Hal said, grinning up at Nigel. 'What do you think he's gettin' for 'is extra five hundred?' He turned towards his other partner. 'How much do you pay your amah, Pete? Does she do everything you ask her to?'

'I don't need a live-in amah, Hal.'

'Oh, yeah. I'd forgotten. You live on your own now, don't you?'

'Yes, as you well know, Hal,' Peter replied, smiling. 'Of course, once this trip is over, I shall be returning to Mid-levels and an amah. Maybe two.' Hal laughed and, delighted, pointed at Peter. Nigel looked sour.

Hal dissected his second yolk with a grin, 'Never you mind, Pete, me old mate. All the crumpet's free 'ere. Like everything else.'

Peter watched the yolk ooze over the edge of Hal's toast. 'Does it ever occur to you to wonder why we are the beneficiaries of such largesse?'

Hal looked up, the yolk dripping onto his plate. 'Why what?'

'Why Agustin is so intent on plying us with freebies.' Peter frowned at Hal, who looked round the emptying dining room with an expression of disbelief.

'I don't know what you are talkin' about, Pete.' He shrugged. 'I don't know why you think this is so strange. Businessmen like to dish out a few perks.' He grinned. 'And get a few in return. Lubricates the wheels.'

'I see,' Peter nodded. 'And what do you intend to lay on for Agustin in Hong Kong?'

'Come on, don't be daft, Pete.' Hal's smile faded and he assumed his reasonable man-of-affairs persona. 'You can't 'ave lived in Hong Kong as long as you 'ave without knowing what goes on in business.'

'O.K. But I'm not in business. I'm in journalism.'

Nigel's knife dropped on his plate. 'Look, old chum, we're supposed to be partners, right?'

'Yeah, that's right,' Hal answered the rhetorical question. 'And if you're prepared to take a third share of the profits, you've got to be prepared to 'elp us make 'em.'

Peter smiled. 'You're forgetting a few facts, Hal. I have not signed a contract. Actually, I have had no contract to read.' Peter's voice took on an edge. 'I've tried living on your promises before, Hal. Or have you forgotten?'

'All right,' Hal said, flexing his jaw muscles. 'Be suspicious if you like. That's just good business. But I'm warnin' you.' He leant forward. 'This meetin' today is very, VERY important.' Peter saw the glitter fade from Hal's eyes and a smile widen his lips. Hal leaned back. 'Agustin's a nervous kind of character. There's no need to make him even more nervous, is there?' Hal and Peter stared at one another. Hal's smiled broadened. 'Okay?'

Peter looked away. He was behaving like a petulant child and he knew it. Hal almost crooned, 'After all, Pete, you're the most important member of the team now.' Hal looked across at Nigel. 'Ain't 'e, Nige?'

Nigel took hold of Peter by the elbow. 'That's right, Peter, Agustin just wants some nice copy and pics to keep him happy. And he can be a very generous man when he's happy.'

Peter shook off Nigel's fingers and rested his elbow on the table. His eyes met Hal's.

'There's only eight days left to gather material.'

Hal waved a dismissive hand. 'Don't you worry about that. We can always buy in some pretty pictures. Dino's got a whole library of Philippines' photos back in H.K. Six by six colour transparencies.' Peter looked quizzingly at Hal, who shrugged. 'Dino was 'ere last year.'

Peter wondered whether Dino could also supply articles to go with his pictures. Nigel glanced down at Peter's bag of gear. 'Pity you don't shoot with a Hassel. Much better definition than thirty-five mil.'

Peter tried to ignore the pinprick of professional jealousy. 'Are you sure you wouldn't like Dino to take over the whole job?' He felt his cheeks redden. No sooner uttered than regretted. He was being childish.

'Come on, Pete,' Hal cajoled, grasping Peter's other elbow. 'You know Dino can't do what you do.'

Peter regretted his shard of spite. He liked Dino and admired his work. 'All right, Hal.' Peter considered his partner. 'But I would still like to see a contract.'

Nigel tossed his serviette onto the table. 'Oh, for Christ's sake, stop whining, Peter. If you really can't lower yourself to tarnish your bloody liberal soul, then piss off back to the Colony. We're not in the business of converting the world. And if that's your bag, then you'd better get another profession. But somehow I can't see you adorning a pulpit.'

Peter had neatly painted himself into a corner. He was not in a position to convert Nigel and Hal to his view of the world and of journalism. He felt Hal increase the pressure on his arm. His voice took on a warmly confidential tone. 'Look, Pete, I understand where you're coming from. Really, I do.' He cast an admonitory glance at Nigel. 'All we need is a nice, colourful issue to please our loyal readership.' Peter glanced at the sincere expression on Hal's face. 'You know the mag. It was you who established the 'ouse style.'

Peter leaned back and looked directly at Hal. He smiled, 'So, not a word about martial law? Nothing about corruption, the suspension of human rights, the detention of Benigno Aquino?' He paused. 'And nothing about gunfights in cafés?'

He knew he might as well save his breath. Peter already knew Hal's answers to the questions.

'Where the hell did you pick up all that crap?' Nigel sounded genuinely pained.

Peter glanced at the questioner. He replied, 'FEER.' Nigel looked puzzled.

'*The Far Eastern Economic Review.*' Peter looked at Nigel. 'The source of all wisdom about the region for all successful businessmen in the region.'

Hal leaned back and gave Peter a kindly look. 'Look, Peter. I've got all the time in the world for Derek Davies. *The Review's* his thing. *Hong Kong Weekly* is mine. There's room for both. And *Hong Kong Weekly* is producin' a special edition on the Philippines for Mr. Agustin. He's the piper, Peter.'

Nigel leant towards Peter. 'So, he gets to call the tune. Get it?'

Chapter Eight

Peter whistled as he blower-brushed the 35mm F1.4 Nikkor. Nigel sulked in the other back-seat corner of the Pontiac. Meanwhile Hal kept up a constant stream of badinage with Chico. As it was still early, they were taking a longer, scenic route to their appointment.

''Ere, what do you think of Maria, Chico?' Hal prompted an answer with a friendly clenched fist pressed on the driver's right arm.

'Very cute.'

Peter stopped his cleaning operation and looked up. He had detected a discordant undertone in Chico's reply. Hal remained tone deaf.

'What's she like in bed then, Chico?' Hal's lips spread in a grin.

Chico shrugged uncomfortably. 'I don't know.'

'Come on.' Another nudge from Hal. 'You tryin' to tell me that a good-lookin' feller like you don't get some nooky from them massage girls?'

Chico gave an embarrassed laugh. 'Those girls are not for me.'

Peter raised the camera and drew a bead on Hal. 'Leave him alone, Hal.' He pressed the shutter release.

Hal pointed at the camera accusingly. 'That's my film you're wastin'.'

Peter lowered the camera. 'It's mine until you reimburse me.' Peter smiled. 'You seem to have trouble reading invoices.'

Hal's hand dropped from Chico's shoulder down to Peter's knee. 'It's all them Chinese characters.' He grinned.

Nigel interrupted. 'Now this is more like it,' He indicated the passing scene. Peter blinked. Was that a sentry box they had just passed? The car lurched up and down as though riding an ocean roller.

'Fuckin' 'ell,' was Hal's reaction.

Nigel was unperturbed. 'Sleeping policeman.'

'Dead policemen, more like,' Hal quipped. Peter looked back and saw a white-striped hump of asphalt. Peter raised the camera and took a shot of the man in khaki drill who stepped out into the road to stare after them. The man balanced an Armalite rifle across his body. Peter lowered his camera and touched Chico's shoulder.

'I thought guns were forbidden under martial law.'

Chico shrugged. 'This is Porbes Park.'

Peter settled for 'Forbes'. It couldn't be Porbes Fark. The car rose and fell over another dozing constable.

As the big car ambled along, warning notices appeared. 'Twenty k.p.h.' and 'no tooting'. Large, detached houses with American style front lawns drifted by. Nigel whistled appreciatively as they passed a white mansion complete with colonnaded portico and green tiled roof. Chico cleared his throat.

'Mr. Agustin's house.' His tone was reverential.

'Nice.' Hal was appreciative. 'Very nice.' He turned back towards Peter, widened his eyes, compressed his lips and nodded in sincere approval.

'I'll bet he has more than one amah to clean that,' Nigel muttered, craning his neck to keep the residence in his sights a little longer.

'You bet.' Hal gave Chico another affectionate push. ''Ere, Chico. 'Ow many amahs has Mr. Agustin got?'

Chico frowned. 'Amahs?'

'Yeah,' Hal forgave Chico his ignorance. 'You know, Chico. Servants.'

Chico shrugged. 'Seven, eight.'

'All girls?' Hal asked, winking at Peter.

Chico treated the question seriously. 'No, two men are married to two of the women. Then there is an old woman and two young girls.'

'Bloody 'ell.' Hal sucked in his lower lip. ''E is definitely loaded!'

Nigel asked, 'How much do servants earn in Manila?'

Chico's reply was immediate and precise. 'Sixty-five pesos a month.'

'Wait a minute,' Nigel's lips calculated as if muttering a silent prayer. 'There's over six pesos to the dollar. The American dollar.' His eyes gleamed. 'Do you realise I could afford nine amahs here? 'He waved his hands. 'No, make that nine and a half.'

Peter leaned forward. 'What hours do they work?'

Chico glanced into the rear-view mirror. 'If the boss wants to get up at five, then somebody's gotta make his breakfast.' He shrugged. 'If he comes home late and feels hungry then they gotta cook too. But... so many people working for one family... it's not so bad. Better than living in Tondo.'

'What's Tondo?' Nigel asked.

'A friend of the Lone Ranger,' Hal lisped and fell back, laughing, against the door of the Pontiac.

Chico smiled and addressed Nigel. 'It's the real poor part of Manila. Life can be pretty tough there, especially for girls. Better to be a servant in Mr.Agustin's place. Or a massage girl.'

Hal narrowed his eyes at Chico. The driver's brown eyes stared straight ahead.

Peter changed the subject. 'So, who lives in Forbes' Park. Apart from Mr.Agustin?' All grist for Peter's mill.

'Mostly rich people. Pilipino or American. A few Illustrados.'

'Sorry,' Peter lurched forward as the car ran over another policeman. A second gate was coming into view.

'Ilustrados?'

The guard saluted Chico, who acknowledged the gesture with a salute of his own. 'They're the families who are from the Spanish times. Pure Spanish blood.' Peter could sense that Chico found the description ironic.

'And do many people still speak Spanish?' His one sentence would get a good work-out. Hal yawned cavernously.

'Not many,' Chico replied

'Got any Chinks?' Hal asked.

Chico was perplexed. 'Chinks?'

Hal persisted. 'Chinks. You know. Chinese.' He drew apart the corners of his eyes.

'Sure. Find a store – find a Chinese.'

Peter murmured to Hal. '*The Review* reckons there are at least two hundred thousand in the country.'

''Ow would you fancy a nice bit of... a nice Chinese girl? Eh, Chico?'

Chico shook his head. 'I don't trust Chinese. They are not true Pilipinos.'

The old distrust.

Peter had learned from Chinese journalists in Hong Kong about their relatives in Malaysia, Vietnam, Indonesia and Burma, who had been made to suffer for their success in business and for resisting cultural integration.

Yet, the Chinese storekeeper in a jungle village would probably be the only trader willing to give peasants credit, cutting marks on a stick, as a record that even illiterates could understand. Of course, when a national leader was having trouble, he could always rouse the fury of those whose debts were outstanding and growing. A dead shopkeeper was a debt cleared. Every so often the peasants would be encouraged to run amok. 'The Jews of South-East Asia' a Review writer had called the Overseas Chinese.

Peter's thoughts were interrupted by Chico's commentary. 'This is Makati.'

Peter recalled a reference from *The Golden Guide*. Makati was the business district. In parts it looked like a building site – its new multi-storey structures staring blindly at the sandy earth through empty vitrines.

''Ere, when do we get to Mr.Agustin's office? We don't need a grand bloody tour,' Hal complained.

As if in reply, Chico spun the power-assisted wheel and the car first dipped and then rose into an asphalt courtyard. The tyres hissed as they span round the back of a low, brick building of uncompromising modernity. The car came to a silent halt outside a discreet entrance of smoked black glass. They climbed out of the vehicle and shook themselves like dogs to ease their stiff legs. Peter hoisted his canvas hold-all over his shoulder.

Chico was waiting by a door which he held open. They shuffled into a darkened lobby, with Peter bringing up the rear.

'Wait here, please,' Chico ordered quietly. He left them, crossing the lobby and pausing before a door of dark, solid teak by an empty reception area. He knocked and listened. After a few seconds hesitation he disappeared through the doorway. Peter gingerly lowered himself into one of a matching pair of hideous leather armchairs. Hal occupied its twin.

Nigel discovered a brochure bearing the legend 'Agustin Enterprises'. Hal hummed to himself as he took in the accoutrements of the space with approval. Time ticked by. Peter wondered whether Chico was giving Agustin a report. After several minutes, Hal broke the silence.

'Oldest trick in the book.' His expression registered disgust. 'Make people wait just to show 'em who's boss. Makes 'em nervous. Who does he think I am? Oldest trick in the book.'

'Why are you whispering?' Peter asked in a voice which seemed to thunder in his own ears.

'I wasn't,' Hal whispered.

'Oh, just knock it off you two.' Nigel nodded towards the door by which they had not entered. 'He'll hear us,' he whispered.

As if he had, the teak door opened to reveal Chico. He beckoned. They scrambled to their feet and filed sheepishly into the space Chico guarded. He slipped behind them and closed the door.

Peter wondered why the office seemed so familiar. He realised that the furniture was a more luxurious continuation of the style of the ante-chamber. Teak and black leather. It wasn't simply the furniture. It was the lighting. He almost expected Humphrey Bogart to step out of the shadows and challenge Sidney Greenstreet. Peter was tempted by the same insane desire to laugh that afflicts mourners at the obsequies of a distant and distasteful relative.

The room crouched in darkness. There seemed to be no windows. The only glimmer of light came from a desk lamp in the shape of a T'ang horse. Its weak yellow glow emphasised the features of the extraordinary face of their Maecenas. The eyes, black in the lamp glow, stared at the nervous trio. Agustin's teak-brown face was deeply incised with the marks of time. Beneath two sad moons bulged pouches of flesh, echoed by the pout of Agustin's lips. The face inspired Peter with the desire to search for his camera. What an exciting yet troubling image.

'Welcome to Manila, gentlemen.' Contrary to his expectations, Peter heard a voice that was gentle to the point of kindliness. Like Chico, the speaker had a Filipino accent with marked American overtones. Agustin rose from his seat. His face had been replaced in the lamplight by a brown hand. Peter could also see a red silk tie and a white shirt. Conservative, in dress at least.

Hal leaned across the desk and Peter watched him grasp Agustin's hand of welcome. East meets West. Third World meets First. Youth and age. Emblematic. Peter almost smiled.

Nigel and Peter took their turns in the brief ceremonial. To his surprise Peter found that Agustin's handshake was cool, dry and quite firm. When Agustin repeated the word 'welcome' Peter felt unaccountably shy, like an acolyte in the presence of some Philippine deity. As he returned to his seat, Peter wondered whether Agustin had any Chinese ancestry.

The creaking of their leather seats ceased as they relaxed. 'How was your trip, Mr. Nicholson?' The face had reappeared in the lamplight.

'Excellent, thanks.' Of course. The airline tickets had been freebies too.

'And does the accommodation meet with your approval?' Peter was at a loss how to reply without sounding insincere.

'Not 'alf, Mr. Agustin.' Hal was not in the least deterred by the question. Nigel inspected his watch-strap.

'Now, what else can I provide to ensure that your trip is a successful one?' Augustin's smile was that of some genie conjured from an Aladdin's lamp. Must beware of rubbing him up the wrong way, Peter reflected. Then banished the reflection.

Nigel cleared his throat. 'About the advertising, Mr. Agustin...'

Their host's face retired into shadow. 'You must go and see my nephew, Joe, in his agency. My cousin is too busy to help at this time. But Joe will give you all the assistance you require.'

Nigel relaxed with a creak of leather satisfaction.

Hal patted his jacket pocket. 'Well, with the advertising under control and our star columnist 'ere, there's just the one outstanding matter. This little document.'

'All in good time, Hal.' The face reappeared. The brown eyes turned towards Peter. 'And you, Mr. Nicholson, what do you require?'

'I hardly know yet, Mr. Agustin,' Peter replied. 'So far I've only been to the resort, the *Intercontinental* and here.'

Agustin listened as though Peter's words were of the utmost profundity. Peter dried.

Agustin filled the silence with a smile. 'So, this is your first visit to the Philippines?' Agustin asked, still smiling.

'Yes.' Peter wondered what bill of goods Hal had sold Agustin about his 'wunderkind' journalist. It occurred to him that they should have agreed tactics before arriving at this point. Limply, he remarked, 'Hal's been here before, I know.'

Hal nodded like a nervous student at a *viva*.

'Perfect.' Agustin rose and moved into the penumbra beside the desk. His voice was now clear and firm.

'It is good that this is your first visit. You will see the islands in all their beauty with the eyes of innocence, like a child.'

Nigel cleared his throat. Hal kept a straight face.

'I envy you, Mr. Nicholson. You will see for the first time the sunset over Manila Bay and the old city of Intramuros. Perhaps Mount Taal or the Pagsanjan Falls. Who knows? Time is short.'

Hal had determined on enthusiasm. 'You're so right, Mr. Agustin. That's just what we want to show our readership of successful businessmen. Just how fantastic this place is.' Hal strove to keep his accent free from too many 'Bristows'. 'All the tourist attractions, the new 'otels. I mean you've got 'iltons and 'yatt's just like 'Ong Kong. Deaches, swimming, sailing, beautiful girls.' Hal had reached Top C. Agustin nodded and turned to Peter.

'Yes, I hope through your words, Mr. Nicholson, the world will experience all the charms of this wonderful country.' The face, softened by sentiment, reappeared in the lamplight.

Moved by his host's evident strength of feeling, Peter rejoined, 'I will certainly do my best.'

'And don't forget the visit to the mine, Mr.Agustin.' This from Nigel. Peter knew he looked nonplussed. Hal filled the breach. 'You know, Pete. That copper mine that belongs to Agustin Enterprises. Up North.'

Peter nodded numbly. He had been outwitted by Hal yet again. The mine was clearly the short straw. Agustin rose to his feet once more.

'Gentlemen, the car and its driver are at your disposal during your stay. Order anything you need, either at the resort or elsewhere. While you are in my country, you are my honoured guests.' Agustin extended both hands towards them, palms upward, in a gesture of hospitality.

'Right then, Mr. Agustin. And many, many thanks.' Hal began to rise from his chair.

'Just a minute, Hal.' At the tautness of Peter's voice Hal froze and looked worriedly at Nigel. He then sank back into the seat.

Peter fixed his eyes on the red, silk tie. 'Mr.Agustin, you are wasting your money.'

Hal giggled. 'You don't want to pay too much...'

'Please!' Agustin's cutting gesture silenced Hal. After a brief pause, Agustin murmured, 'Yes, Mr. Nicholson?'

Peter took a deep breath. 'Do you actually want anyone to read the Philippines edition of *Hong Kong Weekly*?'

Agustin leaned forward into the pool of light. 'Of course, I do.'

'To interest the kind of business reader who could be of real relevance to the Philippines, the magazine must offer more than the usual tourist pap about exotic vacations with sun, sand and sex.'

Agustin nodded. 'I agree. You must not forget the history of my country. We were the first to gain independence from the colonial powers in this region of Asia.'

'O.K. That's important,' Peter conceded. 'But what fundamentally interests *our* readers – the businessmen of the region – is not holidays but a safe destination in which to invest their money – and a profitable one.'

Peter felt his pulse beating fast as he looked into the twin reflections of the lamp in Agustin's dilated pupils. 'And to know those things, they require assurances from the highest level of the administration about what they can expect. Not just in Manila, or Luzon or even in the Visayas.' Peter moved away from the desk and then turned back. 'Who is going to give a businessman assurance about investing in Mindanao? Now that is a big question. Mindanao could be a goldmine. Or is some Moro guerrilla going to sneak up in the night and slit the businessman's throat?' Peter moved away from the desk, turned and moved back towards Agustin. 'And that's not all.' Hal and Nigel both looked tense. 'That's not all. The investors back home may be concerned about the implications of martial law. Some are worried that the President will keep it going; others are terrified he won't.' Agustin showed the hint of a smile. 'People remember the old Congress days before September last year and the anarchy in the country.' He paused. 'And they want to know about the New People's Army. Are they just communists? And what does the government propose to do about them?'

Hal and Nigel were frozen to their seats. Peter knew he had to finish this.

'Above all the world wants to know how a shop window of democracy is making out now that the army has smashed the glass and made off with the display.'

Agustin's face was once more in shadow. He looked up at Peter. 'You have done your homework, Mr. Nicholson.'

'These questions may be unpalatable, Mr. Agustin.' Peter held the older man's eye. 'Unpalatable for a Filipino patriot to hear.' (Peter winced inwardly.) But the people who spend four bucks on our magazine want to know the answers. Tourist information they get for nothing from the airlines.'

The seconds ticked by. Agustin looked up from his folded hands. 'You will read me what you write before you print it?'

Peter refused to look at Hal and Nigel. 'I promise to show you everything I write.' The old man's expression softened. Peter raised a hand. 'But I do not promise to change a word of it.'

Agustin looked down at his hands once more. Hal glared at

Peter. Nigel rubbed his face with his palms. The hiss of the air-conditioner was the only sound. Agustin looked questioningly at Peter.

'I will do my utmost to be accurate and fair,' Peter said.

Agustin stared down at his palms. He looked up at Peter. 'That is as much as any man can ask,' Agustin said and the corners of his mouth showed the suggestion of a smile. 'You say you want to hear the truth from the highest levels of the administration. I will try to arrange an interview.' He rose. 'With the First Lady.'

'Thank you,' Peter moved towards the desk and accepted the proffered hand. As he gripped it, Peter saw in his mind's eye the clear picture of a shadow-man in his fifties, thrashing a projectile in the half-light.

As they walked back to the car, Hal threw an arm round Peter's shoulder.

'Pete, I gotta 'and it to you!'

'Why the fuck?' Nigel asked irritably. 'The silly cunt nearly ruined the whole deal.'

Hal squeezed Peter's shoulder. 'Nigel don't understand the first thing about journalistic whatsits. He'd screw 'is granny for a peso.'

'You're joking.' Nigel shook his head. 'I couldn't get it up for a million bucks right now. I feel completely shagged.' Nigel's appearance confirmed the accuracy of his asseveration.

Hal gave Peter another squeeze. 'Agustin respects us now.' He grinned. 'The old fart.'

Peter slid out of Hal's grip into the back seat of the waiting car with his trusty bag.

Four doors slammed and the Pontiac drifted forward. Hal turned to Peter. 'Ere, Pete.' His brow puckered as Peter turned to face him. 'Who's the purse lady?'

Chapter Nine

'What do you think of the curfew?'

Peter put the question to the cab driver's right ear. Caught by surprise, the man nervously adjusted his pudgy fingers on the wheel. Peter had learned from real foreign correspondents that one of the first lessons they learn is that taxi drivers are a mine of confidential information, with their finger on the pulse of public opinion. In other words, they have an opinion about everything. Taxi drivers opinions' appear regularly in foreign dispatches, their identity protected by the cognomen 'a local political commentator'. Perhaps their most valuable attribute is a smattering of English.

'Curpew?' The driver's brow could be seen in the rear-view mirror to crease into furrows.

'Yes, the curpew.'

The cab slowed among a gaggle of jeepneys; reproductions of Second World War jeeps, disguised by fairground-hued exteriors. By the kerb four passengers were alighting from one such vehicle; girls in brightly-coloured dresses, carrying even more brilliantly hued sunbrellas, their reflections prismatised in the harsh sunlight.

'Me, I don' know.' The driver performed a simulacrum of Chico's shrug. 'My wipe – she likes it.' He turned and grinned. Peter continued to watch the traffic with some alarm. A jeepney bearing a prancing silver horse on its bonnet swept into their lane. Rather than 'Lone Ranger' the vehicle's rear logo boasted the single word legend 'Sexy'. The passengers were anything but. The driver looked at least eighty. He glanced across and gave Peter a toothless grin. Still, where's there's life.

The next jeepney they passed boasted an apple-green, sky-blue and saffron-yellow colour scheme. Its steel studs and chrome panels outshone the sun. Its tail slogan assured doubtful passengers in other vehicles that 'Jesus Never Fail'.

Peter glanced down at his full bag of tricks as the jeepneys dropped behind. He shrugged. There would be ample opportunity to capture them later. Peter returned to the driver.

'Why does your wife like the curfew?' Peter was doggedly pursuing his in-depth investigation. Once more the driver glanced uneasily back at Peter.

''Cause I get home before midnight.' The driver adopted a hang-dog expression. 'She say before she never see me.' He shifted to a more comfortable position.

Peter was inexorable. 'But what about you? Do you like the curfew?'

'The curpew is good,' Peter made as if to ask a follow-up question. The driver forestalled him. 'And the curpew is bad.' Peter held his question back. The driver took up the slack. 'No curpew, more money. Bars, nightclubs stay open on Roxas Boulevard. Now I go home to my wipe.' The cabbie grimaced, then brightened. 'But I no get robbed.'

'Robbed?' Peter was beginning to wish he had learned shorthand.

'Sure.' The cab narrowly avoided a small boy who was risking life and limb to sell a newspaper. 'Before curpew I get robbed three times in one month.'

'Were you hurt?' The driver frowned. Peter engaged in vigorous dumb-show, grabbing himself by the throat and grimacing. 'Hurt?'

The driver shook his head. 'No, but these guys – they had guns.' He pointed at a metal box. 'They smash to get money.'

'And now?' Peter asked, aware that he was promoting his driver to the status of national spokesman.

'Now I go home early to my wife.' The driver grinned at the rear-view mirror. 'She have another kid. I get robbed another way.'

Peter wished he could have recorded the conversation. He settled back on the banquette. Then another thought occurred to him. 'Have you heard of a man called 'Agustin'?

'Mr. Agustin?' The driver glanced back at Peter. 'Sure. Mr. Agustin's a rich man, a big man. Maybe he's a big man with the President; maybe the Purse Lady. I don' know.'

Did that uncertainty suggest a power struggle between the President and his wife? There was no point in pursuing the subject. Taxi-drivers had their limits. The cab now left Bonifacio Drive and entered a multi-lane highway, bordering the ocean.

The driver waved a hand to encompass the scene. 'Roxas Boulevard.' Peter felt the stirrings of real excitement. He drew his bag close to his stomach. He patted the driver on the shoulder. 'O.K. You can let me out here.'

Naturally, Hal had taken the Pontiac and Chico. Now he turned towards Nigel, sprawling on the back seat.

'Don't you worry about Pete,' Hal reached back and patted Nigel's knee. 'So, when we get to Joe's office, you lay it on the line. We want performance.'

Nigel grunted upright. 'It's this bloody, 'mañana, mañana' complex.' He thrust out a belligerent lower lip.

'Yeah, well, you got to do a lot more pushin'.' Hal patted Nigel's knee again. 'You're gettin' plenty of practice.' He grinned.

Nigel switched his attention to the passing scene.

Hal switched his attention to the driver. 'You married, Chico?'

'No,' Chico laughed, 'No, to marry you need money.'

''Ow old are you, Chico?' Hal placed his fist on Chico's bicep and pushed.

'Forty.' Chico's smile was rueful. The teeth he displayed were even and white against his smooth skin.

'Forty?' Hal relaxed against the car door. 'I suppose you're past carin' now anyway.'

Chico carefully placed his other hand on the wheel. The knuckles were pale with tension.

Hal patted Chico's knee. 'You really should 'ave a crack at Maria. She can't get enough of it.'

Chico's eyes were fixed on the road ahead,

'Tell you what, Chico, me old mate. I'll 'ave a word with Mr. Agustin. I'll say 'Chico's a great guy and he really looked after us while we were 'ere. Now that I'm leavin' why don't you let 'im 'ave a crack at Maria?' Hal leaned towards Chico. ''Ow's that?'

'Thanks, but no thanks.'

Hal laughed. Then all conversation ceased.

Nigel experienced a sense of relief when the car swept into the curb. Sometimes Hal was too outrageous, even for Nigel.

Chico cut the engine. 'In there.' The driver pointed out the entrance to the office building with his chin.

Hal and Nigel slowly climbed out into the heat and shook themselves. The car was started. Hal leaned through the front passenger window. 'Just say the word, Chico.' The driver half-lifted a hand but kept his eyes averted. The car skidded away. Hal watched as it joined the traffic flow.

'Wanker,' Hal snapped and turned towards the advertising agency.

Peter flicked the pages of the 'Guide to Manila' he had been given by Chico before they had left Agustin Enterprises. He was appalled by the guide's ugly layout and general shoddiness of production. Photographs were blurred. The 'copy' was a mountain of malapropisms. Throughout, the 'Guide' referred to something called 'marital law'.

By chance Peter discovered a minute picture of the gigantic structure which now confronted him. The image was 'soft' and a double exposure to boot. Below the photograph the title proclaimed; 'Cultural Centre, Manila, built by the First Lady'. An adjacent advertisement announced that Van Cliburn was to be the featured artist of the month. Peter tossed the guide back into the canvas bag.

He considered the severe, rectilinear structure before him with disbelief. It resembled a monstrous, grey sombrero with a deep square rim. He had read somewhere that the First Lady had dedicated herself to a vast programme of beautification. Did she really think this monstrous carbuncle was beautiful? Or that it would beautify the lives of servants on sixty-five pesos a month?

He extracted his wide-angle Nikon and crouched for the obligatory shot of the Centre destined for the projected article on tourism. What he thought was a speck of dust in the viewfinder turned out to be the minute figure of a man, silhouetted against the sky. Good. It gave a sense of the scale of the massive structure.

'Here's one for the Purse Lady,' Peter muttered and pressed the shutter release.

Taking his life in his hands, he dashed to the centre of the highway. Several red and white noticeboards jutted out of the grass divide. 'Wonder if I can get them all in focus,' he muttered moving the aperture ring to F11. He checked the depth of field to be sure.

The furthest notice exhorted him to 'Vote in the Referendum'; the next contained the single word 'Participate'; the nearest insisted he 'Get Involved'. He crouched, uncertain whether the shot wasn't too dull. Just as his right knee began to throb, a green bus appeared, its windows full of wide-eyed secondary-school children. There. That did it. He grunted with satisfaction; then discomfort, as he rose and the blood returned to his calf. He waited until the pins and needles had come and gone.

Eventually there was another inviting gap in the traffic flow. A second, frenetic dash for safety and Peter found himself within sight of the sea. Over a grassy rise, perhaps two hundred paces away, he spotted a group of beached, multi-coloured boats, surrounded by a gathering of thirty or forty men and women. Peter concluded they were local fishermen and their wives.

Peter was apprehensive as he moved down the beach, pretending to check the zoom's aperture. Would the group object to his taking a few shots? A similar-sized body of Hoklo or Tanka folk in Hong Kong would be certain to hurl abuse or even clods of earth to prevent any photographic intruders intruding. Some explained this antagonism as a cultural objection to photography per se; those of a more cynical disposition suggested that a five-dollar bill would quieten any objections.

He was now within twenty feet. A delicious breeze brushed the nape of his neck. To his right, a group of tall palms creaked in the wind. Waves flung themselves against the breakwater which sheltered the boats. He raised the camera and concentrated on the face of a small girl standing alone and staring at him. The image sharpened to reveal a broad smile.

Peter exchanged more smiles with members of the group and indicated his raised camera questioningly. No response. He was about to turn tail when he spotted a large basket, standing apart. His curiosity was aroused. He sensed that he was being watched as he trudged towards the basket.

He discovered that the receptacle contained prawns and crabs, their searching claws fruitlessly seeking purchase in the air. He exchanged the zoom camera for the wide-angle. As he raised the camera again, he sensed that the two nearest fishermen – mending nets – were taking a polite interest. He turned and smiled. They nodded, serious, but not unfriendly. He hoped this was a good sign.

Soon Peter was moving, his trousers rolled, among the outriggers, trying not to include too many competing colours in each frame. Gradually the fisherfolk were transmuted to Ektachrome. If only there were some way to see the images instantly, without having to wait for development in Hong Kong.

He realised that one way the fishermen and women expressed their individuality was by the design of their hats of either straw or canvas. Peter was delighted to discover one fisher-woman sporting a cultural-centre-in-miniature of plaited straw. The wearer condescended to pose, complete with her headgear, with the Cultural Centre in the background. A small crowd gathered to watch the operation. Somebody made a remark which brought a gat-toothed smile from the women and laughter from the group. Peter, now seemingly accepted, searched for his next subject.

He turned towards the water. A slim, red boat ran ahead of the wavelets thrown up by the blustering breeze. He got off three shots before the out-rigger he had chosen drew up alongside the other craft. He must take care not to run through his film too fast. How many rolls had he brought?

Peter paused and raised his eyes to the horizon. The bay was huge. From here it looked out to open sea, with scarcely a hint of horizontal curvature. In the mid-distance lay a coastal vessel or two. Furthest from the shore, American warships – frigates and destroyers – rode at anchor – so many grey, black and white seabirds. A reminder of the political tensions which lay behind this peaceful façade.

Peter recalled having read that when Magellan's ships had

arrived in Manila harbour during their circumnavigation of the globe, a fleet of ocean-going Chinese junks had already taken up all the best parking places. When had that occurred? 1520? 1530? He would have to check.

Peter sighed with satisfaction. He was enjoying himself. It had been a good session. He opened the canvas hold-all and nestled the camera within. As he shifted the zoom to make space, he caught sight of one final shot that he must not miss. He lifted the zoom clear and lowered the bag to the beach.

Fifty yards from shore in the shallow blue-brown waters, two children cavorted in a cascade of frenzied splashing. This was the cherry on the cake. It might even serve as a cover shot.

Peter secreted the camera in the bag once more. He waved at the children, the ocean, the sky and at no-one in particular. He felt a pleasurable sense of goodwill. He had returned to life. Then he remembered. His pleasure could not last. He was not alone.

'God I'm shagged,' Nigel announced, fanning himself with the 'Guide to Manila'.

'What the fuck are we 'angin' about for?'

Nigel raised his eyes to the ceiling. 'They say they're trying to find copies of the invoices they claim to have sent out. No way am I going to return to Hong Kong and hand plates to the printer for a four-colour job without a single peso up front from the advertisers.' Nigel lowered the guide. 'Or are we doing this job for sweet charity?'

Hal leaned towards Nigel. 'Why can't we just print the bloody thing over 'ere?'

'That's why.' Nigel sneered, tossing the Guide to Manila across to Hal. 'Look at it. We'd be the laughing stock of Hong Kong. This first edition would also be our swan song.'

Hal was flicking through the pages. 'Fuck me.' He let the guide fall on the leatherette. 'That's bloody diabolical. They could certainly do with a bit of quality control.'

Nigel was growing more impatient. 'So, what do we do if they don't cough up the money, partner?

Hal stretched out his legs and folded his hands behind his neck. ''Ere, Nige. You know those 'ouses in Forbes Park?'

Nigel raised his eyes heavenward, 'Christ! Can't we keep our minds on the matter in hand for a few minutes?'

'A lovely white mansion with all mod cons and a big, old lawn...' Hal allowed his voice to trail away. He looked up.

Nigel was staring at him in frank disbelief. 'Hal, we have to decide what to do. It's imperative.'

Hal sighed and smiled. 'Three hundred and fifty U.S. a month.'

There was a slight delay before Nigel blurted, 'You're kidding.' His eyes lit up with concupiscence. 'I simply don't believe it.'

'That's not all. Foreign investors who establish their regional headquarters in the Philippines only pay fifteen percent tax.' Hal exhibited his wisdom teeth.

Nigel was now sitting up and taking a good deal of notice. He glanced around. 'I wonder what the rent would be on a nice, little office like this.'

Hal clicked his fingers. 'Peanuts, I'll be bound.'

'So,' Nigel enthused, 'We set up shop over here...'

'But keep an office in Hong Kong,' Hal added.

'And continue to do our printing in the Colony with the Japs,' Nigel concluded.

'Yeah,' Hal agreed. He grinned at Nigel. 'President Marcos needs us.'

'Sounds like just what the doctor ordered.' Nigel's expression changed from excitation to gloom. 'But Susan would never go for it.'

Hal raised an eyebrow and cocked his head to one side. He smiled at Nigel. Slowly an answering smile transformed Nigel's face.

Meanwhile, Peter's next subject had found him.

Five boys in white T-shirts, white cotton shorts and vermilion neckerchiefs. They stood in a cluster, staring at him. Peter smiled and waved. They waved back. One boy sprang up and down. Peter had the zoom handy. He raised it and the boys dived behind the nearest palm. He pretended to take a shot, shrugged, hoisted the camera strap onto his left shoulder and, feigning insouciance, wandered along the Boulevard. The boys duly followed, ever ready to hide.

Peter pretended to give up. To his alarm, the boys emulated his risky dash across the traffic flow. Safe on the landward pavement, Peter entered into the game once more.

He ran round the corner of a modern complex, across a courtyard and hid out of sight in a doorway. The boys pattered onto the pavé and wheeled this way and that, calling to each other like so many gulls.

'Hey,' Peter yelled and stepped out into the sunlight. There were shouts of delight but the boys still held back. Perhaps they had been warned never to speak to foreigners. Peter turned his back, raised the zoom and wasted a couple of shots on the nearest building. The boys' attention was engaged, their expressions serious. Slowly Peter moved towards them until he was only five yards away. He lowered the camera and held it out to one of the boys, who looked quizzically at his friends before accepting Peter's offer. Its weight took the boy by surprise. Recovering his balance, the kid raised and lowered the camera like a weight-lifter.

Soon Peter was demonstrating the camera surrounded by a circle of lads. They had no English and Peter no Tagalog. Peter wondered how he might capture the joyfulness of these children. Then he had an idea. He changed cameras and, placing his camera-bag on the ground, lay on his back beside it, the camera pointing skywards. Curiosity drew the boys into a circle around him. They peered down into the lens. The result would cover the two-page centre-fold of the Philippines' edition.

'Well, that's half the invoices,' Nigel said. He looked up at Agustin's smiling nephew. 'You'd better tell the rest of the advertisers 'no payment, no publish'. Joe's smile never faltered

'You do understand, don't you, Joe?' Hal's voice purred across the office, the descant to the humming continuo of the air-conditioner. 'Our printers in Hong Kong want their money before they start. It's just business. No hard feelings.'

Joe was the personification of unruffled amiability. 'In Manila the printers give me three months' credit, sometimes six.' He spread his palms.

'And if you can't find the invoices, indefinitely,' Nigel said sourly.

'Nigel's got an expensive life-style to maintain, ain't that right, Nige?' Hal was beside his partner, squeezing his shoulder.

'That's right,' Nigel concurred with an emphatic nod.

'Don't worry, Joe. After all, getting the money's just part of Nigel's job. And this is another country. It's your country.' Hal grinned. 'You understand, don't you, Joe?'

'Sure.' The smile did not reach Joe's eyes.

'Mr. Agustin assured us that you would handle the ads.' Hal re-launched his smile. 'And that includes payment.'

Joe blinked and looked down at his hands. Hal's voice resumed on a brighter note.

'Look, Joe, all work and no play makes Hal a dull boy.' Joe received a squeeze on the shoulder. 'What do you advise a visitor to your fair city to do for crumpet?'

'Sorry?'

'Crumpet. Skirt. Girls.' Hal clicked his tongue. 'I'm tired of being cooped up in that resort night after night.'

Joe grinned. 'I hear you been makin' out O.K. with Chico's niece.'

Nigel stifled his laughter as Hal's mouth opened and then shut soundlessly.

Hal struggled to recover his composure. 'Yeah, Maria's a very bright girl. I've been 'elpin' 'er with 'er English. Nice girl.' He nodded. 'Very nice girl.'

'Is she a good puck?' Joe was all polite interest.

Hal swallowed and offered Joe an unconvincing smile. 'I wouldn't take liberties with one of Mr. Agustin's employees, now would I?'

Joe shrugged. Nigel tugged his ear-lobe.

'So,' Hal slapped his palms together. 'I'm lookin' for a bit of action.'

Joe reached for the telephone on his desk. 'I'll ask my cousin in National Security to get you some curpew passes.'

The taxi slowed and halted just beyond baroque pillars flanking the road. Stout walls marched off in either direction while, beyond the walls, Romanesque domes rose, suggestive of some kind of ecclesiastical foundation.

A sign just within the mural perimeter welcomed visitors to Zone 70, 'Intramuros'. Peter now knew that the name meant 'Within the Walls'. Peter also knew that this was the very heart of Spanish Manila.

It was to be expected of any heart which had beaten for four hundred years, that it now required a certain amount of assistance. Most of its vessels were empty – the result of the Japanese-American war – and the remains were kept alive by infusions of tourist pesos, dollars and yen.

The church that Peter had seen from beyond the walls was dedicated to St. Augustine. San Agustin. Like its human namesake it was ascetic and watchful.

With a sinking heart he inspected the series of dull paintings narrating the story of the church in the Philippines. His cameras remained unused during his circuit. He preferred to take shots of the gardens overlooked by the cloisters.

Within the church Peter found the odour of ancient incense oppressive. In a dark chapel, rich surplices stood stiff and ghostly in their glass catafalques. As he perambulated the gloomy interior, Peter almost stumbled over a mourner who swayed in silence before a candlelit chapel. Within, he glimpsed a coffin, buried in floral tributes. He shuddered. It was time to depart.

Peter's next cab dropped him at the *Intercontinental* at the pre-arranged time and he made his way to the coffee-shop. The place was almost empty. He moved to a distant table. The bow-legged waitress brought him his halo-halo. She lowered the fresh green coconut and its contents onto the table in front of Peter.

'Excuse me.' Peter said. The waitress responded with a wary look. Carefully enunciating, Peter asked. 'Can you tell me what is 'halo halo'?'

The waitress frowned and then jabbed her finger at the coconut and its contents. 'Dis.' She was in no mood to play teasing games.

'Yes, I know that.' Peter tried a smile. 'But what does 'halo halo' mean in English?' She waitress chewed her lower lip. Peter repressed the unworthy thought that the staff of an international hotel ought to have a modicum of competence in English.

The waitress's face brightened. '*Halo halo* is 'nice mixture'.' She smiled sweetly.

Peter thought it was time to cut his losses. He raised his spoon and fork. 'Thank you.'

A voice bellowed across the coffee-shop. ''Ere, Pete.'

Hal, with Nigel in breathless attendance, slalomed round the tables, a sheet of paper held aloft in his left hand. The latecomers arrived at their destination. Nigel collapsed into a chair. Hal remained on his feet.

'Guess what!' he demanded.

'They've invited you to replace Marcos.'

'No,' Hal grinned. 'That comes later.' Hal winked. 'No, guess what this is.'

He dropped the paper onto the table.

Peter shrugged. 'I can't wait to find out,' He consumed a morsel of mango.

'It's a curfew pass.' Hal exulted. 'Now you'll be able to get some great night shots of Manila.'

'With nobody on the streets?' Peter now concentrated on cornering a piece of papaya.

'Right. With nobody about. That will show that curfew really works.' Hal was delighted with his own inspiration.

Peter lowered his spoon. 'Hal, have you ever tried taking pictures of nobody? It's only a little easier than taking shots of nothing.'

Hal was searching for a waitress. 'You'll find a way. That's why you're a partner, Pete.' Hal clicked his fingers. 'I'm bloody starvin'.' He moved closer to Peter's breakfast. 'What the 'ell's that?'

'Halo halo,' Peter replied, lifting the spoon with its papaya burden.

Hal peered more closely and sniffed. 'Looks like fruit salad to me.' He frowned. 'Ah Yeot makes better fruit salad than that.'

'That may be. But only someone without the least culinary knowledge could possibly confuse 'halo halo' with fruit salad.' Peter dabbed at his lips with the napkin.

'I'm totally shagged,' Nigel announced as the waitress returned.

'I know what you need, my lad.' Hal twinkled at the waitress. 'Two steaks. Rare.'

Chapter Ten

'This Major Alvarez is going to pick up at ten o'clock.' Hal stretched his arm along the top of the back seat and yawned. ''E's Joe's cousin.'

Nigel looked round from the front passenger seat and tapped the watch on his wrist. 'And we'll have plenty of time for a bit of fun before we leave.'

Hal shook his head at Nigel and raised a finger to his pursed lips. Nigel nodded. Peter noted that Chico had observed the exchange of signals.

'I'll try some time exposures tonight,' Peter announced.

Hal nodded dismissively. He cleared his throat. 'They got some great nightclubs along Roxas Boulevard. Ain't that right, Chico?'

Chico stared ahead as if he had not heard. Nigel and Peter studied the passing scene through their respective windows.

Hal persisted. 'Nightclubs, Chico.' He reached forward, as though to tap the driver's shoulder. He paused and then desisted.

'Yes?' Chico responded.

'Oh, let the man get on with his job,' Nigel snapped, turning towards the back seat. To Peter's surprise, Hal fell silent.

Peter strained to memorize the scenery along the puddled road to the resort. Nearly all the cyclists and pedestrians wore T-shirts and cotton trousers. Occasionally he noted a bright dress on a young girl or a shapeless black outfit on a grandmother. Flip-flops were the universal footwear. Behind the low palms lining the thoroughfare Peter detected flashes which might have been paddy fields.

'I suppose I ought to include something about agriculture,' Peter mused aloud.

'Agriculture?' Hal rounded on him. 'Boy, you sure get some real sexy ideas.'

'Agriculture is really important over here.' Peter knew it sounded lame.

'So's corruption,' Nigel snapped. 'But you're not thinking of a few thou on that, I trust.' Nigel extracted what looked like a long, black pencil from a packet.

'What the bloody 'ell's that?' Hal asked.

'It's a cigarillo. Want one?' Nigel reached inside his jacket.

'No, I do not. And don't light that bloody thing in 'ere. You'll choke us all to death.' Nigel's mouth opened, then shut. ''Ave some consideration for other people for once in your life, Nige.'

'But you smoke bloody great cigars,' Nigel pointed out.

'I'm seriously thinkin' of givin' up.'

The Pontiac slid through the open resort gates. The three graces had gathered at the sauna side to greet them. Maria gave a shy wave. Chico raised his left hand from the car roof in response. Hal slumped lower on the back seat. Sue was holding the third girl's hand. The car slowed and crunched to a halt behind the building.

The three Englishmen trudged up the stairs. Peter could hear the shrieks of children coming from the pool. He glanced down and saw the girls pause beside the car and look up. Nigel waved. He grunted, 'I think we'll be getting some visitors.' Hal did not respond. From Miguel's room there came a muddled shriek, then a dull thud.

'That boy's going to do himself an injury,' Nigel quipped.

'I don't think he's the one being injured,' Peter responded.

The air was heavy with vapour. Peter slipped into his room. The sound of footsteps and doors closing continued for a few seconds and then all was peace.

Peter threw off his clothes and entered the shower room. He considered himself in the blurred mirror. Not bad for his age. When does vanity end?

He returned naked to the bed. His next thought was whether to replace the chair against the door. He shrugged. He made his way to the bed. Nobody was going to rape him. He just needed a nap.

His dream involved Maria, Hilary's black dress and a gigantic penicillin capsule. He struggled to approach Maria but each time he approached she remained a tiny, distant figure. Then another figure joined the dream and Maria was there, close up and wearing Hilary's dress. Even in his dream Peter fidgeted. He wished Maria would get rid of those executive spectacles. She clambered onto the bed, pursued by a gigantic yellow capsule. It drew ever closer. As it rose behind Maria, Peter woke with a start. He rolled over onto his back. A dull thud penetrated the wall behind his head.

'Disgusting little bugger,' Peter muttered. Still, it was none of his business. His tongue felt thick.

There was a knock on the door. Peter held his breath. He covered himself with the sheet. His erection would soon disappear. 'Come in.'

The door opened. The room remained dark. Dusk was approaching. The pale cotton frock seemed to float into the room.

'Yes?' Peter tried to see the girl's eyes.

'You want food?'

'Hang on.' Peter rolled to one side and switched on the tiny bedside lamp. The girl half raised her arm and turned her head away from the light.

'Sorry,' Peter muttered, keeping the sheet over his legs. 'What did you say?'

'You want eat?' The girl was irritating in her timidity. She had nothing to fear. He wasn't Miguel. His mouth required liquid. He checked his watch. Nine forty-five. Too late. The major was due in fifteen minutes.

'No, thanks. I have to leave soon.'

He took a longer look at the girl. What was she hiding beneath that dress?

'You should have knocked earlier,' Peter said, trying to keep his tone light.

The girl looked up. Her eyes seemed even sadder than usual. Peter felt the brief candle of temptation flicker and die.

'Well,' Peter said, all briskness. 'I'm sure Major Alvarez would really prefer me to be dressed for our foray. So, if you don't mind.' He pointed towards the door and made a shooing gesture.

This had more effect than words; with the merest of nods towards Peter, the girl slipped back into the night. There was another bump behind his head. Peter banged the wall with his clenched fist.

'Shut up, you little incubus.'

The military jeep bounced and jounced at high speed along the road to town.

'It's real nice of you to pick us up like this, Major,' Hal called out over the engine roar. He offered the major a foretaste of teeth to come.

The major was the epitome of brisk military discipline. 'It is nothing.' He turned to concentrate on Peter, jammed between his two larger compatriots.

'You wish to take pictures?'

Peter lifted the Linhof tripod and the canvas bag in either hand. 'You wish to take pictures after midnight?'

Peter nodded.

The major displayed a faint sign of amusement. 'It's difficult to take pictures of nobody.'

'But that's just what we want!' Hal burst in. 'A big empty 'ighway in the 'eart of Manila. With nobody on it. They've all gone 'ome to bye-byes. All obeyin' martial law. Get it?'

The major raised an eyebrow and resumed his inspection of the headlit road ahead.

'Major.' It was Nigel's turn. 'What do you suggest we do until midnight?' Every inch the diplomat.

The major shrugged. Peter assumed he might be more communicative in Tagalog. Perhaps the officer, carapaced within a smart drill uniform surmounted by a Thirties-thin moustache and piercing eyes, felt that extra care was needed when communicating with foreign journalists. After all, the responsibility of running the country was no light matter. What was it that Marcos had said in that 'Review' quote from the President's book on the New Society? Something about Filipinos needing discipline. The major was as disciplined as a bottle of bleach. Peter needed a drink.

'President Marcos is a very intelligent man.' The major watched the rocks dissolve in his third scotch. He looked up. 'An honest man. A brave man.' The glass was raised and pointed at Hal. 'Did you know that President Marcos was the most decorated allied officer in the Second World War?' Hal nodded his head. The major resumed. 'They made a film about it.' The major lowered the glass before adding, 'In Hollywood.' He tilted the remaining scotch down his throat. Peter wondered whether the major would be a sentimental or fighting drunk. He opted for the latter. The major fixed his bleary eye on Hal. 'Have you read the President's book on the New Society?'

''Er, no. I'm just a publisher.' Hal's smile was uncertain. 'Peter's read it.'

The major swung round to confront Peter. Definitely belligerent. 'Well, what did you think?'

Peter paused before delivering his verdict. 'From what I've been able to read so far, I can't find much to disagree with.' Worthy of a politician.

The major grunted. 'Discipline.' He clicked his fingers. 'That's what we Filipinos need.'

A middle-aged woman with jowls appeared beside their table. The disco stopped abruptly. The ensuing silence was loud. 'What you wanna drink?' The woman asked, hand on hip. The three foreign friends inspected their glasses. The major's finger enfiladed his guests.

'The same again.' As the military man looked up, the woman's pouches were hoisted in a breath-taking smile. They watched her threading her way between the tiny tables towards the distant bar.

Peter gazed round at the vast emptiness of the nightclub. They were alone – apart from a group of sequinned girls engaged in a game of cards near the deserted bandstand. The major drowned the dregs of his drink. Peter heard ice cubes clink against their guide's front teeth.

'Major,' Peter wondered whether the accumulated drinks had loosened the major's tongue. The major blearily focussed on Peter. 'Major... how long will the Filipinos continue to require discipline?'

The major cleared his throat with a wheezing cough and then laughed. 'You mean – how long will we have this?' He waved his empty glass in an all-embracing arc. He hunched his shoulders and leaned towards Peter. 'I say we need President Marcos and martial law for another ten years.' He raised the empty glass in a toast. 'At least.'

'That's very interesting, Major.' He checked his watch. 'In the meantime,' he got to his feet. 'It's eleven forty and I have some pictures to take.'

Hal also rose to his feet. 'I'll go with you, Pete.'

The major held out a restraining hand. 'There is no need for you to go, Halford. Your photographer can go alone.'

Peter felt his temples flush. Hal had the good grace to look apologetic as he resumed his seat. He frowned at Peter. 'O.K.?'

'Right you are, Chief.' Peter hoisted the canvas bag and the tripod. 'I'm off.'

As if determined to forestall the men's departure, disco music resumed and its thumping rhythm accompanied Peter's escape between two panels of red light which rolled in ecstasy. He glanced back across the room and saw that three of the girl gamblers were now gathered round the men's table.

Peter blinked in the different light as he crossed the Hyatt Regency lobby. 'Hi,' came the greeting from a fair-haired young man Peter adjudged was American. 'Bit late for photography, isn't it?' The man pushed himself upright from his position at the reception desk.

Peter smiled and lifted the tripod shoulder-high in acknowledgement and farewell. Outside, the traffic along Roxas Boulevard was hectic. Hundreds of jeepneys, cabs and limousines were making haste in both directions. Peter made some calculations as he moved away from the hotel, unscrewing the tripod legs as he walked. From his jeep, their army driver strolled over to watch. Peter was not averse to an audience. He made his actions crisp as he attached the lighter camera to the head of the tripod. After a couple of tests with the meter, he attached a remote release and took a time exposure. He also tried triggering the shutter using the self-timer. Peter moved to and fro, glancing at his watch from time to time. The army driver had not taken his eyes from the activity throughout.

First one minute. Then another exposure; this time for two minutes. And finally, with a shrug, a five-minute exposure.

On the stroke of midnight, a red neon sign which dominated the night sky blinked off. Only two vehicles were still scurrying along the Boulevard. Peter was impressed. A demonstration of power.

He took a couple of exposures of the empty street. But how on earth could he convince the readers of *The Weekly* that this was after midnight? He looked for some kind of clue. A bat flitted overhead in the warm darkness. Peter slowly packed his gear. He gave the driver a tired salute and ambled back towards the hotel.

Back in the lobby Peter noticed that the fair-haired foreigner had moved to a table. The man smiled and beckoned Peter over. Peter hesitated. At least it would defer meeting the major for a few more minutes. Besides, Peter liked Americans.

'It's all the fault of those fuckin' Yanks.'

Hal was addressing the major, who nodded in gloomy, sodden agreement. 'Those pigs in Subic Bay. They make whores of our young women to serve the sailors. I know what I would like to do to them.'

Nigel hastily withdrew his hand from a red-sequinned thigh.

The major bleared on. 'One day we will have true independence. One day President Marcos will order all the Americans to quit all their bases in the Philippines.' The Major raised his glass. 'Yanks, go home.'

Nigel and Hal echoed the gesture. 'Yanks go home,' they chorused.

'Drink?' The man who had introduced himself as 'Frank Hubler' enquired. Peter weakly waved a hand and shook his head.

'Look, I'm not trying to get a favourable mention for the Hyatt in *Hong Kong Weekly*.'

Peter gave Hubler a wry grin. He could see just how much the hotel chain needed 'the Weekly'. He asked, 'How is business?'

'Pretty good. House full.' Hubler waved and a waiter approached. The American raised an interrogatory eyebrow.

'Oh, just something soft,' Peter acquiesced. 'Tonic on the rocks.'

Hubler continued, 'In fact, thanks to the low salaries in the Philippines we make a bigger profit than Hyatts in high-salary areas. The guests pay the same price in Manila as they do in Miami.'

'Is the curfew hitting business?' Peter asked. Hubler smiled in reply. He certainly looked prosperous enough in a lightweight Dacron suit, silk shirt and, on his wrist, a gold Constellation.

'It's attracting businessmen. There's all kinds of rumours about big corporations quitting Hong Kong and Singapore to establish regional headquarters in Manila.'

The drinks arrived. Nobody had needed to ask Hubler what he required.

Peter raised his glass in a toast. He sipped the tonic. He looked across at the night manager. 'But what about the nightclubs on the 'Roxas Strip'.

Hubler grimaced and shook his head. 'They're hurting. Trouble is a lot of the girls from the bars and night-clubs have set up shop in the big hotel discos.' He shrugged. 'We do our best to keep it in check.' Peter wondered how Hubler defined 'best'.

The American raised his glass. 'Here's to the tired businessman – far, far from home.'

Major Alvarez patted Hal's knee with inebriate affection. 'Hal, I can feel you are a man with sympathy – real sympathy, for the brown race. You seem to understand our feelings and our hopes.'

One of the girls yawned cavernously. Her companion raised her thimbleful of Coca-Cola. Nigel was frowning as he counted sequins on a scarlet bosom.

'Nine thousand, two hundred and ten.' He prodded the sequin with his arithmetical digit. The girl giggled and crossed her legs. Hal frowned at Nigel. He hadn't even been able to chat to his own companion, let alone count her sequins.

''Ere, Nige,' Hal peered round the bleary-eyed Major. 'I wonder what's 'appened to Pete.'

In the foyer Peter rose from his seat. 'I think I'd better re-join my partners in the disco.' Peter was sorry to leave. He reached across and offered a hand. Hubler took it.

'Wait,' said the American, still in a hand-shake with Peter. 'You must know Fred.' Peter looked bemused. 'Fred Harris.'

Peter looked down and shook his head. 'No, I don't.'

Hubler released Peter's hand. 'No, I guess Fred came here before your time. He came from Hong Kong. He kind of strings for the FEER stringer here.'

Peter felt embarrassed. It was a missed trick. He should have known about Harris. 'I've read his stuff, of course...'

Hubler let Peter off the hook. 'Well, since you're going to be here for a while longer, maybe you should meet the guy.' Hubler grinned. 'He could answer all those tricky political questions I couldn't begin to answer.'

Peter tried to sound enthusiastic. 'Yes,' he said, mustering a smile. 'That would be great.'

'Tomorrow night?' Hubler adjusted a gold cuff-link. 'I'll try and set it up for ten.'

'O.K.' Peter grinned. 'As long as I can get back by the witching hour.'

Hubler's gesture was expansive. 'I think we could find you a bed.'

'I need to shoot a clock,' Peter announced.

Hal looked up. 'Where the fuckin' 'ell you been?'

The catatonic major continued to stare into his glass.

'Your obedient photographer has been working.' In spite of himself, Peter tainted his words with acridity. 'Now I require a clear view of a visible clock.'

Peter looked across the table at his other partner. Nigel's hostess's hands were desperately clenched around a fist-shaped bulge high up beneath the sequins on her thigh. In spite of the air-conditioning Nigel's face was damp with sweat.

'Nigel,' Peter called across the table.

A large buttock lurched backwards into the table. A few drops of coke scattered onto the Major's sleeve. Nigel twisted round and tugged at his choking shirt collar.

'Sorry, Major Alvarez.' Nigel's eyes were an odd shade of blue in the ultra-violet light. 'An accident.'

The hostess was tugging her short skirt towards her knees, rolling her eyes at her sister-in-arms sitting beside Hal.

'Major?' Peter queried.

The officer focussed on Peter and belched.

'I'm afraid I must ask you to direct me to a clock,' Peter apologised.

Outside the hotel, the guardian soldier ground his cigarette into the concrete as the quartet swayed into sight. The major had settled what must have been a considerable bill. Or had he?

They piled into the jeep and there followed a rapid exchange in Tagalog. As the vehicle approached a check-point on the boulevard, the major seemed to have sobered somewhat. The guard outside Naval Headquarters saluted. Somewhat less crisply, the major returned the salute.

Peter's head began to rock to and fro with the hum of the engine. He was all but thrown against the major's back as the jeep squealed to a halt.

'This is the Luneta,' declared the major, pointing towards a large, open park. 'And that is the monument to Rizal, the founder of our Republic.' The finger wavered in the direction of a grey obelisk rising from what looked like bronze figures. 'And that,' said the major as his finger swung upwards, 'is the clock.'

Peter craned his neck out of the window. Above the vehicle, between suspended traffic lights, was a large, rectangular time-piece, whose four neon-lit faces indicated eighteen minutes past one. Each face bore the legend 'Rado'.

Peter clattered into the road. He carefully framed the shot which subsequently failed to make the cut. Bad timing. Although the driver had been able to remain motionless for ten minutes, his passengers did not follow his example. In development the Rizal monument suffered an unfortunate colour shift and every lamp in the park mimicked the star on a Christmas tree. Finally, Peter declared himself satisfied. None of the photographs were fit for the magazine.

They dropped the major off at some anonymous spot in the city. The driver, released from the tension the major provoked and full of beans at 2 a.m., beamed at Peter. Nigel was only sick once on the journey back to the resort. Hal sulked. Peter's eyes began to close.

At this time of night, the resort was clothed in stygian gloom.

They grunted their way up the wooden stairs, their shoes in their hands. Nigel paused to vomit over the balcony. 'Pardon,' he apologised to the courtyard. His breathing was harsh.

There were no salutations as they went their several ways. In his familiar room, Peter peeled off his clothes. It was refreshingly cool. He lay flat on his back on top of the sheet. Had there been a knock on the door, he would not have heard it. He was out like the lights of the resort.

Chapter Eleven

The next rapping that assailed Peter's ears was irresistible. He struggled against the fusillade but was obliged to surface. He blinked. The sun was blazing through the curtains. Peter rubbed his eyes; sandpaper against cornea.

'Mr. Pete, Mr. Pete,' called a husky voice between knocks. Then the door swung open. An oversized Filipino head surmounted by a straw trilby peered round the door. The trilby swivelled until the eyes came to rest on the bed and Peter.

'The Boss wants to see you.' The man's jaws munched the words and an imposing thumb pointed back over the man's right shoulder. It was clear that the man-mountain would remain rooted until Peter gave a response. He made as if to rise; the head disappeared; the door closed.

Peter removed his watch before approaching the shower. Half past seven. Small wonder that he felt wretched. As he hastened to cleanse the night from his skin, he was caught by a twinge of apprehension. Could Agustin have decided to reverse his initial reaction to Peter's show of journalistic bravado? Was Peter to be subjected to pressure from their sponsor? If Peter's bluff was called, his partners would immediately abandon him to his fate.

By now he had showered and towelled himself red. His fingers scrabbled through the remains of his scant wardrobe. He discovered a knitted cotton shirt, underpants and a clean pair of lightweight trousers. (Hold-all by name, hold-all by nature.) He hummed *Travelling Light*. He had difficulty easing the fresh socks over still damp feet. He could hear loud slams further along the balcony. Footsteps clumped by as he slipped his feet into the moccasins. He tugged the door open, while trying to insert his shirt into the waistband of his trousers. He saw a familiar back waiting at the head of the stairs.

'Hal,' he called in what he was surprised to hear left him as a hoarse whisper. He cleared his throat. Hal turned. He looked how Peter felt. Awful. Hal was holding his spectacles in one hand while rubbing bloodshot eyes with the other. Not a molar or canine was in sight.

Hal grunted an inchoate greeting as Peter passed Nigel's room. Not a sound from within. Hal turned and clattered downstairs. They both heard the slap of flip-flops and the sound of hoarse breathing.

'Wait,' Nigel called and laboured to catch up. 'For Christ's sake, what's up?' Strange that panic had assailed all three of them. Was it the unexpectedness of the summons? Or was it the appearance of the giant? He now re-appeared below them, holding a door open and beckoning. They stumbled, a six-legged beast, into the courtyard. The door had closed. Peter was first to arrive. He tugged and tugged at the handle to no avail.

'Push the fuckin' thing,' Hal hissed. Peter obeyed and hurtled into an enormous space.

The first thing that struck him were the dozens of rough, wooden tables and benches, ranged around the room. The second thing was an odour of garlic so pungent that it set off a fit of retching. They each tried to slow the pace of inhalation.

From their left came the crisp sound of frying. In the furthest corner stood Agustin, a large pan in one hand, a wooden spoon in the other. He was looking in their direction. Peter was relieved to note that, however sadly, the little man was smiling.

'Come over, gentlemen,' he called and waved the spoon over the nearest table. It was covered in a stained, red-checked tablecloth.

'I thought we should breakfast together.' He flipped the sunny-side up egg onto its stomach. He looked up. 'Eggs O.K.?'

Three delighted cries chorused. Judging by their exultation, they anticipated that this would be the finest fried egg any of the trio had tasted. Peter felt his head begin to swim. He was overwrought, tired and suffused in garlic. As they threaded their way towards the cloth-covered table, he noticed that the hob on the electric cooker were black with generations of congealed grease and the enamel spotted with stains of a doubtful shade of brown.

Agustin turned towards the table, complete with frying pan,

and tipped a sorry pair of eggs onto a cold plate. The wooden utensil he had placed on the table added another question to those Peter was already asking himself. Hal was then presented with his plate.

'Thanks, Mr.Agustin.' He sniffed. 'Bit of a niff in 'ere, ain't there?' But Agustin had already turned away. Hal shrugged and cut into a yoke's back. Yellow blood oozed onto the plate. Peter turned away and retched. When he glanced back, it was to see that a large blob of yoke had evaded the ministrations of Hal's tongue and congealed on his stubble chin.

Agustin turned with a third plate. Nigel smiled weakly.

'Terrific!' Hal exulted. 'Best egg I've ever eaten.'

Nigel took the hint and split an egg from nave to chaps.

Agustin turned to find Peter on his feet. The short-order cook's eyes widened with alarm as Peter lurched from the table and wove his way towards the exit. Peter choked on his one-word apology before sprinting the final few yards to the door.

Hal shook his head. 'Had a few too many last night.'

Nigel, his cheeks bulging, nodded his head in agreement. The partners avoided each other's eye. The giant, shadowed by his straw trilby, swayed up onto the balls of his feet and flexed his fingers. Nigel's initial alarm abated when he noted the absence of expression in the big man's eyes.

Agustin brought his own eggs to the table and took a seat. 'I want to ask you gentlemen how things are going.' He delicately dissected an egg.

'Oh.' Hal waved his dripping knife towards his partner. 'Great! Great! Ain't they, Nige?' Hal waved his fork towards his bilious associate.

Nigel's nod lacked vigour. His night, passed in dashes from the loo to the sink to the shower, was resuming the chase. He opened his lips, belched and then muttered. 'Most of the advertising's in, anyway.'

Agustin nodded but his eyes were like flint.

Hal picked up the slack. 'Yeah, Joe's goin' great guns.' Hal then added for good measure, 'He got us all a curfew pass last night.' Better to steer away from advertising revenue.

'Yes,' Nigel belched lightly and nodded at Agustin. 'Joe's cousin showed us around.' Nigel essayed a smile. 'Major Alvarez.'

Hal nodded at Nigel. 'Yeah, great guy. A real patriot.' Hal frowned. 'He said a lot of moving things. You know?' Hal offered Agustin sincerity. It was lost on Agustin's bent head.

'So, you gentlemen are getting what you want?' Agustin carefully lowered his cutlery on either side of his plate. 'Now, when do I get what I want?'

Hal stared at the little brown man. He took in the pale-green T-shirt and baggy, black shorts. He frowned at Nigel.

The dyke of goodwill seemed to have sprung a leak. Nigel inserted a verbal thumb. 'We've been working day and night, Mr. Agustin.'

Agustin's patience expired with his breath. 'I want to see something.'

The cloud of unknowing parted. Hal twinkled his assurance. 'Pete told me he's startin' scribblin' today. 'I'll make sure he does.' Hal certainly impressed Hal. Nigel was not entirely convinced. Agustin returned to his egg.

'Just one thing, Mr.Agustin.' Hal's smile made its debut for the day. 'You wouldn't 'ave a typewriter, would you?'

Peter's head and shoulders burst through the surface of the pool. He took a deep breath and drops of chlorination brought on a cough. Only the faintest shadow of garlic clung to his nostrils.

At this time of day, the heat was still bearable and the water not too warm. A haze beyond the palm fronds marking the near horizon hinted at humidity to come. Peter lay back and floated. Up on the balcony, Miguel's door opened. The tall Filipina appeared, tying a sash around her red kimono. Peter checked his underpants which served as a costume. Sagging but respectable. The girl skipped down the staircase. Peter rolled onto his front and dived.

The three diners all looked up as the girl entered and somehow broke the silence in the restaurant. The giant took two steps forward. Agustin raised an index finger. The giant paused, swaying on the balls of his feet. Agustin gestured towards the girl.

She hesitated. Out of courtesy towards his English associates Augustin spoke in English.

'You wish to make some eggs for Miguel?' The girl nodded.

'O.K., O.K..' He waved her forward. 'You go ahead.'

The girl scampered to the cooker, her garment parting at the thighs. She lifted the pan warily, looking over her shoulder.

'Fine boy, your Miguel,' Hal proposed.

Agustin nodded. 'He's learning the business, while he's on holiday from school.'

Nigel started at the sizzle of an egg hitting the hot pan.

Agustin continued, 'I believe in giving my son all the advantages I lacked at his age.'

Hal nodded vigorously. ''E's a lucky lad. Wish I'd 'ad a dad like you.'

Agustin nodded at the giant who brought a tray with coffee cups and a scarred metal pot.

'By the way, Mr.Agustin,' Hal began, his eyes wide. 'What's 'appenin' about the interview with the purse lady?'

The flint returned to Agustin's eyes. A further change of subject was indicated.

'I've told Pete to write something about agriculture.' Hal leaned towards their host. 'I mean, it's really important 'ere, ain't it?'

Something incomprehensible came from the girl's lips. She raised the plate. Agustin waved her towards the door. The girl all but ran as she disappeared with a flash of red.

'A good girl.' Agustin had risen. The giant collected the soiled plates in his huge hands.

'Take your time over coffee, gentlemen.' Agustin departed, leaving them to the garlic.

Peter spun round when he reached the shower curtain. 'What the hell does he expect to see at this stage?'

'Keep your fuckin' voice down,' Hal hissed and pointed a thumb towards Miguel's room.

'Look,' Hal said, lowering himself onto the end of the unmade bed. 'I don't care if you type out the fuckin' Manila phone book. Just let them 'ear the sound of you typing somethin'.'

'No, you look.' Peter confronted Hal. 'I've been here two days.' He raised two fingers. 'Two days.' Peter was even more exasperated by Hal's inability to forestall this importunate demand than he was by the demand itself. Hal was a publisher, for God's sake. He should know the score.

'I know, I know.' Hal's palms pressed downwards in a placatory gesture. 'But don't forget you've got some 'elp from your friends.' Hal tapped the guide to Manila and the *Golden Guide to South-East Asia* which lay side by side on the bed.

'Since when are we in the business of plagiarism, Hal?' Peter's objection sounded hollow in his own ears. He had let himself in for this disaster in the making.

'Nobody's asking you to plague-your-whatsit,' Hal insisted. He lifted the guide. 'Facts are facts.' He paused, peered at the print and intoned, 'The church of San Agustin is the oldest stone-built church in the Philippines.' The book was closed with a slap. 'There.' The dropped book bounced twice on the bed. 'That's a fact. It's either the oldest bloody church or it isn't. And facts are true. And free.' He got to his feet. He appealed to Peter's sense of fair play. 'What difference does it make whether you read it there,' he asked, pointing at the guide, 'or whether you found out from some fuckin' monk?'

Peter laughed. He could see the funny side of it. 'All right. Point taken. Yes, I shall look up reference books. But all the books in the world don't make up for a real, lived experience. I can't even begin-to-beguine an article on tourism.'

Nigel cleared his throat. 'Why not let the shape look after itself? I mean, you've been here two days. So, give your impressions of those two days. You know – a kind of *Philippines' Diary*. On day one we did this, that or the other…'

'Mainly the other.' Peter reminded him.

Nigel chose this remark as a 'casus belli'. 'Look here, Pious Peter. Hal and I are not here to write copy. We've almost finished our job. Just because *your* hat dropped off doesn't mean we don't deserve a little relaxation.'

Punctuating Nigel's address came a thud from Miguel's room. 'Dirty little bastard,' Nigel concluded. There came another thud.

Hal placed his palms together and gazed heavenward. 'She's a good gal.' He grinned at Nigel and Peter. 'Go to work on an egg.'

Hal fell backwards onto the bed, scattering the guidebooks and spluttering with laughter. 'Oh, fuckin' 'ell.'

Nigel looked across at Peter and shrugged. They could not contain a smile. Hal, leaning on one elbow, was wiping a tear from the corner of his eye.

'I'll still need a typewriter,' Peter pointed out.

There came a loud bump against the door leading onto the balcony. Puzzled, Nigel crossed the room and opened the door to reveal a laden giant.

Chapter Twelve

Halo Halo
by
Peter Nicholson

Peter stared at the title. It had presented itself to him, unsummoned. At least it had the attractions of euphony and exoticism. So far, so good. But he pondered on his own role in the article. Was he to adopt the role of 'seasoned traveller'? Or should he be the 'honest debutant'? He rested his fingers on the typewriter keys and stared, hypnotised, through a gap in the curtains at the blue sky. He drifted into that curiously pleasurable mood that afflicts all those who are deferring unpalatable duties. He shook himself and began to type.

> **Whether it is your first visit or your twenty-first, arriving in the Philippines feels like returning home.**

God. What awful drivel. Agustin would probably love it. His gaze drifted back to the blue sky. Once more he was pricked by pleasurable guilt. He got to his feet and drifted out onto the balcony.

The pool looked like every other pool in every other hotel in every other tourist brochure; the water deep blue; the rainbow-splashing children and brown adult bodies laid out like solar sacrifices. The palm trees beyond the resort were made of green enamel and over his head clouds of ridiculous fleeciness floated in caravans. Peter sighed. For the spirit of creation this ambiance was laudanum.

Maria appeared at the entrance to the massage parlour and waved. Joe Conrad had known a thing or three about the trance the tropic drug induced. Maria waved again. Peter nodded and returned to his room. He knew he was delaying his confrontation with the typewriter.

Even if the sky is grey. The blue sky mocked his conceit. But this was supposed to be his diary and the sky had been grey on his arrival.

Now – what was the name of those flowers offered to new arrivals at the airport? 'Sampa…' something. He felt rising irritation. Peter was simply unprepared for the task he had reluctantly accepted. He flung himself onto the bed and snatched up the guide to Manila. On page thirty-three a provocative Filipina with a scarlet mouth sported a garland similar to the one he had worn. Beneath the image was the caption: *Princess Liwayway wearing a garland of sampaguita, the flower of love.*

He read on. The style was execrable but at least the piece offered some of the information he required. He returned to the machine, the guide in his hand. He sought and found a cigarette. He lit it. His right index finger sought out an 'A'.

And the wet season rains fall.

He grimaced and pressed on, cribbing the story of the sensual princess. He progressed famously. At the bottom of his second sheet of Agustin A4, there came a knock on the door.

'Come in,' Peter called. He stubbed out his second cigarette. The girl stood framed in the doorway. She was wearing her habitual cotton frock. Was that the extent of her wardrobe?

'Yes?' Peter objected to the feeling of irritation she aroused in him.

'You want chicken?' As she took a step forward, the unworthy thought struck Peter that, had he arrived with the others, he might have had Maria, rather than this child.

The girl waited. Peter realised he was hungry. He had no reason to reject her services as a waitress

'O.K.' He offered a smile. Not the slightest ripple was returned. As she turned to go, Peter saw Maria sweep past the doorway, carrying a tray with two steaming plates of chicken and rice.

'Oh,' Peter called. She paused and looked round. 'Tell them, no garlic.'

Seconds after her departure his next visitor's head poked through the door. 'How's it coming on?' Nigel blinked at Peter.

Peter waved the two typed sheets above his head. 'About seven fifty.'

'Smoke?' Nigel offered Peter the cigarillo of peace.

'No, thanks.' Peter raised his packet of Pall Mall to show he was catered for. Nigel moved further into the room and perched on the bed. 'I know it's none of my business...'

Peter tensed. He could guess what was coming.

'You're being a bit hard on the girl.'

Peter swivelled round to take all of Nigel in.

'I mean... I think you've really hurt her feelings.' Nigel lit the cigarillo that he had offered Peter from his own.

'I do not believe this,' Peter exclaimed. 'Feelings? What feelings? She is an amenity. Like the pool, the sauna or the bed.'

'Just put yourself in her place for a minute,' Nigel suggested.

'Are you suggesting I should offer myself to guests at the resort?'

'How attractive do you think your rejection makes her feel?'

'About as attractive as I find her, I imagine.' Peter swung round to confront the typewriter once more.

'You bloody little wanker,' Nigel spat.

Peter spun round. 'Look, Nigel. Just because you want to take every sexual opportunity available to you, it does not follow that I should do likewise.' He paused and narrowed his eyes. 'What are you trying to do? Spread the guilt around? You don't have to get me involved to guarantee my silence. I won't tell on you, honest.' Peter raised his hand in the scout salute.

Nigel sighed and collapsed onto the bed.

Peter changed tack. 'Look,' said the contrite Peter. 'I apologise for my attack. It was unwarranted. I'm not quite as pure as the driven snow myself.' He attempted a smile. 'If you think it will make things easier, tell them I've been castrated.'

Nigel shook his head. 'Too late.' Peter looked puzzled. Nigel wagged a finger. 'You shouldn't go swimming in the nude.'

'I really ought to get on, Nigel.' Peter nodded towards the

typewriter. Nigel took the hint.

He paused in the doorway. 'It's not just screwing. You don't think it's just that, do you Peter?' Nigel had turned back in the doorway. 'I mean, Sue's a really nice kid.'

'Which Sue?' Peter asked and then regretted it.

Nigel tugged open the door. There stood the wraith, bearing a tray bearing chicken and rice.

'You're right,' Nigel said, his face impassive. 'It is none of my business.'

Nigel departed and Peter beckoned the girl into the room. She lowered the tray beside the typewriter. He smiled and sniffed the chicken. He smiled again. 'Good. No garlic!'

The girl's face remained impassive. Peter slid the greasy chit across the table and signed it. He paused and looked at the waiting girl. She was so slight. He recalled Maria with her two heaped dishes and realised that she had probably dined with Hal.

He looked at the girl. 'Have you eaten yet?'

The girl shook her head. Once again irritation swarmed over Peter. Why on earth did she have to stand there like an Oxfam advertisement?

'Look.' He was angry. 'Go and get yourself some chicken. I'll sign the bill.'

The girl retreated to the door.

Peter returned to his own meal. After he had consumed as much of the chicken and rice as he could bear, there came another knock on the door.

'Come in.'

The girl was back. Peter noticed a smear of grease on her cheek. With three square meals a day she might even be pretty. Her toes curled over the lips of her yellow flip-flops. He wondered how often her single dress was washed.

'You want mango?' The voice, coming from a zone of habitual taciturnity, surprised him. Without thinking, he nodded; signed the second chit; and watched her depart.

He returned to page three only to be interrupted by the breathless girl's return. A ripe mango on a plate and a steak knife. Peter nodded and smiled. The girl watched him cut into the fruit.

Peter excised the large stone and cut the fruit in half. He offered one portion to the girl. She shook her head; he shook his hand; she accepted his gift. How could people be allowed to go hungry in a country where fruit fell from the trees?

'You want massage?'

The question splintered Peter's ruminations about the injustices of the world economic order. Peter rose to his feet, his lips sticky with mango. 'No. No thank you.'

The girl inspected her toes. Her feet were so dark he could not decide whether or not they were grubby.

'Not now. Thank you.' Peter indicated the table as the girl's eyes came up to meet his.

'I have to work now.' Her head was lowered once more.

'Look...' Feeling something was still amiss, he smiled. 'The mango was delicious. Thank you.'

The door closed behind the girl.

Peter, his fingers sticky with juice, entered the shower room. This could not go on.

Chapter Thirteen

Writing had never come easily to Peter. His doctor father had recently suggested that the cause of this difficulty might be muscular dystrophy. That diagnosis appeared after Peter's letters home had struggled to reach one a year.

He had first conjured with the idea of journalism after he quit the shipping department of Butterfield and Swire. Entry into one or other of the more simplistic tabloids in Hong Kong would have been easy enough at that stage but the emolument would have provoked derision in a coolie. God alone knew why he had opted for photography and the image worth more than a thousand words. If God hadn't a clue, Peter had. His inspiration was one Guy Francis.

Photography was Guy's passion and Guy liked to share his passions. His BBC career had been long and rewarding. After thirty corporative years, Guy fled the Cotswolds and his scrapbooks and departed from England for good. Or ill. Asia, he decided, was to be the mission and Hong Kong his base. So, the man, affectionately known in London television circles as 'Gay Guy', maker of filmed biographies of the artistic and literary lions of his time, went hunting real wild life in the jungles of Indonesia; climbed the tallest mountain in Taiwan; and almost drowned off Northern Hokkaido. It could hardly be said that Guy's chivalrous affair with Asia took the big television distributors by storm.

'They' wanted 'series' and Guy was very much a 'one-show-at-a-time' man. Every two years or so a Francis film would enchant an audience in a fringe viewing theatre at Cannes or Venice. Or Berlin, at a pinch. Then late-night viewing on BBC? (for old time's sake) or New York's Channel 13. But, with a pension and a private income, Guy had no need to temporise with T.V. editors.

How they met, Peter could not now recall. His first memory was of visiting Guy's spectacular apartment overlooking the typhoon shelter in Causeway Bay. For a week their evenings were spent dining on a sampan in the shelter; returning to drinks in the apartment which overflowed with the booty Guy had gathered on his Asian expeditions. His silent man-servant seemed to fulfil all Guy's physical requirements. And, after the first month or so (as men of sixty-three tire of pursuit more easily), the emotional pressures on Peter eased.

So, it was decided that Peter should have his own room in Guy's apartment. No strings. Not that Guy ever completely gave up hope. Certainly, he never allowed Peter out of his sight for longer than he could help. And while they were together the flow of talk was incessant, informative and amusing.

Half of the spacious apartment was devoted to a complete editing channel for sound and vision. Guy took Peter's audio-visual education in hand. Peter proved an adept student in every way but one. But work, Guy acknowledged, proved more fruitful than pleasure. And while Peter openly admired Guy's visionary gift, the compliment was, in some part, reciprocated. They continued to enjoy living and working together.

Asia had brought them together. Now it separated them. On a visit to old friends in the Cameron Highlands, Guy died of a heart attack.

After the three most fruitful years of his life, Peter was toppled into the shark-infested waters, not of Mirs Bay, but of Hong Kong's film world.

The rent on the flat still had another six months to run. Peter's contacts with Guy's solicitor revealed that Guy had left all his worldly goods to his old college at Oxford. They would be pleased.

Guy's body-servant, unsurprisingly, disappeared in silence. Had he resented Peter? He would never find out. Later, it was revealed that the man had entered the service of an Austrian diplomat who lived. alone on the Peak.

After the first days of shocked depression, Peter resolved to take up the reins that Guy had let fall. Feverishly, he ran reel after reel of unedited takes for the incomplete Borobudur epic through the editing machines. Everything had been carefully annotated in

Guy's elegant italics in elegant notebooks. All that was missing was the basic concept of the film.

In spite of the months of discussion about the project and the now frenzied viewing, Peter had finally come to realise that the kernel of the project had died with Guy. It would take years to inform himself of the history and secrets of the vast temple complex. With only three months rent left to run on the flat and his own money running out fast, Peter was in despair. He discovered from the post-mortem behaviour of their film 'friends' how much his privileged position in Guy's life had been resented. For Peter there was not one day's work available.

Aggie had arrived just 'in the nick'. Peter had been on the very verge of dipping into his lucky money to purchase his passage back to the Narrow Land when Aggie – cheerful, ebullient Aggie – fresh from New Zealand – dropped into his twilit world. She was one of that happy breed of antipodeans who chance their way round the globe, always falling on their feet and amazed and consolatory about the misfortunes of others.

At that moment Aggie was the Public Relations' Manager's private secretary at the Hong Kong Hotel. She seemed to know everybody in the Hong Kong media world. In a final defiant gesture Peter had invited all his and Guy's former friends to a final fling in the now almost deserted apartment. It was a gesture meant to prove that he was by no means washed up in Hong Kong. Even as he welcomed the guests and watched them disperse among the vacuum, he knew he had wasted time (and vanishing fiduciary issue) on a bunch of disbelievers. They were takers, not givers.

His grand gesture had, in the event, not been greeted with applause. Au contraire.

Aggie had arrived with Solly. Solly was from New York and had recently rented a few of the pieces of equipment that were all that remained of Guy's former, state-of-the-art collection. Solly had taken a scotch-on-the-rocks in his hirsute hand, asked whether there was a buyer for Guy's Éclairs and introduced Aggie.

Solly's omission of any work offers had hurt Peter the most.

After all; it would not be an act of charity. Peter knew as much as anybody about sixteen-millimetre film equipment. He could strip an Arri or Éclair blindfold. But, in the face of Peter's evident need, Solly had been off-handedly dismissive. For the kind of money Peter wanted, he could hire three, four Chinese techs. Yeah, it was tough, man. Tough.

So, Peter took particular pleasure in Aggie's casual refusal when Solly suggested they leave. Solly was not best pleased to be leaving alone.

Peter was exultant. Thereafter, Aggie and Peter chatted and drank and chatted and wished the dear departing god-speed. The final guest staggered out into the night at three. Peter and Aggie staggered off to bed. At first, they slept in Peter's bed and then they didn't. They moved on to cushions below grotesque masks from Timor and Malacca and a twenty by sixteen B & W portrait of Guy in his best Noel Coward manner. Later Peter calculated that they had made love for thirty-six hours – allowing for food breaks.

When Solly discovered how things were between Aggie and Peter, he swiftly invited his successor to join his company. Peter was in charge of equipment maintenance and of preparing rush orders. At all hours. Solly had been awarded the UPI contract. He found excuses to call Peter in at weekends. Peter prepared for the next stage by teaching himself how to record sound on location. But Solly never allowed Peter to run a single frame of film through the fifteen cameras he serviced. Not even in South Vietnam. Peter's resentment of his treatment grew apace. In bed at night, he complained incessantly to Aggie with no compensatory activity. 'Whiners' were not Aggie's favourite kind of people. The whining increasingly led to rows. Solly waited, silently contemplating the dark hairs on the back of his hands. Peter spent more and more nights alone in the flat he now shared with Aggie. To ct a lng stry shrt, Solly had the last laugh. The end.

Peter stared at the sheet of paper in the typewriter before him. Funny that he never dreamed of Aggie. In spite of their initial bout of passion she had never struck him as the subject of fantasy. Too matter of fact. Too down to earth. Her trouble was the lack of a sense of sin. Lovemaking should be fraught with moral dangers. Peter looked at his watch. He glanced through the window. The sky was beginning to grey over. With his index finger he sought the 'S' key.

'How's it going then?' Hal's teeth flashed round the edge of the door. 'I 'eard you bangin' away.' His grin expanded.

Peter leaned back in his chair and exhaled. He fumbled for another cigarette. His tongue felt like an old stair carpet. Whatever that felt like.

He waved five triumphant sheets above his head. His back twinged.

'There you go. Just under two thousand.' He wished he could muster an ironic cheer. Actually, he did feel rather pleased. He replaced the sheets on the table. Hal snatched them up, his eyes coursing down the first page.

'This is great.' He patted Peter's nearest shoulder. 'Just what the old wog ordered.'

'Neatly put,' Peter muttered as he lit the cigarette.

'Now get your rags on, me old mate.' Hal waved the sheets. 'We've got an appointment with fear.'

Peter slipped his shirt off the back of the chair and filled a sleeve. The smoke from his cigarette curled into one eye, which promptly began to water.

'I'll just point Percy at the porcelain,' Peter announced and struck out in the relevant direction. Hal followed.

'I met a very interesting person today,' Hal revealed. 'A woman.'

'Don't tell me. Kublai Khan's mother.'

Hal shook his head and frowned. 'It wasn't 'er. It was Joe's cousin.'

'God,' Peter exclaimed, 'Joe's family tree must be a sequoia.' Peter searched for his jacket.

'My God!' Hal flapped his arms. 'You could cut the air in 'ere with a bloody knife.' He led the way onto the balcony.

Peter shut the door behind them. 'Where's Nigel? His pages flapped in his left hand. He caught up with Hal at the car.

'You fancy sittin' in the front?' Hal asked, very sotto. Peter shrugged. Hal opened the door beside him. Peter trudged round to the other side of the Pontiac. A heavy drop of water struck Peter's scalp. He blinked when he sustained another blow to the forehead. He dived into the car.

''Ere, watch it!' Hal warned.

'It's starting to rain.'

The silent Chico ignited the engine and the car slid into silent motion. Peter detected the naked face of Maria at the window of the sauna as they passed by. The car's windscreen wipers squealed loudly as the rain drummed on the roof.

Peter secreted the precious papers in a jacket pocket. The car interior soon steamed up. Peter hoped that Chico would avoid the drenched figures on bicycles who swerved onto the road.

'So, like I was sayin'' Hal twisted towards Peter. 'This bird.'

'Joe's cousin,' Peter prompted.

'Yeah,' Hal adjusted his business spectacles. 'Nigel wasn't feelin' too good this mornin'. Hal's vice became confidential. 'You know, Pete. I don't think Nige 'as got enough push. 'E thinks he can just lie in 'is pit, waitin' for Joe to come up with the goods. I know better than to rely on promises.' Hal was every inch the assured entrepreneur. 'I get what I go for.'

For the rest of the journey they witnessed the deluge. The rain completely defeated the gutters of the city. Vast puddles covered side roads and even the main highways were an inch deep in water.

Peter observed a young girl, her dress plastered to her emaciated body, struggle to carry a flailing infant up a steep flight of steps. The rain had soaked the heat out of the air.

They arrived and already the low-slung headquarter of 'Agustin Enterprises' seemed very familiar. Chico drew the car up as close as he could to the entrance. Hal flung open his door and in two squelching steps was home, if not dry. Peter bumped his way along the back seat, clutching his jacket. He noticed that Chico was avoiding eye contact. Unintentionally, the door slammed as Peter leaped to safety.

After the battering of the rain, the silence of the reception area was eerie. They crept across the parquet towards the teak door. Hal shot his cuffs and knocked. The door was opened by the giant. Oddly, without his hat the man seemed taller and more menacing. Baldness can have that effect.

It was almost as though Agustin had not moved from his desk since their initial interview. The two Englishmen conformed to the welcoming ritual. The liquid Agustinian eyes followed Peter as he resumed his place in his 'usual' leather chair.

'You have something to show me?' Agustin's eyes were unblinking.

Peter produced the slightly crumpled sheets from a jacket marked by droplets. Susceptible to the sober ambiance, Peter murmured. 'It's not much, I'm afraid.'

'Please. Read me what you have written,' Agustin murmured and retreated into shadow.

Peter cleared his throat and raised the first sheet. 'Halo Halo,' he announced and paused. An encouraging gesture was performed in the light of the desk lamp.

Peter read on, frowning at a split infinitive. He paused as he reached the bottom of the page. Agustin had reappeared and seemed absorbed. Peter was sure that the material was just too anodyne for someone who had lived here all his life. It wasn't absorption but boredom. Peter felt he had no alternative but to carry on with his recitation. Now he omitted the final page.

'Excellent!'

Peter waited for the verdict to move beyond polite hyperbole. Hal did not wait.

'I knew you'd like it, Mr. Agustin,' Hal chirped. 'Pete's got the gift.' He reached into his jacket and produced his own folded document. Peter winced. It was too soon to tempt Agustin with a contract. Hal leaned forward, then paused as Agustin murmured, 'Mr. Nicholson seems to have made a good impression on others as well as myself.' Agustin was smiling.

'I received a telephone call this morning.' Agustin folded his hands.

'You don't say,' Hal responded.

'From Major Alvarez,'

Hal nodded. 'Great guy.'

'The major was so impressed that he has arranged an interview for Mr. Nicholson with the Secretary of National Defence, Juan Ponce Enrile.'

Peter prayed that Hal would resist the temptation to pun.

'Major Alvarez will pick you up at the resort the day after tomorrow at ten in the morning.'

Back in the car, Hal cheerfully twirled a cigar between his fingers.

'Funny about the major,' Peter mused. The sun was evaporating the rain from the pavements. 'We scarcely exchanged a word all evening.'

Hal interrupted lighting his cigar. 'He was chatty enough to me,' he grumbled. 'While you were out 'avin fun, I was stuck with the bugger. The only way I could get him to shut 'is trap was by letting him write something for the mag.'

'You mean pure government propaganda, don't you?' Peter realised that Chico was watching the exchange.

Hal grew indignant. 'No, of course not.' He exhaled grey smoke. 'It's just a poem.'

'A poem?' Peter was incredulous.

'Yeah. Somethin' about little brown men and little brown women being made out of clay.' Hal drew on the cigar. 'Don't worry, Pete. It may be rubbish but it's short.'

Chapter Fourteen

'No, I'm not goin' all the way back to the resort just to listen to Nige goin' on about Sue this and Sue that.' Hal made a chopping motion with his hand. 'It's getting' on my tits.'

Peter caught Chico's eye in the mirror. 'Where's a good place to eat in town, Chico?'

Chico shrugged. 'There's hundreds of places. French, Italian, Chinese.'

Peter, his mind still on his 'Halo, Halo' article, asked, 'How about some local cuisine?'

Hal interrupted. 'Where does Mr. Agustin eat in town?'

'Local food,' Peter insisted.

Hal gave him a sour look. Chico noted the exchange in the mirror, 'Mr. Agustin eats at the Philippine Columbian Club.'

'What's their speciality?' Peter asked, ignoring Hal.

'You like fish?' Chico asked.

'Fish!' Hal leaned forward enthusiastically. 'I love it.' He tapped his temple, the cigar narrowly missing his hair. 'Good for the brain.'

'Then you could try sinigang.' Chico addressed Hal directly.

Hal cupped an ear. 'Sinning what?'

'Sinigang.' Chico swung the car into the kerb. 'Fish and vegetables. Pick you up at nine thirty.'

Hal belched and gently pushed his plate away. 'What a blow-out!'

Peter nodded, glancing down at his empty plate.

'Fantastic,' said Hal, producing another cigar. He licked it languorously. When the waiter returned, they both ordered fresh fruit.

'You know,' Hal murmured, giving the cigar an affectionate twirl, 'I could really get to like this place.'

Peter smiled and nodded. 'I already do.'

'A paradise for men,' Hal sighed smoke.

'A bit of a fool's paradise,' Peter warned.

'Come on, Pete. You can live like kings 'ere. Don't knock the rock.' Hal's teeth gripped the cigar.

'True. But don't be fooled.' Peter raised a warning finger as Hal opened his mouth. 'It's Agustin who has set us on our thrones. And king-makers can be king-breakers.' Why deny Hal his contentment? A contentment he was sharing? But he refused to allow Hal's delusions to win him over.

Hal withdrew his cigar and laid it in his ashtray. 'Agustin loved the stuff you read 'im today.'

'Agustin's got bigger fish to fry than us, Hal.' Peter rested his forearms on the table. 'He's out to impress somebody a lot higher up the food-chain. Is it the First Lady? On the other hand, this interview with Enrile could be significant. In some quarters Enrile is being touted as Marcos's successor.'

Hal became impatient. 'So what? Enrile. Marcos's old lady. What difference does it make? So long as we do the job right, we can get on the right side of every big noise in the place. In fact, the more people you chat up, the more Agustin gets 'ooked.' Hal grinned and patted the pocket containing the contract. 'Once we produce that big, four-colour edition and get the dough, we won't 'ave to worry about Mr. Garlic any more.'

'Well, once the Philippines edition is done and dusted, Agustin is no longer interested.' Peter suggested. 'I assume.'

Hal leaned back in his chair. He raised the cigar to his lips. 'You know, I should be doing what 'Orientations' did.' Hal exhaled. Peter noticed that the restaurant was beginning to clear. He wondered what the locals did for evening entertainment. He felt a slight chill. He dragged his attention back to Hal.

'Orientations?'

'Yeah.' Their desserts arrived. 'They moved their editorial operation over to Manila. Opened another branch.'

'But don't they still print in Hong Kong?' Peter sliced into the pink flesh of the papaya.

'Yeah,' Hal nodded and swallowed a lychee. 'Better not to keep all your eggs in one basket. Spread the operation. Spread the risk.'

'So, the editorial staff can be arrested in Manila while the Hong Kong end remains out of harm's way.'

Hal grinned. 'You've got it, Pete.'

'As I seem to constitute the entire editorial staff of the 'Weekly' at present, I must say that your scheme does not exactly enchant me.'

Another bite of papaya.

'Don't worry, Pete. As soon as you're banged up, I shall go to the British Embassy and put in a strong complaint.' Hal frowned fiercely.

Peter lowered his fork. 'Where does Nigel fit into all this?'

Hal had the grace to transfer his look from Peter to a distant waiter. 'I'm beginnin' to 'ave my doubts about Nigel.'

'Oh?' Peter awaited the doubts with interest.

Hal shook his head sadly. 'Nigel lacks push. He gets too easily distracted from the job in 'and.'

'But Nigel's a partner. Our partner.' Peter wondered whether he really cared a fig about someone, who from the first had adopted an adversarial attitude towards Peter and who seemed far too interested in fleshly matters. Or should he take this as an adumbration of Hal's future disloyalty to himself? To tell the truth, Peter could not care less about Nigel. But who was worse, Nigel or Hal? Or himself?

'Look.' Hal's tone was confidential. 'Nigel's got personal problems. I reckon 'e's 'eadin' for the rocks with that wife of 'is. In a few months' time, 'e'll be no use to anyone.' He wiped his lips with his napkin. 'Besides, we'll be needin' a Filipino partner.'

'Oh.' The peso dropped. 'Got anyone in mind?'

'Well, with Nigel out of the way, we'll need someone in advertisin' with good contacts in business and the government. Somebody with push.'

'Somebody like Joe?' Peter lowered his fork.

'Hey!' Hal beamed at Peter. 'That's a great idea.' Hal squeezed Peter's upper arm. 'Joe would be perfect.'

'So, I stay over here with Joe and you remain in Hong Kong?' Peter smiled.

'Yeah!' Hal exclaimed. Then he looked appealing. 'It stands to reason, Peter. I mean things could be a bit uncertain at first. At least Hil's job at the hotel brings in real money. And I'll get over to Manila as often as I can.'

Hal's eyes strayed in pursuit of an undulating Filipina derrière, negotiating the channel between two empty tables. 'You can count on it.'

'And I suppose I am allowed the occasional furlough in the land of law and functional plumbing?'

'Listen,' Hal lowered his cigar. 'I'll find out tonight whether there's a chance of both of us settin' up shop over 'ere.' Hal laid a finger along his nose. 'Believe me, me old mate. I'd like nothin' better than to come over 'ere. It's a land of opportunity. Like 'Ong Kong in the old days.'

They were the last to order coffee.

'Course,' Hal inspected the tiny cup. 'Hil would 'ate it 'ere.'

'Would she?' Peter kept his voice in neutral.

'Yeah,' Hal stirred on. 'Hil's stuck in 'er ways. We've been married ten years,' he added gloomily.

'Is it as long as that?' Peter controlled his voice.

'Yeah.' Hal took a ruminative sip of coffee. 'She's still stuck on me, mind.'

Peter had to admit that he was a reluctant witness to the truth of that statement.

'Can't get enough. Funny that. After ten years.' Hal looked directly at Peter. 'You'd never tell from lookin' at 'er, would you?'

Peter's mouth filled with bitter dregs. He made much of inspecting his watch. 'Chico will be waiting.'

Hal raised a hand for the waiter. 'Do the bugger good to wait. Sulky sod.'

When the bill arrived, Hal asked to see the manager. Peter squirmed with embarrassment as Hal wriggled out of paying. Peter knew that Agustin would have certainly paid had he been present, but this abject parasitism, in which he too was complicit, made his flesh crawl. Hal was smiling at his own success.

By the car, Hal placed a firm hand on Peter's upper arm.

'Look, Pete. I'm a bit late for an important appointment.' Hal had already turned towards the Pontiac.

'That's O.K. Hal. I'll grab a cab.' Gratefully, Peter moved

away. He watched as the car disappeared among the traffic.

Hubler was engaged in conversation with one of the most corpulent human beings Peter had ever seen. The man lay back in an armchair in the hotel lobby like a stranded dugong. In one hand he sported a glass of liquid the colour of cold tea. Hubler rose to his feet as Peter joined them. The fat man failed to follow suit. Peter leaned across the glass table and shook the single proffered finger.

'Harris,' the man wheezed.

Peter nodded politely and took a chair opposite the two already in occupation. Hubler was wearing his assistant manager's working clothes; an elegant dark suit, a white silk shirt and the understated gold cuff-links.

'Drink?' Hubler enquired.

Before Peter could reply, Harris interjected. 'Hong Kong Weekly?' His tone was one of such acid incredulity that Peter's hackles rose. He nodded and turned to Hubler. 'A G & T please.' He then added, 'With a miniscule 'g'.'

'I've never heard of it.' Harris produced a wheezing cough, took a sip from his glass and asked, 'What's the circulation?'

'No idea. You'll have to ask the circulation manager,' Peter replied crisply.

Harris raised his eyebrows over his raised glass and looked at Hubler. Peter could sense Hubler's discomfort.

'The Weekly has only been on the streets for a few months,' Peter offered, softening his tone.

'Even so,' Harris snorted. 'Or is it just a hotel giveaway?' The accent was markedly American.

'The cover price is four dollars – Hong Kong dollars.' Peter leaned forward, ready to rise and go. A waiter arrived with his generous gin and a bottle of tonic. Peter decided against bolting.

'And what's your substantive post on the Review, Mr. Harris?' Peter hated to hit below the belt but his own groin was throbbing. Harris, he noted with pleasure, looked down into his glass. Peter introduced the tonic to the gin. It fizzed over the ice cubes.

'There'll always be an England.'

Peter looked up in response to Harris's ironic toast.

'*The Review*,' Peter retorted and raised his own glass.

'Screw the Review,' Harris snorted and drank deeply. The drink was dead. Hubler held out a hand for the corpse and raised an eyebrow in enquiry.

Harris relinquished the glass. 'Whisky sour.'

'That figures,' Peter thought to himself.

The obesity was wearing some kind of traditional Filipino shirt. Across the steppes of his chest rose acres of lace. Sweat stains spread from beneath the bloated upper arms, defying the air conditioning. An ice cube lodged against Peter's upper lip. A second waiter appeared and whispered in Hubler's ear. The assistant manager rose.

'Excuse me, gentlemen. Duty calls.'

As Peter kept his eyes on the departing back, his attention was caught by a laughing group on the other side of the lobby. He recalled a visit to the Hilton Coffee Shop after Solly had won the UPI contract. He and Aggie had clung to each other, weak with laughter, as Solly's elation carried them away into ridiculous realms. Now he felt shabby, trapped with this blob, while elsewhere in Manila there was life and fun. He thought of Hal resentfully.

He realised that Harris was considering him. Peter lowered his drink onto the glass table.

'Been in Manila long?' Peter asked, hoping Hubler would not be delayed.

'Long enough.' The first waiter arrived with Harris's drink. The fat man took it without a word or glance. Sidney Greenstreet in person. A sigh is just a sigh. The waiter knew better than to wait.

'This your first trip?' Harris's tone suggested he already knew the answer.

'Isn't it obvious?' Peter retrieved his glass.

'Tell me,' Harris rolled his glass between his palms. 'What's it like? The first trip?'

'Great,' Peter laughed, feeling like a schoolboy being quizzed by an antique schoolmaster. 'Fantastic.'

'I see.' Harris swallowed half the contents of his glass. 'And that's what you're going to write for *Hong Kong Weekly*?'

'Not just that.' Peter wanted to mount a counter-offensive but was wary of lowering his guard. 'A lot more besides.'

'Such as?' Harris's grin was as wry as his drink.

'There's a few questions I need answers to first.' Peter felt his jaw tighten.

'You mean about martial law and why they're keeping Aquino under lock and key and what's happened to Fernandez?' Harris counted out the questions on modelling-clay fingers.

'Who's Fernandez?' Peter asked, leading with his chin.

'Now, that I admire,' Harris lifted his glass in another ironic toast. 'When I first arrived, I never had the balls to ask a straightforward question like that.'

'Why not?' Peter asked, wondering whether it was an implied compliment or a disguised insult.

'Too scared of looking like the asshole I was, I guess.' Yes, it had been an insult.

Harris drank another mouthful, swilling it from cheek to cheek like a frog with a tic.

'O.K.' Peter made no effort to disguise his irritation. 'So, having proved to your complete satisfaction that I am the arsehole you'd already decided I was, would you mind answering the question?'

Harris looked directly at Peter. 'Fernandez,' he began, his tone temperate. 'Fernandez was the best goddamn journo in Manila. Correction. In the whole goddam Philippines. He wrote a column for the *Manila Times*.'

Peter waited. 'And?' Harris glanced up from his glass.

'Fernandez was kicked off the paper a month after martial law was declared. A week later he disappears. He hasn't been seen since.'

Harris finished his dregs and clicked to attract a passing waiter.

Peter stirred uncomfortably. Hardly the stuff for 'Halo Halo'.

'Was Fernandez a friend of yours?' Peter asked the fat man, whose triple chins gleamed with perspiration. Harris grunted.

'You could say that.'

The waiter arrived. Harris surrendered his empty glass. He looked inquiringly at Peter, who shook his head. The Englishman produced his packet of American cigarettes and offered it to Harris.

'Hey, good to meet a limey with taste,' Harris wheezed and plucked out a cigarette with practised fingers. That explained the cough.

'What happened to Fernandez?' Peter asked as Harris used the Zippo.

'Quien sabe?' Harris gave Peter a sour grin. 'Maybe they gave him an all-expenses-paid-round-the-world-trip. On an unlimited basis.'

Harris tossed back the Zippo. 'He was a damn good journo. Too good.'

Peter wondered how to lift the gloom that had settled over them. 'What about the other journos? On other papers?'

'I think the polite word is 'emasculated'.' Harris shrugged. 'Okay. Back in the Congress days journos and politicians had too many 'cojones'. But a guy is no use without them.'

Sidney Greenstreet out of Hemingway.

'Who's serving as chief eunuch?' Peter attempted to match his idiom to the American's.

'Well, the guy who goes under the misnomer of 'Minister of Information' is called Tatad. He don't like something he reads, he makes a call to the editor and pretty soon there's a small ad in the bottom corner of the back page, 'Wanted – one gutless wonder to write crap. Essential qualifications; a large family of dependents and the ability to take dictation. Desirable – cousins in the Information Ministry. Genuine journalistic experience definitely not required.'

Peter smiled. The little homily was well composed and delivered. He pointed his cigarette at Harris. 'So, what about you?'

'So, what about me?' A question for a question. Harris had to be from New York.

'Yes, you. Just why do they allow you to function?' Peter was genuinely curious. He assumed that some of the harsher things he had read about the Philippines in FEER must have emanated from this particular obese American. He mentioned Hong Kong's finest mag.

'Which very few people get to read over here.' Harris gave Peter a rueful grin. 'Any overseas publication they don't like winds up impounded in a warehouse.'

'But what about Filipinos who travel? Surely they see your stuff.'

'The Filipinos who travel are servants of the system. Somehow, opponents of the regime lose the itch to wander.' The waiter appeared with Harris's fresh whisky sour. 'And yours truly has too many strings to his regional bow.'

'You mean the Hong Kong connection.'

'Hong Kong, Strong Pong.' Harris dismissed the Crown Colony with a backward flick of his hand. 'There's a big world out there, sonny.'

He grimaced as he downed a mouthful of amber fluid. 'I have friends from Los Angeles, California, to New York, New York – via Waterloo.'

He toasted Peter. 'That's in Iowa, by the way.'

Peter tried to picture this bullfrog in a green eye shield, ripping a sheet out of an old Remington and yelling for the copy boy. Harris was a one-man re-run of *The Front Page.*

'So now you'd like to know about 'martial law', right?' Harris waved the damp stub of the cigarette, his fingers shining with spittle. Peter lifted his glass from the table and settled back. Thank God for whisky sour. The fatso wheezed into a more upright position. His arms shook under the strain.

'Anybody who was here before seventy-two will tell you about the good old bad old days. The Wild West with a million weapons and a million trigger-happy boys in the barrio cocked to use 'em. The President that was... correction, that is... is about to lay his future on the line in elections. He has a rival, a pretty tough dude named Benigno – that's a laugh – Benigno Aquino. Now, Aquino is Marcos in spades. Smart, rough, ruthless. Youngest congressman, youngest provincial governor – all the shit that they love over here.' He waved a hand. 'I know. All the shit they got from us. Yeah. You're right. Anyhow, the campaign started to bloody up. Lots of O.K. Corrals. Washington begins to get the twitches. They got a big stake in this archipelago. Like, the navy's kind of attached to the base at Subic Bay and the air force thinks Clark Field is cute. And there's Commie China over the horizon. You get the picture. And Marcos is their boy. Let the Fords eat steak, he says. No, not the Fords. The Fords. The ones who make the cars. And if all this terrible licentious democracy goes on and people keep on killing one another, who's going to be left to buy the cars Ford intends for Filipinos to build for the Philippines market? And while the freedom-loving democrats are busy wiping each other out, the meanies out in the boondocks – the New People's Army – are just waiting to preside over the funerals. So, Marcos and the Old People's Army take over and Aquino is given a long holiday in Camp Bonifacio at government expense. But that leaves the guns. What do we do about the guns, guys?'

Peter took a sip of his now tepid tipple. 'Well, what do we do?'

'Well, the story goes like this.' Harris accepted another Pall Mall and the loan of the Zippo. He luxuriated in lighting up, sure that his captive audience would remain captive. A Yankee whaler yarning to a British wedding-guest. Harris tossed the Zippo back. Peter caught and pocketed it. 'Marcos is smart. That is one fact which is beyond dispute. He was trained as a lawyer and he still thinks like one. In the States he'd make a killing in divorce cases.' Harris grimaced and inhaled. Smoke disappeared into his maw, never to return. 'Of course, this is, as the lawyers say, all hearsay reporting. I was in the States at the time. For my health.' Harris grinned. 'In Waterloo.' The grin expanded to a laugh. 'The way I heard it when I got back was that Marcos had put out a proclamation – or presidential decree or whatever – saying that it was O.K. for people to own guns but that in future they had to be registered. For a small fee. So, half a million guys march round to their local station house, toting their artillery. They fill out the forms; name, address, type of weapon, quantity. They then pay up their five pesos or whatever. As soon as all the forms are signed,

Marcos sends the boys round to all the addresses and picks up a cool five hundred thousand rifles and handguns. And the pesos stay in Marcos's treasury.'

'Is treasury code for pocket?' Peter lit another cigarette.

Harris shook his head slowly. 'I don't think that's it. Oh, he's certainly not a poor man. Not that his family was rich. But Marcos has been in office since '65 and a lot of businessmen get very generous when they're in the market for presidential favours. No, aside from the usual quota of greed that flesh is heir to, I dare say Marcos is about as honest about money as any dictator in history. His problem is, he knows he's right. You've read his book?'

Peter shook his head without prevarication.

'You should. You may not agree with his ideas but he sure expressed 'em well. He really believes he is the doctor the country ordered.'

'Him and the wealthy elite?' Peter felt a twinge of disloyalty towards Agustin.

'Him and the army. Rumour goes that the 'Ilustrados' the old Spanish families – and the other rich, established families were kinda snotty to Imelda when she first came in from the sticks. She'd already had a tough time growing up among step-brothers and sisters. So, I don't think Marcos is allowed to lose too much sleep over the 'wealthy elite', to re-coin your phrase.

Harris looked around. A third waiter appeared.

'Whisky sour,' Harris glanced across at Peter and raised an eyebrow. Peter nodded. 'And a gin and tonic.' Harris inspected the tip of his cigarette. It was burning unevenly. He licked a finger and transferred the spittle to the lighted end. 'Damn things won't burn straight.' One more inhalation and…

'Would you like to hear another story?'

Peter nodded.

'Marcos needed money. For some of his personal schemes. Maybe for one or two of Imelda's cosmetic capers. His problem was not the imposition of taxes. Any government can impose taxes. But how to make 'em stick, that's the problem. Tax evasion was a national pastime. Like Jai-alai. The Filipinos make the French look like amateurs.'

Peter chuckled as their drinks appeared. The waiters obviously had them lined up, just waiting for Harris to click his fingers. Now 'Fats' took a quick sip of fresh bubbles and belched lightly.

'So, Marcos issues another proclamation, decree or whatever, concerning tax valuations. He is going to trust the people with regard to tax valuations. He is going to rely on the people to be honest in valuing their own property so that he can charge a miniscule property tax. Now the rich do not become rich by being totally dumb. They can add up. And they know that, for instance, five percent of two million pesos is a little less than five percent of twenty million pesos. Anyhow, this one poor, wealthy elitist sends in his tax return. Dadada-dada-dada. Value of property two million pesos. 'O.K.' Marcos says, 'You're an honest man and I believe you. Your property is worth two million pesos.'

Peter smiled as Harris performed another disappearing trick with half his whisky. The fat man smacked his lips. Suddenly Harris had become Marcos and Peter was his victim.

'So now the State will compulsorily purchase your property for two million pesos.'

Peter stared for a few seconds at Harris's smug expression and then laughed so sharply, he almost spilled his drink. Heads turned across the lobby. 'Well, the word spreads like wildfire and suddenly Marcos has got a mountain of genuine tax returns filling the treasury. And an even taller mountain of dinero.' Harris tapped his temple. 'Smart.' He chuckled.

On his return Hubler found the two journalists in excellent humour.

Harris wheezed to his feet like an ancient concertina. 'Got to go, Hubler. We didn't miss you.'

Hubler just grinned. Harris swung back. 'Oh, and about the bill for the drinks,' Harris coughed politely. 'Pete will explain it to Mr.Agustin.'

Peter watched Harris roll across across the foyer. He tapped his temple. 'Smart.'

Hubler nodded. 'You betcha.'

Chapter Fifteen

Peter awoke in a more sanguine frame of mind than he had in months. A daredevil taxi driver had got him back to the resort in time. Once he had been paid, the driver locked the car doors and stretched out on the back seat to await the morning. Ten minutes before curfew Peter indulged in another of his nocturnal swims, making sure this time that he was not being observed. Now he stretched, luxuriating in the morning sunshine which was filtered by the curtains. There came a knock at the door.

'Come in,' Peter called, allowing his muscles to relax. A matitudinal massage would not come amiss. The door opened. It was Hal. Peter raised his knees beneath the sheet.

'You're missin' a lovely day.' Hal strode up to the bedside, rubbing his hands and displaying his teeth.

'Yes, isn't it?' For a fleeting instant Peter found himself liking Hal.

'Fancy a trip out of town?' Hal continued to knead his hands. Peter remarked that Hal was wearing the kind of off-duty uniform affected by Hong Kong businessmen under the age of forty; a pale khaki safari suit and brown leather sandals over white socks. Peter noticed the gleam of a gold St. Christopher medal below Hals' tanned neck.

'That's a nice idea.' Peter sat up in bed. 'But I'm afraid I was planning to take a few more shots of Fort Santiago in Intramuros. I missed it on my first visit.'

'Right,' Hal clapped his palms together lightly. 'We'll make a day of it.'

Peter slipped out of bed and strolled towards the shower. 'Is Nigel up for it?'

'I dunno,' Hal said, raising his voice as Peter disappeared inside the shower cubicle. ''E says 'e's still feelin' off colour. I reckon he's been feelin' up that Sue too much. He's not used to so much nooky.'

While the shower ran, Hal availed himself of a perusal of the sheets lying beside Peter's portable. When he heard the shower fall silent, Hal darted to a new position on the end of the bed. Peter returned with one towel round his waist, a second drying his hair.

'How was your evening?' Peter enquired, his voice muffled.

'Great. You should see this 'ouse Isabel lives in. Fuckin' ginormous.' Hal's accompanying gesture lifted him to his feet.

'Er daddy's loaded. One of the richest guys in the Philippines.'

'And Isabel herself?'

Peter slipped on his freshly washed and ironed shirt. Quite a change from his own Hong Kong efforts.

Hal searched for a suitable epithet. His face brightened.

'Nice. She's nice.' He shrugged. 'Bit on the thin side up top. More in your line. But she's crazy about me.'

'What? Already?' Yesterday's contemptuous disbelief had been transmuted by Peter's catalysing mood into an amiable laugh.

'Yeah,' Hal took a deep breath to reveal his patient explication. 'That's 'ow it goes, don't it? I mean, it's either there or it ain't. Right?'

Peter knew it was fruitless to dispute love-lore with Hal. Their amorous records did not bear comparison.

'Mind you, I was glad I asked Maria to wait up for me.' Peter's sunny mood was clouded by piqued jealousy. If only he could embrace Hal's Dionysian indifference to anything beyond the exercise of his phallus.

'A whole evenin' wrestling with Isabel on a carpet builds up a need for relief.'

'I'm sure Maria is happy to serve the greater good.'

Peter wondered whether the athletic Isabel might find him a little more palatable than the importunate Hal. 'Intramuros, Chico,' Hal called from the back seat, his arms draped around Maria and Peter's woman/child in her habitual cotton frock.

Hal chuckled. 'This is the life!'

Peter offered Chico a cigarette. 'We'll let Chico 'ave a fag this time, won't we girls?' Peter calculated how many packets remained in his carry-all. 'Dirty 'abit.' Hal concluded.

Both the grass and the air seemed fresher to Peter in

Intramuros.

'Move over a little more to your right,' Peter commanded, waving one hand to indicate the direction. Hal, Chico and the two girls obediently shuffled across, grinning self-consciously. Peter crouched, watched by two solemn, hand-holding children. 'A tad more. I want to include that notice in the shot.' Would they understand 'tad'?

He included a cannon in the foreground. Peter focussed on the notice board on the wall below another weapon. 'This 1825 cannon fires every six p.m.'

They filed silently past a display of presidential vehicles, protected from the elements by stone arches. They paused, silent, beside the limousine whose sides had been ripped open by bullets. Hal cleared his throat.

'I'm glad I'm not gonna be around next time they fire that fuckin' cannon.'

Peter laughed, in spite of himself. A group of passing Filipinos frowned their disapproval. The girls and Chico looked confused.

Suddenly, Maria ran off across a closely cropped lawn.

'Where's she buggered off to?' Hal enquired. Peter raised the zoom at its full 200 mm extension. He focussed beyond Maria's legs at a white bird with a broken tail. He hurried to catch up with the others. Maria was kneeling on the grass as he arrived. In fact, the bird was not injured. The angled tail was a detail in nature's great design. A rumbling, phlegmy cooing came from the dove as it paraded its amorous intent to a second, presumably female, bird. Peter shifted position so that the two birds were white splashes against the sombre background of a majestic tree. He squeezed the trigger. When he stood, he found that Maria was still watching him. Hal, on the other hand, was bored with birds. He strode away, calling out, 'Come On. Watchin' them pigeons has given me an appetite.' Peter repressed a pun about Hal being 'peckish'.

The open-air café Hal had spotted served sandwiches and coffee. 'There you go,' Hal waved a hand above his head. 'All the pigeons you want. Just keep your 'and over your cup.' Maria, fascinated, stared up at the overcrowded dovecot. The avian foreplay was cacophonous.

The group ignored the bedlam and tried to relax in the sun. Chico accepted a coffee and a cigarette from Peter.

Hal's departure for the 'little boy's room' neatly coincided with the arrival of the bill. Peter felt like a millionaire as he handed over ten pesos.

Which included a tip.

Awaiting Hal's return, Peter pored over the ghastly guide. Apparently, Fort Santiago had served as a prison during the Japanese occupation of the Philippines in the Second World War. Until 1898 and their final retirement to the Iberian Peninsula the complex had served the same function for the Spanish.

Peter felt cool fingers touch his hand. 'We go see Rizal?' It was the wraith.

'What's Rizal?' Hal demanded, looking down at them.

Chico squinted at the grinning face. 'Rizal was the founder of our country. He fought to give us independence from foreigners.' Chico obliterated the cigarette butt in an ashtray. 'He was assassinated by the Spanish.' Chico's face remained impassive.

Once more Peter felt the touch of the cool fingers. He rose. 'Let's go and see Rizal.'

The others followed suit and a flight of doves flashed across the sun.

The fresco was, by any standard, hyperbolic. In the foreground, wearing a dark suit appropriate for a doctor, a slim, brown man lay dying.

Ropes twisted a jacket sleeve out of shape. Rizal's expression was a conflation of pain and ecstasy. In the background, half-obscured by the smoke from their rifles, two lines of soldiers made up the firing squad. Beyond them stood a priest, his eyes pure adamant.

Peter felt a nudge. Hal whispered hoarsely in his ear. 'I'm gettin' an article about this bloke.'

Hal was infuriating. He was breaking bounds, as Peter feared he would. 'Who's the article from?'

'Joe's cousin. Don't worry, you'll 'ave a chance to rewrite it,' Hal grinned.

Peter raised the wide-angle once more. A squad of Chinese tourists burst into the shrine, shattering all decorum with their loud, Cantonese voices. Peter resisted the urge to demand silence. 'M ho chou, la!' The tourists took it in turns to pose before the execution; their faces wreathed in cheerful smiles.

'Hold it,' Hal cried. Everybody froze. Hal cleared an old woman and her two dowdy daughters from the space before the fresco.

'Press, press,' Hal repeated loudly. 'O.K. Pete,'

His face glowing with embarrassment, Peter took two exposures. As the group turned to leave, the tidal wave of noise flooded back higher than before.

'Bloody disgustin'.' Hal sniffed and led them out.

As the Pontiac yawed along the country road, Hal hummed *All Shook Up*. Chico had suggested that they lunch in Tagaytay, an hour's drive South of Manila. The wind whipped up the hairs on Peter's forearm. He began to hum along with Hal. They passed a gnarled old man guarding a heap of coconuts as tall as himself.

'Was that guy selling those coconuts?' Peter asked Chico.

'Sure,' Chico replied, glancing at Peter. 'The farmers sell what they can. Coconuts, pineapples.'

Hal chipped in. 'I could fancy a slice of pineapple.'

The car slid to a halt in a cloud of dust. Chico smiled and pointed.

Peter, camera in hand, followed Hal to the four-foot high hillock. He shook his legs to free them from the damp clasp of his trousers. The farmer wore a broad, circular straw hat and carried a wicked machete. His welcoming stream of Tagalog was accompanied by gestures which did nothing to elucidate his incomprehensibility. Chico came to the rescue. While the haggling continued, Hal raised the topmost fruit and showed it to Peter.

'He says the price is sixty centavos,' Chico translated.

Hal's eyes lit up and he smiled expansively. 'That's fifty cents Hong Kong money.' He shouted back towards the car, ''Ow about a pineapple?' The two silhouettes shook their heads.

''Ow about you, Chico?' Hal was in an exuberant frame of

mind.

Chico nodded, before hurriedly warning, 'Watch out for the bolo.' He pushed Hal to one side. The farmer grasped a pineapple by its crown and, with four swift strokes, reduced it to a cube.

'Jesus,' Hal murmured. 'Will you look at that?' His mouth remained agape.

'They use the bolo for cutting down the brush,' Chico informed them. Peter wondered about the bolo's other uses. So much for rounding up lethal weapons.

The three men bent at the waist to avoid the flow of exuberant juice as each attacked his personal pineapple. The farmer observed them, smiling toothlessly, as the big, curved knife dangled by his side. Chico had a bottle of washing water in the car. They drove on.

From outside, the hotel in Tagaytay was impressive. Peter took both cameras from his catch-all. Slowly, they trooped up the front steps. The weather had changed for the worse and the interior of the hotel was gloom-laden. Maria led the way into the deserted restaurant. Edging between the tables, they made their way towards the impressive windows at the far end of the room. There they gathered and gazed. Silently.

They tried to take in the panorama before them.

Maria breathed the name, 'Mount Taal.'

At first Peter could not quite comprehend what he was seeing. Then he began to disentangle the various components which made up the view.

Within a vast, distant lake rose the rim of an extinct volcano. Then – wonder of wonders – within the rim of the volcano lay another lake. Finally, from the heart of the second lake, a second – live – volcano rose, smoke drifting from its cone. The charcoal-coloured rain clouds were reflected in the waters far below. Peter was filled with wonder that he could have lived for so long in Hong Kong – so close to the Philippines and to this extraordinary place – without knowing of its existence. Enchanted, he raised the telephoto camera. As he focussed, he became aware of the strains of 'Fűr Elise' drifting across the room. Tentative at first, the music gained strength as it progressed. Peter lowered the camera.

Impossible to replicate the reality. He turned.

Maria was seated at a battered upright piano. His own, still unidentified, girl stood transfixed beside Maria. Behind them, his chin resting on his hands, which rested, in turn, on the back of his chair, sat Hal – his eyes fixed on Maria's fingers. Chico leaned against the wall beside the piano.

The music came to an end in the middle of a phrase. Maria's hands dropped into her lap. As clapping broke the silence, Maria wiped her eyes with the back of her hand.

'Fantastic,' Hal enthused. 'That's a great tune.'

Maria turned as Peter rejoined them. He smiled. 'That was lovely.'

'Right!' Hal's chair squealed. 'Let's eat. I'm starvin''

Hal's appetite shifted the melancholic mood of the group as he explored the menu. It was decided to order *adoba*, a spicy dish of chicken and pork.

Chico listened intently as Peter complimented Maria on her pianistic skill. Peter felt drawn to the girl as she raised a smooth, brown hand to brush a strand of hair from her face. Once the food arrived, Hal resumed his role of life and soul of the party, demanding all Maria's attention.

Peter glanced across the table at the child. Was her slight delicacy the result of malnourishment or unhappiness? She was still eating when Hal called for the bill. Peter heard him utter the magic spell of 'Agustin'.

'We haven't got time to waste 'angin' about this dump.' He winked at Peter. Maria had got to her feet,

'What's the rush?' Peter demanded.

'We've got a little poker party tonight, me old mate.' Hal grinned. 'And I've got a great 'and. Full 'ouse. All the queens.'

The return journey from Mount Taal was accomplished in brooding silence. Hal's few manic attempts at jocularity fell on stony ground. The two girls' fingers interlaced as they sat, side by side, on the back seat.

As they journeyed, so the cloud cover thickened. Peter felt a headache coming on. He whistled the first few bars of the Beethoven melody.

Then silence fell. The car paused at the entrance to the resort and, as the girls alighted by the sauna, Maria threw an accusatory glance at Peter and an arm round her companion's slight shoulders. Hal ruminated beside Chico.

Within fifteen minutes of their return there was knocking at Peter's door.

'Come on, Pete,' Hal filled the doorway, the epitome of impatience. 'Let's get out of this bloody place. It's beginning to give me the creeps.'

So, they arrived early at the party. Hal wanted Peter to meet 'Isabel' before the hubbub began. The two men waited. For some reason neither of them felt in a party mood.

'A rich Filipino's home is a castle,' Peter punned to himself. Perhaps he might use it in the magazine.

A servant in the standard domestic livery of white jacket and black trousers had shown them into the vast reception room. The black furniture gleamed dully in dim, reflected light. Against one wall stood a long table, covered in party guise in a damask cloth whose storage folds still showed. At one end of the table two dozen bottles of inebriation gaggled, surrounded by a host of upturned glasses. In the corners of the room dried grasses rose from the necks of gigantic Canton-ware vases. Peter was quite at home among the gaudy masks and other regional artefacts which threw shadows on the walls or glittered in display cabinets. He smiled wistfully at the thought of how Guy might have reacted to these spoils.

Peter reached for his cigarettes. Hal's hand covered his. ''Ere, can't you 'old on a bit? No need to stink out the bloody room.'

The sight of all this wealth inspired Hal's religiosity. His voice had hushed to a whisper. Peter touched Hal's hand and nodded towards a slight disturbance he had detected in a corridor leading from the furthest corner of the room.

Hal turned and, to Peter's astonishment, scrambled to his feet as the slim figure of a girl entered the light. This, Peter deduced, must be Isabel.

Her slightness reminded Peter of 'his' girl back at the resort. But Isabel was clearly older and, up close, her brown skin had a faintly yellow tinge around the mouth and eyes. Any colour would have flattered her more than the black she now affected.

Peter stood beside Hal, awaiting the offer of Isabel's hand before presuming to tender his own. But as the girl arrived beside a neighbouring long, low sofa, she collapsed onto it – a marionette with broken strings; her legs ungainly in the tight skirt.

'Jesus!' was Isabel's first word. Peter looked to Hal for a lead. The 'Weekly' editor retreated, hunched, towards his former seat and flapped a hand to indicate that Peter should also retreat.

'Christ!' Isabel expleted. 'That woman is going to drive me crazy!'

The accent was the by-now-expected Philamerican.

'Isabel,' Hal murmured, his voice freighted with 'respect'. Isabel's hands jerked as though he had bellowed. 'Isabel, this is my friend and colleague, Peter.'

'One of these days I'm going to kill her, so help me.'

Peter recognised that, mingled with a sense of genuine pique, was more than a hint of theatricality for their benefit. In any case, factitious or not, the performance was not be interrupted.

'I told her I wanted to wear the red dress this evening. But she 'forgets' to send it for cleaning, so I have to wear this old rag.'

'It's a lovely old rag,' Hal's attempt at a compliment was brushed aside with contempt.

'I feel like a drink,' Isabel announced loudly. Peter began to rise to his feet but the girl rapidly covered the ten paces to her oasis and flicked a tumbler right way up. Hal avoided Peter's eye as a quadruple whisky cataracted into the crystal.

'Where's the fucking ice?' Isabel asked rhetorically. Carrying her full glass across the intervening space, she spewed a stream of Tagalog into the recess whence she had appeared. There came a distant cry and a faint crash.

Isabel, with impressive composure, returned to the sofa 'I've got a great surprise lined up for you this evening, Peter.' She swirled her drink as she sauntered to her destination. Peter thought it wisest to avoid mentioning that Hal had already unsurprised the surprise.

'Hal tells me that you're a man with a cast-iron resistance to women.' Hal inspected the belouch carpet which covered half the room. Isabel's smile was a sharp as a dart. 'Dear Hal can't say the same for himself.' Hal continued to examine the finer points of the warp and weft. Peter was feeling his resentment rise. Isabel, her smile slurred, resumed her seat, her legs piercing the air like pegs.

'Your friend...' Isabel pointed at Peter's friend with her glass. '... is so sex-mad he even tried to rape me on that carpet.' Hal looked up, alarmed, to find that the half-empty glass now indicated an area occupied by Hal's feet. The feet shifted away from the reported scene of the crime.

'He did not succeed.' Isabel consumed more whisky.

'You gotta admit it was fun tryin' though,' Hal joked. Isabel was basilisk. His smile faded. He was clearly losing his bearings.

An old woman in black and white uniform almost ran into the room towards the drinks table. In her hands she clutched an overweight aluminium container which rattled as she jogged.

'Christ!' Isabel thrust her glass out directly in front of her. 'The ice is needed over here, not there.' The wrinkled old retainer hurried across the carpet and fumbled three cubes of the coolant into the lubricant. She awaited further orders. They came.

'Don't just stand there. Put the ice bucket on the table where it should be.'

Isabel's eyes narrowed as they watched the accomplishment of this task. The battered woman turned to escape.

'Wait!' Isabel yelled. 'Who the hell's the servant around here? These gentlemen require drinks.' She swung her own glass in an arc which included Hal and Peter. A drink was the last thing Peter felt like accepting from this termagant but he knew a refusal would simply prolong the older woman's discomfiture. Prolonged it was nevertheless, as Isabel nagged the wretched servant through the ritual of the whisky, the gin and the mixers. And, finally, the ice. Both men were relieved when the servant was finally allowed to make her escape.

'Who would believe that a couple of drinks would cause so much trouble?' was Isabel's rhetorical question. Peter chose to respond.

'Yes, it might almost have been better to pour your own.' He smiled at Isabel.

He felt Hal shoot him a sharp look before picking up the thread.

'Yeah, amahs are a real problem these days.' Hal turned his back on Peter and concentrated his fire on Isabel.

'Amahs?' Isabel paused, her drink six inches short of its intended destination.

'Yeah. Amahs. Servants. Like that old fart.' Hal nodded towards the distant corridor.

'How many 'amahs' do you have in Hong Kong?' Isabel asked, her curiosity quite genuine.

'Just the one.' Hal and Peter both noticed Isabel's eyes narrow before her head dipped towards her drink. Hal rushed on. 'I used to 'ave more but then they got so... so useless. Couldn't get 'em to do a thing I wanted.'

Isabel seemed to snigger into her glass.

'I keep tellin' Ah Yeot that if she doesn't pull 'er socks up, she'll 'ave to go.' Hal took a tough guy swig of liquor.

'How about you, Pete? Do you have trouble with your servants?' Isabel insisted on drawing both men into the tedious conversation.

'I have the perfect solution to the amah problem.' Peter grinned. 'No amah.'

Isabel's amazement was unfeigned. 'You don't have a servant?'

'I used to have a servant but he left a little while ago.'

Isabel looked at Hal. 'I see.' Her head swivelled back towards Peter. 'Ever had a girl?' Isabel swung one slim leg over the other, delighted with her own daring. Épater les journalistes.

'I trust you mean as a servant?' Peter smiled. He was beginning to wonder when the other guests would arrive.

'Yeah,' Isabel, expectant, inspected her ice cubes.

'As a matter of fact, I did have a lovely girl as a servant once.' Peter looked rueful. 'But she left.'

'Couldn't stand the pace?' Isabel smirked into her whisky.

'I suppose not. She left to get married. She and her husband are now in the States and, from what I can gather from her last letter, doing rather better than her former employer.' Hal's head turned sharply but Isabel chose to pass over Peter's remark to ask another question.

'What's it like, living in Hong Kong?' Hal was not prepared to hazard Peter's unfettered opinion. He snatched the conversational baton.

'Great,' Hal's eyes lit up. 'Exciting – every minute of every day.'

'Not like Manila, eh, Hal?' Isabel tossed Hal the bait.

'Don't get me wrong, Isabel. Manila's great too. But the attractions are different.' Hal struggled to clarify, leaning towards the hook. 'But 'Ong Kong's electric.'

'Would I get a charge?' Isabel asked, leaning towards Hal, her lower lip damp.

'Would you!' Parties every night, boat trips to the islands and all that fantastic Chinese food. You'd love it.'

The light left Isabel's eyes. 'Would I?' She rose and turned to greet the incoming horde. Peter beathed a sigh of more than relief. The Seventh Cavalry was making its belated appearance at the Makati mansion.

Half-way through the banquet Peter made a rough estimate of the number of guests. At each of the ten circular tables in the cavernous dining room were six or eight guests. The cold collation of meats, seafood, salad and fruit might have fed the New People's Army for a week.

Hal and Peter, as guests of honour, perched on either side of Isabel at the top table. Sharing their repast were four immaculately varnished Filipinas, the Misses Philippines from 1969 to 1972 inclusive. Names had been mentioned in the introductions to the journalists but their titles sufficed to distinguish the four queens from each other and their subjects. Like drones, the queens' escorts had been ignored in the presentation as being unworthy of notice. Queens and escorts were the obverse and reverse of coins of frozen good looks. They posed for journalistic inspection, male and female, side by side, their fingers seeking tidbits, their smiling faces erotic masks.

Hal leaned towards Isabel. 'Those blokes don't seem to pay much attention to the girls, do they?'

Isabel glanced at Peter. 'Their lack of interest in the opposite sex is their main qualification as escorts.'

Peter smiled as she looked directly at him. He counted three before leaning towards her right ear. 'Did you know that you have a blackhead in the middle of your right cheek?'

Isabel's hand shot up to the affected area. Her eyes rolled.

Peter smiled. 'Would you like me to get rid of it for you?'

The girl was gone, pushing her way through the gannets jostling around the buffet table. Hal seized the opportunity of Isabel's flight to devour Miss Philippines 1971 in a voracious grin. She too hurriedly departed in the direction recently taken by their hostess. Before long Hal and Peter were alone with the perfect escorts.

'Bloody wankers,' Hal snarled, spitting a sliver of shell onto the tablecloth.

Five minutes later Isabel resumed her place and turned towards Peter. He held his breath. He had already experienced some of the girl's unappetising moods. He was quite unprepared for her opening words.

'Thanks. I hate those bloody things.' Isabel shuddered. A small russet circle embellished her cheek.

'Is it much of a problem?' Peter gravely enquired. Isabel nodded, a small spotty child once again. He took her hand. It was hot and damp. Peter patted it. 'I can recommend sulphur soap. You should use it.' Isabel looked at him suspiciously. 'I do,' Peter added, with quiet sincerity.

Isabel's eyes skimmed the surface of Peter's face. 'You don't have blackheads.'

'Ah! But I did,' he countered. 'Until I had recourse to sulphur soap.'

Suspicion took leave of absence. Trust flooded back into her eyes. 'O.K. I'll try it.' She exhaled as though she had agreed to give herself to him on the reception room carpet.

'Jesus!' The girl stiffened and stared past Peter into the melée. 'I thought she wasn't coming tonight.'

Peter turned to identify the object of this sudden spite. Even in this room, replete with beautiful people, the Chinese woman was exceptionally lovely. Although of 'a certain age', she had skin of a flawlessness which only belongs to the world's wealthiest women or to those whose complexion is their profession. She turned her back on the top table as she paused to engage one of the drones in conversation. Peter could not help but appreciate the full, flowing line of her legs and buttocks in the tight-fitting, blue silk cheongsam. Her profile revealed a bosom which was unusually full for a Chinese. Peter could well understand why the petulant child beside him had not rushed to welcome the newcomer. The crowd shifted and covered the apparition. Peter raised his glass of wine. 'To the Chinese.'

Isabel refused to join the toast. Hal excused himself and departed.

Peter shrugged and sipped the excellent Beaujolais.

Isabel looked up. 'The Chinese only know one thing. Money.'

'Some of them certainly have the knack of acquiring it,' Peter acknowledged.

'They'd sell their own daughters to make a few bucks,' Isabel sneered. 'You really have to watch them like a hawk.' Peter wondered whether she spoke from experience. He glanced back at the crowd now milling beside emptying tables. The Chinese beauty had disappeared.

'Don't you remember the riots in Malaysia?' Isabel's question jerked him back. 'Not to mention how they tried to overthrow the government in Indonesia.' Isabel's body suddenly seemed more angular.

'I do.' Peter placed his glass on the table. 'I also remember how the Indonesians were encouraged to turn on them. Thousands were slaughtered in the jungle.'

'They were traitors. They were plotting to bring communism into the country. They would do the same here, if we gave them half a chance.' Isabel clearly relished her role as demagogue.

'Isabel, you're my hostess but that is no reason to allow you to talk – if you'll pardon the expression – total crap.' Had he had too much to drink?

'Where would South-East Asia be without the Chinese?' He turned to face her. 'Did they not teach you that when Magellan arrived here in 1520 on his round-the-world cruise, he found a fleet of ocean-going Chinese junks at anchor off Manila? They'd been pursuing commerce in the area for centuries.' He turned towards her, warming to his theme. 'And they're still doing it. In every village in this country. Take away the little Chinese store from the barrio and your peasant farmers would be out of credit and into rebellion inside a month.' He made a mental bow to Fred Harris's stuff in the Review. 'And if you wish to remember massacres, why don't you acknowledge the pogroms the poor old Chinks have had to suffer at the hands of Filipinos for hundreds of years. That's the reward for loyalty.'

Isabel's eyes glittered. 'A Chinese is always loyal to China first.'

'Yes, the way a New Yorker of Irish descent is loyal to Ireland. A Yankee Irishman is always threatening to return home and stride over the old sod; a Chinese just wants to go back to lie under it. And what difference does it make if he ends up in an urn in Fujian rather than in Cebu or Jogjakarta?'

Isabel looked up at him, her face revealing a confusion of emotions. Peter excused himself. His bladder allowed him to absent himself.

On his return, he found the tables being cleared by a mixed-gender squad of servants. In a corner of the room a Filipino group was working its way through a Beatles' medley. Dancers spilled out between the reception and dining rooms, their faces dappled by multi-coloured reflectors. Peter stood and observed, one hand holding a glass of tonic water, the other his Zippo.

Hal burst out of the throng partnered by Miss Philippines 1971 – or was it '69? Peter found it impossible to distinguish one queen from another. He watched Hal use his elbows to clear a space. The publisher's glistening forehead gave evidence of what the effort was costing. Peter also noticed that Isabel was observing Hal from her position at the top table. Peter wandered in her direction.

'Would you like to dance?' Peter asked, with a slight bow.

Without a sideways glance, she shook her head.

Peter resumed his old place and inspected Isabel quite frankly, as she gazed past him at the dancers.

Like the child at the resort, Isabel was deceptive. Peter decided that she was not nearly so slim as he had first thought. Her acne was unappealing but very slight. All she needed was fresh air and some exercise. Oh, and sulphur soap.

'What's the verdict?' the girl asked without taking her eyes from Hal's gyrations.

'The verdict is that you are too hard on yourself.'

'How do you feel about being rich?'

'Do you mean 'sincerely'?' Peter asked, recalling the question posed by Bernie Cornfeld when marketing 'The Fund of Funds'.

'No jokes,' Isabel frowned.

'Well, I've been finding out what it's like to be the opposite of rich and I don't think it's too attractive.' Peter took a sip of tonic.

Isabel turned to face him. 'Are you married?'

'No,' Peter grinned. 'Am I about to receive a proposal? You can't buy me with all this, you know.' He waved his glass in a half-circle. 'But you're welcome to try.'

'Is Hal married?' Isabel's question had Peter fighting for his control of facial muscles.

'Who are you hunting, Isabel? Me or Hal? Or will either do?' He took another sip of tonic.

Isabel resumed her survey of the dance floor. The tempo had changed and Hal was threatening his partner's backcombing.

'Hal says he digs the Philippines.' Isabel looked back at Peter.

'I can see the attraction.' He kept his voice flat.

'Does Hal like money?' Her eyes probed his.

'When all is said and done, Hal does have a certain fondness for the crisp and folding.' Peter attempted a disarming smile. 'And all the other good things in life.'

Isabel, determined to keep the initiative, switched tracks. 'How old are you?'

'This is sounding more and more like a job interview.' Peter propped up his chin with an index finger. He fluttered his eyes. 'I'll never see thirty again.'

At last Isabel laughed and the sound was far from unpleasant. Peter rose and held out a hand. 'Come on, it's about time we sweated a little.' And sweat they did. After ten minutes, they went their several ways in search of liquid respite. As Peter bent over the sink in the washroom, his face covered in soap, a familiar voice cut through the sound of running water.

'Cor, there's some crackin' bits of crumpet 'ere tonight.'

Peter groped for the towel. 'Why don't you devote a little more time to your hostess?'

Hal's face appeared in the midst of the material, grinning. 'I reckon that's your job.'

Peter replaced the towel. 'She's been giving me the third degree. I don't suppose you have told her about Hilary?' Peter's remark was an accusation.

Hal grinned. 'She'll find out when the time is ripe.'

'Let's hope that Hil remains as ignorant of Isabel until the ripe time.'

Hal reached for one of Peter's cigarettes. Peter lit both.

Hal blew smoke over the Zippo. 'Now, how would Hil find out such a thing, unless I tell 'er?'

'You're not exactly tight-lipped, Hal.' Peter returned Hal's level look.

Hal laughed. 'You must be 'opin' and prayin' that Hil will find out. You'll 'ave to wait your turn to get your leg over.'

'Don't count your chickens, Hal.' Peter inhaled. 'You're forgetting that nice Catholic girls like Isabel are not encouraged to marry non-Catholic divorcés.'

'I'm not too bothered, Peter. I got the carpet on my side.' Hal winked.

They returned to the party, only to find that the pre-midnight rush was on. While the four queens departed, fully escorted, Isabel encouraged the hard core to hold out until curfew concluded at four. By two a.m. only four hardy couples still shuffled round the floor to the heavy beat of rock waltzes.

Peter was standing directly in front of the bass player, watching his brown fingers crawl over the neck of the Fender. He felt a hand on his arm. It was Isabel. Peter allowed her to lead him down beside the bandstand. Then he followed her into a discreet alcove. A single light shone above the standing figure of a man, casting his face into deep shadow. Isabel left them alone.

'Mr. Nicholson?' The voice was warm but weary.

Peter nodded and a hand indicated the only other chair in the space. As Peter accepted the allotted place, the voice resumed. 'My name is Fernandez. Juan Fernandez.'

Peter blinked. 'The journalist?'

'The former journalist.' The voice seemed to be amused. Ironic.

Peter looked back up the flight of five steps. 'Isn't it dangerous for you to be here?'

Fernandez leaned back against the wall and light picked out the prominences of his face.

'Isabel will keep watch.'

'I should have thought that a millionaire's daughter might be considered an unusual ally in the present political climate,' Peter remarked.

'Isabel is not typical of her class.' Fernandez smiled. 'Besides, she is bored.'

'How about you? Are you bored?'

'I keep busy.'

'Fred Harris will be delighted to hear it.'

Fernandez frowned.

'*The Far Eastern Economic Review* second stringer.' Peter explained. 'He's a great admirer of yours.'

Fernandez shrugged. 'There is nothing left to admire.'

Peter offered the Pall Mall to the journalist, who waved the packet away with a shake of his head. Peter returned the packet to his pocket with a shrug.

'Are you happy to stay dead?' Peter asked. Fernandez looked puzzled. 'Harris thinks you've been killed.'

Fernandez smile returned. 'I hope Marcos thinks so too.'

Peter wished he had lit a cigarette. His mind whirled. This was extraordinary. While the exhausted remnants of the ruling elite danced the final moments of the night away, he was enjoying an exclusive interview with a public enemy.

'I won't be able to quote you,' Peter apologised. 'Correction. I won't be able to quote you directly. The edition's also going on sale in the Philippines.'

'It's O.K.' Fernandez shrugged and smiled, 'We're not interested in hiring English recruits.'

Peter tried to sound casual. 'Who's 'we'?

Fernandez shrugged. 'Just those who wish to see democracy established in the Philippines.'

'From what I hear, you could be in a miniscule minority,' Peter was missing the comfort of a cigarette. 'The people I meet seem to prefer peace to democracy.'

Fernandez flicked the view away scornfully. 'This kind of peace cannot last.'

'How many kinds of peace are there?' Peter wondered.

'This peace is the peace of a dictator. This is the peace of the grave.'

Peter hoped he did not look as unconvinced as he felt. After all, Marcos did not have to hide; Fernandez did.

The Filipino journalist continued. 'Marcos did not impose martial law to bring peace. He took over a year ago because the people were on the verge of kicking him out.'

Peter shrugged. 'That could be another reason.' Why was Fernandez being so forthright? How did he know Peter could be trusted? How could Peter know that Fernandez was to be trusted? Was he being tested? And what if he failed?

'Could be?' Fernandez' tone sharpened. 'Why do you think he's got Aquino holed up in prison?' Peter let the rhetorical question hang. 'And why have so many of the opponents of the President and First Lady quit the country? Every newspaper has been stripped of any writer who refuses to produce pure pro-government propaganda.'

Peter countered, 'And the political gangsters have stopped shooting one another to pieces and their hacks have stopped vilifying political opponents in the press,' Peter countered.

Fernandez lowered his voice. 'Filipinos have always confused liberty with licence. It is true; they do lack discipline. But Marcos and his wife are like animal tamers. They deploy the police and the army as their whips to cow the people.'

'I'm sorry, Mr. Fernandez. Much as I sympathise with your views on democracy, I have seen no evidence of police brutality or soldiers on the streets, except during curfew. Nor have I seen any demonstrations against the regime.'

Fernandez's voice took on an acrid tone. 'No, not so far.' He paused. 'Martial law, as yet, is still an infant. But will the people still be prepared to tolerate Marcos' peace when it reaches adolescence?'

Peter recalled Major Alvarez. How would he feel about being controlled by the good Major for another ten years? Or twenty? Then he remembered.

'Marcos is going to hold a referendum on martial law. Suppose it comes up negative?'

'It won't.' Fernandez drew back into the shadows. 'Marcos has complete control of internal security and the media. The Americans are applauding everything he does, while Mrs. Marcos makes her little trips through Tondo, tossing pesos to the crowd. Marcos, I guarantee, will get over ninety percent.'

'I may have the chance of an interview with Mrs. Marcos,' Peter said and waited.

Fernandez chuckled. 'Be careful she doesn't ask for a contribution to one of her schemes.'

'Contribution?'

'Sure. Imelda can charm the money out of anybody's wallet – for a park, for a cultural centre, for a secret account in a Swiss bank.'

Peter smiled. 'I've seen the cultural centre and the park.'

'You should see the Swiss bank. They are running out of vaults.'

'How come? Are Filipino money men so generous?'

'Every businessman wants to set foot inside the Malacañang Palace.' Fernandez shrugged. 'The tickets come high.'

'What about the President? Is he as expensive as his wife?' Peter remembered what Harris has told him.

'Marcos is a philosopher – a philosopher king. He grabbed total power and he will do anything to cling on to it. Like Hitler, he would take us all down with him to destruction rather than give up what he has stolen.' Fernandez' voice thrilled to its own rhetoric.

'I'm sure there's some truth in what you say, Mr. Fernandez.' Peter was discomforted by the deep conviction of the journalist. Dare Peter push the argument any further? 'But could it be that your judgement is premature? Isn't it a little early to judge the regime? Perhaps you are exaggerating the danger.'

Fernandez slowly got to his feet. 'Embarrassed that this shop-window of Western values is beginning to look a bit soiled?' Fernandez moved to the darkest corner of the room. There was the sound of a closed door opening.

'One thing more you will not print, Mr. Nicholson.' Peter felt a cool breeze creep across the floor. 'If Marcos found me, he would have me killed.' The voice was calm. 'How's that for exaggeration, Mr. Nicholson?' Then he was gone.

Chapter Sixteen

'We cannot give a time frame within which martial law will be maintained or martial law will be terminated, because martial law was imposed out of necessity and this necessity was generated by the existence of a political organisation in the country very different from what we have known.'

Peter's arm was beginning to ache from holding out the tiny microphone but the handsome Filipino was just getting into his verbal stride.

'The purpose of this ideology is to destroy our existing social, political and economic order and supplant it with a new one, probably based on the Moscow, Peking, Cuban or North Korean models or any other such models known in the Socialist world today.'

Peter's attention wavered. The old 'reds under the beds' argument. How weary it all sounded. Hadn't Enrile heard of détente? The Cold War was all but over, never to return. Beyond the narrow confines of the Philippines, people were discussing multi-polarity; the new role of China; the gradual expiry of the Vietnam conflict. But here it was again; the good old 'East-West confrontasi'.

As Peter's mind drifted, he considered his interviewee. This was Juan Ponce Enrile; said by his supporters to be the second most important political figure in the Philippines – although Virata, the man in charge of finance, might feel inclined to disagree.

Like Marcos, Enrile was a lawyer and obviously relished presenting his own cases. Enrile or Virata? Or indeed, might not the future 'widow Marcos' take control of the reins of government, along with everything else? The President was rumoured to be unwell. While Peter's thoughts drifted, Enrile was unfolding arguments for the prosecution.

'...they went even further. They created a military force, known as the New People's Army, and this army had its own regulars, consisting of young men trained as soldiers and armed with modern weapons.'

Peter glanced down at the glossy press photo he had been given of Enrile holding one of a cache of forty-millimetre rockets. Must remember to ask who supplies the arms...

(If Enrile will allow any space for questions.)

'...the bulk of the main part of the Communist Party of the Philippines is still there and we have to dismantle it slowly and gradually and that is what we are doing now.'

Peter and Hal had taken Isabel's advice to carry their passports with them to her party. They had been stopped on their way back to the resort by metrocom police at three-thirty that morning. After a perfunctory inspection of the little blue books, they had been waved through the road-block. Peter had felt fine at eight when Chico had woken him with a knock on the door. The shower had been invigorating and the smell of the garlic eggs not as invasive as usual.

Their journey to Camp Crame had concluded with a warm reception from Major Alvarez. Their wait had lasted for a mere five minutes before they were ushered into the inner sanctum, a large, sunlit, airy office. There, the young Secretary of National Defence had bandied politesse for a further three minutes; consulted his watch and suggested they begin. Peter noticed that Enrile's lips had settled into inactivity. As he raised the microphone to his own lips, he shifted his chair closer to Enrile's desk.

'If one considers the Philippines today, you have instituted a dictatorship.' Enrile blinked once. Peter took a breath and pressed on. 'A benign dictatorship, under martial law. Your new reforms are regarded elsewhere in the region as socialistic – (Enrile's eyes flickered and Peter hastened to qualify his remarks) mildly socialistic – land reform programmes, educational reforms – various programmes which would not be out of place in a socialist country. Are you stealing the weapons of the Communists before they can use them?'

Peter could sense a tension elsewhere in the room, somewhere behind him. He knew that Hal was back there with Major Alvarez and another nameless officer. Peter held his breath and only exhaled as he heard Enrile's opening repartee.

'I agree that here in the Philippines we have established what we call 'constitutional authoritarianism'. In other words, a unitary, centralised political structure.'

Enrile leaned back and placed his fingertips together. 'Perhaps you will respond with: "What is the difference between a dictatorship of the Left and your present system?".'

Enrile did not really require an interlocutor. He could play all the parts. He leaned forward and rested his forearms on the desks. 'It is really a simple question of time. While the Communists want to establish a permanent dictatorship, the Marcos' regime is but a step on the road to democracy. Call it a 'temporary expedient'.'

The explication of the details of this temporary expedient unwound in the warm sunshine entering the room via the windows. Peter gripped his microphone arm in his left hand and felt the throb of his pulse. The monologue wound its way through the details for twenty more minutes without the benefit of any further questions from the interviewer. Peter was numb in arm and brain. Enrile rose to his feet. Peter did likewise. Behind him chairs scraped the floor. Peter could barely feel his 'victim's' handshake. As he slowly re-wound the microphone cord, Peter noticed that Enrile and the majors were smiling and nodding to one another. They spoke in Tagalog. Peter lifted the canvas hold-all to exchange the recorder for his wide-angle camera.

'Would you mind if I took a couple of shots, Mr. Secretary?'

Enrile made a quip about preferring cameras to guns. Peter smiled. It was always the guys at the top who were the most informative and charming – once you had penetrated their protective girdle.

He set the aperture at F4. He dropped back a pace and half-crouched. Enrile looked impressive behind the big desk decorated with toy Filipino flags. Peter knew the first shot was fine but fired off two more for good luck. He stood upright, capped the lens and waved his free hand.

'That's it; all over.'

'Well, I hope you got what you wanted.' Enrile's smile was

broad.

'Certainly, Sir,' Peter oleaginated. 'If only all statesmen were so forthright.'

Enrile's smile broadened. 'That's because we have nothing to hide.'

'Nothing?' Peter smiled in return.

'Nothing.' Enrile remained good-humoured but Peter sensed the unknown major had come closer and was examining Peter closely. Enrile's right arm swept in an arc.

'We say to the world's press, come and look, whenever and wherever you like.'

Peter returned the camera to the bag. He did not look at Enrile as he asked, 'Does that 'wherever' include Mindanao?' A brief pause before Peter added, 'The areas where the Moros are fighting?'

Enrile's smile never faltered. Peter wondered uneasily whether he had not pushed things far too far.

'You wish to go to Mindanao?' Enrile asked slowly, looking Peter in the eye. Hoist on his own petard. Peter nodded. Enrile turned to Major Alvarez. 'Arrange it, Major.' Alvarez bit his lower lip. Enrile looked back at Peter. 'You will be taken there by military escort.' Enrile smiled and spread his hands, as if to say, 'You see how open we are and how powerful I am.' Peter took the proffered hand. Enrile's grip was firm and cool. 'Have a pleasant trip.'

Enrile turned away. They had been dismissed.

Chico drove the Englishmen directly to Augustin Enterprises. There, he escorted them into the funereal office.

'Well?' The little man in the inevitable grey silk suit rose to his feet behind the desk.

Peter hoisted his carry-all onto the chair beside him. 'I think it went well.' He undid the canvas flaps and retrieved the recorder. He depressed the rewind button. He held his breath. The hissing of the tape went on and on. Shit. He had forgotten to check whether the recording had worked. More crackles and hiss. Peter's tension grew. Then the first words came. It was his own voice, testing the machine. More crackles and hiss. Then the relief and embarrassment of hearing his own first protracted 'question'. His nerves untangled. He reached to switch off the machine but Agustin impatiently waved him away.

Peter and Hal were obliged to listen to a re-run of the entire interview. Peter was almost as bored as Hal. He came to just as he and Enrile embarked on the Mindanao section of the interview.

Agustin's face sank back into shadow as Enrile enlarged on his analysis of the problems down in the South. Enrile moved smoothly from North Cotabato to Basilan Island, Zamboanga and the province of Sulu.

'We face the depredations of these Muslim outlaws who defy the government by refusing to surrender their arms. I should like to assure you that, contrary to some inaccurate reports, that the situation in Mindanao is not serious enough to cause me to lose any sleep at night. We have approximately ten percent of our military committed in Mindanao where, we estimate, there are between four and five thousand outlaws.'

Agustin's frowning face re-entered the pool of light and Peter pressed 'pause'.

Hal was also frowning. 'You mean, it might be dangerous down there?' Hal had clearly not paid attention to the original interview. He was now very attentive.

'Who for? The Moros or the army?' Peter asked.

'No,' Hal almost shouted. 'For us.'

For the first time, Agustin seemed displeased. Very displeased.

The old man snapped, 'What is all this?'

Hal snorted, 'This stupid bugger has got Enrile to agree to take us down to Minda-bloody-whatsit, that's all.'

Agustin's fists clenched. 'When are you due to go?'

Peter replied as calmly as he could, 'I'm not entirely sure. Major Alvarez has been asked to arrange transport.'

'It cannot happen,' Augustin snapped. He paused and then resumed. 'It cannot happen until after your return from the mine.' Agustin's lips were compressed in a tight line. He rose into darkness. His invisible voice continued, 'I have arranged for a plane to take you up to the Agustin mine tomorrow. And when you go, you must be prepared for an overnight stay.' He resumed his seat. 'There is too much cloud for you to fly back in the afternoon.'

Peter experienced a sense of relief. Deep relief. The Moros in Zamboanga were little better than pirates. Islam was just a pretext to attack unbelievers and unwary travellers and either hold them for ransom or kill them outright. He shrugged.

'Perhaps in the circumstances, Mr. Augustin, you would be kind enough to make a brief call to Major Alvarez, explaining…' His voice dribbled away into silence.

But if Enrile was half as displeased by the interview as Agustin clearly was, Peter could see he had placed the entire enterprise in jeopardy. For what? Amour-propre? Enrile hadn't needed a demonstration of Peter's superficial researches into the archipelago. Hal came to the rescue.

''Ere, what about the purse lady?' Agustin released his hands before clasping them once more.

'No word yet.' The little man rose irritably from behind his desk. It was the turn of the red silk tie today, enlivened by a solitaire diamond. 'You must be prepared to go to the Malacañang at a moment's notice.'

Seeing Agustin's agitation, Peter asked, 'Look. Mr. Augustin. Would you prefer me to ring Major Alvarez about Mindanao?'

Agustin frowned. 'No, I will arrange things. You go to the mine tomorrow. I know that the Pirst Lady is receiving important visitors from America for the next two days.' He drew himself up to his full height. The solitaire flashed in the light. 'The Fords.'

As the two Englishmen blinked their way back into the sunlight, Hal turned on Peter. 'Are you tryin' to get us killed, you stupid bugger?'

Peter eased his way into the Pontiac and stretched out along the length of the back seat. He yawned – sleepy but contented. Chico swung the big, green vehicle into the traffic.

'I wonder how Agustin gets his kicks.' Peter put the question to the roof of the car and yawned once more. He was reacting to a close call. He now realised he had not the least desire to visit Zamboanga. In fact, if he never came within a hundred miles of the pirate lair, it would be too close. He yawned extravagantly for a third time. 'God, I'm bushed. I'm for bed when we get back.'

Hal sniffed. 'Hil's not gonna be pleased to copy all that bloody guff you got from Enrile.' His face contorted as though he had smelt something noxious. Peter, remembering the lengthy oration, had to admit (albeit silently) that while the interview had been prestigious, 'sexy' it was not.

'Alvarez told me that *Time* was interviewing Enrile last week.'

Hal had heard of *Time*. Peter grinned. 'How does it feel to be playing in the big league?'

'I'm in the big league already.' Hal displayed his teeth. 'At least, I'll be in it this afternoon – with a bit of luck.' The display widened.

Peter yawned again. 'God, how do you keep it up?'

'With stickin' plaster.' Hal squeezed Peter's knee.

'I'd need alabaster.' Peter's quip made Hal laugh. The West Countryman looked up at Chico's reflection in the mirror and lowered his voice.

'Mind you, this is what you might call combinin' business with pleasure. You remember that poof designer at the party? '

Peter struggled without success to remember a designer of any sexual affiliation.

'You remember, 'Hal insisted. 'The one with the tiny bum in the tiger-skin trews.' Hal waggled an impatient finger. 'The one that wanted to dance with me.'

'Who would lead?'

'Yeah, ha-ha. Well, he's agreed to bring some of 'is models up to these falls of theirs…'ere Chico, what's the name of them falls?'

'Pagsanjan?'

'Yeah, that's it. Isabel reckons we ought to get some shots of the crumpet bumpin' down the rapids. She reckons the poofter is the 'comin' thing'.' Hal leered.

'Suppose we're up at the mine or down in Mindanao,' Peter pointed out, testily.

'That's O.K. Isabel can take a few snaps.' Hal looked pleased. 'And if they come out O.K., we'll put one or two in the mag.'

'Why stop there?' Peter sat up. 'Why not invite Maria to write a couple of thoughts on the 'Secrets of the Sauna'?' Chico half-turned. Peter smiled at the mirror and shrugged apologetically.

'There's no need to get aeriated, Peter, me old mate.' Hal was all conciliation. 'It'll be all right. Isabel's got a camera just like yours.'

Peter allowed his head to fall back against the seat. 'I could sleep for a week.'

'You sleep all you want.' Hal patted Peter's knee. 'Just as long as you're up in time for the Ambassador's party at eight.'

Hal shook Peter awake as they arrived at the resort. Nigel received them at the top of the stairs. In shorts and flip-flops he was not an affecting sight.

'Hi, Nigel.' Peter greeted his partner, 'How's the tum?'

'None the better for your asking.' Would the reason for his peevishness become clear? 'Thanks for poking your miserable heads round the door in my hour of need.'

'You've got 'you-know-who' to look after your needs, Nige.' Hal said, with a grin.

''You-know-who' hasn't been near me for the past two days.' Nigel grimaced. 'I've had Marcos's revenge.' Nigel fondled his stomach. 'I might have died for all anyone cared.'

'I'm sorry, Nigel.' Peter yawned. 'But I really will keel over unless you let me get to my bed.'

'I suppose this fatigue is the result of all the hard work you're doing.' Nigel was refusing to give ground.

'Cheer up, Nige, me old mate.' Hal patted Nigel's flabby bicep. 'We're all off to a nice party later.'

Nigel looked dubious. Hal squeezed past him onto the balcony. 'Don't worry, Nige. They've got plenty of loos.'

Nigel finally gave ground and Peter stumbled past. As he opened his door, the last thing he heard was Nigel's plaint. 'It's all that fucking garlic.'

When Peter awoke, the rain was falling from a leaden sky and thrashing across the balcony in irritable squalls. Peter's skin felt sticky. He was sure his breath smelt cloacal. He looked at the time. Six thirty. It must have been eleven or so when he'd fallen face down on the bed that morning. He should have felt refreshed but refreshment eluded him. He reached out and groped for the phone. A loud, husky voice asked him what he wanted. Quietly, 'sans mot dire' he replaced the receiver.

Some indeterminate time later the phone rang shrilly. His first call. He lifted the receiver.

'You call me?' the same husky voice demanded.

'No,' Peter licked his lips. 'No, it was a mistake.'

He was beginning to feel that the whole wretched business was a mistake.

He was always at his most vulnerable during the first minutes after waking. He looked down at the pressure point. Was he to be trapped by his own reflexes? He had never been even remotely interested in 'ladies of the night'. He would follow the sound advice of his P.T. master at school (he of the muscular limbs and jutting jaw). 'Look after your own needs.' Peter swung himself off the bed and strode purposefully towards the shower.

The shower was not at the recommended temperature for such douching but nevertheless he felt more in control of himself under the tepid waterfall. Tunelessly, he attempted 'the Toreador Song'. Balking at the top note, he stopped the flow of water and concentrated on a brisk rubdown with the rough towel.

Peter stepped back into the bedroom. His towel was rapidly deployed. His 'Carmen' stood in the doorway, looking as if she had been blown into the room. The eternal cotton dress was almost unrecognisable. It had been drenched and clung possessively to the curves of the slim body. Unfortunately for Peter's resistance, what had been formerly hidden was now clearly delineated beneath the sodden material. The legs and hips were still 'boyish' but the chest was no longer shapeless. For no reason he could discern, he mumbled, 'I have to go out soon.'

The girl simply stared at him. Water rivuletted down either side of her face. Peter lowered his eyes. Further aqueous streams descended the girl's legs, forming puddles around the rubber shoes. Peter could not risk arranging his towel into a more formal skirt. He retained the damp bundle. The girl shivered.

'You'll catch a chill. Look, there's another towel in there.' He pointed at the shower room. 'Go and dry your hair at least.' He resorted to dumb-show.

The child passed him in silence. Peter shivered as a cool current of air brushed his still damp skin. How on earth could he get rid of the girl without hurting her feelings?

As Peter reached for his clean shirt, she returned, her head swathed in an elegant white turban. Peter felt his teeth chatter. It really was quite cool tonight. The girl's body trembled and she contracted her shoulders.

'Look,' Peter pointed a thumb over a shoulder. 'You go and have a nice, hot shower.' The girl looked uncertain. Peter pointed. 'Go on. Do as I tell you.'

Wordlessly, the slim figure turned, the hands unknotting the turban as she disappeared into the shower room.

Peter dashed for the door of his room and yanked it open. A full-frontal squall threw him back against the outside wall. In two seconds, his protective towel was soaked. He rolled along the wall and tried Miguel's door. It was locked. Trust Miguel to have a door with a lock. Woe betide his prisoner.

Another gust took Peter in the rear. He shook his wet hair and yelled against the furies.

'Come on, you little bugger. Open up.'

Instantly the door was opened a fraction. Judging by the height of the brown eye from the floor, it had to be the captive girl. Her eye and the gap widened. The gale took its opportunity and Peter was injected into the room.

The bulging Bacchus was cross-legged on the bed; tousle-haired, bleary-eyed and naked – an overweight cupidon. A corner of the bedsheet represented the sole concession to delicacy.

'Hi, Pete,' Miguel waggled a toe to accompany the greeting. 'Long time no see.'

'Been busy,' Peter responded, eager to escape as quickly as possible.

'I know. Pop told me.' Miguel's smile informed Peter that Agustin had not spared his ghastly offspring the minutest detail.

'Look, Miguel. I'm sorry to barge in on you like this...' He addressed the kimono-clad girl. What the hell was she called?

'Quita.' Miguel grinned, recognising the reason for Peter's perplexity.

Peter nodded. 'Quita.' He swallowed. 'Miguel, I have a favour I want to ask you.' Miguel turned to the captive and rattled out a gabble of rapid Tagalog. Her expression was enigmatic as she drew the robe round her, turned and opened a well-worn drawer. Her hand disappeared into its recesses. When withdrawn, the hand clutched a bright yellow capsule.

Peter and Quita avoided each other's eyes as the exchange was effected. Peter's hand enfolded the capsule and he watched Quita disappear into the shower-room. There was a brief pause.

Peter started. His nameless girl would be out of the shower by now, sans towel. His own towel clung to his thighs.

He closed his fingers around the capsule. His absurd qualms had tortured him long enough. His abstinence punished the girl and himself.

'Thanks, Miguel.' He turned to go.

'Hey, Pete. You got to take the capsule in the morning if you want pucking at night. Protection takes time.' He drew more of the sheet over his genitalia.

Peter's stomach lurched. 'I know,' he mumbled. Peter could hear the gods chuckling. All this screwing up of courage to the sticking point, only to discover the point had been blunted.

Peter scurried out of the dionysiac cell, protecting his protection from the elements. His wind-assisted re-entry was alarmingly swift. He fought to hold the door against the fury of the wind. He turned, breathing hard, and leaned back to resist the elements.

Naturally, the girl was nowhere to be seen. While he had been gone, so had she. Peter was relieved and, simultaneously, disappointed. Still clasping the precious capsule, he squelched towards the bathroom. As he was about to step inside, he saw the crumpled wreck of the familiar dress, abandoned on the damp tiles.

'Hello?' he called. There was the slightest reverberation. Something was dripping. The girl's head appeared from behind the doorway. She looked apprehensive. He wondered what had produced such apprehension. Then he recalled Miguel. Could he also be a client? His stomach lurched.

'Wait.' Peter rummaged in his portmanteau. He found his remaining clean, casual shirt and handed it to the girl. 'Here. You put this on.'

As the girl relieved him of the shirt, he turned his back and hurried to don his own fresh clothes. Why did he keep his back to the bathroom for the final zipping operation?

When he turned to face the shower, he beheld one of the familiar shirt advertisements. One girl, one shirt. So banal.

Yet, seeing the child's legs at full length added glamour to their slimness. Her damp hair clung in waves around the delicate face with its luminous eyes.

Peter made a show of conferring with his watch. 'I must leave soon.' He extended his wrist to aid her understanding. The girl frowned and inspected her bare toes. She understood.

'Sit down,' Peter commanded. She lowered herself gingerly onto the edge of a chair. 'Are you warm?'

The girl nodded. Did her silences betoken shyness, taciturnity or, simple simple-mindedness?

'How old are you?'

She looked up at him. 'Nineteen.' She rubbed her nose with the back of her hand.

He winced as he realised that the girl was barely half his age. And she might be even younger. Surely, even in the Philippines, sex with minors had to be proscribed. Was her age a falsehood too?

She rubbed her nose with the back of a hand. Winsome. Was that the word to describe her? But with every word or gesture he felt his anticipation ebb. He had never felt the need to indulge in mercantile sex in the U.K. and even less in Hong Kong. Now, with every word they exchanged, his desire slackened

If he really wanted his yellow pill to fulfil its destiny, he should keep the verbiage to a minimum and concentrate on the corporeal. Perhaps he found this tantalising self-torture more engaging than 'the real thing'.

'Why do you work here?' A prize-winner in asinine questions.

Did he expect her to respond that her hobby was masturbating businessmen? The cotton dress should have told him all he needed to know. She probably had a well-rehearsed hard-luck story.

The girl interrupted her perusal of her delicate foot.

'My family in Tondo need money. My mother is sick.'

Peter waited but no further details were forthcoming. The girl raised her leg to scratch the ankle. Peter blinked. He inspected his own toes then looked up.

'How did you get the job?' From Enrile to this anonymous massage girl. All in a day's in-depth reportage.

'Maria help me get the job.' The girl caught Peter's eye and smiled. 'Maria is my cousin.'

Now it only needed Chico to announce that he was related to Agustin to complete the vicious circle.

'But you can't like doing this job.' Peter curled his lip as he made the statement.

The reply was eager. 'Oh, yes. This is good job. Good money, nice room, good food.'

Yet another unreported detail of life in the colourful Philippines. Her left hand tinkered with the second button of the shirt.

He hesitated over the next question. 'Is it part of your job to go to bed with clients?' Was this Peter's latest attempt at aversion therapy?

The girl shook her head vigorously, Of course that was not part of her job, she assured him. Somehow, Peter could not imagine her and her clients completing the Times crossword together.

'No.' She frowned. 'Only give hand-job.' He decided to forego any questions about sinistrality or dexterity.

'You do this for everybody?' Peter fought to retain his urbanity.

'No,' she replied, her frown deepening. 'Only with men.'

Peter was surprised into loud laughter. This evoked banging on the party wall shared with Miguel's room.

The girl stared at Peter, pleasantly bemused by his amusement. The wind still strove to penetrate the window, which shuddered in its frame.

Peter continued to smile at the girl. 'Good for you... what is your name?'

'My name is Miranda.'

Peter Caliban rose and moved towards the girl. She lowered her head. He pressed his lips against the meeting-point of the peak of her hair and her forehead. He about-turned and left her sitting on her chair. He entered the shower-room.

He ran the cold water in the sink and rinsed the plastic cup. He raised his hand and gently placed the warm capsule on his tongue. He gagged before the obstruction was finally swallowed. He considered his reflection in the mirror for a second before returning to the bedroom. The girl sat with both knees raised below her chin. Peter's heart raced. Of course, the sexual interlude had to be effectively concluded by a loud banging at Peter's door.

'Come on, Pete, it's pissin' down out 'ere.' Hal's footsteps ran along the balcony before descending.

Peter bit his lower lip as he slipped on his moccasins, watched attentively by Miranda. He drew on the inadequate jacket. He could almost hear Hal execrating in the car. He held out his fingers and brushed Miranda's lips. He smiled to reassure her. 'You wait?'

She nodded.

Peter smiled again. 'I shall return.' He eased the door open. 'General Macarthur' he quipped, 'when he was leaving the Philippines during World War Two.' He slammed the door behind him and raced down the sodden steps to the car.

Chapter Seventeen

Even the big Pontiac was being buffeted to one side by fierce gusts of wind on their journey into town.

'Well, looks like the little poofter's come up with the models.' Hal beamed back at Peter and Nigel.

'What little poofter?' Nigel asked, his tone aggrieved.

Peter explained. 'A designer that Hal met at Isabel's. And he's arranged to lay on a photo session at the Pagsanjan Falls tomorrow.'

''Ere, how did you know it was tomorrow?' Hal seemed genuinely bemused.

'Because tomorrow's the day I'm due to go to the mine.' He made a moue. 'I know where I'd rather be going.'

'The old boy said it was the only time they could manage.' Hal almost sounded apologetic but fell short. 'Don't worry, Pete. Nige can take my place tomorrow.'

Nigel stirred uneasily in the wine-coloured velvet jacket with matching bow tie. 'I don't know whether I would be up to it, old fruit.'

'You've been up to it ever since we got 'ere.' Hal grinned and dropped a heavy hand on Nigel's knee.

The windscreen wipers struggled to cope with the deluge. As he stared into the beam of the headlights, Peter remembered the girl who awaited his return back at the resort. He settled lower in his seat.

'What's the matter with you, Nige? Don't you 'ave any curiosity about this marvellous country? There's more to it than things that go bump in the night.' Hal frowned at Nigel. Peter noted how the silhouette of Chico's shoulders shifted.

Hal's tone hardened. 'All you've done since we got 'ere is eat, drink, screw and puke. And complain.' Hal's tone shifted to one of sentimental regret. 'I always thought there was more to you than that, Nige. I took you for a man of culture and refinement. I really looked up to you. Really.'

Nigel's face engaged in a titanic struggle between remorse and irritation. Character won through in the end.

'What about you?' Nigel demanded with not a little belligerence. 'You've done likewise. Only, even more likewise. In larger doses.'

Peter shifted uneasily in his seat. The choice of words was infelicitous, to say the least.

Hal glanced across at Chico. 'That's a bit off, Nige.'

Nigel decided to foreclose on further discussion. 'I'll see how I feel in the morning.'

The conversation concluded with the death of a chicken which had unwisely decided to confront the Pontiac. They listened to the fowl bump along beneath the wheels. The journey was completed in respectful silence.

Arrived at the Hyatt, they dashed through the downpour to reach the lobby. As usual, Hubler was in attendance. Peter's stock rose with his partners as he introduced the coutured young American.

'How are you guys getting along?' Hubler smiled as he addressed the question to Peter.

'Fine.' Peter could not resist boasting. 'Enrile gave us an interview this morning.'

Hubler gave Peter an 'I-am-impressed' look and nodded.

'Yeah,' Hal interrupted. 'He said it was the best interview he ever 'ad.' Hubler extended his admiration. ''E said it was better than the one 'e'd 'ad with *Time* last week.'

Hubler offered a round of liquid celebratory salutations.

Nigel placed a protective hand over his cummerbund. 'Just Perrier Water for me.' He winced. 'Gyppy tummy.'

'Yeah, make mine the same.' Hal patted his stomach and gave Hubler a rueful grimace. 'Antibiotics.'

'Well, let's make it 'three of a kind',' Peter smiled.

The waiter arrived. 'Four Perriers' please.' Hubler ordered.

Hal got back on his feet. 'There they are.' Hal hurried to greet the girls. Hubler turned in his chair to view the newcomers.

'Isabel Castillas and the Noval sisters.' He looked back at Nigel and Peter and nodded appreciatively. 'Things are clearly going very well.'

The men clambered to their feet. Hal returned, cupping an elbow in either hand.

A bizarre sheen covered Isabel's face. Her plum-coloured cocktail dress was overpowered by the pink and white silk of the pouting sisters.

Isabel effected the introductions. 'Filomena and Conchita.' Peter did the honours for the masculine contingent. He and Hubler brought more chairs. While the women waited, Hal and Nigel resettled in their own seats.

Hal waved at the other places. 'Make yourselves at home.' An 'h' mysteriously made an appearance in honour of the nubile visitors.

As the three women perched, Hal flicked a peanut into his mouth. He extended a handful of nuts as an offering to Filomena-in-pink. 'Excuse fingers.' Hubler did the honours for Conchita-in-white. Nigel served himself a damp handful of nuts. He tried to toss one into his mouth, missed the target and failed to stop the projectile disappearing into the folds of his jacket.

As the waiter arrived with four small bottles of Perrier and the associated glasses, Peter turned to Isabel.

'Well, Mr. Journalist.' She began. 'How was our honoured Secretary of National Defence?

'Fine.' Peter poured Perrier. 'Did Fernandez get away all right?'

'Sure.' She concentrated on Hubler who was taking the ladies' orders. The sisters ordered discreet vodkas and tonic. Isabel demanded a scotch-on-the-rocks.

'What's your connection with Fernandez?' Peter murmured.

Isabel shrugged. 'A friend.'

Peter moved closer, lowering his voice. 'Not a cousin?'

Isabel was puzzled. Peter sipped his drink. 'He's a bit tough on Marcos and the Pirst Lady.' Peter was going native.

'Nobody could be too tough on her. She's as tough as...' She glanced down before kicking the chromed steel hoop which supported one side of the table. Glasses tinkled and hands reached out. 'She's tougher than that.' The other drinkers relaxed.

'You're pretty tough too. On women.'

Isabel relieved Peter of his glass; took a sip; grimaced and handed the offensive drink back. 'Only some women.'

Peter glanced at his watch. 'Shouldn't we be leaving?'

'Oh, it's only the Spanish Ambassador's. Nobody will arrive before nine.'

The waiter brought Isabel her scotch. She took two deep draughts. 'Got a cigarette?' She extended a peremptory hand out towards Peter. He produced his Pall Mall. He must start rationing. 'You really smoke this shit?' Peter solemnly fixed a cylinder of that description between his lips.

Isabel clicked her fingers at the waiter who was inclined over Conchita-in-white. She glanced upward. 'Bring me a packet of Rothman King-size.'

Peter zipped his Zippo. Isabel reached across and relieved him of the lighter. She traced the enamel emblem on the case with a nail.

'U.S.S. Constellation,' she read aloud. 'I didn't know you were a sailor.'

'It was a present from an American sailor in a bar in Wanchai.' Peter weighed the lighter in his hand. 'Now it's my turn to ask a question.'

Isabel raised an eyebrow. 'Well?'

'What's this all about?'

'What is 'this'? She responded, echoing his tour d'horizon around the lobby.

'This. All this. The international hotels, the big parties in the big houses. Would you really be happy to see all those things disappear?' The waiter arrived with the English cigarettes. Isabel neatly ripped open the cellophane wrapper.

'All that is nothing to me.' Isabel accepted his light. 'I have no freedom. No money. I would be more free in Tondo.' She exhaled a thin stream of smoke. Peter noticed that she was a wet smoker. 'My father has all the money. My mother tells him what to do with it.'

'Does that matter? The rich use credit – not money.' Peter thought that a neat 'bon mot'.

Isabel scoffed. 'Credit? Not *that* much. She clicked her fingers. 'Not even from a Chinese village store.' She clicked her left thumbnail. 'Thanks to that fucking woman.'

Peter checked to see whether the execration had reached the ears of the others. He smiled. 'That's no way to talk about the woman who gave birth to you.'

Isabel spoke slowly and deliberately. 'I wish she was dead. Then I could get a chance to live.'

Peter leaned back, dismayed by the girl's vehemence.

Peter felt his partner's breath warming his left ear. Hal's voice broke the mood.

'I 'ope there's some nice, slow dancin' at this party. This bird's knockers are making my fingers itch.'

Peter's laughed at the sheer incongruity of his two interlocutors.

Finally, there came a general post and Hubler was left alone as the rueful possessor of the bill.

Outside the hotel the wind had all but died away. The only evidence of the earlier storm lay in puddles at their feet and the glistening sheen of car roofs. Chico flicked his cigarette away. It fizzled out.

'We will all go in my car,' Isabel commanded in a voice which carried. Chico closed the door he had only just opened on the Pontiac. Peter was the last to enter the Cadillac. He gave Chico a rueful wave as the Agustin driver watched the black limousine slip into the traffic.

Isabel was between the driver and Hal. Peter and Nigel flanked the sisters on the back seat. The fit was comfortingly tight. Peter was all too aware of the tension in Conchita's thigh pressed against his.

'So, what do you do, Conchita?' Peter asked, just to remind the girl of his existence.

The girl looked puzzled. 'Do?'

It struck Peter that she might very well still be a student.

'How old are you?' Peter asked, smiling. The girl, he noted, was twice Miranda's size.

'It is not good manners to ask a lady her age.' Conchita replied, mock offended.

'Let me guess.' His thigh was pressed even harder against hers. Who was doing the pressing? 'Eighteen?'

'Hey, how did you guess?' She half turned towards him. He was beginning to appreciate the car's air-conditioning. He lowered his voice. 'I know because I am a gypsy. With a crystal ball.'

'Oh,' she exclaimed. 'I bet you're not a gypsy. You don't act like a gypsy.'

Peter smiled and kissed the girl on the tip of her nose. 'Heeeey!' she objected, rearing back in revulsion. Her bosom heaved.

'Hey,' she complained. 'You kissed my nose.' Peter nodded in earnest agreement with her statement. 'Hey,' Conchita repeated. She complained to Isabel, 'He kissed my nose.'

'So? Kiss him back.' Isabel drawled. The girl recoiled at this depravity

Nigel, encouraged by these developments, slid his hand round Filomena's shoulders.

Conchita turned on Peter. 'You! You are just a masher!'

Peter resisted the temptation to laugh aloud at this archaic slang. At the same, he was peripherally aware of Conchita's white bosom.

Within minutes of arriving at the gathering, Peter settled Conchita with a drink and scuttled off.

The Ambassador's mansion was even more impressive than Isabel's had been. To begin with, it was bathed in light.

Isabel linked arms with Peter for a guided tour of what proved to be an expensive and extensive collection of art, ancient and modern.

Peter identified two well-executed and rather gruesome 17th century Ribera oils. He preferred the nearby Japanese ceramics

In a corner of the reception room wide doors opened onto a garden of romantic profusion. The shadowy shrubbery evoked a desire in Isabel to deploy Peter's Zippo. He shielded the flame as she inhaled.

'Who are all these people?'

As she drew her first lungful of smoke, she turned and surveyed the assembled guests with frank distaste.

'Mostly Filipino businessmen and their wives. Wait. I can see two mistresses.' She pointed to their right. 'Those guys are oilmen. Americans.' She peered at the crowd. 'No, no there. There.' She pointed at a tall, well-built, middle-aged man with brutally short hair.

Peter nodded. 'Now, which one is the Spanish Ambassador?'

Isabel drew on her Rothman. 'He's not here.'

'I don't see why a Spanish ambassador should be important in the Philippines of 1973,' Peter said with a shrug. 'What's Spain's interest?'

'Spain?' Isabel looked at Peter and smiled.

'Yes. The country the Ambassador represents.'

Isabel laughed aloud. 'No, Peter. Not the Ambassador from Spain. The Ambassador *to* Spain.' She could see that the joke had gone far enough. 'Among the Ilustrados it is still the most prized position in the diplomatic service. They get to speak Spanish.' Isabel pulled a face.

'But if he's the Ambassador to Spain, what's he doing here in Manila? On home leave?' Peter knew that, in pursuing this hare, he was probably being more than a little naive.

'Leave? The guy hasn't been in Madrid for twenty years.' Isabel raised a cupped hand to her mouth.

'And yet he is still known as the Spanish Ambassador?' Peter was perplexed. 'So, what does he do in Manila?'

'This.' Isabel broad gesture encompassed the congregation. 'He's rich as shit.'

As decorous music began to make itself heard, Isabel led Peter through the horde and back to their little group. As they arrived, Hal swept Filomena onto the parquet floor, drew here bosom to his and closed enraptured eyes.

The businessmen, their wives and mistresses, turned their eyes to the floor show. Peter decided to pursue his tour of the mansion. At a point when the music was barely audible, Peter glimpsed the glimmer of ormolu. He slipped inside the door of the smaller room where he was greeted by an exquisite Empire credenza.

Hands on knees, he bent to inspect the piece.

'Nice. Very nice.'

Peter thought he recognised the slightly hoarse American accent. Peter turned. In a corner sat Fred Harris, his bulk jammed into a large overstuffed armchair. He was looking quizzically at Peter.

'My, you do move in the very best of circles, Mr. Nicholson,' Harris piped in an exaggerated imitation of a Southern belle.

'It's the only way I could be sure of resuming our conversation,' Peter joked, assuming an echoing pose in a twin armchair.

Harris raised a glass to his lips. 'Alone?'

'No, I'm with a party.'

'Has your party added any vivacity to the existing party?' Harris raised an eyebrow and his glass.

'I'm afraid they are doing their damnedest.' Peter replied in a tone of regret.

'And how's the hunting? Happy?'

'Happy enough,' Peter replied, attempting modesty. 'I interviewed Enrile this morning.'

Harris compressed all three chins. He hoisted his glass in a mocking toast.

'Yes, the very best circles, Mr. Nicholson.'

Peter wished he had not abandoned his drink. Faute de mieux, he reached for a cigarette. Gasping, Harris accepted Peter's offer. As Peter deployed his lighter. Harris muttered around his cigarette. 'Get anything?' Harris was poor at pretending lack of interest.

'No.' Peter shook his head. Harris half-smiled into his glass as he drained another dram. 'But he did agree to give us the Grand Tour of Mindanao.'

Harris belched lightly. 'Did he offer or did you request?'

Peter shrugged and replied, 'You could say we met somewhere in the middle.'

'Good luck,' Harris raised his glass again. 'Just remember to duck.'

'Is it really that dangerous?' Being devoid of them, Peter

despised heroics. The fat man responded.

'Enough.'

Peter crossed his ankles. 'What's really behind this 'Moro' thing?'

'Well,' Harris began, adopting a more comfortable posture for disquisition. 'It goes back, as they say, "a long ways".'

'To when Marcos tried to take their guns away,' Peter interrupted.

Harris frowned. 'That was just the casus belli, if you like. No, like I said.' He peered over his rimless glasses at Peter. 'This story goes way back. Kinda familiar to Americans too.' He folded his hands round the glass and rested the whole on his embonpoint.

'As you know, the Philippines proudest boast is that it is the most populous Christian country in Asia... if you can count the Western Pacific as part of Asia. Well, when the Spanish first arrived, they got in cahoots with the local chiefs or whatever up North and pretty soon they'd catholicised most of Luzon and the Visayas. But the South was something else. While the Pope was busy dividing up the world between the Spanish and the Portuguese, Moslems had already moved into the South big time, moving up across the Sulu Sea from the Spice Islands.' Harris crinkled his nose. 'Cute names, ain't they?' He sniffed. 'Well, that was O.K. as long as there was enough room for Christians up North and Moslems way down South. But in the nineteenth century the Northerners began to trek towards the Equator.' He took a slug of whisky. 'I'm not boring you, Mr. Weekly?'

Peter shook his head.

'Well, pretty soon these Northerners run into the Muslims and offer to buy their land. They draw up contracts, all legal like. Sound familiar? Anyhow, the Moros put their mark to them and the Northerners settle in. Well, no sooner had they cleared the land and cultivated it and have this and that growing on it, than the Muslims come back down out of the mountains and say, 'Hey, you Christian landgrabbers – give us back what is ours. You hear?' Harris leaned towards Peter. 'You see, just like the Indians in the U.S. of A, these Moros didn't understand contracts and private ownership. Everything was held in common by the tribe (or whatever) and only Allah could take it from them.'

Peter nodded. Harris was an exemplary teacher. The fat man continued. 'We only lent you that land, Mr. Christian. Now, you just give it back, you hear?'

The mock-Southern accent was execrable. Harris resumed his normal American.

'Land, Mr. Nicholson, good old-fashioned dirt is at the bottom of this little war. That and the oil that may lie under the surrounding waters.' He sighed. 'Add to that a dash of political rivalry between the main groups down there. Plus, some eensy-weensy religious differences – plus and double plus, the Commies stirring up shit, and, there you go, Sweetie, dynamite. Then along moseys Martial I-am-the-law Marcos and says, 'Turn in your shootin' irons, boys.' The Moros figure that the President of all the Filipinos is really a Yankee in disguise. Besides, taking a Moro's gun is like cutting off his manhood.' The chins rested their case.

'Enrile says the government can handle the situation.' Peter hoped the chins would resume their wagging.

Harris grunted a laugh. 'What did you expect Enrile to say? 'The Moros are beating shit out of my guys?'

'But Enrile claims there are only a few thousand Moros and that they only commit ten percent of the army.'

'The numbers of men in the armed forces are a state secret.' Harris lowered his glass into his lap. 'My guess is that they're in deep doo-doo down South and that they're sending in more and more raw recruits.'

'And what about the number of Moros?' Peter realised his cigarette had died.

'Who knows? The number of guys with guns don't matter. For every guerrilla there's ten Muslim villagers ready to supply a hidey-hole or a papaya. And to keep their mouths shut when the army asks questions. Remember what Mao says about the fighters being the fish and the people the water in which the fish swim? It's different for the army though. For every soldier, they need ten more soldiers to supply the papayas – and they get all the logistic problems that go with an over-extended supply line in a war zone.'

Peter recollected the question he had failed to put to Enrile. 'Where do the Moros get their arms?'

Harris shrugged. 'Army surplus, left lying here and there. Or from friends across the Sulu Sea. There's a long tradition of smuggling and piracy South of Zamboanga. Enrile and Marcos play it down because they really don't want to internationalise the conflict.'

'The Russians?' Peter offered.

'The Russians nothing.' Harris wheezed forward, his expression confidential. 'The Arabs.'

'The Arabs? Which Arabs? Not the Saudis, surely?' Peter groped in his memory for shards of articles about Islamic ambitions in South-East Asia.

Harris's wheeze was amused. He placed his empty glass on the tribal rug beneath the chair. He twinkled at Peter. 'The Libyans.'

'Ah, so that's where you're hiding.' Isabel stared at Harris with frank curiosity. 'Don't I know you?'

The fat man strained to lift himself upright, surrendered to gravity and allowed his arms to fall on either side of the chair. 'Yes, we have met, Miss Castillas.'

'Is this business?' Isabel put the question to Peter. He nodded. Isabel sighed. 'O.K. I'll play waitress.'

Harris had his glass extended in the blink of an eye. 'Whisky sour.'

Peter smiled at the girl in plum. 'Gin and tonic, Miss.'

Isabel gave an ironic curtsey and departed,

Harris waited for the atmosphere to re-assemble then shook his head. 'Sad case.'

'What's so sad?' Peter reclined in his chair, 'Just another poor little rich girl.'

'Yeah, I suppose.' Harris was not usually so circumspect.

Peter mused aloud. 'Seems to really have it in for her mother.'

Harris agreed with a nod. 'And makes no secret of it.'

'How about Dad?'

'Weak eyes, knees and mind. But rich as Croesus. And the

kid's crazy about him.'

Harris accepted another Pall Mall.

'She makes Ma sound like a dragon.' Peter flicked the Zippo into flame.

'Ma just stops her from chasing the dragon.' Harris muttered round the clenched cigarette. Peter shuddered inwardly.

He failed to maintain his previous casual air. 'Are you saying that Isabel is an addict?'

'No. Not yet. Ma got to her just in time. Isabel was running with a fast crowd of American and Ilustrado kids - you know, trying to belong.' Harris coughed and swallowed.

'So, her mother prevented Isabel from belonging?'

'She always had.' Harris inhaled. Peter waited for the thin grey stream of smoke to appear. 'Isabel's mother is one hundred percent pure Chinese.'

Peter recalled the vision of the night before.

'Poison coming up,' Isabel announced, bearing three drinks on a tray. She bowed before Harris.

'Thanks, Miss Castillas.'

Peter held out an arm in readiness. Isabel swung the tray further away. 'No, Mr. Nicholson. If you want yours, you'll have to return to the party.'

She smiled. From this distance, Isabel almost looked pretty.

Peter stood. 'I'm sure Mr. Harris wouldn't want me to die of dehydration.'

Harris grimaced. 'O.K. leave. But I'm warning you. She'll be as gross as me one day.'

Isabel laughed, shook a clenched fist and left with the remaining two drinks.

Peter paused in the doorway. 'Thanks for the background information. Now here's some for you. Fernandez is O.K. I met him last night Amazingly, he's another friend of Isabel's.'

Peter wished he had remembered to bring a camera.

Chapter Eighteen

Hal and Filomena were no longer alone when Isabel and Peter rejoined the party. In fact, so many Filipino notables were now whirling wives or mistresses over the once polished parquet that the music had to raise its voice to be heard.

Peter invited Isabel to join the throng. As he drew her closer, he detected that she was wearing some kind of medicament on her skin. Was it an anti-acne cream? Then there was a slight collision and Peter limped apologetically around the tall, fair American.

Dancing resumed and Peter enjoyed the proximity of Isabel. How long had it been since he had held a woman in his arms? Even vertically. When he closed his eyes, he could picture Aggie. He kept the lids closed as he drew Isabel closer.

To his dismay, he realised that he was finding it difficult to conjure up Aggie's features. Then Isabel broke away. Peter opened his eyes to see the extempore dance floor emptying fast. He looked at his watch. It was nineteen minutes to twelve. Ancien Régime and New Technocracy hurried noisily to the limousines awaiting them outside the grand mansion. The race to beat the knell of curfew was without doubt the high point of the evening. One black American vehicle after another swept up to open its bat wings and admit fleeing guests, close to hysteria. Peter wondered who had rescued Harris but the rogue elephant had simply disappeared,

Hal appeared with Isabel. He was wiping his brow with a handkerchief. 'This is a bit of a laugh, Pete.' He grinned. Their Cadillac swung into position at the foot of the steps. Nigel steered Filomena firmly down the curved flight.

Peter leant towards Isabel. 'Shouldn't we say good night to our host?' Isabel threw a quick glance over her shoulder. The dense crowd was pressing forward. 'You must be joking,' she said with a grimace. They pursued Hal and Conchita towards the car.

Peter felt a slight pang of regret that he would now probably never meet the Spanish Ambassador. Why should the thought sadden him? Then he recollected the little office the Weekly was to occupy in Manila. The prospect cheered him. He looked up. The sky was by Munch out of Van Gogh.

Hal's voice jerked Peter back to present reality.

'Come on, if you don't wanna spend the bloody night in Camp Crame.'

'We'll drop the girls first,' Isabel announced. Masculine opinions were superfluous. Conchita yawned fit to bust. Peter made room for her hand to rise and cover the display. The girl was making a point of ignoring him. Filomena was reclining on Nigel's velvet shoulder. Isabel began humming 'The Girl from Ipancma'. Hal allowed his arm to drape itself around her shoulders. Peter sighed. Isabel hummed on.

After the third reprise, the car slid into the kerbside. Twenty yards on, a lantern lit a patch of white stucco wall and the branches of an unidentifiable tree. Peter blinked. He pushed the door open beside him. Exiting, he tripped and almost sprawled onto the road. Conchita meanwhile had bumped her way along the back seat and out through the further exit. Her route had been cleared by Nigel and Filomena who were locked in immobile embrace on the pavement. Conchita turned and regarded her cavalier over the roof of the Cadillac.

'Good bye, Peter. I hope I never see you again.'

Conchita barged between Filomena and Nigel. Peter hit his head as he stooped to re-enter the car. Nigel dabbed lips with a handkerchief as he shut the door behind him.

'What did I do?' Peter wondered aloud, pained in more ways than one.

'Precisely nothing.' Isabel laughed. 'That's your problem.'

'I thought she objected to 'mashers'.' Peter said, ruefully rubbing his scalp.

'Oh, she loves the real thing.' Isabel laughed. 'Poor Conchita. The guys always go for her kid sister. She's worried about being left on the shelf.'

The Cadillac had whispered into motion without drawing anyone's attention. Nigel licked his lips. 'Filomena's a really sweet girl.'

'Yeah,' Hal enthused. 'Fantastic knockers.' He winked at Nigel. 'And she's loaded, Nige.'

Isabel spitefully pinched Hal's ear. 'But for Filomena there's a big price to pay.'

'I know.' Nigel stared through the window beside him. 'I think I'm better off staying single.' Peter winced.

Hal's splayed hand embraced Isabel's shoulder. 'I could marry if it was to the right woman – you know, provided we knew we was really gonna hit it off, like. No good takin' a pig in a poke.'

Isabel looked puzzled.

Peter explained. 'It means a pig hidden in a bag. Something you can't see.'

Hal was impressed.

'Even to see knockers you must pay the price.' Isabel was clearly pleased with her grasp of British slang.

Peter was reminded of something back at the resort. 'I think we'd better be getting back. Fast.'

'It's O.K.' Isabel glanced back over the seat. 'My driver's got a chit. You all brought your passports. Right?'

'Yes. But Nigel and I have got to be up early to fly to the Agustin mine.' Peter realised that that was of no interest to Isabel.

Nigel spoke up. 'Yes, Isabel. And while driving in a Caddy all night might be fun, we have to get a little shuteye.' He added. 'You know. Sleep.' He had suddenly remembered something important awaiting him 'back at the ranch'.

Hal frowned and looked judicious. 'How about we all go back to Isabel's for a quick nightcap? Then her driver can take you back to the resort.' His teeth encouraged agreement.

'Or how about this?' Isabel turned, resting her chin on Hal's arm. 'You all come back to Isabel's for a quick nightcap. Then my chauffeur takes all three of you back to the resort.' She patted Hal's arm. 'We mustn't wear out the carpet.'

Hal's smile faded.

The car crunched to a halt. Isabel led the way into the gloomy elegance of the mansion. She abandoned the trio in the reception room while she went in search of refreshment. Hal inspected a cabinet of Ming blue and white.

'I don't know what they see in all this junk.' He turned his back on the export porcelain. 'And what's the point of showing the plates inside out?'

'Bottom-side up,' Peter corrected. 'It's to display the dynasty characters inscribed on the underside. Sung, Ming or Ching.'

'Well, I wouldn't give 'em 'ouse room.' He produced a large cigar from an inner pocket.

Nigel complained, 'I thought you were giving up.'

'I am. Except for the occasional cigar.' Hal wet the slimmer end with tongue and pouting lips. ''Elps to relax me.'

Isabel returned, propelling a trolley. Kneeling beside a teakwood credenza, she retrieved four glasses to join the bottles. As Hal exhaled a cloud of smoke, Isabel warned, 'This is one for the road.' She poured a Scotch and handed the glass to Hal. Peter and Nigel settled for tonic water.

'Sorry,' Isabel pouted. 'No ice.'

She curled into an armchair. She stretched her leg and surveyed her toes. 'What's England like?'

Peter smiled. 'Tired.'

Nigel nodded. 'Shagged.' His face illustrated the adjective.

Isabel was unswervable. 'Come on. What's it really like?'

'It's an old country.' Peter paused. Isabel waited. Peter expanded. 'Old age does bring on a certain weariness.'

Isabel curled her feet under her thighs. 'The British were in Manila, you know.'

'I've got news for you – in case you hadn't noticed.' Hal smirked.

'No, not now. I meant back in the eighteenth century.' Isabel frowned in her effort to recall juvenile history lessons. 'They conquered Manila in seventeen... seventeen...'

'1973,' Hal said, raising his glass in a toast.

Abandoning the frustrating eighteenth century, Isabel now asked Hal, 'Where do you live in England?'

'Me? I'm a man of the West Country. Can't you tell?' He grinned as he elongated his already stretched vowels to breaking point.

'What is your home like in the West Country?'

'Old. And big.' Hal surveyed the room in which they sat. 'Much bigger than this.' Hal's two up, two down terraced house, watered by Bristolian rains, had sprouted several wings in the years he had been absent in Hong Kong.

'Eighteenth century it was.' As an indigent office worker, Hal had been torn between inhabiting or exploding Clifton. 'Real elegant.'

He had met Hilary at a Saturday night hotel dance with a view of the Suspension Bridge.

Fascinated, Peter watched the reptile of mendacity uncoil itself from Hal's lips. Nigel had lowered his drink onto his right knee.

Isabel's attention was fixed on Hal's domestic arrangements in the West Country.

'Does your house have a garden?'

'Garden?' Hal's nose wrinkled and he thrust the cigar back between his lips. 'You don't call two thousand acres 'a garden', Isabel. We had 'grounds'. We used to go 'untin' in the woods'. Hal raised an imaginary shotgun at an imaginary deer.

'Foxes?' Isabel suggested, lips apart. Hal lowered his weapon to register the change of prey.

'Every week we killed three or four vixen.'

'Not foxes?' Isabel was disappointed.

Hal exhaled smoke. 'Vixen is the name for a female fox.' Hal smiled. 'If you put down the females, you control the population.'

'How do you know which is a vixen?' Isabel's frown showed her puzzlement.

'I used a telescope.' Hal explained. 'You need a close-up view.'

'Hal's family was notorious for the eccentricity of their hunts,' Peter explained. He placed his glass on the table beside him. 'And now, Isabel. I fear we must depart.'

Nigel also got to his feet. 'Here's one Englishman who needs his beauty sleep if he's going to be in the pink tomorrow.' Peter winced at the thought of Nigel 'view, hallowing'. In the pink, indeed.

'Oh, come on, fellers.' Hal pleaded from his unyielding place in an armchair. He raised his glass. 'One more for the road.'

Isabel hauled at Hal's extended arm. 'No, Hal. There's only one road, Mr. Hal, and you've already had your final drink.' Hal lurched out of the chair and enveloped the slim woman. Laughing, they swayed over the carpet.

Nigel coughed – loudly. Isabel's eyes followed the direction of Nigel's. She drew Hal's arms from around her waist.

In the corner by the exit to the corridor stood the Chinese woman who had so impressed Peter at Isabel's party.

'Hello, mother.' Isabel's voice was frigid.

'Isn't it a little late, Isabel?' The woman smiled gently as she moved further into the room. A padded, gold silk house-coat covered her from neck to ankles. Peter was reminded of the flawlessness of her complexion. Tiredness could not tarnish her. As she stepped from the parquet onto the richly decorated carpet, Peter noticed that her feet were small, delicate and bare. The image produced the same sharp, erotic shock as an unexpected hint of perfume.

The woman smiled at Nigel, 'It is not wise to be out after curfew.' Nigel cleared his throat. Peter was not the only victim of the woman's erotic power.

'Do you all have your passports?' She smiled calmly at Peter. Without the smallest hint of make-up, the Chinese woman offered an apparition of exceptional beauty. Peter patted his chest to indicate the document's location. Isabel's face was working. She took two paces towards her mother.

'These are my friends. This is my house. I have invited them to stay.' Beside the composed beauty of her mother's features, Isabel offered a mask contorted by pique.

'Isabel.' The woman's voice was without emotion. 'We do not wish to waken your father. He is unwell.'

Isabel's eyes widened. She looked at her male guests in mute appeal. Peter lowered his eyes. He felt, rather than saw, the girl spin and run into the darkness beyond the most distant corner.

'You will find your car awaiting you outside, gentlemen.' The mother extended her hand. Her fingers were dry and cool. 'My daughter is tired. She has not been well. I am sure we will have an opportunity to meet again... some time.'

Peter's inarticulate thanks carried the trio over the threshold and out into the night where the car awaited, engine purring.

'Phew.' Nigel made the motion of wiping his brow. 'That was a bit on the tense side.'

'What a tragic waste.' Peter looked up at the house as the Cadillac purred awake.

'Yeah,' Hal agreed sombrely. 'I wouldn't mind getting my leg over that.'

Nigel barked a laugh.

Hal had inadvertently reminded Peter of the resort. But Peter was certainly not in the mood for 'getting his leg over'.

It occurred to Peter that their unimpeded progress back to the resort may not have been mere good fortune. The more he considered it, the more he was convinced that the police had been informed of the car's details before they departed from the mansion.

Peter was also convinced that the crunch of the heavy vehicle's tyres would be bound to waken the sleepers in the dark cabanas, crouching in the resort.

'I wish Maria was around,' Hal remarked as he opened the front passenger door. 'Isabel's old lady was a right turn on.'

Peter hoped that the combination of slang and a broad Bristolian accent would outwit the driver's understanding. Peter watched, hand raised and smiling, as the car gently reversed out onto the road. The headlights arced and, in a moment, the men were left darkling.

At the first step they paused and removed their shoes.

'Cor, what 'ave you been dippin' your feet in tonight, Nige?' Hal gripped his nose between finger and thumb. Nigel snorted in his effort to stifle his laughter. Peter looked up. To his amazement, the stars still danced.

'Watch your bloody feet, Nige.' Hal hissed and was answered by another stifled laugh.

Without thinking Peter whispered. 'Oh, just put a sock in it.'

All three men convulsed as they tip-toed along the balcony; pausing every few steps to draw breath.

Peter entered his room still chuckling. The broad white sheet reflected the brilliant moonlight. First, he placed his moccasins on the floor before moving forward on tiptoe. His heart leaped. He was safe. He was relieved that there was nobody in the bed.

But wait. His heart changed rhythm. He now realised that the area of dark shadow in the centre of the pillow was in fact Miranda's black hair. He crept forward until he was beside the bed and then took great pains over the business of sitting.

For some minutes he sat and stared; with every passing second the portrait of Miranda grew more detailed. He continued to stare. Then, Miranda stirred. He sensed her turning towards him. The whites of her eyes shone against the darkness of her skin. She raised her forearm against her brow.

'You want shower?' she gently enquired. Peter said nothing but reached for the edge of the sheet. She did nothing to impede its removal. He looked long at her moonlit body. It was a pity that the girl ever had to wear clothes. Here in the flesh was the real Princess Liwayway. Her fingers touched his hand and he trembled.

'You go?' she asked. Peter nodded. He began to unbutton his shirt and then changed his mind. He would wait until he had arrived at the bathroom.

The sound of running water was harsh at this silent hour. He remembered the paper-thin walls and hurried to cleanse himself.

He returned to the bedroom, the large towel round his waist. The girl held out a hand to guide him to the bed.

'You want massage?'

Peter allowed himself to fall face down on the bed. Miranda carefully removed the towel and the night air cooled his damp skin. He shivered as her fingers brushed his back.

'Wait.' Her fingers withdrew. He hesitated before saying, 'I think we should both have a shower.' Without a backward glance, Miranda rose from the bed and glided away across the room. He heard the sound of falling water.

He gnawed at his lower lip. This was crazy. He who had always refused to engage in paid sex. Was this the time to indulge in a moment of madness? He should settle for a massage. Relief was all he needed.

His heart beat faster, while his excitement slipped down another notch. The constant pressure of his colleagues' sexual obsessions and the temptations on offer elsewhere had begun to tell. Had he survived without market-driven sex just by taking evasive action? And was his evasion driven by morality or simple fear of contagion? Morality or pragmatism?

His courage slipped another notch, as the sound of the shower ceased.

When Miranda re-entered, her head was swathed in a small towel. With a determined, no-nonsense air, she swiftly lowered the sheet to Peter's calves and began to knead the small of his back. The girl's small hands were inexpert and clumsy. Far from relaxing him, her ministrations tightened all his sinews.

'How long have you been a masseuse?' The staccato question brought the kneading to a rallentando and then a halt.

'Oh, long time.' The resumption of pressure from Miranda's busy knuckles against his spine evoked a pained whistle through Peter's gritted teeth.

'Stop!' Peter ordered, hoarsely. The muscles at the centre of his back had gone into spasm. He shifted position and winced in agony. Through narrowed lids, he could see the girl's fingers opening and closing in helpless anguish.

'It's O.K. It will go away.' He felt something brush his skin. 'No, no. Don't touch me.'

The girl stepped back from the bed, biting her lower lip. She was not to know that what she was observing was a recurrent affliction.

'It's all right.' Peter winced. 'It will go away.' He felt fingertips brush his shoulder. 'No, don't touch me! Please.'

Biting her lip, the girl stepped away from the bed.

It took ten minutes for the muscles to relax and the pain to ease. At last, he was able to turn his head. He sighed. Gingerly, he rolled onto his back. Miranda's eyes remained fixed on him.

'I think...' Peter sought the least painful mode of expression. '... you are pretty new to massage.'

Miranda looked down at her feet. 'Yes, I only come here one week before.' She lifted her head and looked directly at him. 'You are my first...' She sought for the correct word. Her face brightened. 'Victim.'

'I think you mean 'client',' Peter gently corrected her. 'So, you are... a virgin?' He felt himself blush.

Her head lowered once more. The girl nodded. Peter eased himself into a sitting position. He beckoned for Miranda to come towards the bed.

She remained fixed to the spot. 'No, no.' Tears appeared. 'I did it.'

'So, I am not your first client.'

'Yes, yes. You are my first puck here.' Miranda raised her eyes and swallowed. The pause was several seconds long. 'I do it with my cousin.'

'Oh, so you did it one time with your cousin?' Peter narrowed his eyes. 'Just one time?'

'No,' Miranda intertwined her fingers. 'Many time. That is why I ask Maria to help me find a job away from my cousin.'

Peter shrugged. 'Why couldn't you just tell your cousin 'no'?' Peter asked, spitefully.

'My cousin live with my family in Tondo. He has good job. Get good money. He say, if I tell my mother, he go.'

Peter was buffeted by conflicting thoughts. He knew he was being unjust, but his mind was filled with thoughts of her, locked in the embrace of her young cousin. Peter knew that his present repugnance at this revelation was just as strong as the tale of incest itself.

Were all men reducible to this simple act? He had never really considered any male sexual activity other than his own. What made him imagine that his own activity was unique and precious – something nobler than a furtive act of friction in a darkened room? Yet, to this girl he probably meant nothing more than that.

But was he any better than Miranda's cousin? In Tondo the cousins had the excuse of affection and propinquity. He, on the other hand, was simply a partner in a mercenary transaction. And he would not even be asked to pay. Miranda was just another cog in the wheel of Agustin Enterprises. Sex as a medium of exchange.

Was all sexual activity reducible to this simple equation? Were casual sex and marriage both to be evaluated by a common measure of exchange? Or was he simply funking sex with Miranda for fear of contagion?

The predictable crux was here. Either he had to definitively dismiss the girl or continue along the sampaguita path. He glanced up at Miranda. Without a word, the girl returned to the bed. She sat. Peter rose and drew her to him with an arm round her shoulders.

As his lips brushed her forehead, her hand fell onto his thigh. Her nipple was cold against his chest as he kissed her mouth. His excitement began as he felt the warmth of her hand against his groin. Gently, he drew her alongside him. Miranda shivered. He struggled to draw the sheet over their cool bodies. He stroked her breast.

The girl lay inert, doing nothing either to accelerate or delay the process. His ardour began to dissipate. Then, a small hand curled over him and he saw, as if a flash had fired inside him, a picture of Isabel's mother. She approached him, her diminutive, perfect feet peeping from beneath her housecoat. She placed her hands on his shoulders and the housecoat fell open. Peter fingers touched her wet warmth. The perfect face was close to his, the eyes closed. He sank into her and then a voice murmured in Peter's ear. 'How big is yours?'

Chapter Nineteen

Peter rolled onto his back and raised an arm over his eyes against the brilliance of the blue sky, glimpsed through the window. The curtain swayed in a gentle breeze. There came the distant yet distinct sound of a cock crowing. He turned his head. He was alone. He raised himself onto his elbows and listened hard.

The girl must have slipped away after he fell asleep. He was perplexed. Instead of being a straightforward sexual transaction, Miranda had become some kind of viva examination in the business of living.

Peter stared at the blue sky. Where did the idea of an examination come from? He closed his eyes and bright window shapes floated behind his eyelids. He could not pretend to have enjoyed what had transpired the previous night but, at least in one direction, he had experienced psychological relief.

He looked at his watch. Eight o'clock. Chico was coming to collect them at nine.

As he slowly turned in the shower of warm water, his spirits began to revive with his revived physical wellbeing. Perhaps he would repeat his experience with Miranda. There was time enough.

He began to la-la *The Toreador Song* from *Carmen*. From the adjacent bedroom came a loud banging. Peter curtailed the aria. Miguel needed his sleep. As he laved his body in soap, his mind wandered to the identity of Miguel's mystery companion before moving on to Maria and, finally, Isabel's mother.

He arrested the flow of water. As he dried his skin, his stomach rumbled. He was so hungry he was even prepared to brave the garlic fried eggs. The knocking resumed.

He realised it was coming from his outside door. Taking the precaution of wrapping himself in a large towel, Peter stepped back into the bedroom. 'Come in.'

Sue took an uncertain step into the room like a two-legged gazelle.

'Hello, Sue.'

Heartened by Peter's cheerful greeting, the girl grinned and asked. 'You want breakfast? I go get breakfast for Nigel.'

'How thoughtful.' Peter thought Sue looked charming this morning. 'Yes, please. The same as Nigel.'

Peter followed Sue out onto the balcony. She tripped down the stairs as he inspected the resort. The door to the sauna opened and Maria appeared, sans the frightful glasses. She gave Peter a radiant smile before turning her head to one side and spitting a stream of white liquid into the watercourse beside the building. To Peter's relief, he realised that Maria was holding a toothbrush in her hand. He waved once more and returned to his lair.

Although he felt lively, Peter guessed that his night's activities before, during and after the party at Isabel's would catch up with him sooner rather than later. He assured himself that lost sleep could be made up during the plane journey. There came another knock on the door. Peter called 'come' and Hal came.

'Well, me old mate,' Hal slapped Peter's bare shoulder. 'You finally got your leg over. I was beginning to think you 'adn't got one.'

Peter smiled benignly as he responded. 'It's quality, Hal, not quantity that counts.'

'You're right, me old mate.' Another slap on the shoulder. 'I thought you was sulkin' because I'd grabbed the best-lookin' bird 'ere.'

Peter could find no meaningful way of repudiating that statement without insulting Maria. So, he just shrugged.

'Maria and Sue are really chuffed to fuck,' Hal continued. 'They're like sisters.'

'More like cousins, actually.' Peter countered. He must bow to the inevitable. Step in the spilt milk.

'Mind you,' Hal reflected as Peter struggled into his socks and shoes. 'I know just what it feels like – to get the wrong girl.'

Peter reached for his shirt. 'I'm quite content with this particular wrong girl.'

Hal was uninterested in pursuing a philosophical discussion. No replies were required. 'I mean,' he continued. 'There's Isabel.

Crazy about me.'

Peter drew on his trousers. Hal paused by the window and gazed. 'But I'd much rather screw her mother.' Hal turned and spread his hands. 'And with this fantastic deal in the Philippines just beggin' for a mover and shaker, I'm trapped in Hong Kong with Hil.'

'What's Hilary's mother like?' Peter could anticipate the response but the question was irresistible.

'What? The Old Bag?' Hal's brow darkened. 'That's what worries me, Pete. They do say a woman gets like her mother as she gets older. You should see Hilary's mother.' Hal's gesture suggested that the lady-in-question's bosom lurked somewhere in the region of her shins.

After a tentative knock, Sue entered bearing two plates of greasy sunny-side-up eggs on a tray. Peter inclined and breathed in. He stood tall and smiled. 'Thank you, Sue. That's fine.' Sue smiled, lowered her tray to the table, turned and departed. Peter lifted Agustin's typewriter onto a chair before zipping it into its case. Hal excised a section of egg-white and relayed it to his mouth.

'If we're going to be isolated miles from anywhere tonight, I might as well try to do a little more writing.' Peter mused aloud. He wondered where the second knife and fork were.

'Great idea.' Hal cut into a yoke and thrust the result into his mouth. 'I bet you'll 'ave a great time up in the mountains. I 'ope you'll think of me flogging down them Pagwhatsit Falls with a bunch of skinny models.' He ingested another forkful of egg.

'If you'd like to change places....' Peter frowned and extended his hand. Hal ruefully handed over the solitary fork

'No, thanks. I can't stand mines.' Hal ginned. 'I'll just 'ave to take my chance with the models.' He attacked his other egg. Masticating vigorously, he asked. 'Lic, Pete. What do you really think of this place?'

'I think a man could starve to death here.' He extended his hand and Hal delivered the knife. 'Thanks for leaving an egg.'

Nothing could dent Hal's bonhomie. As Peter bent over his plate, the monologue continued. 'You know, Pete. After ten years

in Hong Kong, 'avin' to fight every inch of the bloody way…'
Peter finally managed to swallow a forkful of tepid slipperiness.
'I reckon it's about time I 'ad a bit of jam.'

'By marrying the bread?' Peter removed a fleck of yoke from
the corner of his mouth.

'Not just that. No, I meant businesswise. We know Enrile's
gonna read this issue. And Imelda – if she gives us an interview.'
He smiled. 'I bet even Ol' Man Marcos will 'ave a gander. And if
all the top drawer like the mag…'

'Then why not launch a bright, new magazine for the local
market?' Peter interpolated. 'You might call it *Philippines
Weekly*.' Peter gave Hal a bright smile.

Hal was not into irony. 'Right!' he elated. 'You're forgetting
a thing or two, *me old mucker*.'

Peter glanced at his watch. 'In the first place they'll read us
because we have a foreign readership. You don't think Agustin's
taking the mag just to sell in the Philippines, do you? The local
information people will send it around the world and have copies
waiting in their embassy waiting rooms.'

Peter rose from his chair. 'Secondly, this isn't Hong Kong. In
the good old crown colony you can publish more or else anything
you like. We can interview Elsie Elliott or Ma Man-fai until the
Middle Kingdom come – and publish the results. But not here.
Not in the Philippines. This place enjoys the privilege of
censorship, Hal. You have to watch your p's and q's. And I'm not
just talking typography.'

'So what?' Hal frowned before aggressing. 'You're the one
who offered to let Agustin 'ave a gander at all the copy.'

Peter felt his face redden. 'You may remember, Hal, that I told
him 'no changes' and he accepted that.'

'Yeah, but you did promise to be fair,' Hal riposted in a
friendlier tone. 'Now, that's all I'm askin' Pete. Be fair. I mean,
this is a little country, tryin' to make it.' Peter wished he had
remembered to bring his violin. 'You can't expect 'em to be
democratic like us in five minutes, Pete. It took us 'undreds of
years. And after all this…' He paused to wave an all-inclusive
arm towards the unmade bed. '… I think they deserve a chance.

Don't you?'

Peter was rescued from jail by a fourth knock on the door. It was thrust open and Nigel's beaming face appeared. 'What an absolutely fantastic day!' He stepped into the room. 'I'm really looking forward to this trip, Peter.'

'I'll be right with you,' Peter said as he lifted the canvas hold-all strap onto his shoulder and shifted the typewriter to his left hand.

'Very interesting, Hal.' Peter said, pushing past the senior partner. 'But I think we should defer this discussion for a day or two.' He accompanied Nigel onto the balcony as a distant cock crowed.

Maria appeared at the top of the stairway and smiled as she caught sight of Hal. Behind her Miranda stood, expectantly.

He smiled down at her. 'O.K.?'

The girl nodded.

Good. We'll see you tomorrow.'

He started to descend. She considered her toes, curling over the leading edge of her yellow flip-flops.

Peter edged past Miranda as Nigel relieved Peter of the typewriter. Once in the car, Nigel was bubbling over with enthusiasm. He patted Chico's shoulder affably and offered the driver a cigarillo. Chico smiled a refusal before accepting a cigarette.

'I really love this place,' Nigel announced, his head turning from left to right and back again. 'I think I could really be really happy moving over here.'

'But do you think Susan would be happy about leaving Hong Kong?' Peter asked.

Nigel's mouth drooped at the corners. He considered the tip of the cigarillo. 'There's not much that makes Susan happy. Except discussing amahs.'

Peter thought of 'pots' and 'kettles'. 'Well, she won't be lost for conversation in Manila.' He said with a smile.

Nigel turned from his appraisal of the passing scene. 'This trip has really opened my eyes, Peter.' His eyes returned to the passing scenery. 'It's made me realise how deep a rut I'm stuck in in Hong

Kong.'

Peter sighed. He wondered whether Nigel would seriously be prepared to exchange the real gold he earned in a princely 'hong' in Fragrant Harbour for the fool's gold on offer in his imaginary Philippines' paradise.

'Chico,' The driver half turned as Peter called his name. 'How far is the airport?'

Chico glanced up at the mirror. 'Ten minutes.' He was correct to the second.

The pilot was muscular and middle-aged. His smooth brown face and Clark Gable moustache were both shaded by a dark-blue baseball cap with 'U.S.S.' emblazoned in gold braid across its front.

'Hi, I'm Brownie.' The little man's grip was almost painful. 'We've got a Beechcraft over here.' He pointed with a thumb over his shoulder at a bright yellow plane waiting outside a hangar. 'We got another passenger,' Brownie explained as they turned and moved towards the aircraft. He relieved Peter of his hold-all. 'Got to drop this guy off at the mine loading facility at Poro Point.' Nigel followed his leaders. His enthusiasm had tapered off somewhat as they approached the aircraft.

Peter's excitement, on the other hand, mounted as he clambered into the cabin. He stowed his gear behind the seat and followed Brownie's instructions as the pilot helped him strap himself in. The heat was suffocating. Relief accompanied the taxi-ing of the aircraft towards the runway. Peter saw Nigel swallow. They exchanged nervous smiles. Peter had never flown in anything so small before. The roar of the engines as the Beechcraft fled down the runway seemed even louder than in a 707.

Nausea swept through Peter's stomach as a wind slewed the aircraft sideways but then they were airborne. Brownie threw the plane into a steep turn. Below, Peter saw fishponds and multitudes of geese and ducks. The plane straightened and Peter watched the Beechcraft's shadow flickering over the mirrored surface. The twin engines had settled into a deafening steadiness. Talking was out of the question. Peter took a couple of shots with the zoom to avoid reflections. These images would prove useful for his article on agriculture.

Apprehension still lurked but a glance at Brownie's broad back was reassuring. Peter's eyes began to close. He came to as the engine note changed; they were descending towards Poro Point. The plane had landed before the two Englishmen had a chance to be afraid. Brownie assisted the Poro Point passenger to reach terra firma. The big American dwarfed the pilot. He waved at Peter, who nodded. The passengers had not exchanged a word. Nigel was blinking around him with the bewildered eyes of the unexpectedly wakened.

'Poro Point,' Peter murmured as Nigel stared at the installations.

While the Beechcraft was fed with fuel, the three men stretched their legs on the tarmac.

'See that big mother over there?' Brownie pointed to the furthest edge of the airfield. A warm breeze ruffled Peter's hair. He nodded.

'Well, that's an ore truck.' Brownie lowered his arm. 'Carries the ore from the mine up in the mountains down here on the Point for loading onto ore carriers.' His finger swung out towards the bay where the superstructure of a vast cargo ship peeped over enormous warehouses.

'Where does it all go? The ore?' Peter wanted to know.

'Japan, mostly.' It was clear that Brownie had learned his flying and his lingo from Americans. The pilot checked his watch and waved them back towards the plane.

They levelled out at five thousand feet. As far as the eye could see the heavens were draped in a blue shawl, fringed with white. Peter could not stop his eyes closing.

When they re-opened, Peter blinked uncomfortably. The sensation of disequilibrium was created by tremors running through the machine. Peter rubbed his eyelids with his thumbs and hazarded a glance out of the window. He almost started back.

The great plain of mirroring fields of what he supposed was rice paddy or fish farms had been replaced while he slept by the black, rocky teeth of tall mountains only a few hundred feet below. A second look revealed that the crests were covered, in part, in conifers. Peter glanced across at Nigel as the shaking became more pronounced. Nigel's eyes were closed. The knuckles of Brownie's left hand were white with the effort of holding the aircraft steady. Peter hoped that the turbulence was a normal adjunct to the crossing of these high peaks. The crest fell away and the shaking resolved into a throb. But what now lay below was hardly more inviting. Deep rocky gorges slashed the flanks of the mountains. Along one slope Peter detected a narrow, sand-coloured road, curling through a defile – on it, making painfully slow progress, was a twenty-wheeled toy truck bearing what looked like a thimbleful of earth. He felt his heart thumping as he raised the camera for a shot of the road. That ribbon was the only terrestrial way in or out of this fastness. A great terrain for guerrilla warfare.

Without warning, the Beechcraft suddenly banked. Peter grabbed for support. Beyond Nigel's pale profile, he could see their destination. The runway was solid rock. With sheer drops on either side, it ran directly towards the towering face of the mountain. Peter was sure that the plane could not land on so narrow a strip. They circled the immense bowl; a diminutive yellow bird. Above their heads swirling clouds were forming and re-forming over the crests they had crossed. Peter was modifying his claims to 'love flying'.

Nigel's knuckles were now paler than Brownie's. Peter and Nigel exchanged tense smiles. Nigel rolled his eyes. The plane followed suit.

Peter decided that the runway must be dead ahead. Which way was the wind blowing? Might they be smashed into the face of the mountain? It was horrible to be unsighted by the pilot's broad back. Just when he thought his lungs would explode, Peter felt the wheels touch, bounce once and then stay down. The runway now seemed too wide for so small an aircraft. They came to rest a full quarter of a mile from the hangar, which gleamed white against the granite grey mountain-side. Then Brownie taxied gently on.

As they clambered out, Nigel paused and said, 'I was so scared

I forgot to be sick.'

Peter laughed.

They pumped Brownie's hand with enthusiasm. The deadpan little man acknowledged their gratitude with a nod. He cast a weather eye upwards.

'Well, I guess that's it for today.' The laconic remark was accompanied by a tug on the baseball cap.

Where, only a few minutes earlier, there had been a patch of blue sky, there were whirling, shredded strips of cloud. A cool breeze tugged at their ankles.

Peter hoisted the canvas bag so that it rested on his shoulder. Nigel was still responsible for the typewriter. They walked in Brownie's wake as the pilot ambled towards the hangar, hands in pockets.

Nigel spoke for them both, 'Jesus.'

Chapter Twenty

A car to take them on the next stage of their journey awaited them beyond the hangar. They sat, numb, on the back seat and warily took in the grey mountains, while Brownie gave instructions to the ground crew. Then, in a series of rushes, the car carried them to a low wooden building. The driver would depress the accelerator for a hundred yards and then, apparently, lose heart.

The car finally came to rest among wet sand and muddy pools. They were each accorded a painful handshake and a curt 'adios' from Brownie before the car sped back whence it had come, leaving them stranded. To their relief, the door of the building opened and a tall, young Filipino clutching a yellow safety helmet in one hand, beckoned with the other. They negotiated the intervening puddles and climbed after their guide up the wooden steps to the front porch. Somehow the sound of their footsteps on the boards invested the experience with a heavy masculinity. Another door opened. Nigel had to duck slightly as they shuffled into the room. A grey-haired European with antic whiskers rose from behind an incongruous, gleaming, Victorian mahogany desk. He extended an arm over the brass inkwells.

'Good morning to you, gentlemen. You only just made it in time.' His lips spread in a grim, thin line. 'Another half-hour and you would have had nowhere to land.'

Both the visitors shuddered. The grizzled manager waved Nigel and Peter onto chairs of pitiless inflexibility.

'Now, what can I do for you gentlemen?' The accent was basically Scots, with hints of Tagalog and Yankee.

'What have you been told about us, Mr...?' Peter lifted his bag onto his knees. He waited. The silence was eloquent.

'McGee,' McGee responded, accompanied by a thin smile. 'An old Filipino name.' He waited for Peter to smile. 'I manage the mine.'

Peter tried to match this evidence of affability as he reached into the bag for his recorder. He began to unwind the microphone lead. McGee cleared his throat and stroked his whiskers with both hands. There was a neat parting down the middle of his chin from which the beard swept upward, left and right. A van Gogh postman, no less, Peter thought. Salt with a sprinkling of pepper. He decided to keep the thought to himself.

Peter launched the recorder and embarked on a sound test with the lanyard mic in his hand.

'Testing, testing.' He kept his eyes fixed on the volume needle. Thankfully, it moved.

McGee's eyes flickered between Peter's face and the machine. The mine manager was exhibiting distinct signs of nervousness. Those signs increased as Peter rounded the desk and placed the lanyard around McGee's neck.

'And just what terrible things did they tell you about us, Mr. McGee?' Peter asked, clicking his fingers to see whether the needle responded. 'I'm just checking your voice for level, Mr. McGee. We're not starting yet.' McGee nodded stiffly. His voice took on a strangled, metallic quality as though he were addressing a miner's rally through a megaphone.

'I received a call from head office in Manila from Mr. Agustin himself.' McGee cleared his throat. Peter nodded encouragement.

'He told me that a reporter and photographer from 'Hong Kong Weekly' were wanting to visit the mine.'

Peter glanced sideways at Nigel, who was frowning at the change in McGee's vocal personality.

'Right, well, my name's Peter Nicholson and this is Nigel Thompson.' Nigel smiled and raised a hand. 'Executive Vice-Chairman of Hong Kong Weekly Publications.'

Nigel's eyebrows twitched. Peter kept a straight face as he simultaneously switched on the 'play' and 'record' buttons. He raised the microphone to his mouth and continued...

'You see, Mr. McGee, we regard our Philippines edition as our most prestigious to date. So, our three top people are here to handle the issue.' Peter smiled, raised a hand to indicate a pause and pressed 'rewind'. McGee's whiskers curved several more degrees towards the azimuth as the little machine whirred in reverse. Peter pressed 'stop' and then 'replay'.

'…this Philippines edition as our most prestigious to date.' He depressed another switch and the apparatus fell into a pool of silence. Peter and Nigel heard McGee swallow.

'You're no going to use that thing?' The Scotsman's alarm was evident. Peter gently lowered the canvas bag to the decking and moved his chair four feet from McGee.

'Now, there's absolutely nothing to worry about, Mr. McGee. This is just a normal tool of the reporter's trade.' McGee's chair scraped as he shifted nervously away from the approaching Peter. 'This little device saves my having to learn shorthand.' Peter awaited the chuckle that failed to arrive. 'And – you will be pleased to hear – ensures total accuracy. You can check what you have said against the eventual text.'

'I've never done any interviews before…' McGee's voice faded into strangled silence.

'Mr. McGee, I'm just going to ask a few layman's questions. You could answer them in your sleep. O.K.?' Peter's voice had taken on a crooning tone. McGee glanced over Peter's shoulder and frowned at the amused Filipino, who was still stationed by the door.

'Out. Out.' His whiskers bristled as he waved the underling witness of his confusion from the office. The assistant disappeared.

McGee exhaled. 'That's better.' He cleared his throat, plunged into his resources of moral courage and placed one tanned, sinewy forearm on the desk. 'Fire away.'

Peter flicked the machine off 'pause'. 'Just for reference, let's begin with your name and title.'

'Andrew McHugh McGee, mine manager, Agustin Mine, the Philippines.' McGee lowered his voice. 'The McHugh's fra my mother's side of the family.'

Icefloes drifted away in all directions. Peter rested his elbow on his knee. 'I was a bit surprised to find a Scots engineer way up here. How did that come about?'

McGee's eyes lit up. 'I've been a mining engineer all my life. I started in the coal mines of Scotland.' He shook his head sadly as though recalling a departed member of the family. 'Then I took myself off to Africa for a couple of years.' His eyes sparkled. 'And stayed for twenty. West Africa as well as the South. 'Diamonds, gold, coal and copper. Anything that could be extracted.'

His lengthy sojourn in Afrikanerdom would account for further curious distortions of his West Coast brogue.

Peter recalled the treacherous weather conditions on the vertiginous runway. 'Don't you find it rather lonely up here?'

'Oh, yes.' McGee frowned. 'Being in charge is a lonely business anywhere.' Peter saw the man's fingers curl into a fist.

'Wife? Family?'

The Scot was beginning to relax. He shook his grizzled head.

'No.' He looked down and then directly at Peter. 'No woman could stand the life.' He considered the veins decorating the back of his hand. His fingers straightened. He looked up and smiled.

'I'm not the only Scot in the Philippines, not by a long road. There's quite a few engineers. And I've an Aberdonian friend or two in the dockyard in Hong Kong.' He bent forward eagerly, his nervousness all but forgotten. 'Do you not know Gordon Mackintosh?'

Peter regretfully shook his head. 'There are fifty, maybe sixty, thousand expats in Hong Kong, Mr. McGee.'

'Well, I've got Scottish engineers driving a shaft for us just now.'

'How's that?'

'They're working for a British company.' McGee's eyes twinkled. 'One of my old firms. You see, although this is a tunnel mine, we still need to dig a shaft for new workings, better ventilation and ease of extraction.'

Peter shifted the conversation onto his readers' interests. 'Is the mine profitable?'

'Profitable?' McGee's voice became more confidential. 'Have you no been following copper prices? The way the world economy's been going for the last twenty-five years... why, there's no end to it. The Japs canna get enough of our ore.' He shook his head. ''Course, we'd get far more of the profit, if we went ahead and built the smelter.'

Peter scented an interesting angle. 'What would that do?'

'Well, laddie,' McGee settled into his explanation. 'Just now we mine the ore, haul it all the way to Poro Point by road and let the Japs ship it home to their own country. Then what happens?' Peter shook his head. McGee looked pleased at Peter's ignorance. 'They offload the ore into their smelter and then sell the copper back to us, value added. Get it?' Peter was not entirely sure. McGee smiled and continued. 'Now, if we had our own smelter, we could not only supply the Philippines market ourselves, we could export the excess to Japan and elsewhere, value added.' McGee's voice took on a note of triumph. 'Q.E.D.'

'Well, what's stopping you?'

McGee looked over his shoulder and leaned towards Peter as he lowered his voice. 'No single Philippine company can go it alone. The cost would be prohibitive. We need a consortium. Mr. Agustin has spent years putting one together. All he needs is the go-ahead from the Malacañang.'

'What's the hold-up?' Peter contained his growing excitement.

McGee shrugged. 'Who knows?' McGee's eyebrows lowered; his eyes glittered from their covert. 'Mr. Agustin's not the only businessman with a project. I tell you,' McGee winked at Peter. 'I'd sooner be up here than in that whirlpool down in Manila. It's a damn' sight safer.'

'So, is copper the only metal that the company mines?' Peter took a quick glance to check the life expectancy of the tape. Plenty, plenty.

'*Enterprises* is always exploring for other raw materials in extractable quantities,' McGee boasted.

'What about oil?' The question sprang unbidden to Peter's lips.

'Ay,' McGee said, leaning back in his chair. 'There's been quite a fuss about oil. There's been some rumblings concerning Arab interests. But...' He shrugged. 'I think it's all exaggerated. Oh, they'll push up the price a dollar a barrel every once in a while, but there's no way they'd all hold together for really concerted action.'

'So, where does Philippines' oil come from at present?'

'From the Middle East,' McGee spread his palms. 'I suppose with all this Moro nonsense going on down South, the government's getting a wee but twitchy. I mean, with the Moros being Mohammedans and all. But like I said, the Arabs are too busy bickering among themselves to worry us.'

Peter attempted casualness. 'Has there been any actual evidence of oil in the Philippines?

'Oh, ay.' McGee grimaced. 'There's a group of Yanks been prospecting down South. The word is that they found something off Palawan.'

'Where's that?'

'It's the big island to the West of the Sulu Sea.' McGee shifted his shoulders inside his check shirt. 'A bit vulnerable these days. Oil companies tend to run at the first sniff of trouble.'

'Moros' trouble?' By now Peter knew that the interviewee had completely forgotten the recorder.

'The whole area is trouble, potentially. Sabah lies just beyond the Southern tip of Palawan and some say that the Sultan could be supplying the Moros. Then again, to add to the mix, there are disputes between the Chinese, the Vietnamese and who knows who else over islands in the South China Sea.' McGee wrinkled his nose. 'I think Marcos should stick to copper and Mr. Agustin's smelter scheme. Safe as – no safer than - houses.'

Peter relaxed, then leant forward and casually switched off the recorder.

'Terrific,' Peter smiled at McGee. 'A fascinating story.'

McGee raised a hand in alarm. 'Wait.' He leaned forward, lowering his voice. 'You've not got all that down on that wee machine?'

'Yes, but I'll only be using part of it.' Peter cursed inwardly at his casual assumption that McGee would be happy with the interview.

'Well, laddie, you'd better erase all that stuff about smelters... and oil... and the Palace.' A bony finger waved in malediction over the recorder.

'Look, Mr. McGee. I promise you that I will protect my source of information.'

McGee's mouth opened. Peter continued, 'I'll keep the article apolitical and technical. O.K.?'

McGee doggedly refused mollification. His fingers clawed at his whiskers.

'Mr. Agustin will see all the copy before it is published.' Peter felt his face flush with the admission. 'He'll keep us all on the straight and narrow.' Nigel shifted nervously.

McGee's scowl was reluctant to depart. But, finally, he nodded.

'O.K. I suppose I have to trust you. After all, Mr. Agustin sent you and he wouldn't send anyone who would do us harm' The old man rose and hitched his trousers. 'So, what would you like to do now?'

'It would be good to take some shots of the mine, if that's at all possible.'

McGee glanced at Nigel. 'Do you want to go down the mine too?'

Nigel nodded weakly. 'After that flight I could face anything.'

McGee grinned. He turned to Peter. 'There's no much light down a mine.'

'It's all right,' Peter patted the canvas bag. 'I've got flash.'

'You'll be staying the night in the guest house.' McGee moved round the desk. 'Let's away and have some lunch just now.'

The mine manager strode across the office, opened the polished hardwood door and waved Nigel through ahead of him. Peter followed.

A jeep of the original vintage was waiting, its front tyres immersed in a pool of muddy water. Their journey was to be brief. The vehicle skidded to a halt outside a starkly modern bungalow with magnificent views of the vast amphitheatre. In the distance, mountain peaks played hide and seek among the clouds.

Nigel raised impressed eyebrows as they stepped into the reverberative, luxurious lobby of the guest house. Nigel was beginning to feel almost as pampered and important as befitted the make-believe title Peter had awarded him. Leaving the typewriter beside Peter's severely single bed, Nigel took his own small bag of personal effects off to the room McGee had just offered him. When their host was content, he shepherded them to a large, round table by the lace-curtained windows of the guest house dining room. Peter had brought his hold-all, which he deposited by his chair.

Now that he had survived his personal ordeal, the Scots engineer's humour was completely restored.

'Are you in the Philippines for long?' he asked.

'Just a few more days, alas.' Nigel replied. 'It's a fascinating place.'

'Ay,' the Scotsman nodded. 'I've been here the better part of fifteen years and I canna' say I know yet how the place works.'

'At least you're unaffected by the stringencies of martial law, way up here in the mountains,' Peter remarked, one eye on the bowl of what looked like brown Windsor soup a trim waiter was placing before him.

'Unaffected? The curfew is kept up here, precisely as it is in Manila,' McGee insisted, breaking a bread roll between his fingers.

Peter lifted his immaculate spoon and essayed the soup. It was, indeed, what he had feared.

'Terrific soup,' Nigel enthused. He had already cleared the bowl and was dabbing at his mouth with a crisp napkin. He caught Peter's disapproval and murmured. 'Certainly gives you a fierce appetite, this mountain air.'

'Ay, well. It's taken me a heap of years to train the cooks how to produce decent food. They will insist on drowning everything in garlic. I canna abide the nasty, smelly stuff.' He wrinkled his nose. 'Even the mango tastes of it.'

While one waiter whisked away the empty soup bowls, another filled the vacuum with empty hot plates. They were encouraged to serve themselves boiled potatoes, carrots, tinned peas, beef and Yorkshire pudding from Royal Worcester dishes.

'Mr. McGee,' Nigel exulted. 'You're a credit to Scotland.'

The tenor of culinary nostalgia continued as other bowls supplanted the empty main dishes. The dessert was jellied trifle, quivering beneath a coverlet of bright yellow custard.

Peter was mildly surprised to be offered post-prandial coffee, rather than tea.

'What Hal might term 'a blowout'.' Nigel said, leaning back in his chair and patting a stomach straining against his shirt. McGee accepted Nigel's offer of a cigarillo. Peter remained faithful to his own route to cancer.

Just as the small talk had all but dwindled to eructations and murmurs of satisfaction and their thoughts were turning towards a post-prandial nap, McGee had them on their feet once more. Trifle was beginning to seem a grave error of judgment as the jeep was hurled round one rutted bend after another. McGee's enthusiasm for innumerable indistinguishable landmarks failed to compensate for the battering. The jeep squealed to its slippery rest in front of a Tate Gallery reject, straddling a deep hole. Cheerful greetings were exchanged and McGee persuaded Peter to demonstrate his tape recorder to a stout and stumpy Scot in a duffle coat. The ensuing interview of impenetrable technicality was concluded by the engineer asking when it would be shown on the 'tele'. The offending duffle-wearer took Peter's explanation on the chin. He even condescended to share a photograph with McGee by the shaft.

'Would you send a copy of the snap to my wife in Aberdeen?'

Peter could not hold the engineer's eye. 'Sorry. This is reversal film.' His interlocutor looked blank. 'Slides. No copies.' Nigel felt that Hong Kong Weekly had lost a potential reader. The jeep bore them away, first sloshing through a puddle, then rearing over a rock. McGee excitedly announced that the mine was 'round the next bend'.

The young Filipino who had been dismissed from the earlier interview was in attendance at the entrance to the mine.

'When you're done, bring them back to the guest house,' McGee ordered as though his guests had been deprived of hearing. Without a backward glance, the Scot stomped off to the jeep.

'Tough as old boots.' Nigel's admiration was unfeigned. 'What's he like as a boss?'

'He does the job.' The man donned his safety helmet and

offered them his back. 'Follow me, please.'

They stepped over a narrow-gauge railway line and made their way towards another low-slung, wooden structure. Within, they discovered showers, changing rooms and green metal cabinets.

Their new guide opened a double-fronted metal wardrobe and handed each of them a one-piece denim overall, a pair of heavy boots, thick socks and a safety helmet with a headlight.

'Please remove all your clothes except your underpants,' was the instruction.

After they had donned their unfamiliar garb, they were instructed to fit batteries for their lamps around their waists. Peter settled the strap of his hold-all over the unfamiliar denim.

'Hold it.' The guide pointed at the bag. 'What's in there?'

'Camera equipment.' Peter patted the canvas. 'Mr. McGee told me it was O.K. to take some pictures.' This was greeted with a grimace and a shrug.

The man locked their civilian clothes in the cabinet. 'You're going to need flash.' Peter nodded and smiled. 'Oh, and lens cleaning tissues.' Peter shrugged. Maybe the workings created a lot of dust.

They stepped out into the humid air. Cloud now covered every available inch of sky.

The Filipino paused, hands on hips, beside the railway. 'My name is Rosario. I'm a supervisor. I got my master's at M.I.T. That explains my crazy accent.' Peter and Nigel nodded. Rosario half-turned and stared along the tunnel. 'This is the main tunnel of the Agustin mine. We are nearly three thousand feet above sea level. Because we are digging into a mountain, we measure tunnel heights above sea level. This tunnel – the nine hundred, is lower in the mountain than the one thousand and seventy tunnel. So, the world is turned upside down. Get it?'

Nigel shifted uncomfortably inside the coverall. Already his battery belt was chafing his hip. Peter extracted the wide-angle and attached it and the flash unit to the Nikon. He twisted the lock round the hot-shoe and inclined the head. Rosario was already twenty yards away, marching along the rails towards the tunnel. The executive vice-president of *Hong Kong Weekly* vacillated between pursuit of their guide and delay in favour of his partner. Peter hurried to catch up.

Close to, the tunnel entrance proved to be huge. Peter felt like a sinner in a painting by Bosch. Gradually the daylight dimmed, replaced by a fitful procession of lights along the walls. The fixtures disappeared around a distant bend.

A diminutive train, stationary on the track, was awaiting their arrival. Rosario climbed aboard and shared a perch atop the engine with the phlegmatic, silent driver. Peter and Nigel swung up behind Rosario; the cold of the metal immediately penetrated the denim. The train lurched once before gradually easing into smooth acceleration. The passengers lost all sense of speed or direction in the darkness. Peter readied his flash unit. A buzzing light informed him that the device was ready for action. He raised the camera and took a shot of Rosario and the driver. Both men glanced backwards. Peter awaited a recharge. The train drew to a silent halt. Rosario stepped down, the shards of rock scraping beneath his boots. He half turned towards his charges.

'From here, we walk.'

Ignoring Peter's valedictory gesture, the driver stared straight ahead. Peter stumbled after Nigel and Rosario. The tungsten lamps barely grazed the tunnel walls. Peter's left foot sank into a puddle. He cursed.

A hundred yards ahead a cluster of somewhat brighter lights lured them further into the bowels of the mountain. The air was cooled by a silent breeze which pursued them as they clattered on their way.

How high was the roof of rock above them? Peter discharged the flash upwards. Golden-brown stalactites glowed while the adjacent walls of rock were stained green and brown by mysterious liquids. Peter shuddered at the thought of the millions of tons of rock above their heads in this copper-lined sepulchre. In the deeper darkness which succeeded the brightness of the flash, Peter found his breathing was both shallower and more rapid. He peered ahead.

His heart seemed to leap against his ribs as he realised that neither Rosario nor Nigel was in sight. Peter pressed his eyelids shut and then blinked into the featureless chasm. Panic burst out, like a waterfall through a fissure. His boots scraped the rock as he hurried forward. He almost missed the faint glow emanating from the right wall of the tunnel. Peter retreated two paces and stared into the gaping wound in the rock. Nigel must have followed his leader, Rosario, in search of the source of the light. Peter took a deep breath, dipped his head and stepped into the mystery.

'My God,' Peter gasped. Every pore in his body seemed to burst open. In seconds his clothes were soaked. His mouth fell ajar, desperate for oxygen. He had never before experienced such rapid extremes of heat and humidity.

As suddenly as they had disappeared, Rosario and Nigel reappeared. Nigel's mouth opened and shut like that of a fish out of water. His eyes bulged; a large, pale fish in a tiny bowl. Peter noticed that even Rosario's face was streaming with sweat. The young supervisor beckoned Peter to approach the glow ahead. The rubble beneath their feet was treacherous. Peter supported himself by clutching a wooden pit prop jammed against the roof of the cave, just three feet above his head. Grey-brown fragments slithered beneath his boots as the ground began gradually to fall away. Water droplets dripped on helmets and shoulders.

Through the smothering darkness came the clink of pickaxes somewhere up ahead. The sound was everywhere and nowhere. Nervously, Peter raised his camera in the direction of the source of the light, which seemingly rose from below. Through the viewfinder all he could detect was a blurred aureole. He glanced down. The lens filter was drenched in condensation. Pointless to shoot in these conditions. He lowered the camera.

He began to discern shadowy figures. The men were using spades to clear slag from around their boots. Their costume consisted of helmets, boots and battery belts. Their modesty was catered for by pairs of sodden shorts. Their bodies streamed with sweat. Rosario appeared alongside Peter.

'My God,' Peter rasped. 'How do they survive working in these conditions?' He felt his voice failing.

'I have never discovered their secret,' Rosario replied, his eyes fixed on the rodent miners gnawing at the rock. 'You'd better get your pictures fast. You won't last long in here if you're not used to the conditions.'

As if in response, Nigel turned and clawed his way past his companions, towards the cleft in the tunnel wall. He seemed in a semi-conscious trance. Peter hoped Nigel would have the decency to wait until he reached the tunnel before vomiting. He suddenly experienced a wave of sympathetic nausea but fought it off.

At last, he recovered his pack of lens tissues. Rosario helpfully relieved Peter's damp fingers of the pack and did his best to clear the filter. They wasted ten tissues before Peter attempted a single, desperate shot. The condensation dissolved into liquid on the glass. Despairingly he checked the image. The tissue had failed again. His head swam and he staggered to one side of the cave.

'We must get out of here,' Rosario muttered. Peter was feeling limper by the second. Rosario used main force to propel Peter back up the incline; preceded him through the hole to freedom; turned, and hauled Peter through the gap. Nigel, his eyes wide open, was staring down at his feet. Peter retched.

Chapter Twenty-one

Rosario allowed the exhausted Englishmen five minutes to lean against the damp rock of the tunnel and inhale the cool air. There was no dispute when the supervisor suggested they return to the surface.

'We'll take the elevator.' Some strength returned to their exhausted limbs as they slowly trudged along the tunnel to the shaft. A steel cage hoisted them and a quartet of exhausted miners to the next level. This tunnel also had its own railway but Rosario offered them no vehicular passage out of their prison. Peter and Nigel stumbled behind the tall Filipino, occasionally splashing through puddles like a pair of tired children. As they slithered down an incline, a persistent, keen breeze dried their skins, only for an equally persistent drizzle to dampen them again between the tunnel exit and the hut where they had changed their clothes.

Peter caught up with Rosario. 'Tell me; what's the safety record of the mine?'

The young man made a sour face and remained silent. Peter was feeling spiteful. 'With your qualifications couldn't you have got a decent job in the States?' He knew he should not blame Rosario for any failure to deal with the conditions below ground but Peter's pride had taken a tumble.

'I am a qualified mining engineer. I also happen to be a Filipino.' Rosario said, his voice tense. They arrived at the hut. Rosario preceded his charges through the door. 'I suggest you guys just carry your own clothes and take a shower back at the guest house. This place will be full of miners in a few minutes.' He glanced out of the window. 'Yeah, there's the jeep. Right on time.' Rosario unlocked the cabinets and Nigel and Peter sorted their clothes. They relished the feel of the lightweight material as though it was a novel experience. They agreed to defer their showers until they reached the guest-house.

When the jeep regurgitated them outside their destination, they found they were no longer alone. Brownie was in the lobby. He introduced Peter, Nigel and Rosario to a large American who was described as an 'engineer'.

'Hi,' the man said, extending a hand towards Nigel. 'I'm Connors.'

As Peter shook Connors hand, he asked, 'Didn't I see you at a party at the Spanish Ambassador's residence the other evening?'

'Yup.' Connors face crinkled into the smoker's grin which features in so many cigarette ads. 'It's sure a small world.'

Rosario was exhibiting unmistakable signs of impatience.

'How would you guys like to change, so I can get the gear back to the hut? His shrug was apologetic. 'The driver's on overtime.'

The two Englishmen retired to their rooms. Peter gathered up the heavy denim and made his way back to the lobby. En route, he paused outside Nigel's door. He could hear the sound of a shower. Exasperated, Peter slipped into the room, found Nigel's denim rejects and added them to his own horde.

Rosario shook Peter's hand before transferring the awkward burden; smiled a farewell; pushed his way backwards through the guest house doors; and was gone.

Safe in his own quarters, Peter indulged in his delayed shower. Then he opened his bag on the coverlet to check his sorely tried equipment. He knew his cameras were not entirely waterproof. He cleared the smears on the lens filter. More important than any images were the recordings. Tentatively he tested the recorder. To his great relief, he could hear the clear tones of the Scottish mine manager.

He cleared the phone and the lamp from the small bedside table. In their stead he placed the precious typewriter. He inserted a sheet of paper. Then he raised his right index finger, while he searched for an 'M'. Slowly the words 'Martial Law' formed at the top of the page. Peter paused.

Would Agustin be thrilled at his brilliant forensic liberalism? And, beyond Agustin, there lurked other, even more powerful, potential readers. How might Enrile or Marcos respond?

Why should the rulers of a violent country in the Third World indulge the vacuous timidities of Western journalists? Why should Marcos – even supposing he would read the issue – heed appeals to his upbringing in the Western democratic tradition?

The present rulers of the Philippines would doubtless regard Peter's effusions as mere sentimental slop. They held the sword; he doubted whether his pen would actually prove 'mightier'. Peter suspected – nay, feared – that he was simply fighting a pro-forma rear-guard action before succumbing to the strong temptation to 'go native'.

While he wrestled with what passed for his conscience, there came a knock on his door.

'Come in.' He waited. Silence was the stern reply. With a sigh he rose and moved to open the door. An ancient Filipino in 'domestic' tenue looked up. Peter smiled. The man raised his clenched fist to his ear. 'Pone.' He jabbed his other hand in the direction of the lobby. Peter nodded, closed the door behind him and hurried to the front of the building. His stockinged feet had difficulty with the highly polished floor. A white receiver lay on its side on a low, circular table.

'Hello? Nicholson speaking.'

'Hello, Mr. Nicholson.' He recognised the voice battling through the shower of static. 'This is Agustin. I have just had a call from Major Alvarez at Camp Crame.' The line battled against dialling clicks and distant voices.

'Yes. I can just about hear you,' Peter found himself shouting, his hand cupped round the mouthpiece.

'They have arranged transport to take you to Mindanao the day after tomorrow.' There came a sound reminiscent of a pneumatic drill.

'OK.' Peter's spirits lifted. So Enrile had been honest about having nothing to hide. 'Mr. Agustin?'

'Yes, Mr. Nicholson?' The voice faded and then returned.

'Thanks. And I'll have something for you to read on my return.'

The telephonic storm continued to rage. Peter waited for the cacophony to decline. After thirty seconds he replaced the receiver and returned to his room. The auguries were propitious. He could set about his martial law article.

He had covered four sides and was mid-way through a soaring

peroration which would indubitably guide Marcos, his wife and the entire Filipino establishment along Peter's path to liberal-democratic righteousness, when there was a knock at the door.

'Come in,' Peter called. Nigel appeared in the doorway.

'Still invoking the bloody muse?' Nigel grinned and belched.' He came towards Peter and tapped the typewriter carriage. 'Can't sleep a bloody wink with your bloody racket going on next door.'

'Sorry,' Peter sat back and took in the dishevelled Nigel. 'Promised to show Agustin some copy tomorrow.'

Nigel nodded. 'Probably a good move. More diary?'

Peter thought better of revealing the nature of the article in progress. Nigel was clearly impervious to the charms of Peter's missionary zeal. Peter rose and stretched.

'God, my back's sore.'

Nigel collapsed onto Peter's bed. 'Dinner in ten minutes.'

'How do you know?' Peter asked before he could stop himself.

Nigel laid a finger along the length of his nose. 'Investigative journalism.' He grinned. 'I asked the little wog waiter.'

'I've just had a call from Manila,' Peter remarked.

'Hal checking up on us?' Nigel linked fingers behind his neck.

'No, it was from Agustin. The trip to Mindanao's on.' Peter tried to sound casual. How would Nigel react?

'I hope you and Hal have a great time.' Nigel smiled. 'Where should I send the wreath?' He twisted back into an upright position. 'Time for din-dins.'

McGee, Brownie and Connors were already in situ when Nigel led Peter into the dining room.

'Did you gentlemen get what you wanted?' McGee enquired, dabbing butter onto a corner of crusty roll.

Peter drew his chair up to the table. The place setting would have done justice to the Mandarin Hotel.

'Yes, thanks. I've certainly gained new respect for miners.'

'Ay, it's a man's job, no doubt.' McGee smiled grimly. 'Everybody thinks it's going to be cold down in a dark mine, thousands of feet from the sun's rays.' He shared a glance with the nodding Connors. 'But it's as hot as Hades.' He consumed the morsel of bread.

Nigel remembered to show an interest. 'Is that true of all mines?'

'Oh, ay.' McGee again sought Connors' silent confirmation. 'Even down the Scottish coal mines.' He raised his eyes to the ceiling. 'And in South Africa only the blacks can cope with the heat in the gold mines.'

Peter had begun to wonder whether Connors was mute. He turned towards the American. 'You're in oil I gather, Mr. Connors?'

The big man lowered his butter knife. The waiters arrived, bearing bowls of thick tomato soup. Connors leant back in his chair. 'Well, yes. Oil. And coal. And copper. And on the surface, even lumber. You could call me a generalist – a sort of exploitation engineer.' Connors raised his soup spoon.

Peter tried to keep his voice light. 'Not the happiest title in the Third World these days.'

'No, I guess not.' Connors grinned. Obviously, the American believed that the present company was excluded from that world and could therefore discuss it with equanimity. 'A country's got to learn to walk before it can run.' Connors added and downed another spoonful of soup.

'There's surely no need for the Philippines to go through all the same stages of development that we did in the West. That way, they will never catch up.'

Connors looked directly at Peter. His eyes were a very pale blue.

'This country is rich in natural resources, Mr. Nicholson. The West has the manufacturing base which can use those resources. At the present time a country like the Philippines simply doesn't have the know-how to take over our manufacturing capacity. This way, they get foreign exchange for their resources – their copper their lumber to train their people to manufacture their own products. It will happen. But it all takes time.'

'In the meantime, the resources are depleted.' Peter knew he was irritating Connors. So, he pressed on. 'Why not impose a tax on all 'natural resources' sales?' Peter had no idea where that idea came from but he felt the need to rebel against Connors' assured assertiveness.

'What would be the goddam use of a tax.' Connor's voice had an edge. 'It would only fill the bank accounts of Third-World leaders.'

McGee and Nigel concentrated on their bowls, while Brownie vacantly chewed the cud.

'All right, let's look at what's happening while the Third World's waiting to catch up.' Peter's spoon slipped off the edge of his bowl and stained the table-cloth. 'The Philippines has already lost eighty percent of its hard-wood forests since people began 'exploiting' timber. The Indonesians are going the same way. And I'll bet it will spread to East Malaysia before long.'

'So?' Connors eyebrows rose as he raised another spoonful of Campbell's soup to his lips.

'I'm sure you know how long it takes for a hardwood forest to grow.' Connors shrugged and looked away. 'Every tree that is cut down will take a century to be replaced. They're hacking the forest down like it's going out of style. And that is precisely where it is going.'

'You're right about Indonesia.' A waiter was filling Connors' wine glass. 'There may even be one or two Filipino companies in there helping them clear the forest.' Connors raised his glass. 'But here in the Philippines we're helping the government set up reforestation schemes.' Connors eyes crinkled at their corners. 'For future exploitation.'

Peter downed half his own glass of wine. 'Yes, I've seen schemes like that in Hong Kong and even in Britain.' He patted his lips with his serviette. "They replace deciduous trees with conifers. Fast growing, utilitarian, boring, soft-wood plantations.'

'Now hold on.' Connors held out his glass towards Peter. 'Aesthetics plays no part in economic development.' He grinned. 'Not until you have the money to build museums to show it off.'

Peter drained the last of his wine. Connors pressed home his advantage.

'You want the people of this country to ignore the natural wealth around them, so that you can drop in for a few days of cultural tourism? That's just B.S. and you know it.'

'Then what about ecology? The whole balance of life on earth is shifting. And not in our favour.' Peter's ears were burning.

'Who says?' A few sentimentalists. Tell a guy in the barrio that he should be satisfied with malnutrition and poverty for the sake of the view.' Connors raised his glass in front of Peter's eyes.' The glass waved. 'You know what he'll tell you.'

'That's now,' Peter returned. 'But what about the future?' Peter was beginning to feel his brain breaking loose from his skull. 'Future generations?'

'They'll worry about themselves, I guess, much as they always have. Remember, we were all future generations once.' His smile was disarming. Peter raised his glass. Connors' voice was mellifluous. 'So, would you mind informing us what salvationist mission brings you to the Philippines, Mr. Nicholson?'

Peter felt himself flush. Connors smiled. 'In the end we're all exploiting Mr. Augustin's hospitality.'

Nigel forestalled Peter's angry response. 'You're absolutely right, Connors.' Nigel's eyes twinkled as he raised his glass. 'Here's to sensible exploitation.'

The crinkles round Connors' eyes marked his return to good humour. All he needed was a stogy and a stetson.

Peter lowered his glass. 'C-O-N-N-O-R-S. Is that right? I don't want to misspell your name.'

The pale eyes looked murderous.

Nigel's manner became positively boisterous. 'Now, what's this?' He extended a welcoming hand to the waiter.

McGee matched Nigel's animation. 'Shoulder of lamb and boiled potatoes.' Nigel raised a spoonful of what looked like algae from a silver sauce-boat.

'Will you look at this, Peter?' Nigel enthused. 'Real mint sauce, just like mother made.' He allowed the green liquid to dribble from the spoon.

Peter downed the rest of his wine.

'Great little country, the Philippines,' Nigel boomed as he accepted a generous helping of New Zealand lamb.

Connors then passed him the dish of neat, new potatoes, shining with melted butter and topped with sprigs of fresh parsley.

Nigel boomed on. 'Yes, a land of golden opportunity. And, after all, a lifetime's knowledge and experience must be worth a bob or two. Right?'

Connors seemed perplexed. 'Sorry. A dollar or two,' Nigel, said, correcting the currency.

Peter concentrated on the paschal offering. Nigel bounced them through the remainder of the meal – commenting and eliciting comments on every detail. Peter's brain floated on a purple ocean, half-hidden by curling vapours. Foolishly, he passed on the coffee. Two minutes later, mumbling his excuses, he reeled from the table. Nigel engaged the other diners as Peter wove his way out of the dining room.

Back in his room, Peter sat semi-comatose on the cane chair and stared at the typewriter. Where had it come from? It was not his typewriter. Whose was it? He shook his head in bewilderment. He staggered to the bed and lay back on the coverlet.

Miranda appeared beside the bed. She reached across and tugged at the juncture of his belt and his waistband. 'How big is yours?' Her smile was wide but devoid of teeth. Her black mouth stretched and stretched. Peter stiffened as she reached for his zip. 'You want massage?'

'No, no massage,' Peter complained. The hand was now shaking his shoulder but the voice was no longer Miranda's.

'Come on, old sport. Wakey, wakey. Nigel's brought you some nice, black coffee.' Peter forced his eyelids apart. Nigel indicated the cup on the bedside table. 'Black.'

Peter shook his head. His nausea had abated. How long had he been lying here?

'How do you feel?' Nigel asked. 'You've been out for an hour.'

'Not too bad,' Peter replied, holding his head in his hands. 'Considering.'

'Drink your coffee.' Nigel nodded at the cup once more. He watched as Peter took a tentative sip. 'I don't get you, Peter. Why on earth did you go for Connors like that?'

'He looked just like the guy in the Marlboro ad.' Peter said and winced.

'I think I've saved your life.' Nigel beamed at Peter. 'I told him you were pissed out of your mind.'

'Too kind,' Peter smiled faintly and sipped his coffee.

'You're bloody right – it was. Don't adopt that sancti-bloody-monious tone with me.' Nigel snorted.

'Sorry, Nige.' The coffee burnt the tip of his tongue. 'And I'll apologise to Connors next time I see him.'

'One apology is enough for the big prick,' Nigel insisted. 'Anyway, I suspect Connors has marked your card for life. Come on now, drink up and let's away to the Community Centre.'

'What the hell's that?'

'McGee's brainchild. Seems that there about two thousand miners all told up here, including quite a few unmarried ones. The choice was between bromide or entertainment. Pool and other such delights."

Peter nodded towards the typewriter. 'I think I'd better get on with this.'

'Sorry, old sport. I promised McGee that we'd show. He's panting to show off his baby.'

Peter sighed, winced, slipped his feet into his moccasins and reached for the clumsy canvas bag.

'Might get a couple of shots,' Peter explained as Nigel steered him out of the room.

The Centre, while impressive, looked incapable of kindling any but the minutest sparks of joy. Nigel's high spirits inspired two youthful miners to accept his challenge to a foursome at pool. Peter was instructed in the arcana of the game by his partner, who cheerfully conceded to the miners after ten minutes.

'Just my luck,' Nigel complained, winking at McGee. 'Trust me to challenge the local poolroom sharks.'

McGee laughingly commiserated and offered to substitute bowls in the Union Hall to restore their amour-propre. Nigel, full of vinous bonhomie, insisted on personally bidding farewell to all the denizens of the centre. Outside the hall, no stars shone and the still air was deliciously cool. The depths of the hypnotic silence were ravished by the ignition of a jeep.

The banter at bowls was soon transformed into grunting,

earnest competition. Nigel was disgruntled at being worsted by Peter twice. He insisted on continuing. So, they continued and Nigel eventually emerged triumphant with five victories to Peter's three.

While Peter resumed his consumption of black coffee, Nigel entertained the mine manager. Nigel ran through his entire repertoire of Englishman, Irishman, Scotsman and Jew jokes. McGee wiped the tears of laughter from his eyes and slapped Nigel on the back.

'Aye, well, Nigel.' McGee's shoulders heaved once more. 'I've heard every single one of them jokes before.' The corners of Nigel's mouth drooped. McGee grinned. 'But it's the dreadful way you tell 'em. That's the worst imitation of a Scots accent I ever heard.' McGee rocked again. As his laughter dwindled, Peter smiled and asked, 'How far is it back to the guest house from here?

'Well, if you go via the Community Centre about ten minutes' walk up that path yonder. McGee pointed out of the black window.

'It's still not ten o'clock, Mr. McGee.' Peter held up his wrist. 'I think I'd rather get a breath of fresh air than go back in the jeep.'

'Okay. You'll be safe enough. 'The old Scot winked. 'After all, there's nowhere to go up here.' He grasped Peter's right hand. 'Good night, Mr. Nicholson.' Then it was Nigel's turn. 'Good night, Mr. Thompson.' He paused and twinkled at Nigel. 'Usually I toss the caber.' He chuckled and shook his head. The partners watched him laugh his way out into the night.

'How about another game?' Nigel got to his feet and briskly rubbed the palms of his hands together.

'Sorry, Nigel. I really would like to get some fresh air.' He quietly took a couple of shots of another pair of bowlers before resting the camera and hoisting his bag onto his shoulder. 'Good night, Nigel. And thanks.'

'Don't mention it, old sport." Nigel raised a hand. "Look, may I join you?' Peter nodded and Nigel fell into step as they traced the path in the deep silence of the mountain. Behind them the

Union Hall lights flicked off. Elsewhere other faint glimmers marked other huts, scattered on the small plateau. Their shoes scraped the uneven road surface as they strolled.

'What do you really make of this place?' Nigel's voice sounded strangely flat. There was nothing to reflect the sound, of course, Peter realised. Nigel kicked another stone ahead of them.

'Great. Fascinating.' Peter, his eyes acclimatised to the gloom, caught up with the stone and kicked it in his turn.

'What would you think about working here?' Nigel side-footed the stone.

'The thought had occurred to me.' Peter missed his shot. They walked on.

'There might be room for a nice little mag like ours in the Philippines.' Nigel squinted up at the heavens for inspiration. 'Philippines Weekly.'

'Original,' Peter teased.

'No, seriously, old sport. A nice little office in Manila. Dirt cheap.'

'But continue to print in Hong Kong.' Peter prompted.

'Right. Printing here is also dirt cheap but they can't deliver the quality. The Japs in Central knock spots off this place. And we don't want to put all our eggs in one basket.'

Peter kicked another irresistible pebble. 'So, one of us stays here, while the other two return to Hong Kong?'

'No, two over here. One stays in Hong Kong. We'd need a Filipino partner.'

'But that makes four altogether,' Peter protested.

Nigel looked embarrassed and missed his aim. Peter kicked the stone Nigel had missed.

Nigel hastily explained, 'Hal's O.K., I mean, he's got *Hong Kong Weekly* already.'

'I see.' Peter watched Nigel raise his foot. 'And I suppose this Filipino partner would have good connections in business and government?'

Nigel struck the stone a fair blow. 'And advertising. I mean – even you'll admit editorial's not much use without advertising.' They moved on and caught up with the stone. Nigel concentrated on Peter's foot.

'You wouldn't be thinking of Joe, by any chance, would you?' The stone disappeared into the darkness ahead.

Nigel delivered a light punch to Peter's arm. 'Great idea! Joe would be perfect.' He moved on and searched for the stone without success. He shrugged. 'And, if anything were to happen to you, Pete, you'd know I was always there in Hong Kong ready for action.'

'No doubt I would find that a great consolation in Camp Bonifacio,' Peter muttered to himself. They were approaching a red and white barred barrier across the road.

'Seriously, Peter. Do you have any more urgent plans?' Nigel tried to catch Peter's eye as they walked on.

'Not a thing,' Peter confessed and realised it was no laughing matter. It was the bitter truth. A door opened beside the barrier and a beacon shone across their path. A bulbous figure in uniform was silhouetted in the doorway.

'Hi,' Peter greeted the uniform and made his way towards it.

'Hi,' the guard replied, all affability.

'Nice night,' Peter suggested. The guard weighed the remark before nodding.

'When do you get off duty?' Peter sensed Nigel's impatience.

'Midnight,' the guard said and peered hard at Peter, 'You Australian?'

Nigel bristled. 'No, we're British.'

Peter resumed the reins. 'Do you live on the camp?'

'No.'

'So, you'll soon be on your way home.'

The guard shook his head. 'Midnight curpew. I go home pour o'clock.'

Nigel laughed in disbelief. 'But that's crazy. You *are* the curfew.'

The guard's brow puckered and Peter steered Nigel to one side. 'Night,' he called and waved.

Nigel kicked another stone into the darkness. 'Whoever heard of a cop keeping to the bloody law?'

Chapter Twenty-two

'Oh, damn.' Peter dangled the empty canvas bag over the bed. There came a knock at the door. 'Come in.'

Nigel left the door ajar and approached the bed. 'I say – do you happen to have a spare razor?' Peter silently indicated the pile of heterogeneous plastic and metal piled on the rumpled coverlet.

'Oh, what the hell,' Nigel said, rejecting Peter's offer. 'We'll soon be back at the resort. We can shave then. See you at breakfast.' He turned on his heel and departed, humming an excerpt from 'Sweet Sue'.

Five minutes later, Peter, complete with replenished hold-all, bumped into Nigel as they met up at the entrance to the dining hall.

McGee and a steaming tureen of porridge awaited them at their table. Brownie gave them a perfunctory greeting before returning to buttering a blackened triangle of toast. McGee was evidently destined to retire to a boarding house in Glasgow. Nigel would welcome the address.

'Sit yourself down,' McGee ordered. Nigel complied, rubbing his hands and working his chair free with his buttocks. 'Ah, porridge.' He smirked at McGee. 'Wi' haggis to follow, I've nay doot the noo.'

McGee's shoulders lifted while his head shook with pitying good humour.

'That's definitely the worst imitation of a Scots accent I've ever heard,' he insisted, while his face creased into a smile.

Peter politely enquired after Mr. Connors. McGee shrugged. 'Oh, he's being given the grand tour of the mine just now. Then he's off back to Manila.'

In lieu of haggis there came two boiled eggs apiece. Peter consumed his hungrily. His concluding sigh was one of complete satisfaction. He felt his chin. Neither he nor Nigel had shaved.

'Is there a chance of being able to purchase a razor?'

'As a matter of fact, there's a very good chance,' McGee

twinkled. 'There's a general store at the miner's camp down the road a way. He'll be opening just now.'

Peter finished the strong tea while he smoked his first cigarette of the day. Grey wreaths of smoke were pierced by a narrow sunbeam while McGee gave them detailed instructions on how to find the store. Peter rose and made as though to move away. Nigel remonstrated, 'Hey, wait for me.'

They passed the union hall of their previous night's adventures and soon came upon the store, planted, like a dozen other wooden structures, around a broad, open space. Behind the store the flag of the Philippines fluttered atop a gleaming white pole.

'I hope I didn't keep you awake last night,' Peter said as they stepped into the gloom of the store.

'Oh, you mean the typing?' Nigel shook his head. 'Not a bit, old bean. Out like the proverbial.'

The store keeper smiled great expectations at them. Peter idly wondered why the absence of three front teeth should impart an air of idiocy to their former owner. He perused the shelves on either side of the man's grin.

'Ah,' Peter pointed a triumphant digit at a black T-shaped object.

As he paid for the razor with some crumpled notes, Peter detected other notes attempting a clumsy fugue at the back of the store. 'Hang on, Nigel.' Peter said and vacated the premises. He rounded a corner and fell among a group of singing children, aged, he guessed, between five and twelve. Several of them shared the storekeeper's dental affliction without losing their unaffected charm. Now – and more or less in time with one another - they bawled at the top of their voices while covering their hearts with their palms.

Nigel drew up alongside Peter. 'God, what a bloody cacophony.' The only other adult present turned and glared. The children kept their eyes fixed on the fluttering flag. 'Always carry a camera with you.' He hadn't followed his own adage. He took a deep breath.

The air sparkled and the blue of the sky seemed even richer against the pure alto cirrus. A ragged silence fell. The adult keeper then led his charges in a chant in Tagalog. Peter guessed this would be the oath of allegiance. After the following descent into silence, the teacher nodded and, with a chorus of rather more tuneful yells, the children fled into a large hut.

The teacher turned. Peter offered a smile. The Filipino glared, turned on his heel and followed the horde into the school.

Nigel ruefully remarked, 'Well, they obviously know more of their national anthem than I do of ours.'

Back at the guest house Peter raised his trophy at Brownie and McGee. The latter smiled complacently. He knew that the camp could supply all that a man might require.

'Don't be long just now.' McGee admonished.

Peter, lacking shaving soap, drew blood. McGee was evidencing impatience. He extended a gnarled, tanned hand. He grasped Nigel's paw. 'It's been a real pleasure having you.' He frowned with mock severity at Peter's bag. 'Except for that devil's handiwork.'

Peter started. 'Sorry, Mr. McGee. Just one more picture before we depart.' The result was never published. Nor was it ever intended to be.

The mysterious car replaced the jeep and carried them back to the hangar. In spite of their lucullan breakfast, the take-off gave neither of them any qualms. The grey bowl looked less menacing in the intense sunlight and they gazed into its recesses with equanimity. The Beechcraft, as though calmed by the conditions, negotiated the return over the crests without any bumping or grinding. Peter even managed to doze as the sun warmed his face. He awoke to find that the aircraft was circling over the mountain resort of Baguio. Peter managed three decent shots with the zoom. He felt a slight pang of regret as they left the city in their wake. Peter wondered whether he would ever get a closer view of the city. He dozed once more.

He was awakened by a change in the engine note. He squeezed sleep from his eyes. Cold was making him shiver. Raindrops sliced diagonally across the window by his cheek. He stared out at a congeries which he realised had to be in a suburb of Manila. A grey veil of rain swayed between distant storm clouds and a slate-grey sea.

Peter's mood of elation had dissipated. He glanced across the cabin. Nigel was still asleep; head thrown back and mouth agape. Peter hoped the weather would improve for tomorrow's expedition to Mindanao. Rather than ask to enter the southern lion's den, he might have been better advised to request an interview with the imprisoned Aquino. Marcos seemed to be extending generous licence to his most dangerous opponent – if one considers the threat of a trial for treason generous. Was the penalty for a guilty verdict execution? Would that intimidate or infuriate Aquino's supporters? The aircraft heeled over to join the outer circuit. He sighed. Too late to change course now.

'… but the technocrats who now see their plans coming to fruition are enthusiastic. The businessmen, both local and foreign, who are being actively encouraged to maximise their profits, are happy to see their schemes now being put into practice. The mass of the people, on the other hand, will wait and see if the reforms being introduced bring a positive and lasting benefit to them, before coming to a judgement. It is these people the government is addressing in a 'hearts and minds' campaign. For the moment it seems as if the people are prepared to go along with what one government spokesman called 'an attempt to find a Philippine answer to Philippine problems.'

Peter stopped reading and looked up. The face was in deep shadow but the head seemed to be nodding encouragement. Brownie had driven them directly to Agustin Enterprises. After Nigel learned that the pilot was heading for two days of R & R at the resort, he begged off the interview with Agustin. After all, Peter had elected himself to fight the editorial battles. Nigel was looking forward to a few pleasanter struggles of his own once he was 'back at the ranch'.

'As past experience has shown, it is not only a censored press which fawns on an authoritarian regime; it is layers of government subordinates. In the absence of an official opposition, there is an undeniable need for some form of checks and balances on the activities of bureaucrats. In a regime of complex familial relationships this might prove difficult to establish.'

Peter's heart skipped a beat at the thought that Agustin might well be related to the President. There came no reaction from his host.

'The President is clearly a man of high intelligence,' Peter continued, feeling his cheeks glow. What was his evidence for this thick slice of sycophancy? He had never exchanged a word with Marcos. Nor even read his book. He cleared his throat.

'His problem is how to distance himself sufficiently from his own subordinates in order to differentiate between truth and propaganda.' Again, he tried to penetrate the deep pool of shadow. Only Agustin's tie was visible. It was granitic grey silk.

'Is that the end?' Augustin leaned forward into the light.

'Yes. For the moment.' Peter slurred 'moment'. 'I wrote this in the mine guest house last night. It may need a little adjustment here and there.'

Agustin offered no comment. He got to his feet and his head and shoulders were lost in shadow. His voice was soft – almost soulful.

'Peter, you will have to take great care tomorrow.'

Peter found himself wishing for words of approval from Agustin for what he had just read. He found himself wanting to please this seemingly perplexed little man. He sensed that Agustin might be beginning to rue his acquiescence in Hal's seduction. Perhaps Peter could add a final upbeat note to the article? What was it that that American had said at the Intercontinental?

'If this is martial law, I wish they...' Peter cudgelled his memory. 'I wish they would send...' *Export* would be preferable to *send*. 'Export Marcos...' *President* Marcos' would be preferable but unlikely from any American businessman, who only recognised one president on the planet. 'I wish they would export Marcos to the States.' Yes. That would do it.

Agustin's voice, now close to his ear, startled Peter

'Who is this girl Hal has been seeing?'

'Sorry?' Peter was bewildered. To which girl was Agustin referring? Peter already knew of two. Were there others? 'I don't know which girl you mean.'

Agustin reappeared behind the desk. His voice sounded

thicker. 'I mean the girl he brought back from the Pagsanjan Falls yesterday.'

'Hal told me he was inviting another photographer along because I was going to be up at the mine with Nigel.' Peter's lips felt dry. 'Maybe the photographer was female.' He licked his lips.

'And what about the helicopter?' Agustin's voice trembled with barely contained rage.

Peter's head was beginning to spin. 'Helicopter?' He felt like a mischievous schoolboy, caught up in the toils of the adult world.

'You know nothing about the helicopter?' Agustin's voice trembled with the effort to control his anger.

'No.' Peter just managed to stop short of the damning 'honestly'.

'Very well.' Agustin's veined hand cut across the pool of light. 'You may leave.'

Peter lurched away from this sharp dismissal. Outside the office door waited the giant. For reasons he could not fathom, Peter felt on the verge of tears. What enormity had Hal perpetrated to undermine the carefully constructed structure of goodwill they had built with Agustin? Peter pushed open the smoke-coloured glazed door and slouched into the courtyard, shoulders hunched against the drizzle. Watched through the glass by the giant, he untwisted the strap on his hold-all. His fingers closed round the curled sheets in his hand. Crouching in the sodden centre of the asphalt, he thrust the article and its sycophantic pleas into a dark corner of the bag.

The passing cab he hailed on the street beside the offices sped him back to the resort through a slicing downpour. Rather than wait for change, Peter ran from the taxi up the slippery staircase. He burst into Hal's room without knocking.

'Where the bloody 'ell you been?' Hal wanted to know, as he peered around the perching Maria. 'Nigel's been back for ages.'

The Nigel in question lay on Hal's bed in his favourite pair of shorts. He had the air of a man who had had his fill of porridge and Sue. She lay snuggled into his armpit. Peter turned away from their post-coital torpor.

'I've been reading Agustin another article.' Hal chose to

ignore the edge to Peter's voice.

'Pagsanjan.' Hal had at least learned how to pronounce one Tagalog word. He grinned. 'Fantastic.' Hal pushed Maria off his lap. 'Pour Pete a drink, there's a good gal.'

The stained table held ten bottles of San Mig – five empty and five awaiting their fate.

'I tell you, I was takin' my life in my 'ands, goin' down those rapids.' Maria moved into the shower-room to wash a glass. As the water began to run, Hal lowered his voice. 'Isabel was 'angin' on like grim death up at the front of the boat. I was 'angin' on at the back with the models.' He grinned and fell silent. Maria had returned.

'About Isabel...' Peter began.

'She got in a right old tizz.' He intercepted the glass that Maria was handing to Peter and drank a gorgeful of beer. The half-empty glass finally reached its intended destination.

'She'd laid on this big reception for me back at 'er place. By the time she'd messed about makin' the models do the whole trip again, the sun was goin' down.' Maria resumed her place on Hal's bare knee.

'Isabel was gettin' 'er knickers in a right old twist.' Hal laid a palm on Maria's stomach. She raised a hand to adjust her spectacles.

'I've got to get back in time,' Hal mimicked in a girlish falsetto. 'If I don't, that bitch will do something to ruin the evening.' Hal's other hand stroked Maria's buttocks. 'So, I untwisted 'er knickers for 'er.'

'What did you do? Strangle her mother?'

'You must be jokin'.' Hal squeezed Maria with both hands. She squirmed and Peter sank down into a chair.

'What happened next?' Peter asked, suddenly weary.

'I rang Alvarez.' Hal's tongue flicked over his front teeth. 'After your little chat with Enrile he told me to give 'im a buzz if I ever needed anythin'.' Hal shrugged. 'Well, I needed somethin'.'

'Don't tell me,' Peter joked. 'A flying trip back to town.'

Hal bounced Maria on his knee. Twice. 'Right. I drove down

to find a phone with that poofter designer and told Alvarez that we were stuck up at the Falls and needed to get back, urgent-like. So, 'e sent up a chopper.' Hal's grin broadened. 'We jumped in; Isabel took some shots of Manila; we landed smack bang in the middle of 'er back garden; I signed the chitty; and there you go.' He shrugged and smiled. 'Isabel was really grateful.'

Peter twitched with irritation. 'And that's it?'

'Yeah, courtesy of the National Security Forces of the Philippines.' He inserted a hand beneath Maria's posterior. 'Cor, Maria, my leg's gone to sleep. Your bum weighs a ton.' Hal stamped a foot and winced. He levered Maria upwards. 'Pour us another beer, there's a good girl.' Hal lowered his voice. 'I tell you, me old mate, this is paradise on earth.' He rested his elbow on his right knee. His voice became confidential. 'I've 'eard of this place down South.... Seaview or Seamew or somethin'...'

'Cebu,' Peter offered.

'Yeah, well, Cebu's got seven birds for every bloke. High demand, low supply. A man could die happy.'

Peter got to his feet, lifting the strap of his bag. 'Agustin is not best pleased with you,' He looked down at Hal.

'Why, what's upsettin' the old fart?'

'For some extraordinary reason I can't fathom, he takes exception to your calling up military helicopters as though they are taxis.'

'E's only jealous 'cause 'e ain't got a chopper.' Hal winked.

Peter shrugged and departed.

Miranda was spread-eagled across the bed as Peter slipped into his room. She stirred as he tiptoed past the bed to reach the phone.

'Allo?' It seemed as if the husky-voiced operator had never left her post.

Peter whispered, 'I'd like some chicken and rice, please.'

'What you want?' the voice bellowed to encourage emulation.

Peter moved as far from the bed as the telephone cord would allow.

He repeated his order in something closer to his normal voice.

Miranda rolled onto her back, one knee drawn up beneath the cotton frock. She raised an arm across her eyes as Peter gently replaced the receiver. He switched on the light beside the bed.

Courteously Miranda enquired, 'You want massage?' Her voice was heavy with interrupted sleep.

'I'm afraid my present need is for chicken and rice. And a decent shower.' The girl pouted prettily. As Peter made for the water, Miranda went in search of his food. As she disappeared, Peter turned about and rapidly exited to tap on Miguel's door. Peter received a loud, dismissive response.

He was alone with his dilemma. He returned to his room. He needed to think. He entered the shower. After sluicing himself thoroughly, he covered his head with a small towel. On a peg in a corner, he discovered a fresh towelling robe.

He would have to use writing as a prophylactic. That and a large meal. Over-eating, he had always found, was an incitement to sexual inertia. He returned to the bedroom, a towel covering his damp hair; the robe the rest. The steaming plate of chicken and rice awaited him at the small table. Good. No garlic.

No sooner was he seated than Miranda pressed herself against his back and began to knead his shoulders.

'Miranda?' The girl's ministrations were put on pause. Peter smiled up at her questioning eyes. 'I would love a beer.' No sooner said than gone.

Peter had consumed half the rice by the time the beer arrived. Beer and rice, he knew, were a fatal combination. He felt the strong urge to belch. He downed the first drink then held out the glass for a refill. His glass was duly refilled. The kneading was resumed.

Peter smiled up at Miranda. 'Miranda?' The kneading paused. 'I'm sorry but I find your delightful massage a little distracting. Why don't you lie down or something while I finish this delicious food?'

The girl's hands dropped as she turned towards the bed. Peter persisted with his gorging scheme. He could feel his stomach swelling against the knotted robe. In spite of deploying a cunning rallentando, he finally arrived at an empty plate. He pushed it away with a sigh and a light belch. He turned.

Miranda lay prostrate on the bed with one knee raised and her lips pouting. Somehow it looked familiar. Where had Peter seen that pose before? Yes, it was a replica of the posters, scattered throughout the city, advertising the popular 'bomba' films. She lowered her lids as she fixed Pete with a sultry stare.

'Miranda.' Peter frowned at his seductress. 'Would you mind removing your flip-flops from the sheet?'

The girl started guiltily and lowered her feet over the side of the bed.

Peter's blood froze at the sound of a wild howl coming from beyond the pool.

'Jesus,' Peter exclaimed. 'What on earth was that?'

Miranda's hand curvetted in mimicry of the leap of an animal somewhere out in the darkness. She shook her head and smiled. 'Long way.'

'An animal?'

There came another howl, longer and lower than the first and – it seemed to Peter – closer.

Miranda waited while Peter held his breath. As the seconds extended into and beyond a minute, he realized that something had died out there. Died violently. That was the finishing touch.

'Miranda?' The girl looked up at him, her eyes sad and huge. Peter swallowed. 'I'm sorry, but I have to do some writing.'

The girl's eyes were lowered as she rose from the bed and, avoiding eye contact with Peter, returned the plate and the other items to the tray before slipping away into the night.

A paradise for men.

Peter reached down for the typewriter and unzipped the case. Settled at the table, he raised an index finger and searched for an 'E'.

Early the next morning...

Peter was bored with the spare narrative of the diary. The writing reminded him of the sound of a song emanating from a telephone. Somewhere along the way it had lost its highest and lowest notes. Somehow his experiences had lost their relevance. He sighed and typed on.

We took a brief tour of the facilities of the camp. As we made some purchases...

No reader would know or care about what 'we' referred to. Nigel was Peter's secret, kept from the wider world. Yet oddly, he had begun to warm to the overweight, unimaginative, impossible Nigel while they had been up at the mine. That warmth was in danger of spreading from Nigel to Hal. Yes, even to the inexpressibly ghastly Hal.

Peter leant back in his chair. Was it something in the air of the islands which had affected him? True, the trio had shared novel experiences. But the 'experiencers' needed to share a genuine sympathy. This they lacked. Perhaps he had questions to answer about his own attitude. Had he been too judgmental? Or were his judgements justifiable? Then came another question. Which of the two partners could he envisage sharing a life with on the putative *Philippines Weekly*? Both seemed to have their reasons for wishing to return to the Philippines; both said they needed him as a partner. Nigel and Hal distrusted each other. That much he had learnt. And he distrusted both of them, in spite of his present maudlin frame of mind. At the same time, he realised that he held some interesting cards, thanks to the various talents he commanded, slight though they might be.

Peter was at a loss to explain the attraction of the archipelago. Hal and Nigel's reasons were clear enough, falling as they did under the headings 'escapism' and 'plunder'.

Seven women to each man. Signing chits that never required payment. The freeloader's paradise. So farewell Hilary, adieu Susan. Hail, Isabel; hello, Sue Two. Six brown servants standing on the wall. Cheap servants, cheap office, cheap accommodation. This was paradise. The land of plenty. The land of the real 'free lunch'.

They would automatically be enrolled as members of the elite; protected by 'curpew', President Marcos and the guns of the National Security Forces. More spoiled than the denizens of Hong Kong back in the golden Fifties.

Beside the country roads they rose in heaps – the coconuts, the pineapples, the mangos, the Mirandas. Sixty centavos for a pineapple? Locals only pay twenty. An excess of fruit; an excess of people. They both fell into one's lap. And – in this tropical Garden of Eden Peter felt himself ripening quite nicely. The gentlest displeasure from Agustin and he would cave in like rotting fruit. Sixty centavos a pineapple. The man with the bolo. Four surgical cuts and the juice flowed down his fingers. The man with the bolo.

Peter resumed his typing.

> ...at the store we heard some singing. A short walk brought us to a primary school. In the yard squads of children performed the national anthem, before raising their hands in the oath of allegiance.

An etiolated insect with long, slack legs attacked the central lamp bulb with clumsy ferocity. The attacker fell to the floor in a jerky series of dives. Peter stared at the creature. Not the slightest movement. A corpse.

His writing rhythm had fled. He stretched, inhaled and felt his vertebrae creak in protest. He rose and removed the robe. He yawned and trembled. He switched off the bedside lamp. The crumpled bed-sheet glowed in the half-light filtered by the window. Peter carefully lowered himself onto the sheet. He closed his eyes and then re-opened them to stare at the featureless ceiling. His stomach rumbled ricily. He detected a faint, approaching sound. The door clicked open and a cotton ghost drifted silently towards him. He gave an involuntary jerk by way of greeting. The ghost silently took up position beside him.

There was nothing spectral about the warm grip which enveloped his incipient erection. Peter felt slightly ridiculous. But he kept his silence. His mind was still on other things as the spectre began its ministrations. The advent of sexual excitation always caught him unawares. His apprehension fell away as warmth flooded every vein. An animal sound broke the silence. A low growl. The figure in white continued its persistent manipulation. Peter realised that the still, intent figure was actually engaged in an act, not so much of masturbation, as of mensuration; an answer to the question 'how big is yours?'. His hips lifted and the growl was repeated. He was the growler. He gave a muffled cry and fell back on the bed. The ministering devil withdrew. Drums sounded in his throbbing ears. Someone, he realised through his confusion, was knocking at the door.

Miranda had darted to the shadows beside the door as Peter struggled to disguise his discomfiture beneath the sheet. His excitement had disappeared at a speed which put its earlier tortuous arrival to shame. 'O.K.' he called in a hoarse whisper. Miranda spoke in Tagalog. A deep male voice grumbled back in the same tongue. Peter shut his eyes, savouring the final thrum of detumescence. He felt the bed depress as Miranda returned. 'He say Boss want to see you.' The grip on his arm was business-like in quite a different way. With a mingled sigh and groan, Peter reached across the girl's lap and found the switch for the bedside lamp. They both blinked in the sudden light, Miranda shielding her eyes with a slight forearm. Peter turned the watch face towards the light, squinting at the steel hands.

'It's nearly eleven,' he complained. 'What the hell can the man want at this time of night?' Miranda left the bedside and entered the shower room. He heard a tap being turned on. Peter struggled into a sitting position. He leaned forward and grasped his ankles. He was not the bloody man's servant. Did Agustin imagine that he controlled everybody at the resort for twenty-four hours a day?

He became aware that Miranda was observing him with a worried frown puckering her brows. His conscience pricked him. While he could pretend to retain his independence, Miranda could not afford to have that illusion. For her, Agustin was a feudal lord. Any rebelliousness on Peter's part might well involve awkward consequences for this temporary concubine. The girl sat, glum and fretful, plucking the sheet.

'You look prettier when you smile,' Peter suggested. She looked up but snatched her arm away as he attempted to stroke it. Then she pointedly glanced over her shoulder, with a frown.

'You go now,' she murmured, her voice trembling. Miranda

grasped his right wrist with both hands, He bent his arm and drew her towards him. The girl must learn new realities. The small hands released their grip. She was on her feet, in full flight towards the door. She stood beside the door-handle. 'You go now.'

The girl was gasping with agitation. Peter was left in no doubt about the genuineness of the girl's feelings. He began to respond to her nervous tension. In spite of all the anecdotes he had heard from Hal and the hacks at the F.C.C. about the violence of the Philippines, he had never experienced, until this moment, so much as a tremor of fear. Until this moment. Was he to believe that, behind the smiling, welcoming façade, physical danger awaited the importunate foreigner who pushed his luck an inch too far? Certainly, the clues were there in profusion. The curfew, the armed guards in Makati, even the sleeping threat of Mount Taal, all bespoke the threat of violence. But thus far the violence had been hidden behind a screen which shielded the naïve foreigner from native dangers. Now that tremor of fear was beginning to shake his own encapsulated, safe world. He tried to read what lay behind the expression on the girl's face.

The knocking resumed. The girl jerked as though tugged by strings. 'Come in,' Peter shouted.

The door opened in two bites, punctuated by the appearance of a straw hat. The giant's body followed the trilby into the room.

'Yes?' Peter managed to keep his nerves in check.

'The boss wants to see you.' Peter looked away from the bodyguard. 'Now,' the giant rumbled, pointing a thumb over his shoulder.

'Right. I'll have to get dressed.' He sensed that the giant had departed. Without a glance at Miranda, he swung his legs out of bed and strode towards the shower. He counted to one hundred and eighty before reversing the position of the shower tap. He busied himself with a towel as he returned to the bed. Miranda kept her back to the room as she peered along the balcony through the curtains. As she turned towards him, he realised she no longer saw him at all. Fear was blind.

In his haste he dropped the towel on the floor. As he stooped to retrieve it, his foot stepped on something soft and giving. He shuddered with horror and shook his leg in desperation to unseat the corpse of the huge insect from his damp sole. The beast scraped the boards as it flew from Peter's foot. His heartbeat seemed to have doubled its rate. Sex and fear, he realised, had similar effects on the body. He glanced up at Miranda. The girl had returned to her vigil at the window. Peter concentrated on drying his sole. He dressed deliberately and slowly, taking ironic care with the trouser zip. That would be the final ignominy.

'Mr. Nicholson sends his regrets, Mr. Agustin. He cannot attend your midnight meeting. He has caught his prepuce in his trouser zip.'

The shoes completed his tenue. He was ready. The expression on Miranda's face was one of frank relief. He almost expected her to check his appearance – a Filipina version of Hilary. He paused and looked back at the girl.

'No need to wait up for me, Miranda.' Why was he taking it out on her? She was a blameless victim in all this. The girl pushed her way past him onto the balcony. The shadow of a bat obscured a light on the wall of the massage parlour. Peter paused. 'If I see the bat again, I'll assume it's a lucky sign.'

The light went out. So much for luck. Peter closed the door behind him. Along the balcony a beam of light split the night like a beacon. In the beam a grotesque shadow materialised, followed by the grotesquery in person. The giant, now sans straw hat, beckoned to Peter. The Englishman tried to invest his approach with jauntiness as he passed his partners' dark doorways. So, there was yet another room beyond the four he already knew. The giant stepped aside and Peter stepped inside. His partners had eschewed formality in their dress. Shorts were all that separated them from Old Adam.

'Where the fuckin' 'ell 'ave you been?' was Hal's greeting.

Nigel's skin looked greasy in the harsh overhead light. His eyes were black sockets.

Peter realised that the giant had followed him into the space. He noticed that the disposition of the furniture in the room was the reverse of his; so that, instead of standing like guilty schoolboys before a stern Agustin seated at a table, the trio of expatriates huddled at the foot of the bed.

''E's 'avin' a fuckin' fit.' Hal's breath blew hot in Peter's ear.

It was difficult to reconcile the dishevelled figure now revealed to them on the bed with the usually immaculately accoutred businessman who led Agustin Enterprises. On the sheet lolled an unfamiliar brown doll with tousled grey-black hair. An old-fashioned pair of spectacles balanced precariously on one ear. Peter considered that Agustin's maroon pyjamas were probably a mistake.

The trio started as Agustin exhaled gustily. Beside the head of the bed, the giant's hands convulsed. He did not know what to do. Certainly, he did not dare lay a finger on his employer. That would be lèse-majesté.

Peter bit his lip as Agustin began to mutter and moan to himself, rolling to and fro on the tormented sheet. Initially, Peter experienced feelings of alarm but, as the gymnastic display continued, he wondered whether these hysterics were genuine. Then, quite suddenly, Agustin tumbled off the bed and crashed onto the wooden floor. The force of the fall was felt through the three foreigners' feet. The giant took an involuntary half-pace forward and reached down towards his master's recumbent body.

'No,' roared Agustin, flinging out a fist. 'Get back, you bastard.' The big man, bewildered, retreated, as Agustin wallowed among discarded socks and shoes. Peter shuddered at the sound of yet another insect busily attacking the light above their heads. His spine crawled but he did not dare look up. Instead, he stepped forward and bent over the tortured figure on the floor. To his alarm and dismay Agustin flailed out once again.

'Get back, you English bastard.'

Peter easily avoided the telegraphed punch. Agustin, carried forward by the attempted blow, was caught under the armpits by Peter, who found it remarkably easy to lift Agustin back onto the bed.

'Mr. Agustin?' Nigel's voice was high-pitched and tremulous. Agustin glared at him through his crazily-angled glasses.

'You bastard.' He wrinkled his nose but the spectacles

continued to droop. His glanced embraced the trio. 'You greedy, ungrateful bastards.'

After the initial slurring, Agustin's voice was now coming through ten-ten. Loud and very clear. Peter had managed to retain a hold on Agustin's shoulder and now he allowed his knees to relax, bringing him into a position just behind the crumpled figure. He could feel the tension in the corded muscles. Agustin belched and wrinkled his nose again. Peter followed suit as he detected the mixed odour of whisky and garlic. Scots courage with a dash of Italian. Peter's initial apprehension was followed by a prick of affection as the old man allowed Peter to support his weight.

'Why have you done this to me?' The question was directed at Hal and Nigel. 'You ungrateful bastards.' The two men dipped their heads by way of response.

'I invite you to the Philippines. I give you the run of my resort. My home.' His arm completed an arc embracing the room and its somewhat dishevelled contents. 'Have I denied you anything?' Agustin awaited a reply. Nigel, apologetic, shook his head. Hal remained silent.

'I give you rooms, food, drink, girls – anything a man could want. On the house.' Peter was caught off guard as Agustin rolled onto his stomach and reached out towards the bedside cabinet. Agustin's fingers groped among a pile of miscellaneous papers below a tired, wooden lamp. Returning to an upright position, Agustin waved the papers in front of his face. One sheet fluttered to the bedsheet.

'Bills. Bills. Here.' He flung the papers like grease-stained confetti at the men standing before him. Nigel lifted a protective hand while Hal remained silent and inert, avoiding Agustin's glittering eye.

'Tell me, Hal,' Agustin remarked in a voice which closely resembled its usual timbre and volume. 'Have I asked you or your friends to pay for one thing since you arrived in the Philippines?'

Silence replied to the question. Peter's fingers itched to straighten Agustin's disordered hair; to restore his spectacles to their rightful place; to restore his dignity.

'Helicopter,' Agustin muttered and then spat the word out again. 'Helicopter!'

'Look,' Hal opened his gambit, accompanied by a step forward. 'I agree you've been very generous since we arrived in the Philippines. 'Ave I ever denied it?' He extended his hand in a histrionic gesture of appeal. Agustin carefully adjusted his spectacles over both ears. Peter sighed.

'Now, about this 'ere 'elicopter business.' Hal's voice took on volume and colour. 'I don't know why you're gettin' your knickers… you're getting' so upset.' Belying his more confident tone, Hal's lips were dry. 'Major Alvarez told me the army would be 'appy to lay on anything *'Ong Kong Weekly* needed.'

'Why did you need the helicopter?'

Hal's assertiveness faltered, yet somehow managed to stay upright.

'There was an important meeting organised for that evening. With really important people. Some army, some business, some agriculture.'

Hal paused to check on Agustin's response. Would 'agriculture' overturn the helicopter? No response. Hal kept talking.

'Well, with Peter and Nige up at your mine, Mr. Agustin… gettin' some fantastic material, by the way… well, somebody 'ad to go up to the Falls and get the shots. Time's short. And, you know what they say. Time's money, Mr. Agustin.'

Nigel nodded in eager agreement. Hal's volume went up a notch. Agustin remained silent.

'Major Alvarez was 'appy to send for the chopper. I mean, if he'd hesitated – even for a split-second – I'd 'ave taken the 'int.' Hal shrugged. 'But I didn't even 'ave to ask him twice. And… ' He spread his hands. 'We got some great aerial shots of Manila.' Hal continued his attempt at disarmament. 'And, after all, we got the chopper back in good order.'

Agustin's stare was blank. Hal's *joie de vivre* evaporated. He made one last attempt. 'I signed his little chitty, all legal like.'

Agustin's fingers filtered the paper jetsam on the bed. Triumphant, he raised a large, official-looking receipt.

'Yes.' His eyes glinted. 'You have signed.' He shook the sheet violently. 'But Agustin must pay.'

Hal's jaw dropped. His display of dismay was impressive. 'But, Major Alvarez...'

'Major Alvarez knew that Augustin would pay.' He glanced down at the receipt. 'One military helicopter and pilot for two and a quarter hours.' His head jerked upwards and fixed Hal in a barbed stare. 'Do you have any idea how much this costs?'

Hal blenched, silenced by the incalculable. Agustin's voice returned to an approximation of its normal measured pace.

'I do not complain about the money. I complain about your thoughtlessness. Would it not be courteous in a guest to inform his host about hiring this helicopter? The first I hear of this thing is when this invoice is delivered by an army courier.'

'But, Mr. Agustin, I thought the 'elicopter came courtesy of the army.' Hal's face had bleached white. 'Honestly!' Peter winced inwardly.

'That is not the point,' Agustin almost screamed, his eyeballs protruding. 'I am your host.' He jabbed a thumb into his chest. 'You tell me where you go and what you do.' He repeated the stabbing action. 'Me. I call the shots here.' His voice soared. 'You understand?'

Peter felt his sympathy for Agustin ebb.

'You understand?' Agustin's shout was hoarse.

Hal nodded dumbly.

Agustin's voice resumed its habitual measured tenor.

'Not content with costing me thousands of dollars,' Peter now realised that Agustin's drunkenness had been feigned. 'Not content with taking all and giving nothing but words in return, you also make a big scandal with Isabel Castillas.'

'What scandal?' Hal's face flushed in the weak tungsten light. 'I never laid a finger on 'er. And what can you do in a helicopter?'

'She arrived at the Falls with you and others and returned with you alone.'

'The others went back by jeep. Isabel told me she had to get home quick.' Hal held both palms upward and hunched his shoulders,

Agustin rose to his knees. 'And the whole of Makati watches an army helicopter arrive at the Castillas mansion, containing Isabel and a foreigner.' Agustin's chest sustained another blow.

'I don't see what's wrong with that. Isabel was takin' some photos for the mag.' Hal drew himself up to his full height. 'I mean, you wouldn't have objected if I'd dropped her home in a taxi, would you?'

'A taxi does not drop out of the sky,' Agustin replied in his coldest manner. He smoothed down his hair. 'The whole world does not look up at a taxi.'

Hal raised a hand as if to demur. Agustin overrode him.

'Tell me Hal,' Agustin's right fist bunched against his thigh. 'Have you told Isabel about your wife in Hong Kong?'

The insect's frantic clicking was all that stood between the room and total silence.

'Look, Mr. Agustin...' Nigel was stepping into the breach.'

'You,' Agustin's index finger brought Nigel up short. 'Shut your mouth.'

'But Mr. Agustin... ' Nigel disobeyed.

'You,' Agustin's volume increased. 'You are nothing.' Agustin swept Nigel aside with a fierce backhand. 'You I have bought.'

Peter wondered what force could hold back this eruption. No sooner had he wondered than the lava began to flow in Peter's direction. This was obviously Agustin's chosen moment for clearing accounts. The old man's head turned to face him.

'And you,' Agustin hissed. Peter struggled to hold the man's eye.

'You English bastard. You think you are so much better than me, don't you?' The sheer unexpectedness of the accusation robbed Peter of all power to respond.

'O.K.' Agustin jerked his head towards Hal and Nigel. 'You are not the same as those two bastards. You did not come here to rob me.' Agustin's eyes narrowed. 'You say you wish to write the truth. That is worthy of respect. But you must write that you despise the brown race, you white bastard.'

Unnerved by Agustin's fury, Peter failed to notice the man

slide across the bed. For the first time since this terrible scene began, the businessman stood erect. He lurched towards Hal and Nigel, who parted with alacrity to give the fury free passage.

Agustin swung round and, in so doing, tore at his pyjama jacket. He flung it from him.

'You bastard, Hal. You are the worst.' Agustin sobbed the final syllable as he fumbled with the cord around his waist. Then, to their astonishment, Agustin's nakedness was revealed. He breathed sterterously, his fists raised.

The volcano had erupted.

'Come on, you white bastard. I will fight you.' Agustin kicked at the abandoned garments at his feet. They scythed into a corner.

'Come on, Hal. I'll kill you with my bare hands. In a fair fight. Before witnesses.'

Nigel retreated into the shadows; Hal crouched behind a chair.

'Now don't be silly, Mr. Agustin.' Hal's grin was his least convincing yet. 'I wouldn't want to 'urt you.'

Peter seriously doubted whether Hal would be able to make any impression on this fierce little man, whose body, beneath the pouched face of age, was youthful and muscular. He was the personification of a pre-Christian Filipino god; his belligerent stance radiated power.

'Come and fight, you coward.' Agustin strode over towards the chair. Hal did his very best to stand his ground but one foot jerked backwards in involuntary retreat.

'Don't be silly, Mr. Agustin. You're twice my bloody age.' Hal's face was chalk-white. 'I can't fight someone old enough to be my father.'

Hal towered over the naked Filipino.

'You refuse to fight?' Agustin lowered his fists but the eruption had not quite concluded. 'I trusted you and you have betrayed my trust.' Hal's tongue flickered over his desert lips 'You are a dead man, Hal. You have just twenty-four hours to live.'

The giant eased his bulk away from the wall. The diminutive coal eyes surveyed Hal like a snake's tongue. The fingers on the huge hands flexed. In the silence the insect attacked the light, before falling to the floor. Agustin turned his back on Hal. Peter moved beside Hal and gripped his slack arm.

'Come on, Hal.' Nigel waited by the open door as Peter led Hal in a retreat marked by a series of nervous tics.

'Mr. Agustin?' Hal called in a weak voice from the doorway. The inexorable brown back of Agustin refused to budge.

'My God,' Nigel exhaled, as they entered the haven of darkness. They paused outside Nigel's door but he ushered them further along the balcony. 'I'm not going in there alone.' He shuddered.

'It's all right, Nige.' Hal hissed, recovering a smidgeon of bravura. 'It's me 'e's gonna kill. Not you.'

They arrived at the entrance to Hal's den. Hal pushed the door open. He turned towards Peter. 'Come in for a minute.'

Peter nodded his acquiescence and the unhappy trio shuffled into the bedroom. Hal switched on the bedside lamp as Peter closed the door behind Nigel. Hal's face still bore an unwonted pallor.

''E was jokin', wasn't 'e, Pete?' Hal stared across the room.

Peter could not respond to the appeal in Hal's eyes. 'I wouldn't count on it, Hal.'

'Jesus,' Nigel blurted and collapsed on the bed. 'I feel like I want to vomit.'

'Fuck you, Nige.' Hal's voice teetered on the brink of hysteria. 'It's all right for you.'

Peter moved over to the bed. 'There's no need to lose our heads.' Hal sank down beside Nigel.

'I'll 'ave to get back to 'Ong Kong' right away.' Hal pressed his sweating palms together. 'It ain't safe here.'

Peter insisted, 'There's no need to panic.'

'It's all right for you, Peter. 'E only 'ates you. 'E's gonna kill me.' Hal thumped his chest with perverse pride.

'So you keep boasting.' Peter allowed his irritation to show. He relented. Hal had a good reason for apprehension.

'What did 'e say? Twenty-four hours?' Hal stood and carried the chair over to the door. He jammed it under the doorknob. ''Ow can I get away from 'ere without that fuckin' lunatic knowin'?'

'Listen,' Peter struggled to sound a note of warm reassurance. 'This isn't the Philippines of the old days. They don't go round bumping off their enemies anymore.'

'Don't you fuckin' well believe it, me old mate.' Hal shook his head. 'You wasn't 'ere in '69, like I was. It's still there, under the surface. I can feel it.'

Peter occupied the second chair. 'Look, here's what we'll do.' He paused. 'We'll all return to our rooms…'

'You're not getting me back in that place again,' Nigel interrupted.

Hal patted his sheet. 'There's only room for me and Pete in this bed.' Hal patted the top sheet.

'There's really no need for me to stay either, Hal.' Peter said, raising a hand as Hal opened his mouth to object.

'We just return to our rooms and use the chairs.' He nodded towards Hal's example. 'There's no way we can get away tonight without their knowing. Agustin will probably get the big man to keep an eye on us all night.'

Hal and Nigel both shuddered.

Peter, the epitome of sound good sense, continued. 'Agustin was pissed. Not completely, but enough to divulge a few home truths. In vino veritas. But if he really intended to kill you, why would he give you a warning?'

Hal's brow puckered.

'No,' Peter warmed to his theme. 'By the morning he'll have scared us enough. He'll blame booze and we'll all laugh it off.'

Nigel was sitting upright and paying heed. Hal still looked worried.

'Now,' Peter continued. 'In the morning you can ring your friends in the army, Hal, and get Alvarez to pick us up at the resort. We'll be down in Mindanao under the protection of the boys in uniform for longer than twenty-four hours. By then the spell will be broken. Not that I think that Agustin was seriously serious. By the time we get back, he'll be all sweetness and light.'

Hal looked up, bright-eyed. 'You reckon?'

Peter had almost convinced himself. He nodded in comradely affirmation. Nigel rose and stretched.

'The little monkey really had me worried there for a moment.'

'Go on, Nige.' Hal achieved an approximation of a grin. 'You weren't really scared of that little monkey, were you?'

'Don't tell me you weren't, old sport.' Hal looked vex. Nigel looked pleased.

'Not that I blame you, old boy. I was shitting bricks. I reckon that little wog wanted to tear you apart with his bare hands.'

Hal's amour-propre was stung into reaction. 'I'd 'ave knocked the little turd's 'ead off 'is shoulders.'

'Of course you would,' Nigel said, through a thin smile. He moved stealthily towards the door. He removed the chair and opened the exit. 'Pity to lose all those fantastic ads,' he hissed and then he was gone. Hal hastily replaced the chair.

'Wait.' Peter rose wearily. 'I'd better go too. Hard day tomorrow.' He gave Hal a bleak smile.

'They say that tomorrow never comes,' was the bleaker response. Peter blinked.

'I'm sure you'll still be around to plague us.' Peter removed the chair. 'By the way.' He turned towards Hal and looked at his watch. 'It's not too late to book us into the *Intercontinental* from tomorrow. I think we may have outstayed our welcome here.'

'Right,' Hal replied, his buoyancy returning. 'You can ring your nancy friend tomorrow.' Hal grinned. ''Ere, Pete?'

Peter paused on the threshold of the night. 'What?'

'Did you notice 'ow small the little turd's donger was?'

Chapter Twenty-three

Seven thirty. The curtain lifted from the window and Peter caught a glimpse of blue sky. He smiled, stretched and grunted his way into wakefulness. His mouth was dry. He stretched, wondering where Miranda was. He needed a coffee.

Then he noticed the chair propped beneath the doorknob and remembered why he had shut himself in. He also recalled what had provoked his precautions; that yesterday had happened. His heart beat more strongly at the recollection of the catastrophe. He arrived at the moment when the Rumpelstilskinian figure of Agustin had jabbed a vengeful finger at Hal. Peter sat bolt upright.

The threat. He had made light of it to Hal. And now, in the bright light of morning, it seemed even less conceivable that a man in Agustin's position would jeopardise everything he had achieved by ordering an execution. Of a foreigner? And for what? For nothing more than what amounted to a misunderstanding. And the price of a helicopter trip, which Agustin could certainly afford.

He relaxed. The events of the previous day certainly did not warrant assassination. Agustin was no fool. He must know that if anything untoward were to happen to Hal, Nigel and Peter would bear witness to Agustin's fury and the ensuing threat. Were Hal to die within the next twenty-four hours (or even twenty-four weeks) he and Nigel would provide Queen's evidence about Agustin's rage.

He paused. But whose word would the Philippines' authorities take? His and Nigel's? Or Agustin's? Peter pondered. He decided that, on balance, appealing to the Philippines' authorities would simply lead them into a legal and political cul-de-sac. Then he decided that, even if the Philippines' government was not to be trusted, he and Nigel could still have recourse to the Hong Kong authorities.

Corruption might be rife in the Hong Kong police but they would surely investigate a murder. And an investigation would be a major embarrassment for the Philippines' authorities. But what if the Philippines' authorities were still prepared to throw their weight behind Agustin? They might consider him too important a figure to toss beneath the wheels of foreign justice. Perhaps they could not afford the risk that he would possibly reveal much that might have unfortunate repercussions for the ruling elite. Peter concluded that a complaint in Manila would probably lead to political entanglements and a long detention awaiting a trial in which they would appear as witnesses for the prosecution.

Peter shifted uneasily. He imagined that unsolved, embarrassing murders remained firmly unsolved in Manila. In any case, it would be simple to stir up a firestorm of public indignation against foreign journalists 'on the make'. The trail of bills Hal had scattered across Manila would be enough to demonstrate Agustin's generosity and the foreigners' appetite for massage girls, freebies and lucre.

Unnerved, Peter swung his legs out of the bed. He lifted his trousers from the bedside chair. They were becoming grubby. The sharp sense of anxiety returned. He hurriedly dressed and slipped out onto the balcony. Below, darker patches stained the asphalt. It had rained during the night.

Peter knocked urgently at Hal's door. No reply. He turned the doorknob and pushed. The door creaked but did not budge. He knocked again, fearful of waking their antagonists. Silence. Was anyone about? He tiptoed to the balustrade and took a cautious look down. There, beside the massage parlour, was parked the Pontiac. The disappearance of the girls and Hal might mean nothing. Or something dreadful. A hissing sound came from behind him. He turned. The door to Hal's room was now ajar. Maria beckoned.

Hal lay on his back, mouth agape, his breathing stertorous. Maria clutched Hal's shirt to hide her nakedness. The room had a sour odour. The window was still firmly shut against the night and possible intruders. Peter looked down at Hal's gaping jaws. He shook the publisher by the shoulder.

Hal snorted and opened an eye.

'Oh, it's you.' He struggled upright, 'Tough luck, Pete.' He grinned. 'I'm still alive. See?'

Peter was agitated and angry. 'Get packed. We've got to get out of here.' Peter was distracted by Maria, as she slipped back beneath the modest sheet.

'Don't worry, Pete.' Hal's grin broadened. 'I got on the blower this morning to Alvarez.'

'What? Before seven thirty?' Peter consulted his watch. He was surprised that Agustin had not cut off the resort phones.

'It's my fuckin' life we're talkin' about, Pete. Not yours.' Hal spat the words at Peter.

Peter nodded. 'Okay. Point taken.'

Hal's response was another broad grin. 'I told 'im our transport had broken down.'

'What?' Peter was alarmed. 'You didn't ask him for another chopper, did you?'

The grin expanded. 'No, course not.' Hal looked coy. ''E's sending a military escort for us at nine.'

Peter had to join in with Hal's grin. Sheer gall.

'Alvarez himself will pick us up at the Inter at ten.' Hal reclined, his hands supporting his head. 'The plane for Mindanao leaves at ten thirty.'

'For more excitement?'

'Not on your Nellie, me old mate. I'm not goin' out on any patrols lookin' for bloody rebels. That's your job. If they don't bother me, I won't bother them.'

Peter smiled. Hal Houdini escapes again. 'Did you remember to book three rooms at the *Intercontinental*?'

'I booked two. Nigel can piss off back to Hong Kong. I mean... who needs 'im?'

'You didn't ask that question before we started this caper, did you, Hal?'

Peter turned. In the corner furthest from the window stood Nigel, his face a vivid puce.

'You bloody cheapskate.' Nigel spat out the words.

Hal snuggled down on the bed. He grinned up at Nigel who took up the thread.

'I could have been back in Hong Kong getting the layout

ready. But you were happy to keep me hanging round because you weren't paying. Now, as soon as you might have to pay for a room, you want to shunt me back home.' Nigel, Peter noted, was dressed ready for the shunt.

'I kept you 'angin' about? An indignant Hal tugged the sheet. Maria's eyes widened in alarm. 'That's a bloody laugh,' Hal dropped into his falsetto soprano. 'Oh, Hal, Sue is so wonderful. The tightest little cunt in the Philippines.'

Nigel's colour deepened as Hal continued, 'She can't get enough of it.'

Hal dropped down two octaves and sneered. 'Getting' you and 'er apart is 'arder than opening an oyster with your bare hands.'

'You can talk,' Nigel sniffed, jutting his chin towards the crown of Maria's head; all that remained visible above the sheet.

'While Pete and I were risking our lives down in the mine, you were risking yours delving into Maria. Not to mention Isabel.'

Maria's wide eyes appeared above the sheet. It was Hal's turn to explode.

'Now you keep your bloody, dirty mouth shut, Nigel fuckwit Thompson. You've done bugger-all on this trip. Joe set up all the ads. And who was it had to do the follow-up, while you were buried up to 'ere in Sue?' Hal raised his hand up to his Adam's apple.

Nigel patrolled the foot of the bed like a caged bear. 'Oh, and what have you achieved, may I ask?' All you had to do was keep Agustin sweet and get his mark on a piece of paper. Not scribble your own bloody cross all over town and drive the old wog up the wall.'

'I don't take kindly to remarks of that ilk,' Hal remarked, his face expressive of exquisite injury to the soul. Peter blinked. Hal resumed, 'That wasn't called for, Nige.'

'My bloody heart bleeds.' Nigel lifted a corner of his mouth. 'Now, are you going to book me a room at the Inter or not? It's your last chance!'

'N.O. Bloody. T. Not.' Hal compressed his lips into a thin line.

'Right. I'm packed. I'll go into town with you and get the first available flight back to Hong Kong.' Nigel turned away and then paused.

Hal grinned, reached across to the bedside cabinet and opened the top drawer. He extracted a large wallet and began to explore its contents. He flicked his fingers and a folded airline ticket gyrated across the room and landed at Nigel's feet.

''Ere, don't let me keep you. Take yourself and your stupid face back to Hong Kong, you idle sod.'

Nigel's face reddened as bent to retrieve the ticket. Hal sneered. 'You're still not getting' anything out of me, Nige. It's a bloody freebie.'

Nigel straightened and waved the ticket at Hal. 'I suppose you hoped I'd be too proud to take it.' Nigel barked a hoarse laugh. 'In the words of the sage – 'not on your Nellie, old sport.' I'm already out of pocket thanks to your little abortion of a business trip.' He thrust the ticket into an inner jacket pocket. Hal's voice caught him at the door.

'Nige, leave the door open when you go. I wanna let the pong out.' Nigel slammed the door shut. Maria buried her head under the sheet. Hal looked at Peter and winked. Then he assumed a serious expression.

'You reckon this trip to Mindanao will do the trick?'

Peter had no alternative than to nod with what he hoped looked like optimism.

'Do you reckon we've blown it? You can be straight with me.' Hal assumed a serious expression. Peter looked down at the floor. 'I'm afraid so,' He slowly shook his head. 'Once the drink has worn off, Agustin's sure to regret all those silly threats. But he feels we have made a fool of him and I'm sure this particular fool won't be quite so ready to part with his money.'

Hal nodded at his protruding big toe. ''Ow would you fancy an Indonesian issue?' Peter departed.

At five to nine, Hal was in Peter's room. ''Ow's it goin'? Ready?' He seemed out of breath. He held his case in his left hand.

'Ready.' Peter indicated his own kit waiting beside the door.

'Right. Let's go. The jeep's 'ere.'

'What's the rush?' Peter asked, following Hal out onto the

balcony. Peter imitated Hal's anxious glance to the left. There stood the giant. He glared. They hurried away. As they fled past his door, a muffled female cry came from Miguel's room. They clattered down the steps. The jeep awaited, the driver taking a final damp draw on a cigarette. He flicked the butt into the courtyard as he spotted them and an indignant chicken squawked. The driver leaped down and opened the rear doors. Peter and Hal clambered on board, easing their bags carefully ahead of them. It occurred to him that, if all else failed, he could try to place the pics with National Geographic. The driver started the engine. Hal stood up, knees and head bent.

''Ang on a minute,' he bellowed at the driver. Then, more quietly to Peter, 'Gotta say goodbye to Maria.'

'No, wait!' Peter stretched out an arm but Hal had already leaped to the ground. The vehicle jerked forward. Peter saw the giant. The giant saw Hal. The vehicle began to pick up speed.

'Hold it,' Peter heard himself roar. The giant broke into a loping run behind the frantic Hal. The jeep skidded to a halt. Hal's knee crashed against the tailgate as he threw himself on board, his eyes rotating. 'Come on! Let 'er rip,' Hal shouted. The driver crashed into first against the revving engine. The giant seemed to dive to the ground. The jeep bounded forward. Hal looked back and roared with laughter. Rounding the recumbent giant ran the frantically waving Nigel, his case bouncing off his calves.

'Let the fucker get 'is own transport.' Hal laughed and turned his back on his erstwhile partner.

They arrived at the hotel at nine thirty. Compared with the spartan lodging he had just vacated, the room Peter had been allocated at the *Inter* was a sybaritic paradise. He tossed his typewriter onto the bed where it bounced twice before coming to rest. He lay down beside the machine and closed his eyes.

What a complete and utter disaster. How much was one third of nothing? It then occurred to him that, thanks to Nigel, he was richer than that. He was eligible to receive a full half of the proceeds. The thought was curiously uncomforting. With the example of Nigel's fate, he was not in the least certain of the size of his eventual reward for his efforts. Peter elbowed his case to one side and reclined full length on the bed. On the other hand, he had least to lose. And in exchange for a free holiday in a fascinating country and privileged access to the private lives of the elite, he had gained three thousand dollars-worth of bribes from Hal. He yawned. He had not slept too well the previous night. Better rouse himself or he would fall asleep.

There was no point in antagonising Alvarez and inciting him to vengeance just for a peccadillo against the forces of law and order. He yawned and swung his legs off the bed. He wandered into the bathroom. His eyes widened.

In addition to the predictable shower, there gleamed an old-fashioned bath-tub. Luxury. He referred to his watch. Alvarez would be down in the lobby in ten minutes. Pity. He could do with a soak. Instead, he ran some water into the sink and splashed his face. He stared into the mirror. Had the giant had a gun? Would he have killed Hal if he had caught up with him? Peter shuddered. He had stepped through the looking glass into a land where known moral equations no longer added up. He re-entered the bedroom, drying his face on a small, blue towel. The phone rang.

He panicked until he found the phone. Breathless, he picked up the receiver. 'Yes?'

'Mr. Nicholson?' The female voice was young and husky.

'Yes, I'm Nicholson.' Peter was picturing Maria.

'You have a visitor in the lobby.'

Alvarez would be prompt of course.

'Right. Thanks. Please tell him we'll be down directly.'

Peter replaced the receiver. Tiredness surged through every cell in his body. There was no alternative. He had to go through with it. It would at least be a captivating tall tale to tell in the *Foreign Correspondents' Club* back in Honkers. Even if he was just an associate member.

Of course, if Agustin has told Alvarez that we have botched the magazine, we could be walking into a trap. Or, alternatively, Alvarez already knows and has come to inform them that the trip down South is off. They would then be stranded in Manila at the mercy of a furiously vengeful Agustin. How much pull did Agustin have with the army? That was the category of question that Filipinos were posing all the time, Peter realised. Getting the answers right could be a matter of life and death.

So, the question was posed; what exactly was Agustin's relationship with Alvarez? Who knew? Within the next ten minutes he and Hal would find out. It would only require one telephone call from their enraged host to set Alvarez loose. But would Agustin really wish anyone else to know how his 'foreign friends' had shamed him?

Peter was cheered by his next thought. Their 'disappearance' would mean that the Enrile interview would never see the light of day; that the Philippines' armed forces chief's time had been wasted; that his deathless prose would expire with them in Mindanao. Not beneficial for their host.

Another heartening thought. Alvarez would not have been in the least concerned about their reasons for requiring a helicopter. Nor, as yet, did he know that Agustin disapproved of the use to which it was put. Perhaps there was no need for anybody else to be involved. Agustin had simply been ensuring that Enrile's words would be disseminated to the English-language press.

On the other hand, suppose Agustin were to inform Alvarez that, apart from Enrile's magniloquent interview, the issue of the Weekly was brimming with anti-Filipino subversion? That Peter had been revealed as someone who hated the brown race? Or that Peter had distorted Enrile's words? Peter's elation sank. The best he could hope for was that Alvarez would not assassinate them in a crowded hotel lobby.

Peter hoisted his bulging canvas bag, locked the door behind him and moved along the carpeted corridor. He knocked on Hal's door. No answer. Peter laid an ear against the cool, veneered surface. He rapped again. Silence was still the stern reply. A room boy appeared further along the corridor and moved towards him. He made a point of avoiding Peter's eye as he passed.

Peter shrugged, hoisted the bag's strap onto a shoulder and made for the lifts. The doors sighed open on the ground floor. He was pleased to find himself in a crowded lobby. He felt slightly less nervous. His eyes sifted the crowd.

Then he caught sight of Hal in a distant corner. Peter found a route through the congregation of Filipino and foreign businessmen. He came to a halt in front of his partner – who was not alone. Alvarez was at Hal's side. And on Hal's other flank was the 'Third Man'.

Agustin's face was as sad as ever. So, he and Alvarez were in league. Peter strove to keep calm. Would the good major arrest them and bundle them off to Camp Crame?

'Hello, Major,' Peter said with a catch in his voice.

Alvarez looked up. He extended his hand. He then looked at his watch with approval. So, there was a timetable. Peter avoided Hal's eye.

'Shall we go?' Peter wondered how he had managed to put the question. His heart was pounding. What would be the major's answer? Alvarez looked sidelong at Agustin.

The old man looked up. Peter felt one knee give. He managed to control it.

'Mr. Nicholson,' the familiar voice was even and mellow. 'I have received a call from the Malacañang Palace.' The businessman's eyes glowed. 'The Pirst Lady has granted *Hong Kong Weekly* an interview.'

Peter glanced at Hal. Could this be an excuse to keep them in Manila until the giant assassin caught up with them? Hal gave the appearance of being free of all such concerns. His teeth were delivering their best display. They would have put a shark to shame.

'Well?' Peter asked, pointedly. He looked hard at Hal. His look said, 'Come on, say 'thank you' to the nice, kind old gentleman.'

'I don't know.' Hal's shaking head expressed the deepest regret. 'You see, Mr. Agustin, I was really lookin' forward to goin' out on patrol with the army down in Mindanao. Wasn't I, Pete?'

Peter nodded sympathetically. He addressed his own question to Agustin. 'When is this interview scheduled to take place?'

Agustin swallowed. 'Tomorrow morning. At ten.'

'I see no problem.' Peter's smile embraced the trio before him. He drew a breath and then launched. 'Hal and I continue on our trip to Mindanao and, if everything runs smoothly, fly back this evening to interview Mrs. Marcos in the morning.' Peter spread his hands. Voilà. He managed to keep a straight face when Alvarez replied.

'That won't be possible. Bad weather is closing in down South. We could fly you in but there's no guarantee that we could get you back in time for the First Lady. No way.'

Peter's eyes narrowed. 'So, you are advising us against going down to Mindanao?'

Alvarez twisted his hat in his hands. He looked at Peter and nodded. 'For your own safety.' The major almost crooned. The irony of the situation threatened to show on Peter's face. He fought against a smile. The major resumed. 'It is a great honour to interview the First Lady. A great honour.'

Peter's mind whirled. One minute he was in fear for his life; the next, he suspected an elaborate ploy to prevent them from witnessing the war down South. Paranoia was in the very air conditioning they breathed.

Hal cleared his throat. 'Tell you what, Mr. Agustin; we'll stay in Manila and interview the First Lady.'

Peter's attempted intervention was waved aside. Hal turned back to put the point baldly. 'Well, what do you say, Mr. Agustin?'

The old man stared down at the carpet. His 'Thank you, Hal' was barely audible.

'Right then. Time for breakfast.' Hal was rubbing his stomach. He grinned at Alvarez.

'Pity about the trip, Major. I was really lookin' forward to it.' Hal's voice became more confidential. 'We'll make a point of it next time we do a Philippines edition. Eh?'

'I look forward to renewing our acquaintanceship,' Alvarez' valedictory handshake was warm.

Peter partook of the overflow of goodwill. As the two Filipinos moved away, Hal pursued them.

'Oh, Mr. Agustin,' Hal placed a hand on the little man's shoulder. Agustin paused but did not turn. 'I've been ringin' Isabel since I got 'ere and there's no reply. I wonder whether you could give 'er a little message for me. Tell her Hal will be waitin' for 'er in the coffee shop.' Hal murmured in Agustin's ear. 'I feel safer with 'er around.'

Agustin nodded curtly and started to move on. Hal's hand caught him by the shoulder again. 'Oh, and Mr. Agustin. I'll think we'll be stayin' 'ere from now on.' Hal's grip did not slacken.' It's more convenient. For the Palace.'

Agustin nodded once again without looking back. Hal released Agustin's shoulder. They watched the old man make his way through the crowd to the reception desk. Peter saw him point them out to the manager, who scribbled a note on a pad.

'It looks as though Mr. Agustin has returned to his old generous ways,' Peter said, lighting a trembling cigarette.

Hal grinned as they watched Agustin fumble his way out of the lobby. 'Wanker.'

'How can you be sure that Agustin knows Isabel's whereabouts?' Peter asked over their third cup of breakfast coffee.

Hal was drawing a cigar out of an inner pocket of his jacket.

'It stands to reason, don't it?' I mean, Isabel's mum saw the chopper arrive at 'er 'ouse. She and Isabel 'ad what you might call 'a few words'.'

He spat out the tip of the cigar.

'Before I left Isabel yesterday morning, I agreed to give 'er a buzz at 'ome today... in case there wasn't room on the plane down to Mindanao.'

His smile was disarming.

'That was before last night.' Hal puffed an accompaniment to the words as he lit the cigar. 'I reckon Isabel's mum got on the blower to Agustin. 'E must 'ave told 'er to keep anyone from answerin' the phone. For the next twenty-four hours.' He exhaled an exiguous stream of smoke. 'You can't trust Chinks.'

Peter raised his coffee cup. 'I always thought of Hong Kong as a small world. But this place is smaller than you think.'

Hal pointed his cigar at Peter.

'What would you say to Agustin 'avin' it off with Isabel's mum?'

Peter almost choked on his coffee.

'I suppose Isabel told you?'

Hal nodded and inhaled.

Peter shook his head. 'She's just being vindictive.'

Peter wanted to disbelieve. He tried to conjure up an image of the tough little Filipino locked in perspiring embrace with the statuesque Chinese matron and rejected it as too repulsive. Agustin had no place in imaginings in which he himself played a leading role.

'Talk of the devil.' Hal interrupted his partner's erotic musings by pointing his cigar over Peter's shoulder. Peter turned to see Isabel hurrying in their direction. She arrived out of breath. After lowering two smart shopping bags to the floor, Isabel collapsed onto a seat beside Peter. Hal welcomed her with a pigeon-peck on the cheek worthy of Trafalgar Square - or Fort Santiago.

Isabel blessed Peter with a radiant smile, then pursed her lips. 'I hate that bitch.'

Hal smiled a surreptitious 'I told you so' at Peter and patted Isabel's hand. 'What's she done now?'

'She locked me in my goddam room. That's what she's done. I wish she was dead.'

'Right,' Hal agreed absent-mindedly. 'What's that you brought with you?' His teeth gripped the cigar.

'Oh, those?' Isabel dismissed the bags with a back-handed wave. 'Agustin wants you to wear them for an interview or something tomorrow.'

'What's 'them'?' Hal's curiosity was piqued.

'Barong Tagalog. The Philippine National costume.' Isabel responded. 'For men.'

Without another word, Hal waved at a waitress and mimed the bill-signing sign. When she returned, he showed his room key. He scribbled a signature on the bill.

'Come on,' he called, swinging the two bags aloft. Isabel and Peter shrugged and followed the leader.

As they awaited the arrival of the lift, Isabel wanted to know, 'Where's your other friend, Hal?'

'Who? Nige? 'E 'ad some pressin' business in 'Ong Kong.'

Isabel stepped into the lift. Hal was behind her. ''E asked me to send you 'is love.' Hal squeezed Isabel's left buttock.

Isabel giggled. Hal hid her from view in a corner. She giggled again. Peter concentrated on the flashing floor indicator.

'Now that things are back on track, Nigel's absence could present us with certain difficulties,' Peter mused aloud.

'Don't you worry your pretty little 'ead about that, me old love,' Hal said, patting Peter's arm. 'Hil will take care of everything. She always does.'

The lift doors glided apart and Hal led the way along the twilit corridor. 'Come on, we'll 'ave a butcher's at this little lot in my room,' he pronounced, flourishing his key.

Once within, Isabel flung herself on the bed with a girlish shriek, kicking her shoes in different directions. Peter held up a protective hand as the right shoe narrowly missed his cheek.

'Oh, Hal. This is wonderful.' Isabel arched her back like a bow.

'Right,' Hal muttered, as though Isabel had been Hilary. Then he disappeared into the bathroom with the bags.

'So, you've been at home all the time?' Peter asked, bridging the conversational void.

'Yes. My mother and I had such a terrible fight after Hal left last night. I heard her phone Agustin. Then she ordered two servants to take me to my room. By force. I scratched their faces!' Her face shone at the recollection. 'They locked me in but I knew Hal would know how to get me out.'

Halford Puckle. Her Lancelot.

'Honestly,' Isabel continued to practise her indignation. 'You wouldn't believe this was the twentieth century. Can you imagine anywhere else in the civilised world where a mother would lock up her daughter in a room like that? Shit! I'm twenty-three, for Christ's sake!

Peter clucked in sympathy. He reached for his cigarettes. That would make her mother about forty. A nice, mature age. He knew better than to use that description within Isabel's earshot. He hoped he might be able to get some scribbling done today as Isabel smiled at the ceiling and breathed deeply.

Hal returned from the bathroom wearing a stiff, off-white silk shirt, decorated with elaborate openwork lace.

'Fuckin' 'ell,' Hal complained, extending his arms like a scarecrow. 'I feel a right poofter in this lot.'

'It suits you.' Peter could not resist the comment. Hal raised an arm as though to assail Peter.

'You've got to wear yours too, remember. I'm not goin' into no bloody palace dressed like this on my own.'

'Palace?' Isabel exclaimed, sitting upright. 'The Malacañang Palace?'

'Yeah.' Hal grinned. 'Me and Pete gotta chat up the purse lady.'

'My God!' Isabel's gob had undoubtedly been smacked.

'I'd better try on my shirt.' Peter got to his feet.

The phone rang. Hal extended a restraining hand to Peter. He lifted the receiver.

'Yeah?' Hal paused. 'Yeah?' Another pause. 'Yeah?'

Peter hummed 'She Loves You' and winked at an uncomprehending Isabel.

'Yeah,' Hal repeated. 'Right. Don't go away.' He replaced the receiver. Peter moved aside with the other plastic container.

''Ang on, Pete. That was business.'

Hal sat on the bed and took both Isabel's hands.

'Thanks for bringing the Talong Bagalog, love.' They exchanged another peck.

'Barong Tagalog,' Isabel murmured, soulfully.

Another peck. Hal kept a firm grip on Isabel's fingers.

'Yeah.'

To Peter's profound embarrassment, Hal gazed deeply into Isabel's eyes. He spoke.

'Now you gotta clear off,' Hal stood and pointed his thumb over his shoulder towards the door.

Peter blinked in disbelief as tears welled up in the girl's eyes.

'Go?' Isabel wailed. 'But I never want to leave you again, my darling.'

Peter inhaled sharply. Hal looked stern.

'Sorry, Isabel'. You can't stay 'ere. You're not registered as a guest.' Hal was firm.

'Go?' Isabel's shoulders shook. 'But I only just got here.'

'Don't you see. This is just what they want.' Hal calmed the shaking with a hand on either slim shoulder.

'Who?' Isabel snuffled.

'Your mum. And Agustin.'

Peter's mouth fell open.

Isabel, her cheeks tear-stained, stared up at Hal.

Hal cooed, 'Imagine the scandal if those two caught us alone together in a hotel room.'

Isabel brightened. 'Good. I don't care. I want them to catch us.'

'You may not care.' Hal smiled at the tear-stained face. 'But I promise you my wife will.'

Isabel was on her feet in an instant.

'Your what?' she screamed.

'Look, I think I'd better leave.' Peter made a beeline for the door.

'You stay put, Pete,' Hal bawled. Then he returned to Isabel and lowered his voice. 'Yeah, my wife. In 'Ong Kong.'

Isabel howled. 'My mother was right. All foreigners are lying cheats.' She stopped howling and narrowed her eyes. 'You promised you would marry me.'

'I will, darlin', I will.' Hal attempted to encompass Isabel's waist with a placatory arm. The girl span out of reach.

'Don't touch me, you bastard!'

'You mustn't take it like this, Isabel.' The girl turned her back on Hal. Peter saw his partner consult his watch.

'I'm gonna get a divorce from my wife.' Hal pleaded. Neither Isabel nor Peter was convinced. Nor, Peter realised, was Hal.

'I gave myself to you,' Isabel collapsed face-down on the bed. Hal's wink froze Peter's hand on the doorknob.

'That's why I'm gonna marry you, darlin'.' Hal's laying on of a hand on Isabel's shoulder was not shrugged off.

Isabel sniffed deeply into the pillow. 'When?'

Hal consulted his watch again as though seeking a response. 'Oh, very soon.'

Isabel sat up. The tears had probably been the least effective treatment for her troubled complexion. Then Peter found himself swept into the drama.

Isabel swung round to face him. 'Who is this woman?' Isabel demanded. Caught unprepared, Peter produced a fair imitation of a stranded goldfish. Hal came to the rescue.

'She's a cripple.' Hal's voice assumed a reverential tone. Peter bit the inside of his cheek. Hal continued. 'She's spent the last five years in a wheelchair.' Hal studied the pattern on the carpet.

Isabel hiccoughed. 'A cri (hiccough) pple?'

'Yes.' Hal pierced Isabel with his sincerest expression. 'So, you see, my darlin', I can't just leave 'er in the lurch. I'll 'ave to provide for 'er, if you and me are gonna get spliced. You wouldn't think much of me for abandonin' a poor cripple woman and leavin' 'er in penury, now would you?'

Isabel replied, saltily. 'No.'

'Right,' Hal took advantage of her acquiescence to lock her shoulders in a consolatory embrace.

'So, you see that it's important that from now on we do everythin' according to the book. In future I want you to do your best to get along with your mum. Remember she'll soon be my mum too.'

Peter did not dare risk catching Hal's eye. He looked away.

'I think I could even bring myself to like 'er... poor old thing.' He quietened Isabel's heaving with butterfly pats.

'I...' Isabel hiccoughed, 'hate her.'

' 'Course you do... now.' Hal crooned. 'Once I get my divorce and my wife goes back to England, you and me can get spliced. Then you won't 'ave to live with your mum. You'll be able to go out to work and 'elp me pay maintenance to my first wife.' Isabel started. Hal shrugged and spread his palms. 'I won't be able to keep both of you just on my own salary.'

Hal stroked the back of Isabel's hand. She delivered a double sigh.

'Right, my darlin', now you're bein' sensible.' Hal eased the girl off the bed and into a standing position. 'Now, you toddle off 'ome to Mummy and tell 'er that you and I 'ave agreed not to rush things. And to do things above board.'

Hal planted a paternal buss on Isabel's forehead. Her face glistened with smeared tears.

'It'll be better for everyone in the long run,' Hal said, nodding reassurances. Isabel hiccoughed and bent to retrieve her left shoe. Hal patted her rump.

'There's a good girl.'

Peter retrieved the right shoe. Isabel, semi-shod, hobbled towards the door. Peter handed her the missing pairing. She paused in the doorway to give Hal a sad, farewell wave. Isabel hobbled on towards the lifts. Peter closed the door behind her.

'You lying, cheating bastard,' Peter cursed the chuckling Hal. ''My wife's a cripple', indeed.'

Hal rolled across the bed, sobbing with laughter. He got his breath. 'Touchin', wasn't it, though?'

Peter grinned in spite of himself. Hal bounced off the bed.

'Mustn't crease this poofter shirt.'

Peter remembered an earlier event. 'What was the phone call?'

Hal stood in front of his partner and amiably slapped both Peter's arms.

'That was Chico. 'E's down in the coffee shop with Maria.' Another pair of slaps.

'And Miranda.'

Peter felt his pulse thud in his ears.

'Wait.' He grabbed at Hal's arm.

'Have you...?' Peter paused. 'You wouldn't have any more of those yellow capsules, would you?'

'Capsules?' Hal made a show of patting his pockets. 'No, I ran out at the resort.' He grinned. 'Come on, live dangerously.'

Hal fingered the penicillin capsules in his pocket as he closed the door behind them.

'You've got less chance of catchin' it than I 'ave.' Hal assured Peter as he steered him towards the lifts.

Chapter Twenty-four

Peter's discomfiture redoubled at the shame he felt when he caught sight of the girls waiting for them in the lobby. They were wearing their habitual cotton frocks (blue for Maria and white for Miranda) and flip-flops. Miranda was biting her lip while Maria nervously lifted her hair from her nape. Beside them, Chico stubbed out a cigarette in a heavy glass ash-tray.

'Isabel may 'ave the dough,' Hal muttered to Peter as they traversed the lobby. 'But Maria leaves 'er for dead in bed.'

Peter held back as Hal strode forward to the waiting group. Chico frowned as Hal made a noisy show of welcoming the girls. The driver caught Peter's eye, nodded and slipped away.

As Hal led the group across the crowded lobby, Peter hung three paces back. He edged round a group of American tourists waiting for a bus tour to Intramuros. At the lifts Miranda drew near him. His smile was forced. He did not embrace her but thrust his hands into his trouser pockets. Maria laughed a little too loudly as Hal bent her backwards and nibbled at her neck. Peter wondered whether Isabel had really left the hotel. Pointless to seek her in this horde.

The lift finally arrived to disgorge a herd of mutton-dressed-as-lamb American tourists. One of the women, tall and very blonde against her deep tan, glanced down at Miranda. To Peter's chagrin, the perfunctory look reduced Miranda to a nonentity. Why should he mind?

Was it the location? Miranda suited him at the resort. Why not here?

Hal drew Maria into a second, empty lift. Miranda and Peter just squeezed in before the doors closed. Hal's right hand nestled over Maria's left breast. She laughed indulgently and joined hands. Miranda stared at their interlaced fingers. Peter counted floors. He felt for the room-key in his right trouser-pocket.

The lift lurched to a halt two floors short of their destination. A Japanese 'company-man' in a Western suit and a wife secreted behind a grey kimono, entered the lift, to be greeted by stifled sniggers from Hal and Maria. Peter was relieved when the doors parted and he could escape. Just in time, he remembered to hold the door open for Miranda.

'Well, my darlins',' Hal paused at the door to his room, key upraised. 'It's time me and Maria inspected my room for dry rot.' No sooner had they disappeared than Hal's head reappeared. 'Pete, don't forget to book a call for eight-thirty. That's eight-thirty a.m. Tomorrow.'

Peter looked at the time. It was barely one.

'Must look fresh for the Purse Lady in the mornin'.' Hal winked and ushered Maria's buttocks ahead of him into his chamber. With an ironic wave, he disappeared.

Peter made another weak attempt at a smile. The meek Miranda padded along behind him. Peter looked left, right and left again as he inserted the room-key into the lock. He and Miranda were alone.

Once he had closed the room door, Peter hurled the key over the bed. The metal clattered against the far wall and thence onto the thick carpet. Miranda observed his performance with troubled eyes.

'Sit down,' Peter snapped and pointed at one of the deep armchairs. Silent and obedient as ever, the girl occupied the chair. Peter looked away as her skirt hitched up and a few more inches of slim, brown leg were exposed. He made a great business of hoisting his canvas bag onto the bed and fussing with some fresh sheets of typing paper. Unfortunately, he had left the portable back at the resort. He would have to complete the martial law article in long hand. He threw Miranda an angry look. For all he cared, the girl could sit there all night. She appeared frailer than he remembered.

'Would you like a drink?'

Miranda shook her head. She shyly inspected her hands. Infuriating.

'Something to eat?'

She hesitated slightly before refusing once more.

Peter moved across to the telephone. He dialled 0. 'Hello,

room service, please.'

He turned back so that he had a good view of the girl. 'How about a hamburger?'

The corners of her mouth moved without uttering a sound. She nodded. Peter showed her his back.

'Hello, this is Peter Nicholson in room 815. Would you please send up two hamburgers and a pot of coffee for two?' He hesitated. 'Wait.' He placed his hand over the mouth-piece. 'How about an ice-cream?'

The girl's eyes glowed. The skirt rose another inch.

'Hello? Yes. One strawberry ice-cream. And a halo-halo.'

He replaced the receiver and resumed fussing with sheets of unblemished typing paper. He was finding it difficult to adopt a comfortable position in which to write. In the end he compromised between comfort and temptation; keeping his back turned to Miranda and crouching over the bedside table. Although unseen, the girl remained a presence; but, gradually, he forgot her long enough to immerse himself in words.

Biting her lower lip, Miranda rose without a sound and began to edge her way along the wall. Her hand flew to her mouth as Peter asked irritably, 'Do you want to go to the bathroom?' The girl nodded.

Peter sighed, pushed himself up from the bed and strode across the room. He held the door wide open and ordered, 'In there.'

On the threshold she hesitated for a second to take in the lime-green, tiled splendour. She might have been an American tourist gazing for the first time at the Rizal fresco in Fort Santiago.

'Right.' Peter was brisk. He hummed as the door closed. He bawled the 'Toreador Song' to drown the sound of the flush. Then, as he heard the knock on the door, he called out 'Wait'. He crossed to the bathroom door and held the handle tight. 'Come in,' he called, hoping that Miranda would realise what was happening.

The room-boy swung the loaded tray into the room with a flourish. Peter felt the bathroom door-handle beginning to twist in his palm.

'That's O.K.,' he snapped at the boy. 'You can just leave it.'

Peter pointed. The boy nodded and lowered the tray onto the wickerwork table by the window.

Peter signed the chit and smiled. The boy did not respond in kind as he rejoined the outer world, none the richer.

Relieved to see the back of the room-boy, Peter released Miranda from captivity. She seemed harried but her frown was quickly erased by the vision of the food.

Peter enjoyed watching her down the fast food fast. She belched lightly as the hamburger did what hamburgers do. His stomach now full, Peter's attitude towards Miranda became avuncular.

He watched her lick the last spoonful of pink ice-cream as he poured his second cup of coffee. He searched for a cigarette. As he reached into his pocket for his lighter, he caught sight of something on Miranda's leg. A pink scar he had not previously noted interrupted the smooth brown hue of her skin. He retrieved the Zippo.

Miranda watched intently as he flicked open the shield and ignited the fuel. He exhaled his first drag and extended the lighter to the girl. She started in surprise as the warm metal touched her skin. The gadget quickly cooled and her thumb caressed the enamelled legend.

'Do you like it?' Peter asked, inhaling.

The girl nodded. Something in this environment seemed to have scared away the few words of English she had had.

'You can keep it.' No sooner had the offer left his lips than Peter flushed with embarrassment. He recalled that the girl didn't smoke.

Miranda shook her head and returned the lighter, her arm locked stiff at the elbow.

Peter shrugged and accepted the rejection.

The girl rose and began to pack the empty plates onto the tray He felt her hair brush his forehead as she leant over him. He lifted the tray for her. He nodded and muttered, 'Door.' She hurried ahead of him and held the exit wide open. He stooped and placed the tray on the carpet outside. He glanced aside. Miranda's toes were grubby. He stood upright.

A label hung from the handle outside the door. Blank on one side, the reverse read 'Do Not Disturb'. He exposed the reverse. Her heels retreated before him as he returned to the room. They too were grubby.

Peter indicated the bathroom, nodded and slipped through the door. He occupied the seat and counted to fifty. Then he opened the hot tap in the sink and counted to thirty. He then arrested the flow and activated the flush. He ran the tap for another count of thirty. He hoped she might take the hint and disappear.

To his consternation, when he re-entered the room Miranda was lying in a semi-recumbent pose on the bed. Peter took up station in a chair beside the coffee table. He found another sheet of paper and began to write. As the seconds ticked by, Miranda eased herself closer. Soon, she was just behind him, observing every stroke of the pen. He bit his lower lip and continued scribbling but he could not vouch for his coherence.

Peter next took up station in one of the chairs by the bedside table. The girl's curiosity drew her into a position directly behind Peter. Although he gave no sign of noticing, he was exquisitely aware of the warmth of her body, inches from his own. He bit his lip and forced himself to keep scribbling. He realised that this was the roughest of rough drafts and would require drastic surgery in rather less fraught conditions.

It did not help that he knew that Hal would have no qualms about taking advantage of such a situation. He and Maria would probably be on their third round by now. Peter drove away the image of Maria. He shook his head and turned on Miranda.

'Look, would you please stop not looking over my shoulder like that? I find it very irritating.'

The girl started as if slapped. He took her arm and steered her back to the bed. 'Here!' He handed her two sheets of paper out of the sheaf. 'I'll find you a pen.'

She held the ballpoint awkwardly, like a chopstick. She stared at him, wide-eyed.

'Write something.' Peter's impatience was growing. 'Or why not draw something?' He glared at her until her head dipped and the pen began to move. Then he returned to his own muttons and scribbled gibberish, driving the beasts all over the paper.

Half-way down his page, he glanced up. The tip of the girl's tongue was protruding from the corner of her mouth. Sentimentality flooded through him. She was only a kid. A kid whose concentration was now total.

Her dress gaped open as she inclined to her task. Peter turned his attention to Miranda's sheet of paper. The girl was in the process of drawing a flower of some sort. Peter resumed his own task. An easiness settled over the room.

As he reached the bottom of his second sheet, Peter stretched his back and lit another cigarette. Miranda's head was still inclined over her page. Peter rose. The girl did not even look up.

Peter stretched out on the bed, a cigarette clenched between his teeth. He tried his best not to disturb Miranda. He exhaled and traced the outline of the girl's breasts beneath the loose cotton. He had reluctantly come to envy Hal's gluttonous appetite for sex, while convinced that the man was suffering from a psychological malady. Satyriasis. Yes, that was the name for what ailed Hal.

Peter ground his cigarette out in the ashtray. He lowered his head onto the pillow. Sexual insatiability was one thing but Hal's marital machinations were quite another. There he was – planning to divorce one woman in order to marry another for her money. And her mother. Peter closed his eyes and pictured the delicate feet and the flawless skin. He shifted on the suggestive bed.

And then there was Hilary. She was to be abandoned – alone in Hong Kong. He lingered on the image. He traced her outline from head to toe. He shifted his weight as he recalled her breasts. But no man could live by breasts alone. They were a declining asset. And would it be wise to shackle himself to a bosom? Perhaps Hal's restlessness was the way of all flesh. Peter yawned.

His waking was announced by a bad taste on his tongue. He scraped the offending organ against his teeth. Onions. He remembered the hamburger. He blinked. There was something different about the room. He craned his neck and saw that Miranda had moved the lamp onto the table by the window. As he examined her profile, he saw the pink tip of her tongue caress her upper lip. The pool of light in which she worked seemed to emphasize her concentration.

In spite of the air conditioning, Peter's skin felt clammy. He crabbed his way to the edge of the bed. Miranda looked up without a smile. She returned to her task. Peter stretched and looked at his watch.

'God, it's nine o'clock.' The girl was unmoved. Peter licked his lips and rubbed his head. He slipped away from the bed and crossed the room, unbuttoning his shirt as he moved. He rubbed his cheeks. Did he need a shave? And some activity with a toothbrush?

His humming was somewhat off key as he showered away the grime in body, if not in mind. He was warming to the idea of Miranda's presence. He returned to the bedroom and a storm of apathy. Cleansed, fragrant and eager, Peter crossed to the object of his desires. As he neared her, he caught sight of the result of Miranda's labours. Below a bunch of delicately shaded sampaguita stretched a list. He read.

> Name: Miranda Vargas.
> Age: Seventeen.
> Mother: Consuela Vargas
> Father: Pedro Vargas.
> Languages: Tagalog. English.
> Occupation: Sauna attendant.
> Favourite colour: Green.
> Favourite film star: Rock Hudson.
> Favourite song: Sugar, Sugar.
> Favourite real person: Peter (surname unknown)

The girl's face turned towards him as he traced his way down the page. He smiled at Miranda.

'That's wonderful.' Peter reached across and lifted the page from the table. 'Really fantastic.'

Miranda's eyes shone.

'God, you must be exhausted.' Peter murmured, laying a land on her shoulder. The tips of his fingers brushed her collar-bone. He was moved to tenderness. Peter the satyr had departed. But what had the new, tender Peter to do with using a willing young girl? Tenderness was not part of his repertoire.

Miranda shyly smiled up at him. 'You want massage?'

The question solved his problem. The dilemma was unlocked and time moved along its well-trodden path.

'Why don't you go and have a shower?' Peter murmured, stroking her shoulder. Miranda rose. She looked into his eyes and paused. She waited – quite still – as he began to unbutton her dress. He saw the tip of her tongue between her lips. Her small, white teeth shone as though enamelled.

Peter lowered the garment, taking care to avoid contact with her hips or her thighs. She balanced herself with a hand on his shoulder as she raised first one foot and then another to free herself of the dress. Peter held her at arm's length, half-silhouetted against the lamplight. He drew her towards him. She lowered her face against his shoulder as he reached behind her for the catch on her bra. Her nipples brushed against his chest in the cool air. He dropped the garment onto the crumpled frock. Peter knelt to help remove her briefs. The girl was almost hairless. Tenderness was replaced by urgency. He carried her to the bed.

'We can shower later.'

Chapter Twenty-five

The black Cadillac drew up outside the Palace fifteen minutes early. Throughout the laborious journey Agustin had intoned a detailed list of instructions regarding the etiquette to be followed at the Malacañang. Agustin's apprehension fed Peter's. Hal stared in morose silence through the car window. Peter strove to keep his arms at right angles to his body.

He had discovered too late that the Barong Tagalog was double-cuffed. To his horror, he remembered that he had left his only decent set of cufflinks back in Hong Kong, nestling in one of Aggie's shirts. To compound his discomfiture, he had discovered – also too late – that his shirt-sleeves were several inches too long. If he moved his arms the tiniest fraction of a degree up or down, the cuffs would either slip up to the elbow or, alternatively, slide beyond the tips of his fingers.

The Englishmen stared gloomily after the departing limousine. Agustin's worried expression as he peered back at them did absolutely nothing to lighten their mood. Hal raised two fingers in a Welsh bowman's gesture. Peter lifted his hold-all onto his right shoulder. His right cuff slid down his arm and covered his hand.

The guard guided them through a portal and gestured towards distant white stucco. Between the visitors and their destination lay an elegant, formal, European garden.

Through an icing archway Peter caught sight of an iridescent jet of water. He liberated the telephoto camera and focussed. His cuffs shot up to his elbows. In the viewfinder he concentrated on four caryatids, disguised as young, sinuous nineteenth century debutantes, supporting a shallow tazza. On all sides of the elegant display neat parterres reinforced the sense of Enlightenment. Peter circumnavigated the fountain. The shot that was finally included for the Philippines' edition contained a background glimpse of the private entrance to the palace.

Once inside the columned lobby, Hal addressed the guard.

Security seemed very light. Almost casual. Peter inspected the iron and glass doors through which they had entered the building. He soon became aware of the hush which he associated with deep pile carpets. An orange runner fitting that description ran from the doors and ascended the wide staircase they were now mounting. At the end of the ascent waited another guard, Peter adjusted both his wilful cuffs as he stepped into the magnificent reception room, hard on Hal's jaunty heels.

'This knocks the *Intercontinental* into a cocked hat,' Hal muttered as they followed their civilian escort.

The enormous space combined classical severity with decorative elaboration. With its broad central nave and flanking aisles subdivided into 'chapels', the room might have served a large community as a place of worship. But here the focus was not on an altar but on a chandelier of immense size. Even at this hour, it blazed with artificial light.

They followed their leader down an aisle to their left. Half-way along down the aisle they were ushered into another 'capella' with matching banquettes. Hal and Peter sank into one of them, facing back the way they had come. To their right awaited an imposing doorway in a panelled wall.

'Next patient, please,' Hal whispered in Peter's ear. The irreverence of the remark in such a reverent ambiance all but unhinged Peter. He choked, waving the grinning Hal away.

With two minutes to go before their appointed time, Peter checked the recorder by whispering a few words into it and quietly replaying the results. He placed the machine on the seat beside him and re-adjusted his wayward cuffs.

Half-past ten came and went. Hal suppressed a yawn.

'Didn't get a wink last night,' Hal said with a wink. 'That Maria ain't 'alf restless in bed.'

Peter struggled to stifle another laugh. The door opened. They rose as one man. The severely dressed woman of middling years came towards them, smiling. Hal beamed back.

'Mornin', Mrs. Marcos,' he said and extended a gratulatory hand. The woman took it somewhat reluctantly.

'The First Lady has been detained. I hope you do not mind

waiting.'

'No, of course we don't mind.' Hal noblesse-obliged, releasing the compressed fingers. 'You can tell 'er to take 'er time.'

The secretary scurried back to her cell. The two men resumed their seats.

'Is that 'er husband?' Hal wondered, nodding towards the retreating figure.

Peter exchanged the telephoto for the wide-angle. It was time to leave Hal to himself or Peter might regret it. 'Just taking a few more shots.' He got to his feet. Hal shrugged.

Nobody seemed in the least concerned as Peter retraced his steps. He was soon back among the gigantic chandelier and wall-mounted crystal lights. On either side of the entrance, blackamoor torchères added to the palace's electricity bill. A vast carpet stretched the length of the nave. Before each peristylic column, bronze urns on pedestals displayed fresh flowers.

In the most distant corner two men in grey jackets and black trousers whispered in front of an official portrait.

As Peter returned to the ante-chamber, Hal was glumly inspecting his watch. He sniffed.

'She's ten minutes late.' Hal made his displeasure clear.

'This isn't the dentist's, Hal.' Peter reminded him.

'More's the pity,' Hal riposted. 'They give you somethin' to read there.' He glanced past Peter. 'Take a look at this fuckin' Yank.' He nudged his partner. 'Bloody typical.'

A tall figure, wearing a red pin-striped seersucker jacket and sky-blue trousers hovered by the entrance. Beside him one of the duo of grey jackets was guiding the newcomers to their place of asylum. From behind the American appeared a diminutive Filipino, with two aluminium camera cases in his clutches and four naked Leicas dangling from his neck. Peter nursed his hold-all.

Hal nudged Peter once more. 'Will you look at them boots!'

Shiny, mahogany-coloured Texan boots projected below the blue trousers. They were ill-matched to the rest of the outfit, which was surmounted by a pale crew-cut. The newcomers arranged themselves on the banquette opposite Hal and Peter. The cowboy almost dropped the Nagra recorder suspended from one shoulder. The Filipino cameraman's upper lip was wet with sweat. Peter noted the unequal division of labour. It seemed familiar. He glanced sideways as Hal crossed an ankle over a knee. Hal's hands were never full.

The publisher stage-whispered, 'Looks like a right Yankee poofter.' Peter shifted uneasily. The last thing they needed was a squabble with other journalists.

Hal breathed hot air into Peter's ear. 'I hope they don't go in ahead of us.' Hal did not wait for a response. 'Ere,' Hal, leaning towards the Filipino cameraman, opened the conversation. 'What time are you due in?'

'Eleven o'clock,' the Filipino replied, holding up ten fingers and then a single digit.

'I say.' Peter and Hal sought for the source of the sound.

'I say,' Seersucker repeated. He leant forward and lowered his voice.

'Are you chaps English?'

'Yeah,' Hal replied, jutting out his jaw.

'Isn't that a coincidence?' The faux-American leant forward and extended a hand. 'So am I. Bob Young – *L.A.Times*.'

Peter took Bob's hand in some bemusement. Were they double-booked?

'Peter Nicholson, *Hong Kong Weekly*.'

Bob turned towards Hal and, hand extended once more, smiled. Peter made the introduction. 'Hal Puckle, publisher of *Hong Kong Weekly*.'

Hal's chest expanded as the two men locked hands.

Young sat back and shook his head. 'God, is this woman elusive!'

'You can say that again, old chum,' Hal grimaced 'We were due in at ten thirty.'

Young frowned. 'How long did it take you chaps to get an interview?'

Peter shrugged. 'A few days.'

Young seemed impressed. 'I've been here over a month. Mind

you, even the *Time* correspondent had been sitting in the wings for two weeks before they allowed him into the presence.' He lowered his voice. 'Come on. What's the secret? What's your pull?'

Hal kept his face straight. 'I'm 'er cousin.'

Peter was distracted by an eddy of murmurous activity from the neighbouring room. He grabbed his wide-angle and got to his feet. 'It's him!' he whispered hoarsely. 'It's Marcos.'

Neither Young nor Hal was interested in the President. Peter moved out into the main reception area and followed a group of courtiers along the carpet. He paused behind a pillar twenty feet from the President. He raised the camera. A sixtieth at F2. As he brought Marcos into focus, he could see that the President knew full well that his mug-shot was being taken. Peter unscrewed the 85B filter. The Presidential conversazione continued. The group had expanded. Peter realised that the woman wearing a decorative, close-fitting dress beside Marcos was his journalistic quarry. Bit tall for the President. Peter edged closer.

Two men in army uniform appeared in an open doorway hung with silk festoons. They grinned at Peter and posed in a frozen handshake. Not bad. He raised his hands and his cuffs slid back up his wrists. Peter realised that the President was also sporting a Barong Tagalog. With cuff-links.

Another three paces and he would be able to grab some really good close-ups. No sooner had he ventured on pace number one than an arm obstructed his progress. He looked along the obstruction and came upon a broken nose. Its owner jerked the nose back in the direction whence Peter had come.

Marcos feigned blindness as Peter offered him a rueful smile. The nose came closer, reminding him that its owner was also still there. Peter realised this was the moment for discretion rather than valour. He retraced his steps.

Resuming his position beside Hal, he patted the Nikon.

'I 'ope you're not wastin' all my bloody film,' Hal grumbled loudly. Peter bit his lip and pretended to inspect the lens.

'What's *Hong Kong Weekly*?' The seer-suckered one wanted to know.

Hal rose to the bait. 'It's a super four-colour business and current affairs magazine, published in 'Ong Kong.' The rival reporter frowned. Hal added, 'Price four dollars.' And then added. ''Ong Kong money.'

'And produces special editions throughout South-East Asia.' Peter said, smiling. 'Hence our presence in Manila.'

Hal beckoned Young towards him. 'Ere, Bob. 'Ow did you get a job in the States?'

'Oh, they quite like Brits over there. I used to be on the Sketch.' He extracted a card from his breast pocket. 'Look me up next time you're in L.A.'

Hal accepted the card. He patted his own top pocket. 'Left my cards in the 'otel.'

'Where are you staying?' Young asked.

Hal tossed off his reply. 'The Inter.'

'Oh, so am I.' Young seemed to find the information cheering.

Peter noticed the singular pronoun. He wondered where the cameraman dossed down.

'What's your room number?' Young wanted to know.

Hal's shaking head expressed deep regret. 'We're checkin' out as soon as we've done the purse lady. No point 'angin about.'

The Filipino was engrossed in dusting his Leica M4 with a blower-brush.

Young looked crestfallen. 'Oh, what a pity.' He rallied. 'What's the subject of your interview?'

'Oh, the usual.' Peter counted off the subjects on his fingers. 'The beautification of the Philippines; tourism; ethnic minorities; the role of the First Lady in Philippine politics.'

Young frowned and nodded. Peter shrugged. 'As I said, the usual.' Peter shrugged. Then he noted that Hal at least had been impressed. He turned to Young. 'What about you?'

'Oh, much the same range of stuff, I suppose.' Young replied airily, laying some Texan hide across his knee. He traced the incised pattern with a finger-nail. He looked up directly at Peter, his eyes shining. 'None of that stuff really counts.' He grinned. 'The interview is just a blind.' He dismissed the Nagra and its minder with a backflip of his hand. Peter and Hal nodded in unison and leaned towards Young. In response, Young leaned towards them.

'There's this group of stone-age men. Way down South. The Tasaydays. I'm here to write a feature on them.' Young's eyes glistened.

'So, what are you 'angin' about 'ere for?' Hal asked with a frown.

Young leaned towards them and lowered his voice. 'There's one very good reason.' He drew even closer and lowered his voice. 'Until this group was recently discovered, they had had no contact with the outside world.'

'None?' Peter frowned at Young.

'None,' Young nodded firmly. 'They are like living fossils.'

'Don't tell me you speak livin' fossil lingo,' Hal grinned.

'Not a word. What I need is really good pictures.' Young winked. 'Fuck the lingo.'

'Just how big is this group?' Peter asked, his mind tracking back to a brief 'fait-divers' he had read recently about the so-called 'stone-age men'.

'Thirty,' Young shrugged. 'Maybe fewer.'

'So why are you interviewin' the purse lady?' Hal wanted to know.

'Well,' Young's tone became conspiratorial. 'In order to visit the group, you require permission from 'the Minister for Ethnic Minorities'.

'So?'

'The Minister is one of the First Lady's retinue.' Young smiled and shrugged. 'Mrs. Marcos goes really big on ethnic minorities.' He leaned back and gave a rueful grin. '*Time* is after the story too.'

'Funny,' Hal half-sneered. 'I never 'eard of it.'

'Believe me, you will… when me and Pidring here amaze the world.' Young laid an affectionate hand on the Filipino's shoulder. The cameraman smiled. Hal's eyes widened at the sight of a double colonnade of gold teeth.

To their right a door opened. The brisk secretary re-appeared and addressed Hal and Peter in a Bryn Mawr accent. 'This way, gentlemen.' She led the way. 'If you will follow me.' Peter held a hand up to Young and Pidring. Hal strode off without so much as a backward glance.

Peter wrestled with the camera (hanging from his neck) and the bag (hanging from his shoulder). One shirt-cuff retreated up his left arm, the other descended over his right hand. He smiled weakly at the L.A. contingent. The secretary reappeared, hissed and beckoned.

Peter shuffled across the parquet into an office which was small and empty and, from that office, into another, more luxurious affair. Hal was already comfortably ensconced in a large chair. The secretary indicated its companion. 'Please take a seat.' Peter sat.

Two vacant minutes elapsed.

The First Lady entered without fanfare. She was the epitome of simple elegance. Hal stood while Peter juggled his cuffs.

'Good morning, gentlemen,' Mrs. Marcos glanced at her secretarial assistant, who departed forthwith. Briskly.

With no more ado the First Lady occupied an even more imposing armchair at the apex of what had become a triangle. Peter concluded that she did not look in the least like a provincial. Wasn't she from the South? Peter recollected that the President was from the North-East.

Imelda's black hair was swept up in swathes, framing a face of majestic, cubist planes. Her figure-hugging dress could have come from a leading couturier in New York, Milan or Paris.

Hal had already launched into his preamble. '...and Peter 'ere will record the interview on 'is dinky machine. We'll transcribe it word-for-word when we get back to 'Ong Kong. Is that okay?'

The First Lady's voice was a clear mezzo-soprano.

'O.K. But you must remember that I do not discuss political matters. Those are the sole concern of my husband, the President.'

Peter's spirits sank as he imagined column after column on 'beautification'.

'Would you mind, ma'am if I moved my chair a little closer?'

The First Lady smiled and graciously dipped her head. 'As you wish.'

Peter was being rather hesitant with the Sony. Hal stepped into the breach.

'Mrs. Marcos, may I say that that is one terrific dress.' Peter winced and waited for the fusillade of shots in response to this lèse-majesté.

'Why, thank you,' She replied, smoothing the garment over one knee. 'It was designed and cut here in the Philippines. Our local designers are the equal of any designers in the world.'

Peter gently cleared his throat. Mrs. Marcos turned towards him. Peter flicked up the pause switch. The tape began to roll. 'Would you mind giving me a few words for level?'

The First Lady counted slowly from one to ten. Peter nodded and they both settled, Peter launched his first pawn.

'Mrs. Marcos. To foreign visitors your country is already known as one of the most beautiful in the world.' Mrs. Marcos inclined her head in acknowledgement of the compliment. 'They may wonder why you think it requires any beautification policy at all.'

Mrs. Marcos's smiled briefly and gave voice.

'The country has always been a beautiful country. There's no doubt about that. But there is so much disorder and lack of discipline.'

Peter blinked. Mrs. Marcos was breaking her own political embargo in her very first response.

'The people just threw garbage all over the place. There was no orientation, no values, no care – feeling that the whole world was against them. They felt that their neighbours were against them – demonstrating hate and not fostering love.'

Peter risked a glance at Hal. The publisher was lost in admiration of the interviewee. Peter hoped that he would confine his ambitions to Isabel. He re-tuned to Mrs. Marcos. She was, it seemed, just getting into her stride.

'You have to have beautiful thoughts before you can have beautiful surroundings. To have clean surroundings, a clean house, a clean backyard, you have to think of it before you can actually do it. So, this is the true meaning of 'The New Society' that the President is trying to put into the hearts and minds of the people.'

As the flow of words continued, Peter kept a wary eye on her lips and eyes while resting his ears. Pity no-one had revealed to Mrs. Marcos that journalists really appreciate pithy answers. Her manner reminded him of a school matron he had once known In North London.

'... for the New Society. We are all working very hard for it.'

God. She had stopped. The Purst Lady waited expectantly. Peter lurched as he groped for a question that might fit. He clutched at Rizal Park and the plans for Intramuros.

'...I just serve as a glorified beggar for this country. In fact, at the time I wondered how I would raise a hundred thousand pesos, never realising it would reach this much.'

Her eyes widened in innocent accompaniment to her flow. Peter decided that she was indeed beautiful. The skin was without the slightest taint, even this close up. A few milliseconds of inattention from Peter passed unnoticed by the First Lady. Her mind worked associatively and rapidly, linking all her many and diverse projects in a sinuous continuum. She was excited. Pity the readership of *The Weekly* would not feel able to share her excitement. Severe subbing would be required in the coming days. Or weeks.

Peter's forearm and shoulder began to succumb to numbness. Then that same numbness began to invade his brain.

'...I suppose this was when my mission started.'

The lips stopped and closed. Peter jerked to attention.

'Do you think your example might influence the women of the Philippines to try and improve their own positions in society?'

Should Maria try it on top for a change? He coughed and covered his mouth with his free hand. He then noticed that Hal's eyes were rivetted on Mrs. Marcos' face. Hal was enraptured.

'I don't think there is any need for the improvement of the position of the Filipino women. Filipino women, and Asian women in particular, have a wonderful position.'

Peter blinked.

Hal rested his elbow on his knee and his chin in his hand,

'We really don't have to think of women's lib. We have a

place on the pedestal, adored and glorified, so why should we come down from our pedestal and join in building streets or roads?'

Peter recognised the jibe at Chinese women. He thought of the Hakka women on the building sites in Hong Kong. And what about the major projects on the mainland dependent on female labour? Did those women inhabit the very same Asia as Mrs. Marcos? And where was Miranda's pedestal?

'We don't want to be partners.' The voice continued. Peter nodded encouragement. Superfluous. Encouragement was one thing Mrs. Marcos did not require. The First Lady had set aside all the reticence expected of the President's rib.

'For instance, in the case of the President, I have always maintained that he is the head and I am the heart.'

Hal's eyes adjusted to consider that most tender of organs in the female body seated before him.

'So, the role of the President and myself has always been defined. The head is higher than the heart.' Mrs. M. lowered her hand into her lap.

Hal raised his eyes.

The Iron Butterfly fluttered once again. 'The President said, "It will be like a man building a house. I will build a strong, well-founded house. You make it a home."'

Peter felt that this was the apogee of the dissertation. He readied his thigh muscles for departure. He was mistaken. The voice assumed new warmth and force.

Depletion of natural sources?

'The country here is very rich. They say you only have to put your finger in the earth and it will grow.'

Hal guffawed. Peter nervously licked his lips and smiled. His arm had become numbly detached from his body.

He staggered on to 'population control'.

'We don't have winters and this makes people less worried about some very basic necessities of life. It's really a virtual paradise. And what do you do in a paradise? You play.' She smiled. 'So, we get too many children.'

They moved on to 'The trials of the rich and the poverty of the poor.'

'…I can pinpoint more people in the villages happier than the very rich people here. In what place can I have a better birthday than in the palace?'

Peter ordered himself to keep *shtum*. It's just a rhetorical question, Peter.

'I would never spend a birthday here. I would always run back home because I go more for inner wealth than physical wealth.'

All inhibitions had been swept away in the verbal torrent. Now the First Lady was insisting that only Marcos' blood had been shed in the establishment of the New Society.

Hal unexpectedly revealed that he had never heard the grisly tale of the knife attack involving Mrs. Marcos. She took pity on his ignorance. Peter's muscles returned to agonised life as the wide mouth related the events of National Beautification Day. There had been a young man in the crowd with what the First Lady described as 'a sword'. Peter recalled the peasant's bolo.

'When I saw this sword, I said, 'Here am I, very conscious about making things beautiful – how sad to die with such an ugly sword.'

Hal's eyes glowed.

'I never was afraid. While I was being carried from the helicopter to the operating table the people were falling one by one and saying, 'Oh, the First Lady is dead.' And I said, 'No, I'm not dead yet.'

'You were right,' Hal assured her with an encouraging nod. An unexpected silence spread. Peter allowed his left hand to release his right arm and the absent blood trickled back, pricking his arteries with a hundred tiny bolos. The cuff of his right sleeve fell over his fingers and lodged against the microphone.

'You know, Mrs. Marcos, that was a really terrible thing to go through.' Hal's face expressed the profoundest commiseration.

'Thank you.' Mrs. Marcos' smile was angelic. She glanced at her watch. Peter took the opportunity to emulate her. They had been ensconced for three quarters of an hour. He recollected the two men still awaiting their own forty-five minutes. Would she be able to replicate that performance? Peter had no doubts. Poor devils. He inhaled in anticipation of expressions of gratitude. His breath was cut short by Hal's voice.

'You know, Mrs. Marcos, I've seen lots of photos of you but I can honestly say that they don't do you justice. You're so much more beautiful in the flesh.'

Peter hurriedly rewound the microphone lead. But nothing would deflect Hal.

'Did they leave any scars?'

Peter held his breath. This was high treason, surely. To his amazement he witnessed the First Lady unbutton her cuff and roll back her sleeve.

Hal clucked his concern at the sight of the vicious scar that curled along the Marcos wrist. He tutted and then helped her re-fasten the cuff. Even Peter was impressed by Hal's chutzpah.

Hal clicked his fingers. 'Right, Peter. Don't just sit there starin'. Take a picture to go with the interview.' Peter was annoyed. He wanted to kick Hal where it would hurt most and, at the same time, he knew an original photograph was a sine qua non. Why hadn't he had the courage to propose it? A quick glance at the First Lady's smile confirmed her approval of the request. She shifted into what was clearly a favourite position while Peter scurried about the room in his best Antonioni imitation. In all he threw off eight shots.

'Fantastic,' Hal crowed. 'Beautiful.'

Mrs. Marcos smiled and rose from her chair.

'Oh, Mrs. Marcos,' Hal cooed. The First Lady froze.

Peter sensed that they were risking all the goodwill they had enjoyed up to this point. They were definitely overstaying their welcome.

'Could you do us a tiny favour?'

Mrs. Marcos paused – her lips thinner. Hal, his calcium on gleaming display, pressed on.

'As you know, we're devotin' this whole edition of *Hong Kong Weekly* to your country. Of course, this interview with you is the real cherry on the cake but we'd like to cover one area of your personal passions in greater detail.'

'Personal passions?' The lady's eyes were wary. 'Yes?'

'It's about these people down in the South.' He frowned. 'The Tawayways.'

The First Lady frowned and then brightened. She gave a delicate chuckle. 'You mean the Tasaydays.' She stroked her lower lip with a finger. 'Yes?'

'Well, Peter here...' Hal glanced at the photographer, interviewer-hod-carrier and general-factotum. 'Peter here was wonderin' whether we might run a little feature on them. Mainly photos, you know – since they don't speak any English.'

Mrs. Marcos' smile out-beamed Hal's. 'You must understand, I am not the Minister for Ethnic Minorities. But I will make enquiries'.

She extended a hand. Peter took light hold of her smooth softness.

Imelda leaned towards him. Her voice was a musical murmur. 'You know – you should wear cufflinks with the Barong Tagalog.'

Peter felt his face flush. At least Hal refrained from kissing the extended hand. Mrs. Marcos turned away. They passed in lockstep through the brisk secretary's office and returned to the ante-chamber.

Young looked at his watch. 'My God. You've been an age.'

'Sorry, me old mate.' Hal could not budge the broad smile on his face. 'Fascinatin' woman. Great sex life.'

The guardian of the inner sanctum tapped her foot. Young nodded angrily at his blameless technical assistant, who took up his Leicas and prepared for battle. Hal stood back and bowed Young out of the waiting room. 'Next patient, please.' Young threw Hal an angry look.

'Oh, Bob, me old mate.' Hal winked. 'Best of luck with the Tawayways.'

Chapter Twenty-six

Peter concluded that Agustin's expression betokened suppressed excitement rather than constipation. The millionaire stared at the recorder as it unwound its tale on the back seat of the Cadillac. Only the giant, masticating beside Chico on the front seat. was inattentive to the pronouncements of the First Lady.

To Peter's relief the play-back was curtailed by Agustin waving at the ever-vigilant Chico. The hearse-sized vehicle glided away from the kerb. Peter switched off the machine.

'You know, Mr. Agustin, she's a real cracker, that Mrs. Marcos.' Hal tossed the comment at the little man curled in the corner.

Agustin's eyes left their dream world and refocussed.

'Cracker?' Agustin repeated with a frown.

'Yeah. You know. 'Good lookin'.' Hal translated: 'A knock-out.'

Agustin allowed Hal a micro-smile.

Hal was all buoyancy. 'Well, after that, I reckon it's time to celebrate. Tell you what, Mr. Agustin. I'll treat you to lunch."

Agustin's eyes widened.

'But could we go back to the hotel first?' Hal plucked at a sleeve. 'I'd like to get out of this fancy dress.'

In the hotel lobby Hal addressed his flock. 'Look, as we're 'ere why don't you all go on up to the restaurant? I'll be with you in a tick.'

Meekly, Augustin allowed Hal to shepherd him into an express lift. Hal and Peter returned to their respective rooms.

Peter held his breath as he turned the key in the lock. Maybe he would surprise Miranda in bed. His skin prickled. But the bed lay virginal beneath its coverlet. Unslept in.

Peter called Miranda's name. He checked the bathroom. It was a puzzle.

While he changed, he glanced about the room for a note or some other sign but it was if Miranda had never existed. A pang of nostalgia caught at Peter's throat. The previous night now seemed prehistoric.

He supposed that she must have become bored with waiting and had returned to the resort. Had she had enough money for a cab? Then it occurred to him that she might be elsewhere in the hotel and would return soon. But did he really want her to return?

The child's vulnerability had evoked his protectiveness. He was in danger of becoming ensnared. If he was – as now seemed likely – to establish himself in Manila, there would be bigger fish to fry than Miranda. The thought both lifted and shamed him. He shrugged. At least he had rid himself of that damned Barong Tagalog.

Hal's quarters were equally unheeding to his second rap on the door. A room boy swung into the corridor, a drinks tray balanced on his left hand. Was he heading for Hal's door? The drinks swung past without a pause. Peter raised his knuckles to rap for a third time.

The door opened. There stood Hal, resplendent in his grey suit. He patted Peter's cheek and pouted.

'Right you are, me old mate,' was his greeting as he closed the door behind him. He flicked his room-key into the air, caught it and slipped it into his trouser pocket. They set off in lockstep.

'How's Maria?' Peter asked. Perhaps he should let Hal know about Miranda's disappearance. Then he thought better of it. He had had an ample sufficiency of Hal's jibes.

'Maria?' Hal looked puzzled. Who on earth was Maria? 'Dunno. Maybe she's gone back to the resort.' Peter exhaled. Of course. The two girls had obviously returned to the resort together. Hal nudged Peter's ribs with an elbow. 'What do you reckon on that Mrs. Marcos, eh? A right cracker. I wouldn't roll over 'er to get at you.' Another nudge. Peter forced a smile.

Hal paused at the entrance to the restaurant and shot his cuffs. The unlikely partners peered at the many crowded tables for a sight of Agustin. The pullulating congress gave off the odour of expense accounts and chicanery.

Peter took in the itinerant businessmen, probably on a stopover during their regular round from Korea to New Zealand, laughing among possible victims and their mercenary, nocturnal partners. These men, downing fine wine and draping an arm around a partner-for-the-nonce, were to be his rivals or colleagues.

That was for the future; at the moment, dressed as he was, he felt distinctly out of place. Nevertheless, he smiled inwardly. Soon he too would be wearing silk suits, shirts and gold accessories. He was consoled by the thought.

They paused before the centre-piece of the vast space - an elaborately staged Russian buffet. A 'maître d' accosted them.

'Mr. Agustin,' Hal frowned. The man offered an inclination, turned and moved away. They pursued his swallow-tailed jacket along the winding carpet. The head waiter stopped, stepped aside and waved an arm in the direction of Agustin, who sat in isolation, the giant on guard behind him. Chico was nowhere in sight. Peter felt sure that the girls had been returned to the resort.

Hal took a seat, moved his chair closer to the table and rubbed his hands. 'Right,' He grinned. 'What's it to be, Mr. Agustin?' Their patron nodded towards the buffet. Hal shrugged and contemplated the à la carte menu. Once he had scanned the prices, he decided to settle for the buffet. He nudged Peter and raised his serviette.

'Remember who's footin' the bill,' Hal muttered, got to his feet and made for the cornucopia.

Agustin indicated the path Hal had taken and rose to his feet. Peter did likewise. The two men slowly moved towards the buffet.

'What did you think of the First Lady?' Agustin asked behind a raised hand.

'A remarkable woman,' Peter mumbled. 'Remarkable,' he repeated, more loudly.

They had arrived at their culinary destination. 'She is very interested in tourism.' Agustin said with an accompanying finger-tap on the side of his nose.

'So it seems,' Peter mumbled, spearing a chicken breast and carefully lowering it onto his plate.

'Was my name mentioned?' Agustin wanted to know.

'It came up quite naturally in the course of conversation,' Peter lied, his concentration on a display of large prawns. Hal was of no assistance, having disappeared around the far end of the table. 'What's that?' Peter said, frowning at a what looked like potato salad.

It was Agustin's turn to frown. 'That? That is potato salad.' As if to encourage Peter, Agustin engaged with the salad. Peter did not like potato salad. He liked prawns but he did not want Agustin to think he was a gourmand. He eschewed the prawns and emulated Agustin.

The older man led the way back to the table. The giant stepped away and drew out Agustin's chair. Peter, dejected, resumed his place. His sparsely stocked plate struck the double damask and a fork leaped and tuned an upended wine glass. Hal finally returned, his plate a teetering feast.

'Now that's what you might call a buffet,' Hal declared, with a grunt of satisfaction.

Agustin turned to the late-comer. 'Thank you, Hal.'

'You don't 'ave to thank me. Just tuck in.'

'No, I was referring to what you did earlier today. Peter tells me that it went well.'

'Yeah,' Hal agreed, his jaws working. He transferred the contents of his mouth into the other cheek. 'She was O.K., once I broke the ice.'

Peter was surprised that someone with Agustin's advantages should be seeking reassurance; and especially not from a group of foreign hacks he could buy and sell ten times over.

'Congratulations.'

Peter almost choked at the proximity of the voice. He turned. Major Alvarez smiled at him.

Hal waved at a passing wine waiter and ordered a bottle of 'Bernkastler Green Label'.

'I hear from the Malacañang that the interview was splendid.' Alvarez smiled broadly.

'Goes without sayin'', Hal said, grinning.

Hal's wine arrived and the party sat in watchful silence as the waiter massacred the cork and spilled ice water from the bucket onto the table-cloth. The waiter, ducking his head, hurried away. Alvarez raised his glass.

'To a successful edition of *Hong Kong Weekly*.

''Ear, 'ear,' Hal responded and swallowed half the contents of his glass.

Agustin sipped. Alvarez reached inside his jacket and produced a brown envelope which he held across the table and offered to Hal, who sniffed. 'What's this?' the gracious publisher wanted to know.

'My humble contributions to *Hong Kong Weekly*.' Alvarez's smile was rather forced.

'Oh, right.' Hal dropped the envelope beside his plate. He lifted his glass and devoured the dregs. Hal poured himself another glass. Agustin refused any further wine. He blinked as an envelope appeared beneath his eyes. 'What is this?'

Hal tapped the envelope against Agustin's glass. 'Just a copy of the contract. Now that I've got the major's stuff and we've done the Purse Lady, there's nothin' left to do but sign.'

Agustin pushed the envelope aside with the back of his hand. 'This is a good meal, Hal.'

Hal grinned, 'A bargain at the price, I'd say.'

'Right,' Agustin raised his glass. 'But I don't pay for the meal until after it is finished.'

Hal managed to control his voice. 'It's not the same, Mr. Agustin. You can't expect me to order a print run of fifteen thousand copies of a four-colour mag without your signature on the contract. Can you?'

'Why not?'

''Ow do I know I'll get my money? You might change your mind.' Hal tried for a smile and missed.

'Even if I did, you would still have fifteen thousand magazines to distribute throughout South-East Asia.' Agustin's lips smiled thinly. His eyes did not join in.

Peter sighed. 'Touché,' he thought.

'But the edition's all about the Philippines!'

'You convinced me that such an edition would sell well in the region.' Agustin stared at Hal. Hal blinked. Peter leaned forward.

'There's really no need to argue,' Peter interjected. 'I'm sure Mr. Agustin will be happy to sign once he's seen the proofs.'

'Yeah, that's right.' Hal leant back and extracted a cigar from his inside pocket. 'I'd forgotten about the proofs. Forget I spoke, Mr. Agustin.

'I need to see the proofs quickly,' Agustin said, placing both hands on the tablecloth.

'You will.' Hal smiled without showing a single tooth.

'It's in everyone's interest that this edition be well received.' Peter smiled. 'Once it's off our chests, Hal and I have plans to move our regional headquarters from Hong Kong to Manila.'

'That is good to hear,' Agustin replied without conviction.

'Yeah, with Pete and me workin' flat out, we'll 'ave the proofs back 'ere in under two weeks.'

Agustin leaned back against his chair.

'O.K. Two weeks. But Mr. Nicholson will go back to Hong Kong alone.'

Hal extracted the unlit cigar from between his teeth.

'But why?' Hal produced his Dupont.

'Peter is the editor, Hal.' Agustin shrugged. 'After we receive a proof copy of the magazine, I will sign the contract right before your eyes.'

Hal sulked. 'OK. But if I stay, I'm not goin' back to that resort!

Agustin ran a finger around the rim of his glass.

'You may remain here, if you wish.'

'Right! I do wish.' Hal's spread hand inflicted a blow on the table. 'Pete can leave as soon as he can take a flight. Even tomorrow. No need to waste any more time or money.'

Agustin turned and flicked his fingers for the captain. The red-coated Filipino nodded and hurried over with the bill. He laid it piously before Agustin.

'No, Mr. Agustin,' Hal laid aside his lighter. 'I'll do that. This is my shout.' Hal clicked at the captain, who hesitated. Agustin shrugged and nodded. Hal signed the bill with a flourish.

'Ain't credit wonderful?

In a curdled atmosphere, the group broke up. Hal stared after their sponsor and his Goliath.

*

'Fuckin' wog wanker!'

Peter looked up from the Alvarez envelope at the figure reclining on the bed.

'To which wog wanker are you referring?'

'I bet he wants to run it past Mrs M. before he signs.'

'Can you blame him? Do you imagine Buck House would let any Tom, Dick or Halford publish the transcript of an interview with Her Maj without running an eye over it? And it seems the Palace here is taking quite an interest in our little publication.'

''ow do you figure that out?' Hal raised himself onto an elbow.

'Here are two official portraits of 'Her Most Beautified First Lady'.' Peter held aloft a pair of cellophane packets. 'Put not your trust in foreign snappers.'

'Let's 'ave a butcher's,' Hal ordered, holding out a hand.

'This could be the cover,' Peter ruefully acknowledged. Respectfully, he wafted a six by nine transparency in Hal's direction. Seated below a portrait of the President in a heavy gold frame, Mrs. Marcos smiled tenderly at the camera, her dress of white silk. About her neck a circlet of what seemed to be lustrous snow-flakes gleamed. To her right Peter recognised a Borobudurian deity with an uncanny resemblance to Mrs. M. in its general shape, full lips and broad yet delicate nose.

'I suppose we could take sycophancy up another notch by printing the other shot on the back cover.' Peter tossed over the second portrait, which landed on Hal's stomach.

Hal made a growling sound as he considered the Purse Lady in green silk, five diamond bracelets on each wrist, a challenge in her sidelong glance.

'She's a really nice-lookin' bird,' Hal nodded. 'And loaded, I'll bet.' He raised the portrait higher and frowned. 'Could do with a bit more on top, though.'

'You know, Alvarez's stuff isn't half bad.' Peter admitted. 'A little too obviously ethnic but nothing to be ashamed of.'

'Great.' Hal swung his legs off the bed. 'I'm fed up with all this work. Let's go and find a bit of fun.'

Even though the sun still bathed the streets, 'José's' off the Boulevard was an inkwell. Hal and Peter groped their way past the blackout curtain and felt their way towards a table.

A short, fat woman (predictably wearing black) waddled towards them, boasting a gat-toothed grin.

'Two nice, cold beers,' Hal ordered, displaying the appropriate number of digits.

The bar was a vacuity until the moment when the juke box bellowed into life. From hidden depths four girls sashayed into the diminutive space between the tables and the bar. They began to gyrate. Hal had his back turned to the dancers. He grimaced at the volume of sound. Peter's attention was caught by a tall girl in pink with revolutionary hips. Impressed by the rear view, Peter wondered what she would look like in front. She obliged. Peter was even more impressed.

Something had taken place at the Inter. It was something that had totally surprised him. He realised that he had become as one with the foreign businessmen, the luxury tourists, the whore-mongers. Something had been triggered in him.

He now realised he had acted badly towards Miranda. But somehow, at this moment, he could not have cared less about the girl. He supposed she and Maria were safely back at the resort. He was in no hurry to find out.

Now that they were on the very edge of completing their mission, he felt heady. He had interviewed two of the most important political figures in the Philippines. He had met fascinating sources of information. He had been spoiled mercilessly by Agustin. Treated like royalty. This was something like.

He glanced back at the sensual bar-girl.

Her eyes were dark (what did he expect, blue?). Not only were they dark, they were large and lustrous. He could tell that the eyelashes were factitious. But he judged that her breasts were not. And, in a land where women were universally short, this whore's limbs were worthy of a chorus line.

The beers arrived. Hal, with all his usual grace, grabbed one of the glass tankards and downed half the freezing amber. He left his finger-prints in the condensation. The drink-bringer waited. Hal ignored her. Peter, grinned crookedly, produced his roll of pesos and paid.

'Ah, that's better…' Hal sighed. Peter vacated his chair and crossed the floor. Without missing a step or a beat, the girl turned to meet him, deserting her erstwhile partner, a short, rotund local. The trap had been sprung.

As if by magic, the music changed to a slow rock-blues. Peter sighed as the girl slipped between his encircling arms. They met. He had guessed right. Her breasts were all her own. Peter closed his eyes and sighed.

He was bumped. He looked behind him. A grinning Hal was circling them with a small, unsmiling girl in his arms.

'What is your name?' The girl's breath was hot in Peter's ear. He did not hesitate. 'Hal.' He pressed himself against her. 'Yours?' He lightly kissed her ear lobe. 'Thea,' came the breathy reply.

Peter stroked the girl's back. He could detect nothing beneath the sere, pink cotton blouse other than the smoothness of skin. He glanced down at the equally smooth brown flesh, gleaming beneath her pink mini-skirt. They spun. Thea caught him between her thighs. His instincts took over. They turned again. The very world turned. The girl's lips parted and Peter found them irresistible.

'Go on. Get stuck in, mate,' Hal growled from two yards away.

Peter gave Hal the evil eye. The tiny girl was gazing up at Hal in wonder. The music exited with a long fade. The quartet then removed to the darkest table in the darkest corner by the bar.

Hal casually introduced his partner as 'Dolores'. Equally casually, he omitted to mention Peter's name. With grudging reluctance, Peter introduced Thea to his grinning partner – but without identifying Hal by name. The woman in black re-appeared with a round of drinks; lagers for the men, the statutory thimblefuls of coke for the girls. Hal nibbled Dolores' neck and stroked her right breast; Peter released a few more damp notes. The waitress revealed her gat-teeth and departed with her reward, borne on high on a small, wet tray.

Peter turned his attention to Thea. Their lips conjoined once more and her tongue flickered out to caress his. He carefully placed a hand on her bare thigh. Her hand closed over his.

Peter and Thea turned as one as Dolores gave a piercing shriek. She was staring wide-eyed at something below Peter's eye-level. Tearing her eyes away, she gabbled something to Thea in rapid Tagalog. Not content with words, Dolores held out both hands and made a circle of her fingers. Then, for good measure, she crossed herself.

Hal grinned at Peter. 'Always gets 'em like that, the first time.' Hal grinned.' She'll get used to it.' Dolores gabbled some more. Hal's eyes twinkled. 'It's not my fault she's got small 'ands.'

'Come on. Let's dance,' Peter suggested rather too sharply and dragged Thea onto the floor. It was too late. The sexual tension between them had fled. Hal had once again succeeded in triumphing over a rival.

Thea was going through the motions but her distraction was evident. Her mind, one might say, was no longer on this client. In parallel, Peter's own interest went into a decline. Hal and Dolores joined them on the tiny dance-floor. Peter ground his teeth as Thea stared at Hal. At the end of the number, Dolores accompanied Peter back to the table while Hal and Thea remained in situ. Peter winced as he saw Thea's tongue flicker over Hal's lower lip. Dolores' fingers slipped along his thigh and palped the material covering his groin. Disgusted, Peter pushed her hand away and stood, almost knocking over his drink.

'How big is yours?'.

Peter marched blindly towards the blackout curtain.

''Ere, Pete.' Hal called. 'There's no need to rush off.'

'I'll rush off if I want to.' Even in his own ears Peter sounded like a ten-year-old. 'You big prick!'

Hal's raucous laughter drove him into the night and haunted his dreams.

Chapter Twenty-seven

Had Peter really been in Manila just four hours earlier? He lay on the truckle bed in Aggie's flat, staring at the crumpled Barong Tagalog, hanging from a peg behind the door. His skin also felt crumpled in the overheated, humid room, redolent of damp wool. There was no question of running the air conditioner. The cost was prohibitive.

He recalled the cool evening silence of Agustin's resort. Even with the window barely ajar up here on the sixth floor, the bedlam from the street was intrusive. Restaurants leant their weight to the fetid congregation of odours in the dank stillness. Against the constant hum of the world outside, Peter could detect a distinct, dry click coming from the wardrobe in the corner of the room. In his absence the bastards had re-colonised the apartment. He decided to leave them be. Within a month – or two at the outside – he would be back in the Philippines. He frowned. But not without a cast-iron contract. He had learned that much from his dealings with Agustin. And with Hal.

Peter shifted uneasily as he recollected their last meeting. Had it been just this morning?

Thea it was who had answered the door to Hal's room at the Inter. The girl's hair had been tousled; her long body wrapped in a bath-towel – the very essence of 'Playboy'. Before Peter could take evasive action, the girl had leant forward and brushed his lips with hers. He realised that her eyelashes were genuine, after all. The girl's eyes opened and they descended three inches as she lowered herself from tip-toe. Peter's heart had lurched at the poignancy of the smooth, brown skin in the chilly morning air; at the sadness of the 'might have been' and 'now never would be'. He had realised that he was morally no better than Hal. He would happily (more than happily) have grappled with Thea as Hal had done. His priggishness had deserted him; had left him for good; had left him flat.

Thea led him into the room and, with a little wave of adieu, entered the bathroom. Peter crept towards the bed. From the bathroom came the rasp of Thea hawking into the sink. The spell had been broken. He realised that the sound had woken Hal, who was blinking at him.

'Bit of all right,' Hal grinned and nodded towards the source of the ugly sound.

'Bit noisy for my taste,' Peter replied.

'Thea's even more restless than Maria,' Hal complained. 'Couldn't get a wink all night.' He raised himself on one elbow.

'I'll need my plane ticket.'

'Oh? Right. You won't mind if I don't come with you?' Hal reached into the drawer of the bedside cabinet. 'Got a few matters to clear up.'

A toilet flushed.

'Thanks,' Peter managed to grunt as he accepted the folded ticket.

'Chico will take you to the airport.'

'Right.'

'Look, Pete...'

'Yes?'

'No 'ard feelin's...? He nodded towards the bathroom.

'I told you. She's not my type.'

'She's certainly no Miranda,' Hal chuckled. 'By the way, where is Miranda?'

'Where is...? Seems to me that I should be asking you that question.' Peter placed his hands on his hips. 'All right. Let's put it another way. Where's Maria?'

'I dunno. I told 'er to go back to the resort.'

'Just how did you tell her?'

'What do you mean?' Hal frowned. 'Like I said, I told 'er.'

'Well, I have a suspicion that you must have upset Maria for Miranda to disappear with her.'

'Well, Pete me old chum, you can suspect all you like.'

'You don't deny it?'

Hal grinned. 'I 'aven't got the fuckin' energy.'

Peter sensed someone moving across the carpeted room behind him. His spine tingled and gooseflesh crept along his forearms. A towel brushed past him and then the girl was between them, reclining on the big bed. Two droplets of water shone like jewels on her left shoulder. Her black hair was lank. Her face glowed as she looked up at Peter.

Hal laid his hand on Thea's shoulder.

'Right,' Peter muttered, half-turning. 'I'd better be off.'

'Oh, Pete.' Hal's voiced lifted and arrested Peter's transit to the door. Warily, Peter turned and faced his partner.

'You know there's not a lot of time to get out the proofs...' Hal raised an admonitory eyebrow. Peter nodded.

'You won't let me down, will you, Peter?' Hal frowned. 'The future depends on this.'

'I won't let us down, Hal.'

'Yeah, right.' He smiled. 'Us'. His expression lightened. 'I've phoned Hilary. She'll be transcribin' all the interviews and such.'

'My God, Hal, you really have got a nerve.'

Hal grinned, 'Yeah, I 'ave, 'aven't I?'

Peter shook his head, turned and made for the exit.

'Oh, Pete...' Hal paused. Peter stopped without looking back. 'Don't forget to give Hilary all my love.'

Peter reached the bedroom door. He could not resist a backward glance. Hal's hand tugged at the knot on Thea's towel. Before Peter could avert his eyes, the garment fell and he was presented with a vision of the girl's nakedness before it was enveloped in Hal's embrace. Peter stirred in Aggie's bed at the memory. There was a smear of sweat on his upper lip. He tasted salt. Like the Cantonese for lechery – haam sap – wet and salty.

At least his departure had had a touch of dignity. He left as he had arrived – in the Pontiac with Chico at the wheel. Peter had insisted on sitting beside the driver. He read the absurd speed warning once more and wound down the window. Chico and Peter exchanged a smile.

As the green torpedo yawed towards its destination beneath a lowering cloud cover, Peter fingered the Zippo on his jacket pocket. He was down to his last packet of Pall Mall. He bit his lip as he remembered his intention to give the lighter to Miranda. Large spots of rain struck the windscreen with spiteful, audible force. Manila was looking its least inviting. The sagging cables swayed in the gusts. The car window was raised again.

Outside the busy terminal building Peter shook Chico's hand. What could they say? The driver looked embarrassed. His dour looked changed to one of muted pleasure as Peter pressed what remained of his peso roll into Chico's hand.

'And would you please give this to Miranda, Chico?' He handed over the Zippo.

Chico smiled, nodded and was gone.

A profound, ineffable sadness engulfed Peter as he moved towards the terminal building with his luggage.

The same reception team waited in the open space by the same arrivals' gate. The trio of beaming girls displayed the same look of eager expectation, their garlands of sampaguita at the ready. He tried to shake off a sense of foreboding.

The tannoy farted into life. Peter's heart leaped. Was someone calling his name?

'Would Mr. Peter…?'

If only the hubbub would quieten. Where should he go to find the source of the announcement? No need. The crowd parted for a large, pink-faced businessman carrying a dramatic new briefcase. The new arrival extended a hirsute paw towards a beaming Filipino wearing a Barong Tagalog. Beside them a younger Filipino displayed a large, white card bearing the legend, 'Mr. Peter Mathieson, Corduroy Co.' To the businessman's evident delight, two smiling girls stepped forward and draped his shoulders with white garlands. Mr. Mathieson sniffed suspiciously at the blossoms and frowned.

Peter murmured, 'It's sampaguita, Mr. Mathieson.' He smiled to himself. 'The flower of love.' Perhaps the Philippines' edition of *Hong Kong Weekly* might serve an educational purpose after all.

Peter felt a prickling sensation in his groin. He swung his legs off the bed. Something sounding like dry twigs scrabbled under the bath as he entered the ancient shower-room with its miniscule white tiles. He urinated directly into the water, hoping the noise would keep the roach at bay.

As he stared down, he looked back over the events of the day. Given the urgency of the situation, he had fully expected Hilary to be at the wheel of the big Ford, waiting for him at Kaitak. To his annoyance, Hilary had not appeared nor had she responded to his phone calls. In the end he had had to take a cab. The driver had not been best pleased at having to wait while Peter raided his cache of Hong Kong money up on the sixth floor. The lift was hors de combat and he finally arrived in a state of perspiring exhaustion from the porterage of his luggage. The driver had been placated with a two-dollar tip.

There came the sound of a telephone. Peter quickly returned to the bedroom. Another click came from the direction of the wardrobe. He shook his head with frustration as he raised the receiver.

'Yes?' He could not exclude the irritation from his voice.

'Hello, Peter. This is Hilary. Is this a good time?'

It was the same warm, gentle voice with its slightly flattened vowels. Peter became attentive.

'I'm so sorry I wasn't at the airport to meet you,' Hilary apologised.

'That's all right.' He hoped he sounded convincing.

'There was a bit of a crisis.'

'Crisis?'

'Yes,' Hilary said and then paused. Peter could hear distant but distinct Cantonese conversation. 'Nigel and Sue have broken up.'

'What?' Peter's shock was quite genuine.

'I've been seeing both of them – trying to talk some sense into Nigel.'

'I see.'

What on earth did Nigel think he was playing at? Sue was all he had left.

'So, does that mean Nigel's out of the picture for the Philippines edition?' Peter was ashamed to have asked quite the wrong question at the wrong moment. There was a click on the line and an answering clink from the wardrobe. He could picture Hilary wearing her black negligee on the double bed in her elegant bedroom. Without cockroaches.

'How's Nigel taking it?' Peter asked, trying to get back on a conventionally empathetic track.

'It's not him I'm worried about.' Hilary sighed. 'It's Sue. She's so conventional. This has been such a terrible shock for her.'

Peter wondered how the equally conventional Hilary would react to lurid tales from Manila starring Halford Puckle. Correction – will react when Hal files for a divorce?

'Has Nigel given any reasons?'

'Some.'

'Oh?'

How much had Nigel revealed to Hilary? He was precisely the type to pour his heart out to the nearest sympathetic audience. And Hilary was certainly sympathetic. But, from the sound of it, Hilary was as yet unaware of Hal's future plans.

'Well, with all those beans being spilled, I can well understand why you didn't appear at the airport today.'

'Yes, I'm sorry.'

'It really didn't matter. I got a cab.' His forgiveness was genuine and somewhat sentimental.

'Look, I think I'd better come over now. To get the material.'

'Now?' Peter looked round and the litter of his arrival. The flat was a shambles.

'Yes. Make up for lost time.'

'But the flat's in a mess.'

'I'll just pop in for a couple of minutes for the interview tapes and the cassettes.' She paused. 'I'll take the film in tomorrow morning.'

'Well, O.K. If you really don't mind.'

There came a click on the line and the phone went dead. An answering click came from the wardrobe.

The room had darkened. Beyond the windows a bank of storm clouds scudded over the host of television aerials etched against the sky. Across the courtyard a light flicked on. A dumpy, middle-aged Cantonese in dark shorts and a white singlet opened a refrigerator door and withdrew a bottle of Vitasoy.

Peter flicked on the bedside lamp. He clambered over the bed to draw the curtains. His pot-bellied neighbour had lit a cigarette. Inspired to emulation, Peter fumbled for a Pall Mall from the remains of the remaining packet. With the Zippo gone, Peter would have to resort to matches They were in a pocket of his jacket. His jacket was hanging in the wardrobe. Peter shuddered. He licked his dry lips. As he reached for the wardrobe door, another dry rustle almost froze his blood. He flung the door wide open and took two rapid steps backwards. The door bounced on its hinges before coming to rest. Peter peered into the gloomy interior.

In the dark corner behind his best and only pair of winter shoes Peter thought he detected movement. He tip-toed forward on tingling feet. A huge antenna waved from behind a black shoe. Mustering the little that was left of his courage, Peter crept forward and gingerly lifted the shoe out of the wardrobe. If the creature was still clinging to the shoe, it was totally out of sight. Peter's heart thumped as he imagined the gigantic body scurrying over his knuckles and up his arm. And in summer, the beasts would fly. Slowly, carefully he raised the shoe to eye level.

Three inches at least. The creature's body was dark russet in colour; the lighter-coloured legs were hooked over the rubber heel. Raising the shoe higher, he stealthily crept towards the bathroom. Holding his breath, he lifted the shoe high over his head before releasing it. The cockroach literally exploded on contact with the tiled floor with the sound of a pistol being fired. He shivered and retreated back into the bedroom and collapsed on the bed. The sound must have been from the exploding air trapped beneath the creature's winged carapace.

Eventually his heart-beat returned to something akin to normality. He lay staring at the ceiling for five minutes, before venturing to return to the wardrobe. Gritting his teeth, he patted the pockets of his jackets. Not one but two boxes of matches. He shook the Hong Kong version. It rattled. From the depths of the wardrobe came an answering rattle. Peter slammed the door shut and fled to the bathroom. He stumbled over his abandoned shoe, exposing the flattened corpse of his enemy. He stood back against the wall.

'This is ridiculous,' he said aloud, his voice distorted in the ceramic echo chamber. Teeth clenched, he despatched the stubborn corpse to a watery grave with one sharp blow on the shoe. He flushed the toilet twice. Just to make sure.

He returned to the bedroom and a normal heart-rate. He set about tidying the room. Of course, with no amah and no wife, the place was a pigsty. Maybe it would be better to concentrate on the sitting room. Everything was so untidy. Hilary would be shocked. She probably had had no occasion to visit a bachelor pad since embarking on her very amah-ed, Hong Kong life.

Opening a dresser drawer, Peter flung in yesterday's shirt. He deployed his unwashed singlet to dust the visible surfaces He closed the bedroom window against the rising tide of noise from the street. He sighed and switched on the air conditioner.

When the doorbell finally rang, he was fully dressed and adding a few finishing touches to the restoration. Peter hoped he looked reasonably presentable as he moved to answer the ring on the doorbell. At least Hilary did not flinch when she caught sight of him or the sitting room.

She was wearing powder-blue. A powder-blue suit of the finest linen.

'Hello.' Her smile was warm. There was a silence. For once Peter was lost for words. 'Do I look odd?' She asked, glancing down.

'No, absolutely not.' Peter stepped back and waved his guest in. 'Was I staring?'

'Yes, you were rather. I hope it's not the outfit. First outing today.'

Flattering. Or was it? Hilary would happily wear something new for an expedition to Central or the office. No need to jump to any conclusions.

She had moved to the centre of the small sitting room and was revolving slowly.

'Please, take a seat.' Peter offered, slightly flustered. Do you have time for a drink?'

'Well, yes. Just a little one. G & T?'

Peter was relieved to find an inch of gin and the last bottle of tonic. How long had the ice been forming? 'Sorry, there's no lemon.'

'Thanks,' Hilary said as she accepted the offering. 'This was Aggie's old flat, wasn't it?'

'Yes. I'm here on sufferance.'

'Aren't we all?' Hilary said with a shrug. 'Why aren't you drinking?'

'Oh,' Peter started. He had begun to consider Hilary's calves. She was wearing a much more flattering pair of white court shoes. The heels were a great improvement. 'I'll see what I can find. Stock's rather low. Only got back this morning.'

'I know.' She smiled. Peter disappeared into the kitchen. He realised that liquor supplies were now exhausted. Luckily, he finally discovered a half-concealed bottle of Seven-Up. Peter detested the stuff.

'What's through here?'

Hilary's voice came from the innards of the apartment.

'Bedroom and loo.'

'Oh?' You've left the light on.'

'That's all right. Nothing can get in. Window's closed.'

'Sounds like the air-conditioner's on.'

'It is. Because I closed the window.'

'It'll cost a fortune. I never have it on except at night.'

'Nor do I. Normally.'

Hilary nodded and disappeared in the direction of the armchair in the sitting room. Peter followed and lowered himself into the chair's twin. He twirled the sickly-sweet drink around the ice.

'So, when did it happen?'

'Nigel and Sue?'

Peter nodded. From where he sat he had an oblique view of Hilary's pristine jacket. The lapel had jutted forward and Peter could just see a bra strap. Warmth crept up his thighs. Why did he find Hal's wife so desirable? Why had Miranda had the opposite effect? Clean versus unclean? Amateur versus professional? His moral response was so skewed. Hal could at least make the proud boast that he was open to anything in skirts. Or out. No qualms.

Omnivorous. A healthy appetite and no indigestion.

A vivid recollection of Thea, naked in Hal's arms, invaded Peter's imagination. He glanced back at Hilary. Her hand rose and adjusted the jacket lapel.

'I think it's tragic,' she murmured and took another sip.

'Yes.'

Hilary recrossed her ankles and considered her tanned feet inside the flattering white shoes.

'I mean, just because Nigel goes to bed with some whore in Manila, there's no need for him to break up a perfectly good marriage.' She frowned. 'Nor give up the day job.'

Peter almost choked on the 'Seven Up'. He cleared the bubbles from his throat.

'Don't you agree? It's crazy!' Hilary turned towards him and the wilful lapel dipped forward. 'I think it's tragic.' She took another sip.

'Yes.' Peter was lost for words. Where was this conversation going? There were questions to answer. He looked directly into her eyes.

'Yes,' he replied. 'And no.'

'What do you mean?' Her brow creased.

'I mean – yes, it's important if a man goes to bed with a whore in Manila and no, Nigel's marriage was not perfectly good.'

'It was as good if not better than many marriages I know.' Hilary's lips compressed into a tight line.

'Maybe it was missing something,' Peter suggested with a frown.

'What?' Hilary tossed her head. 'Sex?'

'Love.' Peter replied. 'Maybe even romance.'

'Nonsense. Men generally follow a pattern. They dress up whores in romantic clothing. But a whore is a whore and sex is sex.'

'And what is marriage?'

'Marriage is a partnership. Through thick and thin. No matter what.'

'Even if it means that a man feels driven to use whores?'

'Men are just children with a toy between their legs.' Hilary curled her lip and took another swig of her drink. Peter was becoming alarmed – both at the conversation and the rapidly diminishing drink. Had Hilary been drinking before she arrived?

'But Sue doesn't share that attitude, does she?'

Hilary considered Peter. Yes, she had definitely imbibed before her arrival. She answered, 'No, she doesn't. More fool her. Sue's a conventional little fool. What sort of life can a divorcée have in the Colony? And it isn't as if Nigel would have the courage to stay away.'

'You think he'll go back to her?'

'Of course. If the little fool will have him back.'

'You sound rather bitter about the whole business, if I may say so.'

'Bitter? Of course I'm bitter. I can imagine just what Sue is going through.' Hilary rose from her chair. 'The loo's through there, you say?'

Peter nodded. Hilary bent to place her glass on the arm of the chair. She seemed indifferent to the wayward lapel. He caught her staring at him staring at her. Her smile was knowing. She left the room.

Peter shook his head. Hilary was in the strangest mood. It was as though some imp were speaking through her lips and exorcism was required.

From the bathroom came a shriek. Peter leaped to his feet. Hilary was staring into the bowl, her face white under the tan. Peter pushed past her. It was the corpse of the cockroach. He forced a laugh.

'It's only a dead cockroach.'

'Are you sure it's dead?'

'Quite sure.'

'But it's swimming.'

'Look, I know it's dead because I killed it.'

Hilary shuddered. 'I still need to go to the loo.'

Peter paused for a second, took a deep breath and tore a double sheet from the roll. Gritting his teeth, he bowed into the bowl and grasped the roach inside the paper. As the water soaked its way up the sheets, Peter's sensitised skin could feel the hard shell of the beast. Hilary raised both hands to her mouth as Peter turned.

'I'll just toss it out of the window,' he announced, astonished at his own sang-froid. As he left with the carcass, Hilary closed the bathroom door. Peter watched the white, wet bundle turn through the six floors of air and strike the courtyard. He shuddered and closed the window. Time passed. Finally, the flush flushed. The seconds ticked by. After a minute of silent inactivity in the bathroom, Peter crossed the bedroom and tapped on the bathroom door.

'Hilary?'

'Yes?' the voice was very, very small.

'Are you all right?'

'Yes.'

'Are you coming out?'

Silence.

Peter turned the door handle. He pushed the door open but stayed outside. All he could see were tiles and end of the bath.

'May I come in?'

Silence.

Peter ventured into the room. Hilary was seated decorously on the lid of the loo. Her eyes were shut and her head rested against the pipe leading to the tank. If anything, she was paler than before.

Peter grasped her upper arm and lifted her gently to her feet. She slumped against him. He half-carried, half-dragged Hilary into the bedroom. Her lowered her onto the coverlet.

'Cockroaches sometimes have this effect on people.' His tone was one of masculine concern. 'Has this happened before?'

'Never like this,' she murmured and her head slumped to one side, away from Peter.

One of her shoes had come adrift and was lying, abandoned, in the middle of the parquet. Peter retrieved it and placed it neatly beneath the bed. He eased its companion off the owner's other foot and placed it beside its sister. He tidied Hilary's legs, side by side on the bed. Breathing quite hard, Peter considered Hal's wife. Poor old Hilary. Alas. Poor old Sue. Poor fool Nigel.

Hilary gave a sudden start, her legs straightened and she was fast asleep. Peter took a moment to consider his course of action.

He borrowed some money from his store. He slipped out of the flat and took the lift. On Waterloo Road he purchased gin (small bottle), six tonics and the smallest bottle of brandy he could find. He returned to the flat.

He peeped into the bedroom. Hilary had not budged. Peter stacked the tonics in the fridge and poured himself a brandy. He grimaced at the taste. One-star Portuguese rot-gut from Macao. He turned his attention to the tapes and film cassettes that Hilary had come for.

When he eventually heard the feeble sound of her voice, Peter looked at his watch. She had slept for nearly an hour. Outside, the storm clouds had darkened further. Perhaps they were related to the clouds he had left in Manila that morning. A gust of wind rattled the window. He heard her call.

'Peter?' The voice was faint and seemed far away.

'Peter?'

He tasted the brandy on his breath. He pushed himself out of the chair and walked to the bedroom door. He looked in. Hilary bestowed a faint smile on him. Her clothes were neatly folded on the bedside chair.

'I couldn't rumple my new suit, now could I?'

Peter shook his head. Only her face was visible. She had slipped under the sheets. He noticed that the room was cold. The air conditioner gurgled and hissed on.

Peter smiled and walked rather awkwardly towards the bed. He sat down with great care. Hilary's bare arm appeared and reached across. Her warm hand grasped his cold fingers.

'You're cold,' she announced.

Peter smiled and shook his head.

'Then you're nervous.'

Peter nodded. His teeth chattered.

'There's nothing to be nervous of, Peter.' Her voice was soothing. Her fingers left his and laid hold of the covers. His weight was holding them in place.

'Don't, Hilary.'

'It's only sex, Peter,' Hilary murmured and rose from the sheet into the lamplight. The sight of her breasts struck Peter with the force of a blow. In the cool air her nipples were as firm and large as raspberries.

'Don't Hilary.' The breasts first lifted and then dipped like grapes before Tantalus. Beneath lay the shadowy, suggestive regions he had never explored. Hilary moved across the bed and stared into Peter's eyes.

Peter felt Hilary's teeth against his upper lip. Her tongue sought his. He clenched his fists against the small of her back.

'Hold me,' she breathed.

Peter offered her a comic face. 'My hands are cold.'

She smiled and drew one of his hands from behind her back.

'There,' she said, as though to a small boy. She took his open palm and guided it to her right breast. Peter began to throb. The raspberry pressed into his palm. He lowered his lips to taste the offered fruit. Hilary helped Peter extricate himself from his clothes. At her insistence, he allowed himself to be pushed back while her busy fingers unzipped him.

'Did you have a girl in Manila, Peter?' Hilary asked as her fingers closed over his penis. She stroked him sensuously.

'Did you?' Hilary repeated.

'Yes,' Peter gasped and swallowed. Hilary slowly sank back onto the pillow, Peter still in her grasp.

'Was she pretty?'

'Hhhm.' Peter mumbled, taking further unfair advantage of Hilary's right breast. Hilary allowed herself to sink back onto the pillow. She retained her hold on him.

'Was she pretty?'

'Hmmm.' Peter nodded at the breast. His left hand sought out the regions beneath the sheet. His temples drummed.

'Did you go all the way with her?' the fingers kept up their rhythm.

'Yes,' so this was her exorcism. He was playing the part of Hal.

'Did she do this to you?' Her hand was unrelenting.

'Yes,' Peter's words rose from somewhere deep within. 'Yes.' His fingers were slick with her arousal.

He tore the sheet aside. Hilary raised her hips to meet him.

Peter placed a hand on either side of her body and lowered himself onto her firm stomach. He reached down.

Her fingers closed over his hand.

'And did Hal have a girl too?'

Peter froze.

The fingers curled around him once more and resumed their rhythm.

'Come on, you can tell me. I won't mind.'

Peter allowed his body to fall to one side of Hilary. He felt a pain shoot through his groin. He winced. Hilary released him. She raised herself on one elbow. Her hand reached out to stroke his cheek. Peter turned aside.

'I'm sorry,' Hilary murmured, her breasts still heaving, still beautiful in the dim light. Peter saw the tears glistening on her lashes.

'If you wanted to know about Hal, why didn't you just ask Nigel?'

'I did.'

'Did you do all of this with him too?' His attempted smile was a failure.

Hilary's face was turned towards the shadows. Her shoulders heaved.

'I think you'd better take what you came for and leave.' Peter was surprised at his own cruelty.

Sobbing erupted and Hilary's body rocked to and fro on the disordered bed.

'Poor Sue,' Hilary moaned as her tears stained the pillow-case. Peter left the bed and switched off the air-conditioner. It was quite cool enough.

Chapter Twenty-eight

Every available channel on Peter's naked skin was running with its own rivulet of sweat. He stared out of the open lounge windows, his mood as grey as the sky beyond the aerials. Inspiration would not come. He experienced that curious tingling sensation of guilty pleasure which comes from staring at nothing when there is work to be done. As Hilary had meekly reminded him last night – her hands gripping the plastic bag of tapes and films – his two major articles were required at the printers by five o'clock. It was only a question of tidying but what was engaging Peter's mind at the moment was more than mere distraction. He chewed the end of his ball-point as a stabbing pain reminded him of the task at hand. He glanced down at his groin with distaste. At the top of the damp page on the table before him were the words 'Dear Miranda'. But how on earth could he express what he had to say with any delicacy? Why not just throw some words onto the page and worry about the finesses once there was something to finesse? He sighed and began to scribble.

I think you had better go and see a doctor. (Great beginning!) Some days after I slept with you in my room at the Intercontinental, I developed the symptoms of gonorrhoea. As you were the only girl I slept with in Manila and I was disease-free before my arrival there, I can only conclude that you too have the disease. Do not think that this alters my feelings towards you or that I disbelieve what you told me of your behaviour with other guests at the resort. I do advise you to consult a doctor as soon as possible. My own doctor has given me some black and red antibiotic pills. They will solve the problem but I must not have sex until I am better. That will take at least two weeks. When I return to Manila, I hope I will see you again. Many thanks for all

you did for me.
Yours sincerely,
Peter.'

P.S. Perhaps you should ask your cousin to see a
doctor too.

P.P.S. Perhaps you should avoid your cousin in
future.

P.P.P.S. May I suggest you always wash your hands
after work

Peter stared at his final postscript for two seconds before
collapsing with laughter. He crumpled the paper in his hand and
tossed it in the bin.

Why on earth should he wax so pompously pious towards the
little bitch? She probably visited a pox doctor at regular intervals
anyway. He must have coincided with her when the next visit was
due.

He wanted to pee but he knew the experience would be
painful. He recalled the French slang for what ailed him – 'dur
pis'. Much more appropriate than 'clap'. There was absolutely
nothing to applaud in this condition. The pain retreated.

Peter smiled. Hilary would never know how close to disaster
she had come. Of course, had she caught it now, with Hal in full
cry, there would have been a great to-do. Grounds for divorce, no
doubt. Peter chuckled.

Poor Miranda. He sighed. It was, he supposed, an occupational
hazard. Could he really blame her for bending the truth an inch or
six? It had really been up to him to take the necessary precautions.
Caveat emptor.

Except Miranda had been 'on the house', as Agustin had so
neatly put it. Just another extra, free, gratis and diseased.

When she did visit a doctor, he hoped she would get a more
sympathetic reception than he had received chez 'Jones, Jones
and partners', pox doctors to the expat community. Dr. Jones
Senior had been a medical version of Hilary, but rather older and
less attractive.

'Are you married?'

'No longer.'

'That's just as well.'

'Hear, hear.'

'Present this scrip to the receptionist outside. Follow the instructions to the letter.'

'To the letter. Roger.'

'Where did you pick up this thing?'

'In Manila. With a pulsating Pilipina.'

'I know you're trying to make light of this but I think I should warn you to stay out of other people's beds for the next fortnight. Then present yourself for a final check.'

'These pills will do the trick?'

'Yes. But there are antibiotic-resistant strains of this disease so I shouldn't treat this too lightly in future.'

Peter gave his sacred word to the good doctoress.

Only after Peter had about-turned and departed did he recall where he had met the good lady before. She was one of Aggie's friends and he had met her at one of Aggie's 'orgies'. Quite innocent affairs, really, but everyone pretended to be that little bit wickeder than they were under the guise of being a little bit drunker than they were. So, he had kissed Doctor Jones repeatedly in the darkened bedroom where the coats had been thrown. Free with her kisses she might have been; free too with her hands but, in spite of her inebriation, Peter had been quite unable to get here off her feet and onto the bedful of coats. It must have been Christmas last year. Before he and Aggie broke up.

The front doorbell rang. Peter inhaled through his teeth with irritation. The bell delivered its imperious clamour once more – this time for ten seconds non-stop. Peter growled and got to his feet. He listened and only heard the constant rumble of the Waterloo Road traffic. He resumed his place, noting the damp buttock marks on the cheap leatherette. This time the bell pealed for fifteen seconds. Probably some door-to-door fish salesman. Peter marched on sticky soles to the front door. He would have to exercise his Cantonese.

'Uei?' he called. 'You go away.'

'Pete?' a woman's voice called. Aggie's voice.

'Oh, Aggie.'

'Come on, Peter. Open the bloody door before the neighbours roll out.'

'You've caught me in the shower. I'm naked.'

'So much the better. Open up.'

'Hang on a tick.'

Peter raced into the bathroom, switched the shower on full bore, leaped in, leaped out and wrapped the bath-towel round his waist.

'At bloody last,' Aggie breathed as she breezed into the flat. 'My God. This is a pigsty.'

'I gave it a good tidy last night.'

'Why?'

'Why what?'

'In whose honour did you tidy it? You never so much as raised a duster in anger while we were together.'

Peter had to admire the woman. Even in this humidity, she had the appearance of someone returning from a long walk in the clean, fresh outback. Her fair hair struggled attractively against the ministrations of her hairdresser. Her white T-shirt was provocative over her flared jolly-jack-tar trews. A dozen ethnic copper and brass bangles jangled on her left wrist; three gross of silver ones on her right. Aggie dropped her monster sun glasses into a white shoulder-bag. She reached across the dampness with her scarlet lips and imprinted a chaste kiss on Peter's cheek.

'I only got back from Manila last night,' Peter mumbled, as though responding to an accusation.

Aggie produced a small mirror and checked her lipstick. 'How was the trip?'

'Fruitful.'

'I hear the dollies over there are a dime a dozen.'

'That's the pineapples.'

'Nice?'

'Yes. The pineapples were super. So were the coconuts.'

Aggie ran her finger-tips along the border of the sideboard, her talons catching the Swatow lace runner. She inspected her fingertips with distaste.

'Great job you did. You always were a dirty bugger.'

To his amazement Peter felt an unexpected tear prick the corner of his right eye. His sudden fit of melancholy must have been infectious. Aggie lowered her voice.

'Maybe that's why I've missed you.'

'Drink?' Did he really say that?

'Yeah, right.' Aggie replied, draping her bag over his chair.

'Don't sit in that chair!' Peter shouted as her tailored bottom began its descent. Aggie froze.

'Why ever not?'

'That's my work chair.' Peter hurried across and guided Aggie onto another station. 'Those are all my papers.'

'What're you writing? Nights of passion in the hotspots of Manila?' Aggie was flicking through Peter's martial law article. Peter retrieved the ball that was the rejected letter to Miranda from the floor and slipped into the kitchen.

Aggie's voice pursued him. 'I'll just have a Seven Up on the rocks.'

Peter portered the drink back; the ice clinking as he tried to balance on bare feet. Aggie looked up.

'Don't they have any sun in Manila? You're paler than a ghost.'

'I was there to work – not to create a sun tan.'

'There are lots of ways of avoiding a tan, Sonny Jim.' Aggie pursed her lips. 'See, I'm still jealous.'

'I don't believe it.'

'I'm here to prove it.' Aggie rose and took a deep breath which all but overwhelmed the doctor's proscriptions. Judging by visual evidence, Aggie could give Maria a run for her money.

'I'm sure you could,' Peter smiled and raised a palm in what he hoped would be construed as a polite check on any further advances.

'A tan isn't everything,' Aggie asserted as she advanced towards her prey.

'I would love to demonstrate just how unimportant a tan is but I have a five o'clock deadline at the printers in Causeway Bay.'

'And I've got a deadline with Solly at seven this p.m.'

'I wondered when Brooklyn's answer to Tyrannosaurus Rex was going to make an appearance.' Peter tightened the towel. The freshness of the shower had been replaced by damp stickiness.

'That's just it. The monster and I are through – washed up – kaput.'

'Who washed up whom?'

'The washing up was mutual.' Aggie's right eyelid trembled. She rubbed it with a knuckle like a small child. No recriminations. If he wished to extract the gory details, Aggie would have to be horizontal.

'We're having our final dinner tonight to try and patch things up.' Aggie looked directly at Peter. 'I want to patch up some things but not others.'

Aggie crossed the parquetted gap in three swift strides, pursing her lips at Peter. They struck the cheek he had turned.

'I get it.' Aggie stepped back, her blue eyes hurt and fierce.

'No, you don't get anything.' Peter attempted to reach out for her arm; Aggie shrugged back out of distance. Peter let his hand drop.

'How long do you need to finish this job?' Aggie's new manner was business-like.

'What? All of it?

'Yeah. All of it.'

'Two weeks.'

''Til publication?

'Or not.'

'And then?'

'It's 'publish or be damned'.'

'If it's published?'

'I'll be leaving to set up shop in Manila.'

Aggie looked down at her feet to consider this.

She looked up again. 'I wouldn't want to quit Hong Kong,' she said with a frown. Then she raised her head. 'What happens if they don't publish?

'U.K.'

'Christ! Britain? The Narrow Land?'

'It's nobler to be a nobody in the U.K.'

'They get plenty of practice.'

Peter took Aggie's arm.

'What about Manila?'

'I'm sorry, pet. I've been there. On my way to Hong Kong. It's a dirty, corrupt, violent shit-heap. No way. I'm not giving up a great job and way of life that I've struggled to get for years only to go and be your 'little woman' in the Philippines.'

'I take it that's final?'

'You could stick around Hong Kong, you know, Pete.'

'What? And work for the egregious Solly again?'

'There are other jobs.'

'Not for me there aren't. This place is great if you're a solicitor, a banker, an engineer or even a civil servant. But films? Journalism? Art? Forget it!'

'There's always P.R.'

'I don't have the boobs for it.'

Aggie flushed. 'Thanks a million, Peter. I must remember to add that to my C.V.'

'I'm sorry. I was annoyed. It wasn't meant to be personal.'

'Sexist remarks never are.' She sighed. 'O.K. you've got your two weeks in the flat. I reckon I can let Solly fuck me for another fortnight.' She sobbed once, bit her lip and left him alone. He winced as the front door slammed in a salutation to the neighbours. Peter squeezed the ball of paper in his hand.

The phone rang. Peter dropped the letter into the waste-paper basket as he picked up the receiver.

'Hello, Peter Nicholson speaking.'

'Hello, Peter. It's me.'

'Hello, Hilary.'

'Sorry to interrupt the muse.'

'Join the queue.'

Hilary's voice changed tack to worry-ward.

'How's it coming?'

'I'll get there, don't worry.'

'Fine. Look, why don't I pick you up?'

'I'll meet you downstairs.'

'Four fifteen?'

'Four thirty would be soon enough.'

'I've got to pick up some pics at the processor's en route.'

'Fine.'

'Pete?'

'Yes?'

'I've already transcribed Mrs. Marcos.'

'Wow. Did your fingers catch fire?'

'It's not half bad. Particularly that stuff towards the end.'

'Could you understand all the local references? For spelling?'

'Perhaps you could check the transcript with me later this evening.'

'Your Hilton or mine?'

'There's no need for that. After we're through at the printers, I'll drive you home and let Ah Yeot feed us.'

'Just as well you're driving. The Beast's got a dead battery.'

'Right. Four fifteen, outside the flats.'

'Right.'

'Oh – and Pete …'

'Yes?'

'I'm sorry about last night.'

'So am I Hilary. In so many ways.'

Peter lowered the receiver onto its cradle. Efficient lady. He sighed. Did all marriages go flat after ten years? His own had lasted far fewer. He still wondered what Hilary saw in Hal. Although he now had to acknowledge a grudging liking for the Bristolian felon, he could think of only one thing to recommend Hal to a woman and there were still twenty-three other hours in the day.

Peter sighed. After all, what had Aggie seen in him? At the thought, he recollected his two-week reprieve and scurried back to the table. He lifted his watch from atop the sheaf of typing. Better get a move on.

At four fourteen, Peter stepped forward to the edge of the kerb in Waterloo Road to be greeted by a dead cat. He retched, stepped four paces to the left and waved at the Granada with the brown envelope containing his 'oeuvre'. Hilary was smiling at him as the car slid to a halt. Peter opened the passenger door and climbed in. Hilary's dress was a cool pastel green. It matched her eyes.

'You've just run over a cat.'

'Oh, don't. How horrible!'

'It's all right. I was only joking.'

Hilary frowned and gunned the engine. The car lurched out into the traffic stream.

'You'll have to get onto the flyover.'

Hilary nodded. Peter had always found the sight of a pretty woman at the wheel of a car titillating.

'You look very cool.'

'Thanks.' Hilary glanced at him and smiled, 'It's so damned hot.' Their eyes met for a moment. Hilary frowned and looked away.

'The traffic's been awful today.'

'And every other day.'

At the entrance to the cross-harbour tunnel, Hilary produced her white leather bag from beneath her seat to pay the five-dollar toll.

Peter frowned. Hilary was driving with bare feet. More titillation. Hilary wound up her window to give the air-conditioning a chance to function.

The Granada dipped down into the tunnel. Having queued for ten minutes to enter it, there was now no car in sight. Peter turned and considered Hilary. She glanced at him. Peter leaned across the gear-lever and kissed her. Her knuckles whitened on the wheel as he brushed her breast with his left hand.

'Does that mean I'm forgiven?'

'You are – if I am.'

'There's nothing to forgive.'

Peter sighed. 'I think Hal is a very fortunate man.'

'Why don't you tell him that?'

The car rounded the upward curve into the daylight. The solid greyness was beginning to fragment. Over Repulse Bay the sky was tinged with blue. They turned left towards Causeway Bay. The car slowed and then stopped by the kerb. Hilary slipped her feet into her shoes and opened the driver's door.

'Shan't be long.'

The processor's was just round the corner from the old days in Causeway Bay. Peter adjusted the rear-view mirror. Through the narrow gap between multi-storey apartment buildings, decorated with washing on bamboo poles, the harbour shone like a brazen tungsten shield. Peter manoeuvred the mirror back into place. Hilary reappeared, holding aloft a large, brown paper envelope.

'What took you so long?' Peter quipped.

'Why on earth did you take so many?'

'Well, if the mag doesn't want them, National Geographic might.'

Hilary's smile seemed a little tighter as she swung away from the kerb.

'Who's doing the layout?' Peter asked.

'The printer has found somebody.'

'Somebody? Who? His cousin?'

'As a matter of fact, yes.'

Hilary peered at the crush of vehicles at the next intersection, all hooting in impotent fury. She added her note to the medley.

'He works for Nigel, oddly enough.'

'Hal really is a cunning old sod.'

Hilary spotted a gap and shot through it, narrowly missing an old woman who hopped back onto the kerb, losing one of her black felt slippers in the process.

'Silly bitch,' she hissed. 'They've got no road sense.'

There speaks the genuine article, the Hong Kong tai-tai, thought Peter, but kept his counsel.

The Granada swept into a side road, narrowly missing a hawker's trolley laden with corn-on-the-cob. A stream of obscenity pursued them. They arrived at the cul of the cul. Hilary braked and cut the engine.

'There may be trouble ahead,' Peter remarked, nodding towards the Opel whose exit the Granada partially blocked. Hilary shrugged as she bent to retrieve her shoes. She climbed out into the landscape of vegetarian refuse. Peter shrugged in turn and followed her along the pungent street. Picking their way through paak choi stalks, soft drink cartons and spittle, the foreign devils arrived at the entrance to a well-worn fifteen storey edifice.

Hilary marched without hesitation into a dark tunnel. Ten paces in, she stopped and pressed the lift button. The tiny vehicle responded immediately. Hilary stepped inside, Peter hard on her somewhat grubbier heels, clutching his day's work in its brown envelope.

'Awful things happen in lifts they tell me,' Peter joked. The joke fell flat. 'Floor?' he asked.

'Eight.' Hilary gave him a bleak smile. 'Not too awful, I trust.'

'Don't worry, I'll protect you.' Peter smiled at Hilary. In the tight space her scent brought some relief from the earlier odours of the street.

'Thanks for the protection,' Hilary murmured as they left the lift. She rang the bell beside what seemed to be the entrance to a perfectly ordinary apartment. Beside the heavy door with its spyhole a plastic board reassured all visitors that this was indeed the Fuk King Printing Company.

'A rose by any other name...' Peter murmured in Hilary's ear. The door opened and they were assailed by the racket from a machine which lurched to and fro in a distant room. A smiling Chinese with a shining pate bowed them in. East met West at the counter.

'Hello, Mr. Choi,' Hilary lifted the envelope from Peter's fingers and placed it on the plasticked counter.

'Good day, Mrs. Puckle,' Mr. Choi, beaming, greeted Hilary.

'This is the last of the copy, Mr. Choi, except for the two interviews we discussed. And these...' she dropped her own envelope on top of Peter's offering. 'These are the photographs.'

'Very good. Very good.'

'Yes, they are,' Peter concurred. Mr. Choi wheezed and inclined his head.

'Do you have a light box, Mr. Choi?' Peter wondered. The proprietor frowned. 'To view the pictures.'

'Oh, yes, yes.' Mr. Choi waved her towards the next room.

Hilary glanced back at Peter. 'Coming?'

Peter produced what remained of his pack of cigarettes. He patted his pockets.

'In a moment. Have you a light, Mr. Choi?'

Hilary slipped behind the counter and on towards the noise. Mr. Choi produced a book of matches. The cover had a white background with red and gold Chinese lettering. In English was the name *Wing Chung Peking Restaurant* and an address in Kowloon.

'My company plint.' Mr. Choi beamed, pointing at the lettering on the matches.

'Excellent work, Mr. Choi. I hope you can do as well for us. When will the first proof be ready?'

Mr. Choi beamed. 'One week.'

'O.K. I'll go and see the pictures.' Peter passed the smiling Choi and went in search of Hilary.

She was leaning over the light box, peering at the transparencies through a loupe.

'Wonderful, aren't they?' Peter asked, slipping his left arm around her waist.

'Yes,' Hilary replied, straightening, her eyes bright. 'Wonderful.'

''National Geographic' standard, would you say?'

'Oh, much better! *Hong Kong Weekly* standard.'

Peter laughed. 'Touché.'

'Now, Peter, comes the time of reckoning.' Hilary clicked open her bag and produced a white envelope.

'What reckoning? Don't tell me I owe Halford any more money?'

'No. This is what Hal says he owes you.'

Peter frowned and gave Hilary a long, searching look. Her eyes widened in response. Peter relieved her of the envelope. The gum came unstuck at the first tug. He opened the flap. Inside were ten five-hundred-dollar notes.

'Very generous.' Peter's smile was crooked. 'but partners generally don't get paid until after the issue has appeared.'

'Partners?'

'Yes, partners. There's going to be fifteen to twenty thousand each in this when Agustin puts his cross on the contract.'

Peter held the envelope out to Hilary. She shook her head.

'I'm sorry, Peter. I know nothing of any partnership. Hal

phoned me from Manila last night and said I was to give you five thousand dollars for your work on the mag once I had received the articles, the cassettes and the pics.'

Peter bit his lip. He was in a white rage. Like Nigel, he had been out-witted. If he returned the money it would never reappear. Hal had double-crossed him, as he did everyone else. Even Hilary.

He looked at her and smiled. 'He'll do the same to you some day. You know that, don't you?'

'I expect you're right,' Hilary murmured, her face very pale. 'That's no reason not to take the money, Peter.'

She was right. Peter knew it wasn't her fault. She was just obeying orders. He snatched the envelope. 'Just don't expect any further input from me. We're through, Hal and me.'

'But you're the editor. That's part of the deal.'

'Tell Hal to find another sucker.' He paused and frowned at Hilary. 'I hereby promote you to the editorship of *Hong Kong Weekly Philippines Edition*.'

'Won't you come back with me and just check the Mrs. Marcos interview?' She moved closer. Once again, he inhaled her perfume. It would serve Hal right if he did accept.

'I think I'll pass, Hilary.'

'Wait and I'll give you a lift home.'

'Who needs lifts? Peter waved his white envelope. 'I'm loaded.'

Chapter Twenty-nine

Encouraged by one-star Portuguese brandy, Peter raised the receiver. The dialling tone reverberated through his befuddled skull. He'd give Halford Puckle a piece of his mind. But first he had to find the number of the hotel. He lowered the receiver. But what was the number for international enquiries? He shook his head. It did not clear.

Poor Hilary. She was the ultimate sucker. Nigel and he had a small enough stake in this business. Hilary had devoted ten years of her life to the rat. Now here he was, gnawing at the bonds which tied the twain together. Not fast enough to make it a clean break. No, trust Halford Puckle, mastodon, to extract the last milligram of advantage from the girl, before flinging her on the reject pile along with all the rest. Hilary's one consolation was that she had a job in Hong Kong which would keep her in court shoes and custom leather bags for the foreseeable future. So, of course, did Aggie. She and Hilary had a lot in common. Of course, he could exercise his own options now. He felt sure he could revive the embers of Aggie's affection. He better had if he wished to stay on in the flat. But he wasn't sure whether he wished to return unto that particular breach. Even at the end of the effort of repairing it, he would still be in the Solly circle. Aggie had made it clear that she had no intention of changing the essentials of her way of life. Peter blinked. It was also clear that men were not among the essentials. At least, Peter now knew that Solly wasn't. Nor, come to that, was he. As for his relationship with Aggie, how could it survive anywhere but here in the Colony? It was clear that he was a refreshing change from the standard banking, commercial, cheese-cutter wearing brigade who would swarm like bees round a bright, bosomy blonde from Down Under; just as Aggie had offered relief from the unmerry band of spoiled colonial daughters, expatriate secretaries on the make and very bored wives.

Hilary wasn't a bored wife. Peter took another slug of brandy.

He swallowed air along with the fiery liquid. He needed another bottle.

Peter pushed himself off the bed and found his old flip-flops. In the dark of the stairwell, he stared at the glowing red eye of the 'lift coming' light. He fingered the folding envelope in his pocket. At least he would be able to last a few days longer with Hal's five thousand. But who could he ask to put him up after Aggie kicked him out? He couldn't think of pretending that he wanted to stoke up their former affair; not just for free lodging. Nigel would be out of the question.

Odd. After all these years there was nobody he could turn to in time of trouble. A shooting pain reminded him of another little problem. The course of capsules would last just long enough. A final check with the doc, the old witch, and he could return to his nearest and dearest in Britain with a clean bill of health – if not wealth.

The lift opened. Peter blinked in the expiring tungsten light. A Chinese lad of sixteen or seventeen was already inside, staring at the floor. Peter almost slipped as he stepped into the lift. He checked the floor indicator as the door closed, Five. It really was painfully slow. Four. He would buy some Martell or Hennessey this time round. Forget the firewater. The young lad reached across Peter and flicked on the 'Emergency Stop'.

'Nei tzou mat lan yeh?' Peter asked angrily. 'What the bloody hell are you doing?' The boy turned towards Peter and held out a hand. Peter's heart thumped as he saw the blade of the knife wink in the weak light.

'Nei bei tsin ngor, gwailo,' the boy rasped. 'Give me money, foreign devil.' His hand trembled. Peter was scared but the 'gwailo' appellation had upset him.

'Diu lei. Ngor mo tsin,' he shouted. 'Fuck you. I haven't got any money.'

'Bei tsin. Bei tsin. Seung sei ma? Ngor daasei ley.' Give me money. Do you wish to die? I shall kill you.'

'Ngor mo tsin bei-a,' Peter spat. 'I haven't got any money to give.'

The boy reached towards Peter's right trouser pocket from

which the corner of the white envelope protruded. Peter grabbed at his wrist. He could smell the boy's breath – an admixture of ginger, garlic and catarrh – a poisonous effluent in this confined space. He winced as another pain stabbed into his groin. Peter looked down and saw the knife blade withdraw, bright liquid red.

'You stupid little cunt,' he roared and brought his fist down hard on the boy's neck. Then he fell back into a corner.

The boy's knife hand slashed upwards and there was the sound of tinkling glass. All was pitch black. Peter slid to the floor. The boy trampled on Peter's legs in his desperate effort to reach the envelope. Peter felt the money being dragged from his pocket.

'No, no,' Peter moaned as consciousness escaped. His leg was soaked with blood and urine.

The lift whirred into life. It bumped to a halt. The door opened. He heard shouts and the scuff of shoes. The door closed once more as Peter passed into pain-filled darkness.

Bells splintered in Peter's head. His body floated aimlessly to and fro. A leaf on a throbbing tide. Then, more shouts and whirling lights, rushing this way and that, round bends and through swing doors. And always the cacophonous Cantonese trumpets raised in alarums and excursions. His arm was lifted and then all was drowned in liquid peace; deep, dark and warm.

'How much money did the thief get away with, Mr. Nicholson?' The first face that Peter saw in the hospital was that of a young Chinese police inspector.

'Money?' Peter closed his eyes. Then he remembered. He tried to sit up and winced.

'Don't tug at the stitches, Mr. Nicholson,' another voice exhorted from the other flank of the bed. This voice belonged to a young Chinese doctor in a white coat, a stethoscope round his neck.

'Never mind about the money,' Peter slurred, 'What about...?'

'Oh, you're still intact, Mr. Nicholson. Your assailant's aim was not all it might be.' This was concluded with a thin smile.

'What sort of shot did he make of it?'

'A superficial slash in the groin, stopping short of anything crucial. Long but not deep.'

Peter lowered his head on the pillow. 'A great souvenir of Hong Kong.'

'I hope you were not intending to leave the Colony in the near future, Mr. Nicholson.' The doctor was the epitome of Harley Street urbanity but 'The Colony' sounded absurd on Chinese lips.

'How long will it be before I can get the hell out of here?'

'Out of Queen Elizabeth? A matter of days. But you lost quite a lot of blood. So, I suggest that you give yourself a couple of weeks for your body to get over the shock.'

'Suits me,' Peter smiled. 'Oh, doc.'

The doctor gave his patient a less than friendly look.

'Sorry. I meant 'Doctor'. While we're on the subject of my groin...'

'Yes, Mr. Nicholson?'

'I had a little contretemps with a different kind of attacker while I was in Manila recently. My private practitioner, Dr. Jones of Jones, Jones and partners, will I'm sure enlighten you as to the prescription. If it helps, the capsules were black and red and the course is to last ten days.'

'I see. I'll prescribe sufficient to last until you can return home.'

'Thanks.'

'Now I'll leave you alone so that the Inspector can pursue his enquiries.' The doctor frowned at the end of his stethoscope, 'Though I'm sure the groin injury in Manila would make a better story.'

Peter winked. The Inspector leaned forward. 'European or Chinese?'

Peter sighed. The he realised the inspector was referring to his assailant.

The first call came from Nigel. 'Hello, old sport. How are you feeling?'

'Hello, Nige. Nice of you to call.'

'Not really. Not after all you've been through.'

'How did you find out?'

'You're a celebrity, old bean. Page the first in the good old

Morning Post.'

'Page one!' Peter smirked.

'Well, yes. But right down in the corner.'

'True to form.'

'Well, how is it?'

'Oh, coming along nicely, Nige.'

'Is there anything we can do?' Peter's ears pricked. 'Sue was fearfully upset when I read out the report.'

Peter hesitated but decided to chance it. 'How is Sue?'

'Oh, blossoming. Literally ballooning by the minute.'

Peter could detect the pleasure in Nigel's voice. 'You're not having another kid, are you Nigel?'

'Well, not me, old boy. It's Sue.'

'You sound pleased.'

'I'm bloody delighted. Didn't know she had it in her. If you know what I mean.'

'Congratulations.'

'Look, I tried to ring you for three days after you made the Post but no go.'

'I was in Queen Elizabeth.'

Nigel cleared his throat. 'How bad was it?'

'Not too bad. The stitches prick a bit and so does the pubic hair. They shaved it all off for the op.'

'Serves you right, you old lecher.'

'Talking of lechers... have you heard anything from Hal?'

'Don't mention that bugger to me. Screw his own mother for a dollar.'

'You know what he did to me?'

'No,' the lie sat uneasily on Nigel's lips.

'Didn't Hilary tell you?'

'Well, she did mention about you and Hal falling out.'

'Falling out!' Indignation produces pain, Peter noted. 'Thrown to the wolves. Stabbed in the back!'

'I heard it was elsewhere.'

Peter chuckled. 'So, Manila is out?' He awaited Nigel's answer with interest.

'It always was, really. One can't have everything in life. And

I've got this fabulous little secretary in North Point who does things on the side for me. So, I've decided that 'Home is where the heart is'.'

'Why don't you drop by, Nige, for a chat about not so old times?'

'Righto. I'll see if I can slip away from the office soonish.'

'Good.'

'Right.'

'Right.'

The phone clicked and Peter heard the dialling tone. Two days later a huge hamper of goodies was delivered by the Shanghai Store in North Point. 'Love from Sue and Nigel. Get well soon.'

When the phone next rang, Peter was limping about the flat, doing a spot of desultory dusting.

'Hello, Peter Nicholson speaking.'

'Hello, darlin'. Nice to hear your polished tones. I thought you were at death's door.'

'Who's been misleading you?'

'I just bumped into Hilary in Central. We only got back last night.'

'From somewhere nice?'

'Bali. Solly persuaded me that we needed a few days away from Strong Pong. I wasn't in the mood to argue.'

'I'm sorry you were forced into the position of holidaying in Bali while I was having a ball in *Queen Elizabeth*.'

'If you're going to be sarky, I'll ring off.'

'O.K.'

'O.K. what? I ring off?'

'No, silly. I'm glad you called.'

'How are you managing?'

'Fine. I'm keeping your flat nicely dusted.'

'You shouldn't be doing housework. How about I come round and 'do' for you?'

'It's no good, Aggie. There's only one bedroom with only one bed. I don't want to burst my stitches.'

'Is this a brush-off?'

Peter decided it was time to get serious. 'Aggie, I can't hang around Hong Kong. I've got just about enough bucks to last me until I recover and then get me back to dear old Blighty.'

'You don't have to worry about loot. I've got more than enough for both of us.'

'My pride can't afford it, Aggie.'

'So, you won't let me into my own flat?'

'I promise I'll leave the key with Ah Wong.'

'You could at least drop it round to the office.'

'I'd just as soon not.'

'So, this is it?'

'I'm afraid so, Agatha. The Colony's good for you and good to you. And you're great for it. But I've been here too long for its good and mine.'

'Don't forget the key, you bloody pom.'

The phone went dead.

With only four days to go before his plane was due to leave Kaitak, Peter received an unexpected present. He had walked down to Ah Wong's little store in Waterloo Road. On the way back, he had glanced into the letter-box in the filthy lobby to the block. He had no key but he was able to extricate the brown paper parcel which projected from Aggie's box by half an inch. The parcel was addressed to 'Peter Nicholson, Esquire'.

Back upstairs, Peter opened the container with care, sitting on the edge of the bed. His hands caressed the shining four-colour cover of the latest edition of *Hong Kong Weekly* price $4 HK. That meant $60,000 for Hal to set himself up in Manila with Maria, Thea and Isabel. Not to mention Isabel's mother.

There was Mrs. Marcos in white posed against the portrait of the President. It looked fine. Peter turned over the magazine. Yes, there was the Lady again, first and last. Alpha and Omega. Peter sighed and lay back on the bed. He began to delve within.

Inside cover, full-page four-colour ad for Agustin Enterprises. Nice block. Rotten colour. Too much info. Facing title page, *Hong Kong Weekly. Publisher and Managing Editor.* That's new. *Halford Puckle. Editor Hilary Brooks. Brooks?* Must be Hilary's maiden name. Peter smiled to himself. Here was the index of contents. He settled back to read the interview with Mrs. Marcos.

During the first answer he blinked. What was this line about the need to beautify pubic places? He knew all about that. Wait. There it was again. And again. The word appeared over and over. There would be 'L' to pay. Wait. Here was a gap, as though the typesetter hadn't known how to spell a word. More typos. The whole interview was strewn with the mangled corpses of words.

Makati was consistently translated to Ireland as 'Makarty'. Peter giggled. And what was this riddle? Rowcharse Bullifard. He mouthed the words. Oh, yes. It meant 'Roxas Boulevard'. Terrific. Peter burst out laughing when he came across the article on 'Marital Law'. He hadn't had so much fun in years. He tossed the magazine across the bed. A white compliments slip fluttered onto the coverlet. Peter plucked it up and read, 'I hope this speeds your recovery, Love, Hilary.'

The phone woke Peter from a contented doze. He lifted the receiver.

'Hello, Peter Nicholson speaking.'

'This is Mr. Puckle calling from Manila. Will you accept the charges?

Peter paused. It was tempting.

'Do you accept the charges, Mr. Nicholson?'

'No.' And Peter replaced the receiver. He had to wait two more minutes before the phone rang again.

'Hello, Peter Nicholson speaking.'

'This is Mr. Halford Puckle ringing Mr. Nicholson from the *Intercontinental* Hotel in Manila, the Philippines.'

'This is Nicholson speaking.'

'Hold on.'

''Ello? 'Ello! Is that you, Pete?'

'Yes, it's me. How are you?'

The line seemed to splutter.

'I'm fuckin' choked, if you must know And you know why '

'I can guess, Hal.'

'How could you do it to me?' And us being partners, an' all.'

'We were never really partners, Hal.'

'Yes, we were.' The voice took on a certain urgency. 'We still are. I've even found a nice, little office in Makati. Everythin' was goin' great. Why did you do it?'

'I didn't 'do it', Hal.'

'Don't give me that shit. Who else could 've done it?'

'What does your new editor say?'

There was a pause. Distant yet distinct Tagalog rattled over the line. ''Ow could you let 'er?'

'She told me you were buying me out.'

'She didn't give you any money, did she?'

'Just five grand.'

'Five bloody grand. I'll strangle the bitch.'

'It's all right, Hal. I don't have it any longer.'

'No. The bloody 'Onkers and Shankers' 'as, I'll be bound.'

'No such luck.'

'I know why she's doin' this. Bloody Nigel told 'er about Isabel and she thinks this'll fuck up my chances in Manila. Well, you can tell bloody 'ilary from me that 'er little scheme won't work. I'll figure out some way to get back on top – if it takes my last cent.'

There was a pause in the harangue.

'What did you do with my five thousand bucks?'

'It was stolen by a kid with a knife.'

'What?'

'In a lift.'

'Did 'e 'urt you?'

'A shrewd thrust in the groin. No lasting damage.'

'I wish he'd cut your donger off, you wanker.'

There was a loud click and distant Tagalog once again reigned supreme. Peter smiled and replaced the receiver.

It appealed to Peter's sense of fictional form that his last meeting with Hilary should take in the very same locale as the historic rendezvous that had set the wheels of the Philippines adventure in motion. He spotted her as she filtered through the traffic jam at the end of Queen's Road, opposite the hotel. Peter transferred his single piece of luggage into his left hand.

As befitted so sad an occasion, the sky over Central was azure, brilliant and cloudless. An ABC of a sky. Hilary waved. Peter waved back. She was wearing something pink which set off her tan. Her white court shoes added interest to her calves. Peter suppressed an unworthy thought. As she stepped onto the pavement, Peter caught her by the elbow and steered her towards the coffee shop.

'Thanks for coming.'

'Thanks for asking me.'

The sweat coagulated under Peter's armpits as the couple lightly stepped into the refrigerated coffee shop. They just beat a Chinese couple to a small table in the corner. As they settled into their seats Peter could not suppress a wry smile.

'Now. I've been saving the best until last.' He stared into her green eyes. 'Why did you do it?'

Hilary lowered her bag to the floor and raised her chair so that a chair-leg was inside the strap. Peter smiled. Hilary reciprocated.

'Why did I do it?' Hilary drew a deep breath. 'It was the last throw of my dice.'

'Has it worked?'

Hilary looked down. Peter saw that her lashes were wet.

She sniffed. 'That bastard!'

'Why on earth would Agustin have footed the bill for the magazine after all that had happened?'

'He had no option. Hal threatened to distribute the magazines, errors and all, in Hong Kong and also despatch copies to newspaper editors all round the world if he didn't get his money.'

'I'm astonished that Agustin fell for that. Mind you...'

'What?'

'I always suspected that Agustin had a kind of perplexed affection for young Halford. Even though he threatened to kill Hal.'

'When?' Hilary's eyes widened with anguish.

'It's a long story. I may tell it to you one day.'

'Don't worry. Nigel confessed to all of your misdeeds. He needn't have bothered. I've known about Hal's extra-curricular activities for years. I caught him with his hand inside another girl's blouse while we were on honeymoon.'

'Then why did you stay with it so long?'

'Did? It's not over yet.'

Peter raised his eyebrows. Hilary lowered her eyes as the waitress approached.

'*Leung booi gaafei, m goi sai.*' Peter ordered. He raised two fingers. The waitress sniffed and departed.

'Do you really think he'll come back?'

Hilary shrugged.

'I knew all along that Hal was a shit. But he was such a lively shit. Even when he was bedding my best friends, he still made me feel alive. He was always so full of plans. Of course, it was mostly wind. I had to do all the dirty work.'

The waitress arrived with the overheated coffee. She poured two cupfuls, generous to overflowing. Peter and Hilary left them to cool.

'He started from nothing. And that's a fact. Not exactly 'rags to riches'. But we were just a couple of kids when we got here with a few dollars between us. No real qualifications or experience. We just wanted a good time. Together. Hal did everything and anything to earn money. Nightclub bouncer. Advertising salesman. Even encyclopaedias. He can work hard.'

'Putting wind to good use.'

'At first I put up with it all because, well, it was good between us.'

Peter nodded.

'By the time he lost interest in me we had a different arrangement.'

'Lost interest? But... ?'

'Where do you think he gets all the energy for all the others? I wouldn't have left him with any.' Hilary showed Peter a boastful, bitter smile.

Peter spooned a little sugar into the cool coffee.

'For the last ten years we've been partners. We've built that magazine up between us into a going proposition. Not a big circulation, I grant you, but growing. It was a bit of a joke to begin with but thanks to Hal's flannel and my attention to detail it was beginning to work.'

Peter lifted his cup. A droplet splashed into the saucer.

'I never minded the girls. Not after the first few years. I didn't mind the money wasted on luxuries for Hal – the silk shirts and suits. I got my share of the goodies. But I did mind when Hal took you and Nigel on as partners. I'm the only partner Hal ever had on the magazine. I built it with him. There were just the two of us. When I knew beyond any doubt that Hal was about to discard all those years of my life, I decided to save the magazine by threatening to destroy it.'

Peter sighed.

'I hoped, of course, that Agustin would throw Hal out of Manila. I hoped Hal would come back. We could have survived one lost edition. We've done it before. Now there's nothing.'

Hilary's hand made as though to raise the coffee-cup. Her shoulders trembled.

'Hilary. I really am so sorry.'

Hilary looked up. 'Hal's filing for divorce, you know.'

'Will you fight it?'

'No,'

Hilary took the coffee cup, made as if to lift it, then changed her mind. She reached down and opened her bag. In her hand was a tiny lace handkerchief. She dabbed her eyes.

Peter extracted his crumpled packet of Pall Mall and offered it to Hilary. She shook her head and then looked up.

'Is it the girl in the pictures?'

'Sorry?'

'The one that Hal's going to marry in Manila. The one in the towel.'

Peter took the unlit cigarette from between his lips. 'No.'

'I'm glad. She looked like a whore.'

'Hilary?'

'Yes.'

'Would you mind if I write to you after I get back to the UK?'

'I'd like that.'

'And if you ever get back...'

'I've got the offer of a very good job here. In a hospital.'

Peter looked at his watch, gave Hilary a rueful smile and clicked his fingers to attract the young waitress.

'*Siu jiee. Maydan. M goi lei-a.*'

Epilogue

The time is October 1983. The place is a modest cottage near Kingston-upon-Thames. In the evening glow of an open fire a man and a woman sit in opposing armchairs. They are reading the Sunday papers.

Peter and Tessa have been married for not quite nine years. Life has settled into a gentle pattern. The friends of the shipping agent and his picture-editor wife describe them as 'contented'. Others, not so benign, suggest they are in something of a rut. Their needs are as modest as the cottage they inhabit. Their sense of well-being is considerable. Theirs, they often tell their friends, is 'a good partnership'. Halford, their cocker spaniel, lies asleep on the hearthrug as his parents read in the dim light; Tessa the news pages, Peter the colour supplement.

Tessa looks up. 'Gosh, terrible goings-on in the Philippines, Peter.'

'Hhmm?'

'Do you think Marcos had anything to do with Aquino's death?'

'Hhmm?'

'Well, I think he did it. What a monster!'

'Yes, dear.'

'Weren't you there once?'

'Where, dear?'

'The Philippines.'

Peter looked up.

'Yes. You know I was. By the by, there's an article about Manila in the supplement.'

'It sounds a horrid place.'

'I suppose it is.' He frowned. 'Now.' Peter returned to his reading.

Halford sat up and yawned cavernously.

'Good God!' Peter leaned forward in his armchair. 'Would you believe it?'

'What's wrong, Peter?'

'You remember that chap I went to Manila with? The one I told you about.'

'Oh, you mean Halford.' She smiled down at the dog.

Peter handed the supplement to his wife. 'Just read the caption.'

Tessa scanned the double page for clues. To one side was a photograph of demonstrators with placards carrying the messages; 'Marcos Must Go' and 'Who Killed Ninoy?' She frowned.

She passed quickly to the opposite page. There, the colour photograph depicted a middle-aged 'European' with a dense moustache surmounting a picket-fence of teeth. The man's arms enfolded four Filipinas wearing minimalist puce silk dresses disguising little.

'Just read the caption,' Peter exhorted.

Tessa leaned towards the light and read aloud:

'One man who really knows how to cater for the requirements of visiting businessmen from the States, Europe or Japan in his nightspot in Makati is a 43 year-old expatriate Englishman... Peter Nicholson!'

Tessa lowered the supplement. 'What a bloody cheek!'

Peter gave his wife a wry smile. 'I think I may have rather a torrid time in the office tomorrow.'